GW00470156

SHOTGUNS

V.

CTHULHU

Double-barrelled action in the horrific world
of HP Lovecraft

Edited by Robin D. Laws

Published by Stone Skin Press 2012.

Stone Skin Press is an imprint of Pelgrane Press Ltd. Spectrum House,
9 Bromell's Road, Clapham Common, London, SW4 0BN.

ISBN 978-1-908983-01-5

A CIP catalogue record for this book is available from the British
Library.

1 2 3 4 5 6 7 8 9 10

Printed in the USA.

This book can be ordered direct from the publisher at
www.pelgranepress.com

Contents

Save a Barrel for Yourself

A Preface

We're used to thinking of H. P. Lovecraft's horror tales as the genteel territory of doomed and scholarly men, whose instinctive reaction to physical threat is the fainting spell. Those wanting action in their mythos tales, conventional wisdom tells us, should look to Robert E. Howard's rip-roaring confrontations between heroic protagonists and inhuman expressions of cosmic horror.

Yet when you look at Lovecraft's stories, you see, amid the antiquarian narrators and literary references, a writer fully capable of heart-racing action.

The rooftop chase from "Shadows Over Innsmouth" stands toe to toe with any pursuit scene, in or out of the horror genre.

Walter Gilman's hand-to-hand struggle against dimension-hopping witch Keziah Mason in "Dreams of the Witch House", with its apparently climactic strangling by crucifix chain, presents as muscular a confrontation between man and monster as an aficionado of the weird could ask for.

In "At the Mountains of Madness", the flight from the shoggoth brings sudden physical terror to the mind-blowing metahistory discovered below the Arctic wastes.

Then there's the little matter of a certain nautical ramming action, as performed by men of the commandeered schooner Emma against the risen Cthulhu himself. That famous scene from "The Call of Cthulhu" constitutes the kind of action set-piece filmic blockbusters are made of.

We associate the action sequence with escapism. Lovecraft decouples this connection; his protagonists' physical efforts are no less protected from futility than their mental explorations. Gilman's triumph goes unrewarded. He fails in his ultimate objective, the saving of a kidnapped infant's life, and is soon himself destroyed. Robert Olmstead may get away from the fishy denizens of Innsmouth, but not from the monstrous genetic heritage that will eventually claim him.

This collection plays with the action side of Lovecraft's writing, and of the mythos tradition as taken up by others. We recruited a phalanx of rising neo-Lovecraftians and asked them to give us fresh mixtures of action and cosmic dread. Whether they embraced the bleakness or allowed their heroes to blast tentacled foes left and right was a choice left up to them. Shotguns, they were instructed, were optional. Nearly all included them.

Blasting firearms and ferocious hand-to-hand struggle are all well and good, but the iconic horror action sequence remains the flight from relentless pursuit. Kyla Ward's "Who Looks Back?" resounds with pumping blood, the exhalation of breath, and the exhaustion of muscle as hikers in New Zealand's Waimangu valley confront an underutilized Lovecraftian entity.

We know what happens when Norwegian sailors enter Cthulhu's south seas domain. But what of the region's islanders? In "The Old Wave", Rob Heinsoo explores the impact of the mythos on its earlier inhabitants. He delivers the atmosphere and thrills of the exotic tale without succumbing to the pitfall of exoticizing his central characters. Along the way he pulls off a tricky voice shift and brings us ever closer to the green shark's devouring maw.

Fragmented perspective and a scattergun prove a troubling combination in "Lithic." Dennis Detwiller invokes the mythos with a minimalist, allusive touch, as his shattered narrator comes to terms with what he saw—and what reached out to him—on the fringes of a Vermont resort town.

If horrific events become all the more shocking when they arise in prosaic, familiar locations, Chris Lackey's "Snack Time" proves that the principle goes double for siege action. Chris finds new reasons to be terrified by a classic pack of Lovecraft creatures. When they pursue the protagonist to a take-out joint, the barrier between mundane and insane shatter like our conception of Euclidean geometry.

Himself a researcher of grimoires, Dan Harms drafts as his action hero the historical figure John Georg Hohman, 19th century compiler of the magical recipe collection *The Long-Lost Friend*. Set in snowy Berks County, PA, "The Host from the Hill" shows how a nose for occult books might lead one to an alarming letter, backwoods ritualists, and an excitingly rendered aerial battle.

Steve Dempsey situates the potentiality for violence of his story "Breaking Through" in the contemporary London drug scene. It starts with a brutal baseball bat beatdown, carries its protagonist into a flash-mob mystery, and concludes with... well, let's just say there are trains and squishiness.

No collection of action-oriented Cthulhuiana would be complete without a visit to the classic Delta Green milieu. Delta Green, as seen in games and fiction, fuses the Clancyesque guns and paranoia genre with mythos terror. "Last Things Last", by one of Delta Green's original creators, A. Scott Glancy, brings all the tradecraft, ballistics lore and brittle professionalism you'd anticipate from such arrangement. That he brings us a touch of pathos amid the dread might not be so expected.

In "One Small, Valuable Thing", Chad Fifer wraps his take on the mythos under a seamless layer of contemporary hardboiled crime story. His action sequences arrive with the force our anthology concept demands. The story plays with our awareness of its inspiration without having to underline it with a usual litany of direct references. Along the way, it finds a straight-faced modern analog to the aforementioned Lovecraftian fainting spell.

Martial arts explode on the hot streets of late 60s Oakland, CA, in Nick Mamatas' "Wuji." Fresh elements of time, place and milieu bring bone-crunching immediacy to a tale exploring the cosmic toll of personal transformation.

With its gleeful sense of play and hybridized western-steampunk pedigree, Natania Barron's "The One in the Swamp", leans to the romp end of the action-horror spectrum. Yet when the horrors appear, they're no mere monsters in a shooting gallery. They maintain their sense of menace and visceral nastiness.

If anything distinguishes the work of *Tour de Lovecraft* author Kenneth Hite more than his affinity for mythos horror, it would be his nose for piquant historical detail. When presented with the brief for this book, he combined those two loves, delving deep into the archives to find the inspiration for "Infernal Devices." This time-spanning, viewpoint-hopping tale takes as its point of entry the origin of the shotgun itself.

In the nomadic wilds of a modern American city, the needs of flight and fight are never more than a millisecond away. Dave Gross grounds the weirdness of his tale "Walker" against a tellingly drawn backdrop of Seattle street life. The story's voice shifts to match the uncertainty of the characters' perceptions and loyalties.

As per my publisher's instructions, I honored a longstanding tradition of Cthulhoid anthologists by writing a story of my own, entitled "And I Feel Fine." While I was at it, I figured I might as well destroy the world.

Speaking of the apocalyptic, Larry DiTillio lets out all the aesthetic stops in "Welcome to Cthulhuville." It partakes of the unhinged wildness of a Robert E. Howard mythos tale, cranking it so far past eleven that it breaks through into a gobsmacking realm of surreal, tentacled experimentalism.

Who says terrifying violence and exquisite lyricism can't go hand in hand? Ekaterina Sedia proves the contrary with "End of White." A corrupt fecundity gradually suffuses a world of doomed Bulgakovian reverie as soldier Coronet Kovalevsky chooses, rather than join the Bolsheviks, to while away his days in a deceptively sleepy shore-side Crimean town.

Together these fifteen stories show that action and horror go hand in putrescent hand. Strap on your armor, count your bullets, and brace yourself to turn the page. Mayhem is about to rain down.

— *Robin D. Laws*

Who Looks Back?

Kyla Ward

Who looks back on the Waimangu track?

Not Kelsie Munroe, running light over gravel, the slope gentle but the surface potentially foul. The track's made for walking, not running or driving. There is a road proper for that, for ferrying tired tourists back from Lake Rotomahana. You're meant to walk one way down the length of the valley, taking in all its steams and smokes, and weirdly-coloured sinter. But Kelsie never walks where she can run and Lewis jumps.

Lewis Zabri keeps her pace for now: brown skin abreast of freckles, black stubble beside red hair. They dress much the same; singlets, shorts and runners, packs strapped into the small of the back. Kelsie is taller and can beat him over short sprints but this is four kilometres of up and down, winding and in places rough. Lewis keeps himself loose and breathing easy. He knows she's planning something.

The valley of Waimangu, New Zealand, is the youngest landscape on earth. Nothing here, not the trees, not the streams, nor the cliffs themselves, existed before the eruption of 1886. The ground split, swallowing everything, then spewing it out again as boiling mud. Forest and farmstead, whole villages died. For kilometres around, there was not a single living thing. On the walls of the Visitors Centre, blurry black and white photos show weirdly peaked hills and plains of ash. It's gone green now: first the extremophile algae, then lichen and ferns, then melaleuca spilling down the slopes in a long, slow race, the reclamation marathon. The algae was first to reach the bank of Frying Pan Spring. But Kelsie, or maybe Lewis, will catch up soon.

You're not meant to run and definitely not to leave the track, risking a scalding, broken limbs or damage to the unique terrain. But Lewis and Kelsie leap, climb and throw themselves off things as a matter of course and the terms of this race have been agreed: first to the lake via the Mount Haszard lookout. Ahead of them and still a serious drop below is where the track and creek first cross. The climb to the lookout begins there, but Lewis sees no reason to wait. Running straight at the guard rail, he extends hands and flips himself over the cliff in a perfect *saut de chat*. He doesn't so much as glance over his shoulder.

Kelsie is not impressed. She trains in *parkour* herself but this isn't the terrain. Lewis can say what he likes about the zone and the flow, but terrain is king. She knows this and that's why she'll win. He's risking a spill for a gain she'll more than make up at the lookout, if the map approximates reality. Worse yet, this close to the Visitors Centre he's risking the rangers seeing him.

Three metres below her now, Lewis adjusts automatically to the crunch and mealy slide beneath his feet. So long as he stays off the algae, he'll reach the start of the climb seconds ahead of Kelsie and that gain he'll keep. Ribbons of colour unwind beside him, pink rock and water a startling green. Steam sifts across his field of vision and there is frantic noise around him, an all-encompassing bubble and hiss. One part of his mind feels the heat and moisture and yes, some fear; the other only registers angles, surfaces, opportunities. He is in the zone, feeling the flow. The goal of all his training is to clear his mind of the artificial clutter of modern life and here, now, he is almost free. That's why he'll win.

Kelsie burns on down the track. Despite his pretensions to this or that philosophy, Lewis never really thinks, or else thinks that everywhere is just like London, where no one gives a damn. But sometimes people do care. They care about travelling together. They care about sleeping together. By God, a whole lot of them care when someone tic-tacs on the shrine at Tanukitanisan Temple and what was the point of that? They had to leave Japan overnight and it didn't even make the blog. Then again, nor will the stunt she's banking on today, for which she's carrying an extra kilo.

Twenty metres, ten: Lewis vanishes ahead of her into the steam. She can hear the creek: is that the creek? It sounds like voices. It's like from out of the ground, from the weeping black ferns and deliquescent rocks there rises a deep and liquid dissension. The warmth envelops her, damp upon her arms and face, sulphurous in her eyes and nose. For a moment she runs blind.

Lewis rejoins the track and not a moment too soon: Kelsie is coming up fast. Here, the valley narrows sharply and the banks seem to be rotting, a foul, yellowish slough choking the creek bed. He peers ahead for the turn-off and sees only the wildly swirling fog. Is he motion then, with nothing to mark his passage? Can there be motion in a void? Yes, there can: so long as Kelsie comes behind. Grinning just a little, he eases, anticipating her sight of his back. She takes all their games so seriously, even in bed. Then something shifts beneath his feet. The gravel is suddenly live as well as warm. The fog billows and the noise of the creek rises sharply around him: *is* that the creek roaring? He does not stop, cannot, as directly in front of him, something forms from the white.

Kelsie knows that sound isn't the creek. Its voices have not vanished, merely retreated behind the encroaching rumble of a truck on gravel: she has Australian ears, accustomed to country sounds. A bank of wind hits her face, clearing the steam and she sees Lewis running slow and beyond him a large, white utility bearing the park logo. Coming straight at him, at her. Behind the cab she glimpses ridiculous things, white and shapeless with reflective face plates and Lewis is—oh no, he's not! Not slowing or swerving, Lewis guns straight into the path of the moving vehicle and vaults. Hands and foot on the bonnet, next step against the windscreen. Even though the truck is jerking, skewing to a stop, he executes the move with perverse bloody brilliance. Straight over the top he goes and through the white shapes, revealed by their reaction as men in thermal suits. In the instant of their shock, before they even imagine her presence, she shifts balance and angle, and leaps out across the water.

Lewis sees angles, shapes, the moving flat of the truck bed. His pulse sings as he leaps to the ground and keeps running, unfaltering. Yes, yes; that was perfect! Did those guys even *see* him? By those shouts and grinding, clunking gears, oh yes they did. A grin splits his face as he rounds the bend and sights the turn-off.

Kelsie grinds uphill through ferns and bushes, wincing as she pushes on her right ankle. Her leap covered the distance as she saw it, but seeing isn't believing down here. Solid is slurry, ferns anchor foam. Her ankle stings and she's not sure if it's burn or graze. Either way, she's committed: their rules don't compensate for accident, pursuit or even biohazard. It's win or lose and she is not losing today, there's too much at stake. So she climbs a bad climb. Exposed rock to fallen log: it's an obstreperous sign of her progress that the plants get bigger. The pink and yellow cools into grey; spindly trunks and spiking tussocks block her view of the stream, but she can still hear voices. And not shouting scientists and squealing rangers; the old voices, that the Maori tribesmen must have heard to mark this place as the realm of monsters. While Lewis was psyching himself up, she read the placards in the Visitors Centre. Then suddenly, startlingly, she is out of the bush with hard-pressed earth beneath her feet. Before her the path to the lookout swerves up a steep defile. But she is alone and whether Lewis is ahead or behind, she has no idea.

Lewis would say he was ahead: ahead of the utility and its shrouded occupants. What the Hell were they doing, dressed up like that? The cluttered part of his mind noticed machines in the back of the ute, the monitors and probes. It made sense they'd check the valley regularly, though he would have thought they'd use the access road for that. But here he turns up the hill and here the Klu Klux Rangers cannot follow him, if that's what they're shouting about. It's true they could reverse all the way back to where the climb rejoins the main track and wait for him there, but surely they've got somewhere to be! Another blast of air strikes him from down the valley. He hears a new note in the creek, a warbling, high pitched sound.

Kelsie ploughs up the path but she's spent her best. If by some miracle Lewis is behind her now, she'll abandon her plan and take the track down to the lake. But how to tell? The vegetation here is thick. Strange flowers rise aside of the path: purple trumpets on stems like giant foxgloves. Huge tree ferns, the biggest she has ever seen lip over her head and reach for her feet with long, black tendrils. Branches bristle with inch-long thorns. Still, a faint whispering rises from the earth, punctuated by the rasp of her feet and controlled breath. Then suddenly by screams.

Lewis looks up to see the white utility, with its doors swinging and machines falling as the vehicle flies through the steaming sky. Rangers fall too: foolish, flailing space men, mission aborted. One remains braced in the driver's seat: Lewis sees him clearly as the truck rotates. That's a whole truck up there, spinning slowly as though something wraps it, carries it amidst shifting coils. And, as the nacreous mist thickens, something does.

Kelsie all but stumbles towards the lookout. She's made it: there's a bench concreted firm into the ground and there's the cliff. Ferns, flowers fall away: the valley lies before her, a snaking, smoking rift down to the metallic sheet of the lake. Nothing in that view suggests a source for the dreadful sounds, the mash of flesh and branches. It was behind her then, the accident. *Lewis, oh my God*. And she turns. She begins to turn back, as branches crack and wind flattens, and something huge and whistling like a train churns up the hill. Into her view drops a white utility. It drops from the sky right before her eyes, crashing, sliding away down the cliff as something in the air loosens and billows, shooting away with a furl resembling the feeding fringe of a coral polyp as much as steam or clouds or a weather balloon: what the Hell is she *seeing*?

Lewis hasn't stopped moving down the main track. This was where both truck and terror came from, but they aren't there now and he can really put on some speed. His is the discipline of pure motion, but maybe there's something in this headlong rush of a small, brown boy being hunted through the London alleys. The track bends and bends again; on his left Mount Haszard and on his right the creek, bubbling with increased vigour. And his cluttered mind suggests that if what he saw *was* an explosion, the freakish herald of a volcanic event, then in all likelihood he's running right into it. Where is Kelsie? If he was so far ahead that she didn't see the horror, then she might well have continued on up to the lookout. He's closer now to the exit than the entrance: when he reaches that he'll head up and meet her. They're bound to be safe on the mountain.

Kelsie had the rope and carabineers in her pack. This was her plan: an assisted fall from the lookout, ten metres down onto what they called the Terrace, then a straight though possibly scalding sprint to the shore. She'd take risks when it counted. Confined to the remainder of the path, Lewis would have lost minutes and been lost in wide, white-grinning admiration of a stunt so worthy of himself. Then she could have told him she was through. Now she goes through the same motions to deadly purpose: there are people down there, she can hear them. Anchor on the bench and on the largest tree, though that wouldn't be worth much: quickly, quickly pull the sleeve in place so the cliff doesn't cut the cord as she goes over. Climbing was her first love, in the erosion gullies around the farm: her first attempt to escape. Her second took her to London and where hasn't she been since then? Stepping off into air, she looks down.

Lewis hears another rumble. A thrashing, boiling, torrential sound: in the direction of the lake, pure white striates the sky. There's been no geysers in Waimangu since just after the eruption, when they claimed it held the largest in the world. What's this then, what is this? It's *incredible*! In all his travels, running round and round the world in search of its edges, he's never seen the like! The entire lake must be rising and even as he runs, as the track beneath him starts to shake and the outrunners of the wind hits, there's as much delight in his whoop as fear. Until he realises that the wind and the whistling are coming from behind him.

Kelsie drops into ruin. The valley floor is made up of smashed sinter, broken rocks, raw scars scraped through the undergrowth and white wreckage steaming, all of it steaming. A white figure flails, caught half in metal, half in water the same unearthly green as the spring. Rumbling, roaring, human screams a tenuous thread of sound. Kelsie is shaking, everything is shaking and as she lands, nice and light and square, she's nearly flung off her feet. Not even unhooked she is turning, stumbling, drawing the rope across the heaving pink and yellow ground. Inhaling an overwhelming smell, like eggs boiling in a rusted kettle, she reaches down and hauls on wet fabric.

Lewis slithers in blood-warm water, popping and stinging against his skin. There was nowhere else to go as something that wasn't a trick of the light, nor a current of superheated water or anything else but a creature came hunting. His entire body knew it and that wracks him beyond the heat and acid. He keeps himself loose and floating: going with the flow, but he isn't alone. Slick like rubber and obscenely buoyant, white corpses follow the current, floating swiftly towards white Hell.

The ranger's name is Ahere, her skin darker than Lewis where it isn't burned, her eyes a brimming brown. Crying and hugging Kelsie, she tells her things: a seismological blip, a bloom on the thermal map, an early morning expedition in full heat-wear down to check the lake. A new vent had opened, yes, but there had been nothing to suggest more until the thing emerged. *Hīanga*, she says, we put the lines down and it comes, we put the lines down and it catches us! She points frantically to a strange, circular mark in the sinter, a circle at least a metre across with five deep indents that Kelsie assumes was caused by some part of the utility. All she really gets from Ahere's story is that the lake is dangerous. But there's no going back the way she came: the whole cliff looks unstable and she doubts Ahere could make it in the best circumstances. Whatever Ahere saw, whatever *she* saw, they have no choice and apparently there's a reason. Ahere is saying they'll be safe.

When Lewis was a little boy, he loved dinosaurs (raptors, hunting him through the alleys). Ruins too, the temples and tombs of all the ancient civilisations, but keep digging and you reach dinosaurs, their big, stone bones tomb and temple both. To go back further takes more than science or even imagination, but clawing at foam and slurry, Lewis realises that this isn't the youngest landscape on earth: it's the oldest. Go back further and it was all like this or near enough, a fury of earth and water. Near enough for that thing, maybe; that primal, elemental thing. Maybe life on earth did not begin with cells, but with fire and air. The cluttered part of his mind runs on like this, the other is crawling in the sludge, out of the creek but keeping low. It wants to find a hole and crawl inside: the other is telling him he needs to find the widest open space, where the rocks won't fall on him. That's what they said in Japan. He can only hope Kelsie is safe.

Kelsie was going home. From the North Island of New Zealand, Sydney is a hop across a puddle. She was going home and not like she swore to her father she never, ever would. She got the news two days ago in Wellington: her grant had come through and she had a whole new life of work and study waiting. But how to tell Lewis she's sick of living in hostels, tired of waitressing in shitholes to fund the next leg of the trip, while he blogs and preaches *parkour*. She knows he wants to climb Machu Pichu, has tagged Easter Island and Antarctica as stations in his quest for who knows what, and perhaps he will. But she's going to die in New Zealand with a stranger staggering on her arm, as the earth shakes beneath their feet and through the steam, the whistling rises once again.

Lewis runs. On the path but hunching, nearly on all fours. The hunter is still out there: he hears its whistling, its rush. He pushes, burning all his last and, miraculously, there is Kelsie paralleling him through the steam. All this, and neither has gained so much as a step! He lopes along the gravel, she jogs across the world famous Warbrick Terrace, deep crimson flashing under her feet. Her hair flashes: she is magnificent, she would be flying were she not hampered by a pale and lumbering thing. A monstrous form, a homunculus or golem with gleaming white skin. And fly she must, for through the clouds the hunter is coming: he feels its wind, sees the mist clear. And as it comes, his shrieking, cluttered mind sheers clean away. He sees angles and surfaces. Instinctively he understands that little warm-blooded things scuttling through ferns don't interest this hunter. How could they threaten it? How could they even feed it? It's the monster it seeks, with its unnatural contours: he yelps and changes course.

Kelsie hears Ahere shriek and feels her suddenly sag against her: thinking she's stumbled, she yanks her up and then sees her face plate is shattered. Her nose and eyes have vanished behind a web of cracks and there is blood. Are there stones in the air now? She grabs Ahere, reaching into her core for one last effort and oh my God there's Lewis sprinting towards her, Lewis with his stubbled head, arms and legs pumping crazy. She lets go of Ahere's arm and sees Lewis raise his, a sharp, black rock in his hand. It freezes her brain. She can't comprehend what she's seeing, match cause and effect. Only when the second flint strikes the helpless woman, opening a gash in her thermal skin, does she leap to intercept him, grabbing his arm, hauling at him, her height and weight costing both their footing and bringing them down.

She's in his arms now, rolling and thrashing; he laughs and rolls with her, all heat and sweat and hair. Slipping, sliding, seeping crimson; he's hard as a rock, licking permanganate from her skin.

He's below her and she strikes him hard, no longer thinking of Ahere but rather of his grasping hands, his grinning mouth, of being dragged and used, and assumed. Of needing to win so she can finally, finally not need him.

Something passes over them, the two little mammals rolling in the mud. Something screams in agony and the crimson drenching them is at blood heat.

Kelsie stares down at Lewis and things click back into perspective. He's still grinning but he's shivering and what comes out of his mouth isn't words. She could leave him here, she really could. In light of what he did and the trouble she'll have, perhaps she should. But she can't. Somehow, she has to get them all to the lake. Looking around, she can no longer see Ahere so presumably she's followed her own advice. Aching weary but somehow no longer terrified, she staggers up and then offers Lewis her hand.

He had rather lie here, wet and happy, but everything is shaking and they had better find shelter. Somewhere quiet and dark where the water makes no sound. He stays close to his mate, gaze darting through the undergrowth and ears peeled for the hunting cry of the things below, that strike from above. Their voices are everywhere, but only the whistling counts.

Up ahead, Kelsie sees black and white. Black the fringe of unbelievably stubborn vegetation: white the boiling lake. There's no escaping there. Then part of the black resolves into a roof and windows, wheels, and she realises what Ahere must have meant. Running off from the dock, directly ahead of her and Lewis lies a road, and parked upon it is a small bus. The access road and the bus that takes tourists out of the valley! A broad and stable slope, solid walls and engine: this is their way out and always was. Where is Ahere? There's no sign of her here. Oh please, let her not still be back there...

He knows the artificial hollow is a trap. They can't go in there: he takes hold of his mate to pull her away. She resists him, chattering shrilly as though it's he who doesn't understand. He does understand, the hunters are waiting for more white monsters! Now she is grabbing him, dragging *him* towards the unnatural planes and sharp angles, and what is that dark substance streaming across the ground like water, yet solid? He twists out of her grasp, makes a blow of it, a stunning blow to the side of her head—and misses. She has jumped clear of him, landing on the black.

Kelsie screams as the bus explodes upwards in a geyser that holds a shadow, a writhing, tubular shadow that crushes windows and seats. Shrapnel scatters but she is already running, uphill again but she will not give in to what she saw and will not die in the grip of a nightmare. Lewis pursues her; she hears him ploughing through the bush at the side of the road, chuckling in his madness. She veers away from him, though it costs her speed, and now she is shrinking from the whistling in the air, from the steam-shadow hurtling, coalescing into solidity right above her.

He gathers up all his strength, all his superbly honed muscle, and makes his leap. Although he no longer considers it as such, this is the pinnacle of *parkour*: a *passe muraille* such as hearsay finds impossible to believe, that makes the witness gasp and the practitioner sigh. Not to scale a wall, but to interpose himself between his mate and the thing with the whiplash body, the grasping tendrils, the·five-pointed sting. It is not fully material, not at its full strength when he hits, so the impact sends that sting plunging into the tar. But it solidifies around him, lifts him up with a billow and swarm, and does not fade as it carries him out, over the edge of the world.

At his yell, his triumphant scream, Kelsie glances over her shoulder.

Who looks back on the Waimangu track? Anyone who does will never really leave. When the rescue team finds Kelsie, she has painted herself with sulphur and antimony, and is using her pitons to punch the five points into the road, again and again.

Old Wave

Rob Heinsoo

The first time I paddled across deep waters I became a man, killed a turtle, and lost the girl I loved to a trader who brewed weak beer. My friend Grinner and the other boys were proud to have finished our initiation and to paddle alongside the grown men on a kaala voyage. But every stroke brought us closer to Sunward Island where Rain would marry a man who already had two wives. My uncles slapped my shoulder and said that Rain's new husband, Windhope, had always been good to my own mother when trading. Rain was sure to speak up for me if I wanted to enter the kalaa trade myself some day when I had wives and full canoes of my own. They talked like we always talked, expecting our life on Sweetwater Island to go on forever.

It was my first kalaa, but most of the men paddling away from our home in our four largest canoes had lost count of their kaala trips, either north with the Red-Shell necklaces or south carrying a White-Shell armband.

On this trip to Sunward, two days to the north, our Chief carried a Red-Shell kaala necklace named *Many Yams*. *Many Yams* had come to us three moons earlier from the chief of Coraldown, the next island south of Sweetwater. *Many Yams* had brought us strong crops, pleasant rain, and good fortune. Or at least that is what Chief would claim when he passed the necklace on to Wide Man, the chief of Sunward.

Rain rode in our Chief's canoe, shaded in a reed pavilion beside *Many Yams*. The other three canoes in the kaala expedition, including the one I paddled with my friend Grinner and our uncles, rode low in the water under heaped bundles of dried yams wrapped in banana leaf. By giving Wide Man the yams along with the Red-Shell necklace, our Chief would show that he was the biggest man this year, especially wise when giving away one of Sweetwater's daughters, since status and power flowed to the most generous kaala-givers. We all felt good about ourselves because Wide Man had already fallen behind. We had expected him two or three weeks earlier, carrying a White-Shell armband that would have come to him from the north, but he was late.

As we paddled toward Sunward, I thought about the nights Rain and I had spent under these canoes, on the beach far enough away from the village that we imagined no one could hear us. Once Rain had told me I was "beautiful in the dark." We both laughed because we knew I was ugly everywhere else. I was taller and stronger than full-grown men, but my mouth twisted and my eyes scared children. Mostly Rain liked me for my voice. I wasn't called Singer for nothing. It was a name I worked hard to keep, especially since I had spent most of my childhood called 'Rock.'

Where most people in Sweetwater lived calmly and avoided trouble, I loved fighting. When I was seven years old, a year after my father died, I had broken three older boys' arms and heads with a rock. One boy, Fisher Bird, nearly died. People called me Rock for years until my voice and the fact that I never hurt anyone again let me grow a new name. I learned all the fishing songs and as many paddling songs as I could learn without being on a kaala voyage. I even knew the women's planting songs and weeding songs and a couple of the birth songs. Men weren't supposed to sing the women's songs, but people said that songs were luckier when I sang them, so no one minded. Grinner said, "Singer's voice is the opposite of his face. Shut your eyes and listen."

I shut my eyes as I paddled and told myself to give up on Rain. She had not looked at me once since she slipped inside the shade made of reeds. Even when we stopped to trail our hands in the ocean to find the north-ripple current, Rain kept her back to me. So I kept my eyes closed and let the sun burn away the memory of our nights.

When it was just me left in my head I started singing a strong-paddle song, just to myself, the others were all laughing and sharing some joke, so no one could hear. For some reason I changed the song and sang in the voice of a turtle, a coughing grunt instead of words. There was a knock on the bottom of the canoe and I knew we'd hit a grandfather turtle's shell as it came up to breathe. I opened my eyes, handed my paddle to Grinner and dove over the side away from the outrigger. I curled back under the canoe's track and found the dark oval of the turtle as it sunk toward darker water. One flipper, then the tail, avoiding the beak, I fought grandfather up toward where I could hear my uncles cursing me. I got a breath and yelled "Turtle!" and the curses turned to cheers.

> For three moons on Sweetwater
> *Many Yams* brought twins.
> On the first day of paddling,
> She called the turtles in.

A day later, still on the water, Grinner and I were excited to see Sunward for the first time. We were so eager for the moment when the Chief would launch into the *Arrival Song* that we were already whispering it to each other so that no one else could hear. Not the real words, of course. Grinner was filling in the song with new words, lines about what the girls on Sunward would be saying to each other when they saw us row into the island with the giant turtle on our boat, how they'd never seen one *that* big. He was trying to make me feel better about losing Rain. I did feel better, rowing in the sun with my best friend and a prize turtle and uncles who were speaking to me as if I was an adult.

We were still humming and laughing when we saw the smoke from Sunward Island. "The feast fires have started," said Kano. "They realized we were coming, this time. That's good."

Grinner splashed him and said, "You like it when the food is ready and you like it when the food is half-cooked, so long as you can bloat." Kano shook his fat fist as if he was angry but he didn't mind the joke. We all helped him eat, sometimes it was more fun to watch Kano eat than to finish our own food.

I realized that we were paddling slower and that the Chief hadn't started the Arrival Song, even though we could now see the full sweep of the island and our song would be able to break on the village.

"What's wrong?" I asked a man named Two Hooks. He'd placed his paddle atop the canoe and was staring at Sunward, shading his eyes for a better look.

"I don't know. There's something...."

"Oh, it's the smoke," said Kano. "Look, the cook-smoke has colors." He was right. I hadn't seen it before because I was too excited, but the cook-smoke wasn't just white or black. In places the smoke rising from the cooking rings on the beach held coiled lines of color, shifting ropes of blue or orange and pink or a touch of yellow. The colors disappeared if you looked hard. I'd never seen anything like it, but how did I know what they cooked on Sunward?

"It smells funny," said Kano. "Not bad. Just, I don't think I've smelled this before. It's good, actually, like fruit-meat-beer-smoke."

Now we all laughed, since Kano had managed to say that it smelled like all three of his favorite things. A couple of seconds later the Chief started the Arrival Song, his powerful voice calling out to us to answer. We sang as we paddled toward the island and forgot about the strange smell. By the time we swung around the point, Wide Man and twelve of his most-favored fishermen were singing back to us from the beach.

Friend! Where have you been! We feast, we drink
But it's not the same without you.
Together now, together we can dance!

I had been preparing myself for greeting songs and an eventual
fuss over the great turtle I'd caught. But the giant pink shell on
Wide Man's head distracted us all. I say it was pink, but that may
not be true. It wasn't white. It wasn't red. It glinted.

I got my first look at the shell when Wide Man jumped off
the beach like a man twenty years younger to help us pull our
canoes out of the water. I thought, "Well I don't even know what to
call *that*." It had spikes and prongs like a *king-shell* and soft ridges
like a *yam-snail*. There were more openings than I thought a shell
could have and one of these holes was placed so that the shell rode
on top of Wide Man's head. He never stopped beaming as we sang
the *Sunward and Sweetwater Song*.

Our Chief promised to hand over *Many Yams* and I knew that
this was when we would get to hear about great events in *Many
Yams'* kaala line through the islands: the splendid harvests, safe
births of twins, and all the other good things that came from this
Red-Shells' kaala-luck, a list that would include my lucky turtle-
hunt for at least this telling of *Many Yams'* story.

But Wide Man was too excited about his own news to listen.
Our Chief was staring at the head-shell too and he didn't really
protest when Wide Man broke into *Many Yams'* story with a wave
and said, "Yes, yes, we are glad to welcome *Many Yams* among us
and will increase his fortune before sending him up the line of
kaala. But look at the magnificent kaala prize I will bring you!"

He rose on tiptoe to acknowledge the shell with his stocky
body. "She is *Ocean Mother*! Her story goes back grandparents
and grandparents and grandparents ago, even though we had not
heard most of her stories before receiving her from Molawa. I
know that she is late to sail to you and your people. I hope you
will not think less of me because I have kept Her good fortune
among my people longer than we expected. By the time I bring

Her to you, in one moon, or two, Her fortune will be tripled again. Come, let us carry your goods to the feast rings. You can clean up and then we will eat, such a feast we will have tonight!"

Of course we were tired from the trip. With the song finished, the ache hit our muscles. But I was not so tired that I had forgotten Rain. She had hung back in the pavilion on the canoe, as she'd been told, waiting for the moment when she could join the First New Family song. But Windhope was missing and Wide Man was trundling up the hill, placing his hand along the shell to keep it from falling off… Not so perfectly fitted, then.

"And for our sister? What welcome for our sister?" I asked.

Wide Man turned back. "Oh! Windhope's bride! Rain! I am terrible. A new wife! Quickly, fetch Windhope and his wedding musicians!" Several of the dozen men at his side scattered. Within ten minutes, before our yams were even half-unloaded, Windhope and his family were clustered on the beach singing the songs to welcome Rain, promising her several excellent weddings. Windhope was still a strong man, despite his notoriously bad attempts at beer, and his flashing smile and calm humor struck me as steps in a dance he had danced before. He knew what he was doing. Rain was already smiling at a joke he had spoken low so that only she could hear it. I turned and filled my arms with banana-leaf bundles.

To give Sunward its due, the feast started well. From up close the cook-smoke looked normal but the smell was just as Kano had said: fruit, meat, beer, all good things. The cooks laughed and said we would have to wait for the feast for explanations. I felt better when the Sunward women thanked me over and over again for the turtle. It was already baking in the chief sandpit, they'd pulled out lesser fish to make room for it. Soon people were telling the story around the fires. Several men from Windhope's family asked me to teach them my turtle song. I put them off, saying that it was time for a kaala and for a wedding, that we could share fish songs later.

Finally the women carried in the food. None of our dried yams had been brought to the cooking circles and now we knew why. The yams on the plates being carried up from the cook-rings were twice as big as any I'd seen. They were rich orange, soft yellow. The texture was good and the juices seemed like meat. So many different tastes. In a yam?

Wide Man laughed and gave in to our questions. "It's the gift of *Ocean Mother*!" He'd finally removed the shell from his head. It rested on a reed mat at his side, propped up on a heap of just-harvested giant yams, spiky with roots. Up close *Ocean Mother* turned out to be a shell armband after all, like the other White-Shell armbands that came to us from Sunward, but bigger, as if the person whose arm was right for the band was twice as big a normal man.

"Sometimes when *Ocean Mother* finds favor with a village, as she loves us here on Sunward, she brings something new, a gift that no one could have thought of! We call them New Yams. They grow twice as fast and twice as big. So the women have more time to sew and help with the nets."

"And make new dances!" called someone in the back, and everyone laughed, though we were laughing at the dirty joke and a few of the men from Sunward seemed to be laughing at us.

I took four or five bites of the New Yams. They had an aftertaste. I only half-chewed my last bite and then pretended to cough and took it out to bury it in the sand. In the corner of my eye I saw something moving in the dirty yams beneath the great pink shell. Something skinny and black and slow. A worm? Or roots settling?

I moved to the far side of the circle where I couldn't see the New Yams or the shell. Maybe I was done eating. The wedding musicians came to start the dances of the First Wedding of Windhope and Rain. I sat with my face to the flames, found a gourd of beer, then another.

By the time I threw aside my fourth gourd, I'd watched all the wedding dancing I could stomach. The kaala songs I'd been ready to sing, songs in honor of *Many Yams*, seemed to have been forgotten. Wide Man and our Chief were still talking about *Ocean Mother*.

The problem with weak beer is that you can't get drunk and forget your life. I needed to get away. Five beers at home and I would have been asleep, but four beers here and I could walk smoothly, two steps from the fire, then ten, then twenty. I made thirty steps from the fire without Grinner calling out to me or anyone from Sunward running after me in protest. Ah! I had escaped!

I walked slowly down the beach feeling sorry for myself. I felt sorry for Rain. I even felt sorry for our Chief, who looked uncomfortable sitting beside Wide Man. But mostly I felt sorry for myself. My stomach hurt. I'd been using beer to scrape at the taste of the New Yams. "They taste like everything but shit and earth and yams, and that's not right," I said aloud, and realized that Sunward beer must be strong enough, since I was talking to myself like a drunk man.

I kept walking and turned off the beach toward the village. The paths were clear in the dark and there were night-fires and people dancing in one of the yards. Children who were too young for the feast and some of the Sunward people who weren't part of this kaala trade or the wedding had gathered in the center place to sing kaala songs. This happened in our village, too: everyone loved kalaa because it brought new things and news of relatives on other islands, so everyone danced and sang kaala songs even if they weren't directly involved in the trades between the big men.

A couple of the Sunward men nodded to me and made the sign for turtle. I stood in the shadows, happy to just listen at first. I let the familiar rhythms of kaala song roll through me and soothe the thick knot in my stomach.

A young girl wearing a white feather necklace was making up the funny verses that come before the main chorus. She was good at it, making fun of everyone while sounding respectful, and

I started feeling better. But then she sang about the New Yams, and I realized that she wasn't singing the song of the shell that was receiving its feast. The Sunward people were still singing the song of the shell they'd had for months, *Ocean Mother*. I lost the rhythm for a moment and thought about returning to the beach, but the chorus was coming, the verses that went into every song for White-Shells traveling south. Alright. I could sing the chorus. The line would start at Sunward, go north to Molawa, and so on, tracing the path that *Ocean Mother* had already taken through all the kaala islands until the path swung back around and finally reached Sweetwater.

I was thinking as the chorus began that it must have been a very long time since *Ocean Mother* had been at our island. There were kaala shells that got lost for awhile, or stuck between feuding trade partners. And other shells that entered anew, though Wide Man had said *Ocean Mother* had a long history. There was a story here. Perhaps I would get it from someone after the song.

Together we sang, "Blessed in Sunward, given from Molawa, thanks to Turtle Pond Island, back to Flying Fish and Green Fish and Shark and Solstice, Solstice, Solstice," we caught our breath as others kept up the Solstice-weave in many beats. This was always my favorite part of the song tracing kaala north, after this the verse slowed down as each distant island got more time inside the beat. The laughing girl with the white-feather necklace was still the leader. She danced while banging two coconuts together. Huh! The song was getting raucous even before reaching North Star, not the way we sang the song at Home, but clearly Sunward danced hard.

"Redrocks! Redrocks! Redrocks!" we yelled. Some of the singers had stopped using words and were just making noise, but the girl's voice was still clear. "Redrocks beside the smoking bay," she sang, in a higher voice than I had thought she could find. What smoking bay? We were all dancing now.

"Then Lady's Island, Lady's Island, Lady's Island," sang the beautiful girl with the white feathers. I was dancing with my eyes closed, willing my pounding heart to wash away the sickness in my stomach.

"Paj-cross! Paj-cross! Paj-cross!" screamed the dancers. My eyes snapped open and I fell, banging off a door-post. "Paj-cross?" I said. "Not Paj-cross, it's Black Bay, next." But no one was listening. There were more men and women now dancing among the children, they had joined while my eyes were closed. I got to my knees and tried to catch the glance of a woman who had smiled at me earlier, expecting her to be as surprised as I was that these children were singing the song wrong. But her eyes didn't focus, she screamed "Paj-CROSS!" with everyone else.

White-Feather Girl held a crescent *guaraj* shell in her hands above her head. She danced with her eyes closed and a smile I did not expect to see on a child. She reminded me of Rain for a moment, standing on the beach at midnight with her naked arms raised to the stars.

"Gsesh-na-rahgnan Gsesh-na-rahgnan!" screamed the girl. I stumbled around the doorpost looking for the edge of the dancers. This gsesh-thing was not a place at all. The rest of the dancers echoed the call anyway.

"Lhir-kna-ral!" screamed White-Feather Girl, in the beyond-high voice that she had used earlier. I caught a glimpse of her surrounded by the tallest dancers and she reminded me of Rain again, of Rain in the wedding dance with Windhope. But this girl was dancing with five grown men and women. They started moving together and the audience screamed the name of another place that was not a place, and then another.

The wrong vomited from my stomach and smashed out my front teeth.

Light moon, sweet moon, slip past your husband's warriors
Light moon, sweet moon, to hold us on these waters
Sweetness, to feel your hands,
Light hands, bright hands,
Guide us to our waters.

I woke with roots pressed into the mess in the front of my mouth and the voices of my uncles singing around the sound of the paddles. I was propped off the bottom of the canoe by two reed mats. Mine and Grinner's, I realized. The thin crescent moon wavered, twinned by double-vision. There was a touch of morning on my left.

We were paddling south towards home? At night instead of waiting for the morning? Grinner was paddling beside me. I tried to sit up and ask him what was going on but the bindings tied into my mouth wouldn't let me talk right.

"Heyo, sweetness wakes," whispered Grinner. I heard the flash of his smile as much as I saw it. I felt around in my mouth.

"Careful there," said Grinner between strokes. I gained my seat, found my paddle in the bottom and caught up with the stroke. "You're finally really scary-looking. I know how much you wanted that. But I bet you hit the guy who hit you even harder, eh? Knocked him off Sunward, maybe?"

"Why are we paddling the night songs?" I grumbled, around bloody fibers and twitches of pain.

Grinner understood me. "Well, it's not just that you got drunk and beat up in the village. The Chief had already decided to leave, no one knows why. Maybe we got cheated this time. Or maybe Chief finally figured out that Wide Man screwed his wife the last time he came to visit. Or maybe..."

"What?" I asked.

"Maybe it was just too strange. Right?" Grinner looked puzzled, like he wasn't sure if it had been strange or not.

I didn't know what to say, so I nodded. I could feel that I had lost two of my teeth. There was blood in my mouth and another taste I was having trouble figuring out. It was slipping away, a dream. But that seemed wrong. It hadn't been a dream. It had been real. I reached in and pushed on the place where my teeth were missing. The pain woke me hard.

And there it was. The taste behind the blood was the taste of the New Yam. That was clear. The end of what had happened in the village? I had no idea. It was lost or hidden, somewhere back behind the squirmy taste of the New Yam.

I looked for our Chief, but his canoe was just a shape on the water. I heard his voice and he was singing clearly enough. The uncles in my canoe seemed tired and more or less happy to be going home instead of being scared or sick. So I rowed like someone thinking normal thoughts and stayed quiet through the next day it took us to follow the South-Spiral current home.

Home from the kalaa, I listened as Chief and my uncles told the story of the visit to Sunward. They talked mostly about Rain's wedding dance, which was clearly what the women wanted to hear.

I held new herbs tight against my mouth and kept listening. No one said anything about the *Ocean Mother*. Or the new yams. Or Wide Man's plan to bring us the *Ocean Mother* in a few moons.

I was the only one who had gotten sick. I asked everyone, but we hadn't brought any of the new yams with us, and the rest of the men weren't even sure what I meant. When my mother and others asked me how I lost my tooth, the Chief told them I'd gotten in a fight again. Everyone thought I had probably gotten in a fight with Windhope, so when they were assured that wasn't true, they'd lost the story they wanted to hear. People seemed to feel better that this time I'd gotten beat up and hadn't hurt anyone.

It was alright with me to be left alone. At first I couldn't talk so well without my teeth. I was worried that it was going to affect my singing. If I lost my voice, who would I be?

For a week, I took smaller canoes out by myself, instead of fishing with the other men. Everyone, even Grinner, thought I was upset about Rain. But actually I was upset about what no one else claimed to remember, the taste of the New Yam. When I wasn't eating or drinking, when I was just hauling nets on the beach or falling asleep or shading my eyes and looking north, I had moments when I could feel something in my stomach, thin like a root or a worm.

One day when the nets were in and I was just waiting, I sat on the edge of the canoe and looked at my reflection. The breeze on the water made my face look even more wrong than usual. I heard a deep roaring thrum in the distance, like the sound of a conch shell being blown. The breeze stopped but there were still things wrong with my face and I could feel something moving in my stomach.

I threw myself on my back in the canoe and braced myself against the sides. For the first time since coming home, I started to sing, but this was not a song that I knew. "Ancestors, *help me fight. Grandfather, fight alongside me. Grandmother, sing beside me. Ancestors, help me....*"

On my back in the canoe I saw five white birds of a type I had not seen before and have not seen since, swoop past, so fast that I forgot my illness and leapt up to watch. Standing and watching as they disappeared in the distance, I thought for the first time about what had really happened to the little girl with the white feathers.

They'd been taking off her clothes as she screamed names I could no longer remember. Two of the men had started to fuck her and another had a knife and was cutting. The sickness in my stomach had tried to swallow me but I'd vomited it out. I hadn't thought of White-feather Girl since. I hadn't truly thought about Rain, either. We had left her there in Sunward in a village that was dancing for the *Ocean Mother.*

"Ancestors... *help me kill the Ocean Mother.*" That was the last verse of the first new song. I felt the long-whip thing inside my stomach die. This time I didn't need to vomit it out. It had just been a ghost of a bad thing. My heart started filling with other songs that the ancestors could have known.

"Your voice *is* different. But it's not bad. Just different," said my mother, two weeks later when she walked out to the spit to bring me fish soup I hadn't asked for and a bundle of berries. I think she was worried about me, spending so much time in the trees.

"Every singer should lose a tooth," I said. It was my first smile that day.

After the song on the water, I had asked the ancestors for the songs that I would need to fight the *Ocean Mother*. These new songs were about spears and throwing things and standing when hurt, about resisting fear. Sometimes they were about jumping and running. And when men had been with me a of couple days, they found that the songs were also about killing, and death, and dying without failing, and things that had nothing to do with the way we had lived before.

I hadn't intended to teach anyone else. I started with the idea that I could fight alone. But a day or two after I sang to the ancestors, one of my uncles failed to come back from fishing on a calm day. We found his boat and he was gone. And the day after that, another man went out alone and disappeared. He had also eaten the New Yams.

I didn't want Grinner disappearing, so I taught him a few of the songs. And of course Grinner talked with everyone. Men who had been at Sunward felt better just humming the new tunes. So one by one or three at a time, uncles and cousins and brothers began visiting me where I was fishing from the point. They asked me to teach them.

As soon as they learned three or four songs well, every man said what I thought: they felt like they already knew these songs. They were familiar already, not entirely new, something our grandfathers might have heard of, or their grandfathers. I thought to myself that it went back further than that, but I didn't need to tell people what to think. I just needed them to sing.

Soon we started doing the things I was singing about, or some of them anyway. We didn't sing my new songs near the village, but in the trees we practiced throwing spears and stabbing and running until we collapsed.

Until the others collapsed, anyway. After the third week, I decided to stop pretending to be tired, and to stop missing sometimes on purpose to make people feel more comfortable. The new songs suited me, and with the taste of blood always in my mouth it didn't feel like I needed to be calm like a man trying to avoid being called Rock. I threw three times as far as the other men, when I wanted to. When no one was around to see, I sometimes took a spear that was close to breaking and ran toward the water. I threw north, just to watch the spear disappear, a far flash of black.

One moon into my new songs, people in the village started calling the spit where we practiced Singer's Point. I didn't stop them. So the Chief caught up with me on the beach one morning as I was about to go fishing with a few of my new brothers. Chief looked over my head but his two brothers looked at my hands and my eyes. Once I had thought they were dangerous men.

"Naming a place after yourself is a bad idea, Singer."

Naming? Naming a place?! I had forgotten until that moment, the strange names of the places that didn't exist, Gsesh-na-rahgnan and the other names White-Feather Girl used that night on Sunward. The terrible names swam into my memory but our new songs stabbed them until they became like stumps of something broken. They wanted to bite but they weren't truly there, not for me.

I can't say what happened to my face as I remembered the names. But the Chief stepped backward and both his brothers turned in different directions. One brother kept turning and walked away, pretending to be interested in another man's nets. The other brother backed down the sand until he could put his hand on his canoe.

The Chief spoke again before I could. "Well. That's good then," he said. "We can talk later. All good."

I had no need to look in his eyes because I did not want to see him afraid. "It will be good," I said. "Very good." Chief turned to walk to his canoe.

"Chief," I said. He stopped, not wanting to. "When did Wide Man say he was bringing you the pink shell?"

I watched as the words broke inside him. It was less important, now, to avoid seeing his fear. It was more important to show him that I was not afraid. "How soon?" I asked.

Chief was a brave man, really. He must have remembered more than the other men. He unclenched his teeth and said, "It could have been last week. Next week? It could be moons."

I waited.

"Wide Man wanted to keep it longer than usual and I said that was fine. And that's when he said that he might bring the shell sooner. So we left. But we dragged you from the village first."

"I will be honored to take a Red-Shell kalaa to Sunward," I said. "Kano's father has one, a necklace named *Day Flyer*. Or you could give me a Red-Shell. And when I'm there I will see how they have done with the *Ocean Mother*. Maybe I will take it away so they do not have to bring it all the way here. I will pass it on somewhere else, somewhere people want things like that."

The Chief's hands shook as he took a Red-Shell necklace named *Twelve Paddles* off his neck and handed it to me. "Take *Twelve Paddles* and *Day Flyer*, Singer, take them both. They will bring you luck."

"Good, they are good kalaa shells. I know their songs. I will give them to Wide Man if he is still in the village."

It felt right to talk like that. We knew that I would not be giving the shells to Wide Man. We had stopped pretending that everything was alright. But it felt better to use words that offered hope.

"You should find Rain, Top Woman, Green Eyes, Mirror Tree. All your sisters and aunts. Let them know they can come back. Ask them, please…" He said this even though it was against all the marriage treaties to bring our sisters home. I thought better of him then. Old Chief was willing to change.

As we walked toward the village I hummed the *Four Strong Spears Song* in the deep thrum that had become my voice. Old Chief said, "Will you teach me that song?"

One spear can break
Two spears can miss
Three spears might run
Four spears. Four spears.

Four strong spears never break
Can't miss
Will not run
Four strong spears
Kill so that the people live.

When we could not find the north-ripple current, when it had disappeared in a splinter of warm water going east and odd cold swells, I realized there would be no one left on Sunward to bring home to Sweetwater. We had brought five canoes and more paddles and spears than warriors, in case there were aunts, sisters, and friends we could take away from the island.

I tell you this now, about the currents days from Sunward, to make you understand why I am not saying everything about what we found on the island. There are things that must be faced and killed that it is still not right to talk about. What came to Sunward destroyed the ways of the ocean far away. I will not let my words become like those ripples.

What I can tell is that the smell of the pink shell knocked Dzo and fat Kano out before we got off the beach. We left them with a guard and the rest of us changed our breathing to keep out the worst of it.

On the path to the village we found ways of dying that the flies would not touch. Two of our men went crazy, so that Grinner and I had to kill them ourselves, and no one thought we had done wrong. The men who died had not been singing with me on the spit until the night before our voyage. I hadn't wanted them along but they had sisters who had gone to Sunward to marry.

The dead children we found in the dancing circle were worse. The other new men began crying and Old Chief's strongest brother killed himself by smashing his head into the doorpost of the hut where I had lost my teeth on the night of the feast. I realized that the men who had not learned all the Fighting Songs would be dead soon unless we took them back to the canoes. We circled the six weakest men and walked them back. Kano had recovered. He leaned on his spear and promised to guard them and teach them *Song Against Fear*.

As we marched back toward the village, we lit torches. I taught Grinner and the twelve men with us a song the ancestors had just sung for me. You know it: *We Are Warriors*. But before that moment none of us knew the song, or what it meant.

We walked into the jungle that had grown from the New Yams and killed things that had once been dogs and other things that should have been women. We heard a conch shell blowing from where the jungle met the sea. It made a sound like the island sinking, like waters crashing overheard, but we could feel our toes digging into dry sand. We sang louder to step above fear.

We found Wide Man facing the water on a high cliff. He wore *Ocean Mother* around his waist and blew into a funnel that sprouted up to his mouth, sending the sound of the conch thundering out onto the ocean. There were things and once-men beside him that tried to kill us but they had no war songs. The blood in my mouth carried me up to Wide Man.

"For Rain. For everyone," I said, and rammed the spear through him. *Ocean Mother* screamed and broke. I had some idea of twisting Wide Man into the dirt but he slipped off my spear and ricocheted from the cliff into the water. The sharks clustered beneath the cliff foamed over Wide Man's red body. I turned to kill the things left on land.

Burn an end
To what is dead
And should not have been
Burn until ash is clean.
Burn.

I'd relaxed when the last of the corpses went into the fire. We had been careful to avoid breathing the smoke. There was nothing we could do about the wrong-jungle and most of the village. Maybe it would recover. Perhaps not.

We sunk the two canoes we didn't need, so that nothing we had missed could follow us home, and paddled south toward Sweetwater.

Five hours later, heading into evening, the storm hit us from the north.

"Well, at least it waited until we'd finished the fires," yelled Grinner as he took down the sail. "We could all use a bath. You more than me!"

The smell of lightning competed with the blood and ashes in my hair. "No choice. Just keep running ahead of it," I said.

"We're all ahead of you, Chief," yelled Kano from the back of the outrigger.

I opened my mouth to yell that my name was Singer, looking back over my shoulder, when I saw our slowest boat, the one that had most of the new men, disappear without being hit by a wave. It was a long way off through the rain and the wind but I watched between peaks. There was no sign of the canoe or the men.

I put down my paddle, motioning that everyone else should keep trying to keep the canoe turned into the waves, and took up my grandfather's harpoon with its heavy obsidian point and its strong fiber rope.

Here it came. A great green shark rose from the middle of the seventh wave from our canoe, throwing itself out of the water in a leap. Everyone looked up and saw the shark spread against the sky. It hit the storm wave smooth, with hardly a splash, sliding back into the wave leaving black foam in the air and on top of the water, a dirty-blood mark almost twice the size of our canoe.

I raised the harpoon and sang *We Are Warriors*. I would throw the moment the shark showed itself closer. But in the canoe beside me, Grinner screamed. He vomited so hard that he folded in place, smashing his nose against my knee.

To find a spot for the throw, I had to kick through my uncles and brothers. They flopped and spun in the bottom of the boat or fell off between the outriggers, twitching like fish caught on the points of giant spears.

I knew, then, that Grinner and the rest were not prepared for this shark. They did not realize that an old grandmother shark coming from the bottom of the ocean to find its pink shell armband could easily trade fins for arms and its long fish body for something more like a human face. See! Here it came again, rising now from a wave just two lengths away, still the same shark teeth, pink and glinting rows opening wide as it spread its arms and dropped toward the canoe, as if it were the green wave itself that would drive us down.

My harpoon disappeared into the black between the teeth. The shark screamed. I could not hear it because my ears were full of blood but I felt the scream and then the impact as the skin of a great green arm smashed into the side of the canoe as the shark fell into the water, this time in an explosion of blood and blackness.

The canoe was tipping over so I threw my body onto the outrigger and smacked it back onto the water. Then I felt the harpoon's rope where it had wrapped around my body, I had a second to jump far from the canoe before I was dragged down. As I went into the dark, something snagged in the coil beside me, the body of one of my friends. We fell together and I pulled the knife from his belt to saw at the rope around us. When the rope parted and I lost grandfather's harpoon, I did not know which way was down. The body of my brother went one way, so I kicked the other.

I surfaced into the rain within sight of the canoe. I climbed back in and rescued three men from the water. As the rain died off and the storm dulled to a squall, I looked at the knife still in my hand. Grinner's knife.

Paddling past Sunward
Straight on to Molawa,
Slaying in Turtle Pond Island,
Good War for Flying Fish and Green Fish and Shark,
Deliverance for Solstice, Solstice, Solstice.

I have two wives now, as is right for a Chief. My first wife makes me laugh, which reminds me of Grinner. My other wife is from Coraldown, the southern neighbor we had to take when we became Good War Island, so that someone would properly fish and farm. I know she hates me a little, but I hate myself a little, so that is alright.

When we sail south we carry spears. We break White-Shells and show people why they must not sail south any longer. We teach them a few of the war songs so that they can survive long enough to warn us if *Ocean Mother's* children should appear. We teach them that they will be giving us yams and fish in return for their protection. We take some of their children back to Good War Island with us to teach them the rest of the songs.

When we sail north, we carry all our weapons, war canoes full of men and women singing the songs of the ancestors of war. I used to carry *Twelve Paddles* and *Day Flyer* around my neck in case we met someone to talk with. But the currents have gone insane and the stars are wrong. Who can say whether the places we burn are places we used to sing kalaa for or places the *Ocean Mother* vomited into our lives?

Sometimes I fish alone and try to remember my father's songs, or the song for planting yams, or the strong-paddle song that called grandfather turtle. I could teach them to my children. I sing, but all I bring up are tears and the taste of blood and the songs that came after.

Lithic

Dennis Detwiller

I'm going to try one more time to put it all in order. Even now, I can feel it slipping away, moving in my head in waves. Things spin and snap into place, seeming so clear, so perfect; but only for a moment. Then they fade and drift and disappear. But, for now, I have something. Something to hold on to.

Listen.

I was on the phone with Nan again. Two years of my life leading to one long, messy breakup spread across the northeast from New York to Vermont. The place I fled to lick my wounds.

New York was full of places I didn't want to go and people I didn't want to see. It was winter break, and Nan was staying. I ran home to Vermont. A place Nan and I always talked about visiting, but now, would never see together. It was smaller than I remembered. Like everything there had been shrunk by half a foot behind the scenes in some weird conspiracy.

"What's wrong with you? You don't sound right," Nan said, a wash of noise in the background.

"I'm trying to get my head together," I said. And I was.

Still am.

Through the phone, I could hear Penn Station. A million snippets of time rushing by the receiver as Nan waited for me to speak. The ghost-whispers of a million lives.

For some reason, it made me hungry.

The memories show up, and I really don't know what to do with them. They smash and pile up and collide and combine, and I don't know how to sort them. This happened...after Nan. It must have. I was home in Vermont. Home again.

I think.

"Don't go up on Indian Hill no more," the man said, touching my shoulder. I wasn't paying attention, I was looking up at the mountain, and I turned and found myself face to face with him. This was...I don't know when. It was evening. Early evening.

It was clear, his voice, and not slurred, though his breath was a wave of liquor. I was buckling the belt on the rent-a-cop suit and crossing on the corner of Ulysses Street, and I jumped a little when he stopped me. It had been a long time since I was in town and I wasn't expecting to see anyone. I wasn't expecting to be stopped.

Anyway, I didn't know him. Then at least.

He was that age homeless people become when they've lived outside for too long, a prematurely aged look that hovers between thirty and sixty, depending on the time of day and how deep in the bottle they are. We didn't get many homeless in Stoveton. Vermont was well outside the area friendly for year-round outside habitation, and you got used to the idea that past freezing, everyone was inside somewhere, tucked in, listening to the storm. It's what gives the area that "everything in its right place" feeling that the tourists go nuts for. It isn't hard-headed New England pragmatism that keeps the streets perennially clean, it's the fact that homeless people die in Vermont in the winter.

Most got the hint and headed for more southern climes.

He looked at me for a moment, eyes a lucid blue shot with red, and then moved his hand away. As he did, I saw a thousand bouncing fleas on his jacket and I jumped back a little, self-consciously wiping the jacket where he had touched it.

He stepped backwards, hands up. Was he old enough to think "peace" or young enough for a simple "dude"? I couldn't tell. He didn't seem dangerous. In any case, I'm a big guy. I had a foot on him, at least.

As I looked at him, he seemed to shrink. He turned down the utility road next to Sharkey's Pizza and walked away fast, a single unlaced boot flapping in the dirty snow behind him. He didn't look back.

For a moment I wondered what his life must be like. Digging through dumpsters behind Aces. Eating stale, frozen bagels out of fragrant plastic bags. Sleeping next to laundry exhausts and heated patios, under piles of papers and in crawlspaces. Burrowing into things for warmth. I tried to place myself in his world. But it all fell away as I thought about it, failing to come together in any clear narrative. Still, that lifestyle seemed familiar. Somehow.

"How do you know where I'm going?" I shouted after him.

I feel like I saw him more than once, so that could have been another day, or a dream.

There was a night on Indian Hill where I almost killed someone. This memory is old. Tommy something. He'd been goading me all night. Mocking me. Pushing me, even though he was small, scrawny. We drank and listened to Radiohead and watched the stars, and at one point, it was like someone whispered something in my ear, and it was on.

I looked up at Tommy and he was looking at me, smirking. And it was like it wasn't Tommy. His eyes were lost in shadow, and his uneven teeth were lit with red and yellow from the fire. It wasn't Tommy.

People talk about their first punch. They say it hurts. They say it's ineffective. This punch was neither. It didn't hurt. Tommy went flying. He rebounded off one of the stones, rolled and then dropped into the fire, still rolling, pant cuff flashing with a momentary flame.

And then I was on him. I beat him for a long time. I don't know how long. I recall scraping up clots of earth and yellow grass and shoving it in his bloody mouth, up his nose.

For a second I felt the pulse of a million dead generations. People half-naked and starving on the mountain who gathered together there to appease something unseen and sleeping. They fought, they fucked, they killed. We had hit a current there, at that moment. We tapped into something alive and older than anything.

Finally, somehow, I brought myself under control.

When I looked up, wheezing, Tommy was nothing but a broken lump of blood and dirt beneath me, shaking and bleeding. I saw a ring of faces, all lit by fire from below, staring at me. They didn't look human. All their faces were illuminated with something other than the fire.

Anyway, no one tried to stop me. Nothing came of it. I signed his yearbook later that year like nothing had ever happened at all.

Maybe it hadn't. It's all so disjointed.

When I was growing up, Indian Hill was called the stoner's garden. It was about three miles from town, and by the time we were sixteen, we were tooling up there in a 4x4 to blast music and get drunk and smoke up. Everyone went there. All the kids from town.

I spent a million drunken nights there in various states of adolescent disrepair. Once, I woke in my underwear, alone, on one of the stones in the middle of August, covered in dew. It was that kind of place. A place to try a drug for the first time, or to lose your virginity, or lose a fight. It was our clubhouse. Sometimes it got so you couldn't think, being up there. Too many people, too much energy, too many drugs.

Other times, we'd simply camp out near the ring, watching the stars and passing the bottle. It was the only local hang-out where we could get away with the things our teenage selves wanted to do. It was our place.

Some time after New York, I found myself working up on Indian Hill, like an ellipses bracketing my life. I lived the cliché. Small town boy launches himself for wonderland, only to smash into the same small town on the far side of the arc. It didn't seem like such a stretch. The Grove was putting a ski run up there, and due to insurance concerns, they'd fenced off the area around the stones and put up a guard shack.

At dusk every night, I'd hike up the Booth road, take the cut off, and march up Indian Hill through the pines. Every morning I'd catch the first fuel truck down to town, drag my ass to my mom's house, crash out and do it all again.

(I haven't seen my mom in some time. I can't recall the last time clearly. Every night in the house seems the same now.)

I rode that shack five nights a week, reading scripts and books on film-making, biding my time. Soon enough, I'd be back in New York, running around with a camera, playing pretend for twenty-six thousand a year. Nan would be there. But I didn't like thinking about that.

After New York, it was something like a vacation from people. It was nice, for once, to sit alone in the dark with the knowledge that nothing human was around me for miles. And to get paid for it, not so bad. I didn't mind the dark.

Anyway I remember a lot of nights on Indian Hill. It seems to be all I can focus on, now. It's hard to think of anything else for some reason.

I also remember finding an animal, when I was...younger. Maybe half the age of when I was working up on the rise. This was near Indian Hill, in the woods. 1995? 1996? I don't know. I was little. Years before Nan, New York and the guard booth.

Why am I thinking about this? It's hard to think about this.

I'd walk the woodlots on the lower mountain when I was little. Summer break. Wandering through silent woods, listening for animals in the underbrush, spying on the few people I'd come across. You didn't see many people up there, then.

When I heard this, I knew it was something special. The noise was bad. Something small and in distress. The noise carried.

Anyway, I followed it through the ferns for ten minutes, maybe twenty. Finally, I thought I had it boxed in, near a deadfall and some old trees. Something furry and small and making noises in the underbrush.

There was something wrong with it. I thought it was a cat. It wouldn't let me see it. I caught a glimpse of it in the brush, something grey and white, but it skittered away from me, making noises that were wrong. It sounded like something in pain, something squealing and mewling but trying to be quiet at the same time.

I chased it. It's what kids do, after all.

I caught one clear view of it, pulling aside one of the big ferns in time to reveal it, frozen in fear, in the middle of a clot of dirt next to a rotting stump.

It wasn't a cat. It was a rat. A rat as big as my arm. Grey and white. Something was wrong with it. The front third of its body was knotted with some transparent grey web. Something like a cord of latex filled with pulsing curd. These webs went down its throat, up one nostril, and kept its mouth open so that it left a constant pool of dribble as it went. It was wheezing with terror.

It looked up at me, almost resigned to its fate, trembling with exhaustion.

I stopped in my tracks, terrified to go any closer. It ran off into the woods. I never saw it again. Never thought about it again, until now.

I could find it now, I suppose, if I looked for it. It's still here, somewhere, I bet.

What a strange thought.

One of the millions of evenings on the hill, I let myself in the gate, and carefully pulled it shut. It was winter, but still early. So there was standing water during the day at least.

The road, what of it there was, was ripped up. Mud flung everywhere in frozen chunks, the grooves from giant tires cutting patterns in the earth like maps. My boots squelched as I climbed the incline, trying to keep out of the deeper mud, preferring the frozen edges, which cracked under foot.

Martin was there, outside the shack where I knew he would be, but he didn't see me. He was flushed red when I came up the rise, and a plume of white poured from his lips as he flicked the cigarette out into the pines. He leaned his head back, put his hands on the small of his back and stretched, letting out an audible grunt.

Martin was built like a leprechaun linebacker. He was tiny, but strong and wide and a little bit scary looking, with a ruined nose and thick cheeks crisscrossed by burst capillaries. Anyway, he was old, or older than me. That's about all I really knew about Martin.

We'd exchanged some forced pleasantries in front of the company man, once, and since then, it'd been hand-off after hand-off. Nothing much more.

"Missed some shit today," Martin said when he saw me, obviously pleased.

I raised my eyebrows and stepped past him to the shed. Checked the fuel on the heater, and put my stuff down. Unperturbed, Martin just kept on talking.

"Some nut was up here. Took a crowbar to the bobcat. The cops just hauled him off."

I stopped.

"One of the Dowdys?" The Dowdys owned a house on the far side of the run, and they weren't too pleased with the construction. There had been words on more than one occasion.

Martin shook his head.

"No. Like I said, some nut." Martin surveyed the road going up the slope towards the stones.

"How'd he get to the site?" "Didn't come in the gate. Must have hopped the fence." Martin turned and looked at me with a smirk.

"Huh," I said, thinking about the man on the street this evening.

"Anyway, he didn't stop shit, they hauled off the second stone before the whistle blew."

For a moment, I felt light-headed.

"Where did they take it?" I asked.

"What?"

"The stone? Where did they take the stones?" Even in the memory, the fact seemed important, monumental. Vital.

He glanced down and smiled with a look on his face like an adult talking to a child. He shook his head.

"Kid, who the hell cares? Not me."

And then I was alone for the night. Whatever night that was.

The memory fades away like a dream when you first try to recount it. I used to write them down, but my handwriting is poor. Gibberish is all I get from those half-sleep composed notes. Anyway, the thought, it was about Martin, Martin and Indian Hill.

I try to focus on Martin. I close my eyes and all I see is the back of a naked man, face down in the winter mud, his head split open like a gourd with pink-white brains spilled out.

It is night, and his skin glows blue white, as the blood and heat leave his body. His head juts mist as the warmth inside him spills out to fill the night.

And a voice inside me is muttering a million different things. Threads of thought so fine they form an unbroken wall of ideas so complex and interwoven that looking at them simply throws into focus how incapable of understanding them I am.

I'm weeping there, in the memory, I think. If it is a memory. The voice is there too, muttering, chanting, speaking to me, but it is too much. Someone else is speaking.

"I'm sorry, I'm so sorry..."

It's my voice.

I'm thinking too much about Indian Hill. I need to think about other things, but it's like the further they are from the Hill, the more difficult they are to focus on.

I think about Nan. Even though it hurts, I think about Nan.

There was a time when Nan was calling me. The phone was ringing but I was far away. My head aching, my hands raw and numb. From my vantage point, inverted on the bed, I was looking at four stretched squares of light crawl across the ceiling in time-lapse. Everything felt wrong. Time was like a greased rope, spilling out of my hands and into the black, I was dropping with it.

My face felt puffed, my nose was raw, my eyes nearly swollen shut. Was I crying? Who knows.

The phone rang again, and each time it would reach its peak, the sound would shake through the air, shaking my head, shaking my fillings, blurring my vision. Each time it stopped, I thought it would be the last, but it wasn't. It kept ringing.

I felt exhausted. Cracked open and hollowed out. Empty. Nothing could bring back the order to my life now. It was too late. Too much had happened. It was beyond me now. I was just reacting. Everything was jumbled up already.

Something had happened on the Hill.

Finally, after what seemed like hours, the ringing stopped.

I slept.

I dreamt of swimming in warm water. Floating around me in the current were the prone bodies of others, people drifting along in an amber river, still. As I watched, through the blurred water, I saw them twitching, as if asleep.

What a strange dream. I don't like thinking about it.

And just like that, it fades away.

Night on the mountain comes on like this: first, everything settles, then it fades.

On this night, it wasn't winter yet, but there was some snow, and moment to moment, it seemed to bleach the warm colors out of the world like a photo fading in time lapse. The yellows and reds thinned, leaving purples and blues, split by black pickets of trees, until the sky at the forest's edge was the only bright thing in the world.

I had been up here a thousand times. A million. I had seen the play of light before dusk in rain, in heat, in winter. I felt I had seen all that Indian Hill had to offer me, still I watched it, arm propped up on the plywood table in the shack, with the lights out.

Finally, like some magic trick, someone turns it all down, all the colors. For a few minutes, as the last of the air fades to black, I sat in silence in the booth, in the dark, listening to my breath. Finally, with a click, I snapped on the lights.

All that's left by five-thirty is the guard shack; a wave of light in four directions from the windows, the dim pearly glow of nearby snowbanks, and silence. You couldn't see the town. There were no other lights except the shack.

I turned the heater up, spun the egg timer for thirty minutes, folded open my book on Tarkovsky, and began reading, but the page seemed uninviting. I kept starting and stopping and turning back to the beginning. The words seemed to drop from my mind as my eyes tracked them.

This could have been any of a hundred nights. A thousand.

Then this other time, I'm running in the woods. This is recent. I think. I'm running with a slung shotgun and a flashlight. Every footfall the shotgun swings away from my shoulder, and every other footfall, it smashes into my shoulder blade. But I don't care.

I'm very, very frightened.

My feet are screaming. My back, bent. I'm stumbling on snow and branches and over deadfalls, flatfooted and without any grace—terrified. I've dropped the gun and the flashlight more than once, and scrambled to pick them up just as quickly. My breath is coming out in plumes that are lost behind me before I can even see them.

It feels like I'm surrounded. In the dark, just past my vision, it feels like a crowded room. Like a theater after the lights go down, like I am the main attraction. I am being watched. I am the focus of something terrible which waits for me in time.

Confusing. Is Martin here?

Sitting on the mountain seems to take up much of my mind.

Guarding something as ambiguous as a proposed ski-run is difficult to picture, so I'll walk you through it. The timer goes off, you pick up the shotgun and flashlight, and walk the run. The shotgun was standard now in podunk assignments, as Vermont was going through a nasty resurgence of its Black Bear population. Having been chased by one the previous summer at Yale Lake, I didn't need to be told twice. Anyway, everyone local knew their way around a scattergun.

The flashlight didn't do much. I mean, it's big and heavy, but the light is pathetic in the face of the night. It's like walking along the bottom of the ocean. Your breath in your ears, the crunch of snow and pop of twigs, a dim light plucking a tiny circle of normal out of the black.

Thanks to the recent snow, you could find the footpaths. There was the main run, from the entrance to the stones, and then a skein of boot marks tracking an octagon around the perimeter of the fence. I followed that one. Walked it. Maybe it was a mile all told. Didn't see anything except trees and snow and dark.

When I cut back on the far side to walk to the stones, I stopped, shifted hands, trading the shotgun and light, and began up the hill.

About five minutes up, the men had been to work. The old growth trees that had crept in in all the years of my youth around the stone circle had been plucked like rotten teeth. A nearly perfect rectangle of cut trees swept past the stone circle like a frame pointed at the sky. The ground, which was once covered in thick yellow grass was bare mud, torn up by construction equipment.

In the center were the stones, or what of them were left. There were nine when I was a kid. Nine big rocks cut at strange angles worn down over time. Older than the United States, older than the Indians. They were carved and cut and graffitied by a million hands throughout the years. I myself spray-painted my name on one in the summer of 2005, the year I graduated high school.

That stone was still there. Others, two of them, had been plucked from the ground leaving an ugly black and brown squelch in the ground. Each of these holes had been marked by pickets of snapped paint-sticks, painted with fluorescent orange to mark them.

I stopped at the peak of the hill, huffing. I shone the light around up there, marking the stones and the lack of stones. It felt wrong, unbalanced. But I didn't know if that was just the artist in me. For no reason at all, I wandered over to one of the gaps and looked down into the hole.

It was a three foot deep slack of mud, which sunk in an uneven pyramid to a black gap, about the size of my fist, in the center. I shone the light down the hole, but all I could see was black. It seemed wrong too. I had leaned up against the rock that had been there for *years*. It was cool all year round, tall and grey and flat, well mostly. If you leaned back facing the center of the ring, and looked up, a slight dip in the stone seemed to frame a star in the center of the sky.

No one knows who put them up. The Indians have stories. Back in high school I dug up some books on the stuff and poked around. It's a habit I have. I find something out of the ordinary, I latch on, and I read about it. Or at least, read about it as much as I can. Then I think about it. The summer I became interested in the stones, I read seven books on them. I have a notebook somewhere.

First off, the Indians didn't build them, and that's according to the Indians. Rogue Vikings, a moon-faced white people who feared the sun, some unknown pre-native civilization, take your pick. The whole of New England is peppered with them, stone forts, old rings of stones, gullies and gunnels and fences of chipped rock—monolithic structures which thumb their nose at modern science. Some of the rocks are huge, three, four tons. They were standing when Champlain blew through here in 1609, dropping a flag along the way, and they were standing when the state was founded.

Strangely, no one really seems to care too much who put them up. It's amazing what people choose to ignore when it bothers their pre-established sensibilities. It's also useful when you want to knock them down. There's no definitive culture to protect. Some Indians might raise a stink, and some sad little faux-Wiccans, but past that, there's no one left to stand up and complain. It's a shame, really. The rocks are incredible.

Some studies, for instance, of the rocks at King's Chamber (another site in Vermont) dated it 10,000 years *before* the Indians got here. Trouble that. It was ignored. I mean, they printed it, but no one looked any deeper. Who was I to complain? I didn't really take it upon myself either. Just because I read a few books and took some notes, didn't make me any better. I just went along with it like the rest of them. Complaining about it didn't help.

I still think about them a lot.

This must have been a dream.

I was on the mountain. It was a warm and clear and a spring or summer morning. Nan was there. We were walking together in the pines, holding hands. There were no bugs yet. Birds were crying in the trees, there was a clear, warm grey white light and the shadows that the sun cut divided the world into a grid of darkness and light.

Nan turned from me, releasing my hand, and began walking up Indian Hill towards the stones. I stopped, refusing to follow. She didn't look back. In fact, I couldn't recall seeing her face at all. Her back was to me, wearing the same green sweater torn at the sleeve, the same capri pants. I knew it was her. But I couldn't see her.

I wanted to see her face, but I didn't want to go up the hill. She continued up the rise until she was nearly a hundred feet away.

The tug was sudden.

My right arm was suddenly pulled forward with a shocking force, causing me to stumble forward, arm outstretched, barely keeping my feet.

It was only then I realized that my hand wasn't just my hand. The skin at the ends of the fingers kept going, snaking out from my finger tips like it had run like hot wax, congealing into a messy knot of muscle and fat, forming a rope of flesh that tumbled to the ground and coiled up the hill towards Nan.

The hand she had been holding with mine was connected by a hundred foot rope of grey-pink flesh.

I don't remember what happened next. Maybe I woke up.

One morning, pre-dawn, on the run. Don't know when. I was standing outside the booth, taking a piss down the run when I heard it.

As I stopped peeing, I heard a thin, high sound—something far off and distant and directionless. I zipped quick, unable to identify the noise, worried someone might be coming, but as I moved, the sound vanished beneath the crackly and shuffle of my clothes.

I froze in place and listened again. A moment later the sound, a voice, maybe a child, or a woman or a man singing. High and thin and far off. It floated through the air and seemed to hover for a moment before vanishing. There were no words I could pick out. No structure. No pattern. Just a voice that rose and then faded. But some birds can sound like people. But it was too cold and too dark for birds.

I stood still and listened again. Waiting.

While I was waiting, I don't know how long, the dawn came. Slowly filling the gaps in the air with light. Finally, with my legs getting stiff and my fingers growing numb, I went back into the booth to warm up.

It never occurred to me to go up the hill to the stones. Not then.

I think.

This was before the homeless guy maybe. Near there at least. It wasn't a dream.

I climbed from the cab at about eight in the morning, and the town was already up and about for hours. I skirted the plow-

line to the salted sidewalk and considered myself in the glass of
Griffen's. My hair was standing in sleep-spikes, my eyes were deep
and bruised with lack of sleep. I looked ruined. My bed was two
hundred yards from here, up a rickety set of steps, in a room with
a whistling water heater and frayed quilts. It sounded like a dream.
Like heaven.

I turned to walk home and found myself facing Armin Dowdy,
no more than fifty feet from me, moving at a clip in my direction.

Everyone knew Dowdy. He was the terrible old man from our
childhood. His house bordered the garden. He'd run up on parties
on the stones three or four times a year, scattering kids with his
screams. He was frightening, tall and thin and scarecrow-like,
forever in insulated overalls and a down vest. His was older now,
thinner, but none of his presence had left him. He saw me, and
I saw him and without thinking I turned back and stepped into
Griffen's.

With my back to the door, I found the paperback rack and
began searching it. The door opened behind me with a BING
and I kept my eyes down. Then, silence. The clerk was lost in her
magazine and the music playing was soothing. I tracked titles but
all the words seemed jumbled. Reversed, mixed-up. Gibberish.

"You're guarding the run," Dowdy said to me. His voice was
close behind me. For some reason, I didn't turn. I pictured him, a
tall old man hunching down to speak into my ear.

"Don't turn around. I can see it hasn't got ya yet," his breath
was warm and smelled of coffee and denture-cream.

Confusion, now. I smirked a little, uncontrollably. A picture
formed in my mind. Crazy. Dowdy had slipped off his rocker
quietly somewhere along the way. What was he? Seventy?
Dementia. Burning out slowly up on the hill in a big ratty house.
Losing his mind piece by piece. I didn't turn. I was confused,
embarrassed.

"I don't know how many in the town been taken, hard to tell
in winter," I could sense him turning his big head to look around.

"You listen up. Don't let no one touch you. No one. Skin to
skin. Don't you do it."

I turned to look at him and was startled to see his eyes filled with fear.

"I can't talk you off the run. You be careful. It'll come for you soon."

The old man exited the door with a bang, and was gone.

But maybe that was earlier?

Once, I dreamt of warmth. A womb-like warmth and nestling close to others. Other people in a dark liquid. There was a sound like a drum. Something banging away somewhere else in the warmth, shaking it, shaking me. It felt safe, but also tomb-like, enclosed, buried.

I opened my eyes and in the blurred half-light I saw a dozen naked bodies, floating in a yellow-brown gel, mouths open and filled, eyes alive and searching in the murk. The next thing I knew I was wobbling in front of my bathroom mirror, face covered in cold water, eyes wide and blank and frightened. I ran cold water through my hair and slowly came back to reality.

Then I went downstairs and made myself a turkey pot pie and watched the news.

One night, I opened the gate at four-forty, expecting to find the last dregs of workers leaving the area, and Martin or Davis at the booth, instead, I found no one. The trucks were gone. The booth was closed and locked, but no one was there. I locked the gate, unlocked the booth and got in to get it over with.

I would ignore the strangeness and simply mark the countdown. Then, back to school.

This is one of the few moments I can track with any certainty.

A night, in the booth.

I felt it right away. Even before the first timer went off, I could feel it. The buzz at the base of your neck when someone is watching you. I sat staring at the same paragraph again and again, eyes flicking glances out the window into the dark. I had read nothing. The idea of being watched had spun up to a monstrous size in my mind, consuming all else.

Finally, unable to stand it, I stood, picked up the shotgun, slung it, and grabbed the flashlight. I stepped out into the dark and clicked on the light.

"Hello," I said to no one at all and felt immediately embarrassed. What was I doing? There was no one to hear me.

With a muffled DING the timer sprung in the guard booth and I spun and came within a fraction of a second of shooting blindly at the door, cutting it up with shot.

My breath huffing out of me, I let the shotgun hang from its strap and stared in wonder at the safety of the booth. I put my hands on my knees, the shotgun spun and dropped and butt first, dangled in the dirt, and I laughed, shaking. How would I explain a booth peppered with shot in the morning? God. What was I doing?

That's when I heard it. The soft crunch of footsteps in the snow. I didn't look up, but the shaky humor faded from me quickly. I sat there, leaning on my knees, huffing out pillars of smoke. Was I afraid? I don't know.

Finally, not really moving, I looked up to the left.

Past the edge of the light of the shack, maybe thirty feet away, stood a person. She was short, maybe five feet tall, and a woman, that much was clear. You couldn't see much. She was dark, and it wasn't just the light. Her skin was dark, and there was a lot of it, because she was nude. She was covered in black chunks of mud.

Standing in the snow at night, nude, watching me.

My breath caught in my throat as I watched her watch me. She stood still, but in the silence, I could hear something else. It sounded like a rubber-tire dragged along grass, a slow, low hissing sound.

Suddenly, I flicked the flashlight up on her. For a moment, she was there, clear as day. Naked, brown with frazzled, mud-stained black hair. Dark eyes. Pearl white teeth pulled back in a grimace. An Indian.

Next, she was in the air as if she had leapt backwards eight feet, then ten, flying backwards, hands flailing out in front of her. She made no sound, but her form vanished in seconds into the black of the trees, up the run towards the stoners' garden.

I stood there for a long time, in the dark, shaking.

I remember some of it, now.

Some morning, when Thomas showed up, everything was in order. My face was fixed in a bored expression I had practiced the last few hours. I hopped the fuel truck down the mountain. What nobody knew is I spent the night in the shack curled up in its base, avoiding the windows, a shotgun clutched in my hands, waiting for any noise. I didn't walk the perimeter. I didn't check the stones. I didn't leave that booth. I didn't even pee.

When I was off the hill, the feeling of relief was palpable.

I didn't sleep when I got back. I ate, went upstairs, and sat on the bed, rolling the night over in my head.

It was difficult to place last night's events in any order. I could still see them in my mind, but there was a powerful urge to discard them. To cover them up with other things. Had I seen what I thought I had seen? Was there a naked woman up there that night? Was it a trespasser?

I had to know.

It's almost clear now.

I went up the mountain with a box full of slugs in my jacket that night. No more shot. I didn't think it would do any good. This is still when I thought it was under control. I had suspicions, but they were so crazy, I didn't even really believe them, though my body did. On some primal level I was terrified all the time.

When I made it to the booth, I loaded up the shotgun, left the booth and marched up the hill before the sun went down. The march was slow. A new snow had fallen. The garden was clear of all but one stone. Eight muddy holes, criss-crossed by a thousand muddy footprints, truck and bobcat tracks and picket fences.

I sat on the last stone. It was a huge, low, hill-like stone. It was the stone I woke on so many years earlier after a night of drunken partying. I sat very still, breath pouring from my scarf in gouts. Shotgun on my lap. I placed the flashlight on the rock next to me.

From my vantage point, I had a clear view of all of the holes.

I decided, then, that I would spend the night here, just to see what might happen. Though then I really didn't know why.

Nan is yelling at me. She's marched from the living room to the bathroom and saying something hurtful. But now I know this is not real. Nan was there, sometime in the past. Some other point before all of this, but this here, this moment, is not real.

I know this because she throws a box of letters at me, letters I wrote to her, I think. The box hits me and tumbles and catches the air and scatters papers everywhere. She slams the door.

On the ground, in front of me, a dozen letters are all arrayed all over the ground, staring up at me. Every line on them is gibberish. A jumble of letters which seems to shift and change as I look at it.

I know.

On the last night, when the first thing slithered from the hole, I was asleep. I had nodded off. It was a slow sound, broken by a squelch and a pop, waking me immediately. I clicked on the light. Unsure if there had been a noise at all or if my imagination had startled me from sleep.

It had gone full dark a few hours before, and as the stars spun through their tracks and nothing happened, the fervor I had felt in waiting for something had faded. My eyes closed sometime after seven.

I grabbed the flashlight and clicked it on, pointing it north, but all I saw was empty, muddy holes and the night sky cut by the tops of pines further down the mountain. Then someone said something.

The voice was low, keening. It took a moment to realize it was terrified, that voice, wheezing. Barely under control.

My light tracked around until it found the woman. It was the same woman I had seen earlier. Muddy, naked in the snow. She was an Indian. She was curled on the ground near one of the holes, lips drawn back in a grimace, wheezing, mumbling words in a language that I didn't know.

I stepped forward, and she seemed to shake convulsively. I brought the shotgun around and pointed it at her. She didn't react to the gun, she just stared at me with crazed eyes. Eyes that reminded me of something I had seen years before.

I crept up on her like that. Shotgun in one hand, flashlight in the other, in a shuffling gait.

I was only a few feet from her when I saw it.

A clear, grey white tentacle tracked from the shadow behind her, curling into the muddy hole from one of the stones, emerging from it like a worm from the ground. It slid lazily back and forth, easily fifty feet long and as thick as my thigh. Inside it, when the light crossed it, I could see liquid pumping through it.

Dennis Detwiller

When the light hit it, it shifted as if it could feel it, sliding back and the Indian woman was pulled from her feet with a scream.

My mind dropped through my feet and the fear was on me in a way I never thought possible. The tentacle was attached to the back of the Indian woman's neck. It held her like a marionette... attached.

The sliding sound woke me from my revulsion.

Other tentacles had emerged from the ground. One, with a tip barbed and cut like a lamprey, was almost at my boot when I saw it.

I opened up. I pumped a 10 gauge round into it, and it flailed back, spraying the ground with a grey-white soup which seemed to melt the snow beneath it. The smell was like a swimming pool gone over in high summer. A whiff of chlorine filled with the swampy stink of green. There were screams; the Indian woman was yanked back as if an invisible giant had swept her off into the dark.

I ran down the rise and fired three times, cutting one tentacle that popped up in front of me in two with a single shot, leaving an end flopping in the dirt, when I was knocked from my feet.

I was struck by something big which hit me from the side with the force of a linebacker's tackle. The air left me, the shotgun fell. The flashlight went flying through the night air in arcs, landing in a drift, pointing up towards the ceiling of naked pines.

The Indian woman was there. The Indian woman had struck me. Her face was a mask of tears. Her mouth moved soundlessly. She was sorry, she was exhausted, she was not in control.

Something was *in* her.

I scrambled backwards like a crab until my hands fell on the shotgun. The tentacle LIFTED her off the ground by her neck, making her look as if she was floating, her eyes rolling back in her head and her hands opening in front of her in a strange gesture like a cat in repose. She crossed the ground I had crab-walked in a second, landing with a leg on either side of me, her face a mask of terror and regret.

I rolled, pulled the shotgun around and pushed it into her chest. Fired.

There was a huge explosion. Her eyes rolled in her head, and her lips pulled back in a grimace which was more of a grin. With a shake, her body dropped, hollowed out by the slug, like a sack of wet flour. I was covered in a soup of grey white jelly mixed with blue black clots of blood, which flooded from the hole in a gout. The tentacle roiled back until it was a dozen feet off the ground, two dozen. It looped, and curled and tracked me, covered and pinned and screaming.

I went to fire again, but the shotgun was empty. But that's not important right now, I think.

Not important.

In the gap between my memories and the world, something hovers. It is alive and terrible, and has slept a long, long time. It speaks to me, and uses me and makes me whole. It has taken me into it and has made me real. I sleep in it in the cold mountain and it keeps me warm.

I gave myself to it before I knew it even existed. I gave it blood on the mountain and worshipped at its stones and made the proper ablutions. It heard my pleas even when I didn't know I was making them. It heard me and watched me and waited.

It took me, one night on the mountain, and now I am with it forever. It speaks to me from time to time. It manages me. It works through my memories, it keeps me from going mad by moving my mind from subject to subject.

SLEEP it says to me. A word so complete and total, so encompassing it washes away all that has come before in my life like a wave of white. Erasing all want, all need, all time.

I will sleep soon, and when I sleep, I will forget. But not forever.

Nothing human lasts forever. Does it? Please. Is there someone there with me in the dark.

Hello?

Listen.

In the Pacific, there is a fish which poisons its prey in such a way that it causes the fish to flail about, to swim in circles and to let off a distress chemical which calls other bigger fish for it to feed on.

It waits, this predator, until the other bigger fish get close, and then it feeds. The poor bait fish can be poisoned dozens of times in this manner before succumbing to death. Bloated with the poison, mind reeling, body reflexively going through a terror-dance, it can sometimes last days in this stupor.

I think about that fish a lot, beneath the water, screaming.

I can't remember why.

Snack Time

Chris Lackey

I was in a bit of a hurry.

I was actually running for my life down an empty street in Los Angeles, when I noticed a police car parked in front of a donut shop. A cop was just walking out with a bag in his arms. I ran up to him.

"Officer, Officer!" I shouted. He was in his mid-thirties and a bit overweight. He had a mustache, which seemed to still be in fashion for police officers and firemen. His name tag read "Officer Bluthe."

"What's the problem?" he asked, annoyed.

"I...uh..."

I panicked for a second. I didn't know what to say. I couldn't tell him what was really going on. That would sound crazy.

"My friends were...attacked." The truth.

"Where are they? Did you see who attacked them?"

"Well yeah. It..." I had to softball it. "It was a dog." Okay, that'll work, I thought. He looked around, worried. I knew he was buying my story.

"Where is the dog now?" he asked—a good question.

"I don't know. It was chasing me. I think it might still be around." I was sure it was. "It's really big like a St. Bernard, but it looks more like a Rottweiler." I was laying it on pretty thick. Sure, it was big and doggy, but not like any dog I'd ever seen.

"Okay. How bad are your friends hurt?" the officer asked.

They were dead.

"I don't know. But we should get out of here quick," I said very calmly. I always keep my head in crisis situations. I guess that's why I'm still alive.

At that moment I started to feel a little dizzy and nauseous. I could see the officer was feeling it too.

"Okay. Let me call this..." Bluthe said, but he was interrupted. I was looking over at the donut shop, to the side of us, when something moved at him. I couldn't see what happened next because warm liquid sprayed in my face and in my eyes. I heard him hit the ground as I ran blindly in the other direction. I tasted blood.

I wiped my eyes as I ran, and almost slammed into the donut shop's front door. It wasn't a chain store—it was one of those places that sell donuts and Chinese food. I never understood why there are so many Chinese/donut shops in Los Angeles. Someone told me it had to do with deep fryers, that you use the same ones for making donuts as you do egg rolls. I never checked into it.

As I was saying, I was running into a fast-food-Chinese-and-donut-shop, covered in blood. I got inside and pushed the door shut behind me. I wiped my face a few more times, trying to get the blood out of my eyes. When I thought I could see well enough, I looked for the beast through the glass door. Nothing. All I could see was the cop's body laying on the ground about fifteen feet from the squad car and ten feet from...his head. I started to panic.

"Oh, my god!" yelled someone behind me. Heh. I swear I jumped out of my skin. Probably the worst startle of the evening. Well one of the worst.

I spun around to see a chubby, teen-aged, Chinese-American kid with a name tag reading "Nick", standing behind the counter. He took a step back. Oh yeah, I thought. I'm covered in blood and look like a lunatic. Normally a 49-year-old, skinny, balding, white guy isn't that intimidating, but when covered in blood—that's enough to give anyone pause.

There was also a rather dirty looking, bearded man (homeless, I presumed), and a thin, older, Hispanic woman wearing scrubs under a jacket. I think she was a nurse. Everyone looked terrified. Of me.

"Kid, call the cops," I said very calmly—though I honestly didn't know what the police could do. Maybe they had enough firepower to take the thing down, but mostly I just wanted more people around to distract it.

Nick walked over to the phone without taking his eyes off me, slowly picked up the receiver and dialed 9-1-1. I thought about asking him if we could lock the door, but I didn't think it would stop the hound.

I looked back outside. No sign of the beast—or of anyone. Los Angeles can be like that: a city with millions of people where at times the streets are totally empty. You can actually be alone on a typically busy street, and I really felt it then. I felt very alone.

"Are you okay?" the nurse asked hesitantly. She was cautiously walking towards me. The homeless guy just sat there drinking his coffee.

"Yeah, it's not my blood," I said a little too casually.

"Oh…" she stammered as she stopped walking.

"Hold on. I didn't kill anybody. There is this really big, rabid dog out there. It attacked that cop," I explained as I jabbed my thumb over my shoulder.

"Officer Bluthe?" Nick said, almost shouting. He ran and looked out of the front doors. The whole front of the place was glass, but filled up with those poster-sized stickers with pictures of donuts and Chinese food.

"Oh, god," he whispered. The nurse walked over and looked out one of the windows. She gasped. I felt bad for a moment. This was my fault. If I was more careful... If I anticipated the opposition better... those fanatics. My friends and I had a plan that night. We knew there would be opposition, but we thought we could handle it. We were wrong. They overpowered us. They had machine guns! Where did they get machine guns? And in the confusion of the gun fight, the summoned hound had no one to control it. All my friends were devoured or riddled with bullets or both. I managed to get out with my life, but the beast seemed to be on my trail. Officer Bluthe, Nick, these poor people... all affected by what I had done. Or didn't do.

Then I felt the nausea again, only for a split second, before it appeared. It's a kind of sickening feeling, a vertigo. Then the beast slammed into the glass and bounced off. The nurse screamed and I felt myself just shake hard for a moment. I couldn't believe that the glass had held. Perhaps my luck was beginning to change.

The thing lay on the ground stunned. That was the first time I really got a good look at the creature. To call it a hound now, seems a gross misinterpretation, but nothing else really comes close. It moved like a dog, it had four legs, a head, a mouth and eyes... but that's where any real similarities ended. Its bone structure was different, the joints were odd and misshapen and the skin was textured like a rotten lizard. My head throbbed as my poor brain fought with the cognitive dissonance, but I couldn't look away. They call it a Hound of Tindalos. I think. The taxonomy is sketchy on these sorts of things, so I'm still really not sure.

It was still conscious, but stunned. I knew I wouldn't have an opportunity like that again, so I bolted out of the front door and towards the fallen police officer. I crouched down to unclip the holster and pull out his pistol. I spun around, ready to shoot the fallen beast with every last bullet in the gun — but it was gone.

Oh no. I blew it. I kept spinning around and aiming the gun, thinking the beast was going to try to sneak up on me. I needed to move, get my back up against a wall or something, but the police car caught my attention—more specifically the shotgun inside it. I need that, I thought. But it was locked into some kind of holder.

I leaned over the cop's body and rummaged through his pockets, while keeping an eye out for the hound. I really didn't know what the thing was capable of. I'd heard stories about the Hounds of Tindalos, but it was already doing things I didn't think were possible. I thought it could only slip into our world through the angles of our universe, but it seemed to be popping up anywhere it liked. But then why didn't it appear on the other side of the glass—the side I was actually on? I pushed the thought out of my head as I pulled out the cop's keys.

I moved over to the squad car and checked the handle. It was open. I sat in the driver's seat and something poked me in the back. It was my dagger—my magic dagger. I'd forgotten I'd crammed it down the back of my pants when things went south back at the mansion. I didn't know it yet, but it was going to be very important that I had it. At that point, however, it was just a pain in my lower back.

I started going through the keys, trying to find the one that would unlock the shotgun. Finally I got the right key, grabbed the shotgun and took some ammo. As I got out of the squad car, I tucked the pistol into my belt and ran back over to the shop. Thankfully, Nick hadn't locked me out. As I stepped inside I saw him standing tensely behind the counter.

"Stay away!" yelled Nick, brandishing his own shotgun. Oh no, how does everyone have a gun?

"My god, put that thing away!" screamed the nurse.

"Nick. Calm down. I'm on your side," I said quietly and calmly. "My name is David Daniels. I work at UCLA. I'm a professor. That thing... is some... it's a government experiment gone awry."

"It just walked into... nothing!" he said angrily. I know he wasn't mad at me, he was mad at this thing for twisting his view of reality. When dealing with the supernatural, some people get quiet, some get angry, and some even pass out. Nick was angry, with a weapon. Not a good combination.

"I know... It's unsettling. But the animal is... equipped with state-of-the-art... stealth technology."

"What, like in Star Trek?" he said with the shotgun still pointed at me. At that point I couldn't tell if he liked Star Trek or hated it.

"Yeah, sure, Star Trek—but much more dangerous. Please, can you aim that thing somewhere else? I don't want you to put it down. I actually want you to shoot that damn thing if you can see it. Shoot it. Blast it and don't think twice."

"I have to go now," said the nurse. She began slowly walking towards the front door.

"I don't think that's a good idea," I said, moving to block her exit. "It's still out there."

"I have to go home. My husband is waiting for me. I have to get him his medication..."

I wasn't sure how to handle the situation. I'm not really a people person, so I pointed the gun at her. "Sit down," I screamed. Then she screamed at me. Then Nick was screaming. But the homeless guy didn't scream. He just looked a bit concerned.

"Put the gun down or I will shoot you!" Nick yelled at me.

"This is a life-or-death situation. If she goes outside she'll die!"

"So you're gonna kill her?"

I realized I might have been a bit overbearing, so I lowered my shotgun and put it on the floor.

"Sorry...sorry," I stammered.

And, as if on cue, that bend in space/time happened, but inside the shop. It was hard to focus on the hound. It was standing a few feet from me, but it looked like it was yards away. My perceptions were confused. I wasn't sure where to aim. Nick, however, seemed to have no problem. Before my eyes could even focus on it, I heard the deafening boom of his shotgun and saw the beast jerk over. It rolled across the floor and faded away.

The homeless guy finally got up and moved to the back of the restaurant. He still took his coffee with him. The nurse just climbed up on top of a table and started doing this strange staccato scream. Nick started yelling. I couldn't tell if he was screaming in fear or for victory. I looked at him and he was smiling, but still screaming. It was very unsettling.

"I got him! I got him! I got him! HA!" He screamed. Nick may not have been all there, but he had some great survival instincts.

"It's okay. Everyone has to calm down. We're going to be okay," I said.

With a crazed smile on his face, Nick shifted his gaze to me. He looked at me for a moment, unchanged, then his face melted into an expression of confusion. The nurse got quiet.

"What's your name again?" Nick said skeptically.

"David. Professor David Daniels," I said, hoping the police were going to show up soon.

"And why do you know so much about this? Did you make that monster?" He walked out from behind the counter to me and vaguely waved his gun in my general direction. I looked over at my shotgun still on the floor.

"Oh, no. No. I... I worked in another department." Even I didn't believe that one.

"Sure," Nick said skeptically. I was a bit worried, but I didn't think he would shoot me. I knew that if the police arrived and got us out of there, my contacts in the department could make all of those problems go away. In my side work into the world of the paranormal, I managed to bring a few police officers into the fold.

"Nick, I'm sorry about your friend. Officer Bluthe. I lost some friends tonight, too. I keep thinking about what I'm going to tell their families. About what happened..." I trailed off. Nick relaxed a bit when I said this. I thought that letting Nick see a bit of my "sensitive side" might win him over, though I had no intention of contacting any of my associates' families. Why bother?

"Can I leave now?" asked the nurse, still standing on the table.

"I think we should wait until the police arrive. But you can get down off that table," I said with all the nicety I could muster. She gave me a dirty look and stepped down.

"Here it comes again," said the homeless guy. I didn't know what he was talking about until the wave of woozy hit me. The hound wasn't dead.

It manifested on the counter behind Nick and leapt to a table. I noticed there was an old scar on the side of the beast where Nick had shot it. At the time, I thought it must have healed quickly, but now I realize it stepped out of time and space to heal somewhere and lick its wounds. I guess when time doesn't matter, you can wait until you're feeling better, then pick up where you left off. Amazing.

I dove for my shotgun as the monster leapt from the table. Nick spun around, lifted his shotgun and fired at the thing, but it moved too quickly. The hound jumped into Nick, knocked him to the floor, then landed on me.

The hound had me pinned. I couldn't reach my shotgun so I went for the pistol in my belt, but its hind foot trapped the gun. I saw Nick scrambling away from me and I screamed, "Help!" The nurse was screaming, I couldn't see the homeless guy, and I couldn't see where Nick was off to. All I could see was the hound. It looked right into my eyes. It didn't snarl or growl. The beast just held me there for what seemed like an eternity. But in a second, the hound looked up behind me and then leapt off and over the counter. I heard a blast and felt hot gunpowder hit the top of my head and shoulders. Nick was shooting way too close to me. My ears were ringing.

I scrambled up and ran into the kitchen. The nurse followed me. Nick shot again into the dining area, then ran after me. I lost track of the homeless guy.

"It's gone again! What the hell?!" Nick screamed at me.

I needed a new plan.

I stood there looking around for an idea. Nick was sliding boxes over to barricade the door. The nurse just sobbed quietly and homeless guy was back there already. Still with his coffee.

"That's not going to help," I said to Nick with too much resignation. But this didn't phase him. He just kept moving boxes. I stood there, not knowing what to do. I stared for a moment at a tray full of pink-frosted donuts. I love pink-frosted donuts, I thought. I got very scared at that moment. I started to think that I would never get to eat a pink-frosted donut again. So I picked one up and took a bite. I didn't think about it, I just did it. I went to a happy place. I thought about my friends alive and laughing. I thought about my parents and sister on our family vacation riding in the back of the station wagon. I thought about when I started working at UCLA and how happy I was to be there, almost skipping across the campus, to the Library, where the books were.

The books.

And then it dawned on me, I needed to do the spell. I knew how to do it, I had it memorized for crying out loud. It was relatively simple, as advanced space/time mathematical formula go. Unfortunately, it did seem like our best shot.

I heard the sirens in the distance getting closer. Thank god, I thought. Something to keep it busy for a while. I needed to hurry. The hound would go through these guys in minutes.

You see, at that point in my life, I had been thrust hip-deep into the world of the occult for almost ten years. It started off innocently enough when I began looking into the death of my estranged grandfather. It appears that he was an investigator of the bizarre, and that he uncovered a few groups people, one of which was called the Order of the Key. This group of almost fifty people prayed... or questioned... or looked for guidance from an ancient god called Yog-Sothoth. When my grandfather died, he bequeathed his papers and research to me, and I became part of that world. I didn't ask for it. It just sort of happened to me. I'm a victim of life and its illusions of control. I find myself just going from point to point. Connecting the dots. It's not so bad, really.

"Nick. Do you have a marker here?" I asked him. He was done with his boxes just sitting on the floor with his shotgun across his lap.

"What?"

"A magic marker! I need to... do some math... to figure out how to... shut down its cloaking technology."

He had to know I was lying, but what could he do? Call me out? He just gave me a cold stare and pointed to a cabinet.

I rushed over and looked inside. It had a mess of odds and ends and a few magic markers. I grabbed one and looked around in the kitchen for a space to make the circle and symbols. As I spun around looking for a suitable spot, the nurse stabbed me in the leg with a kitchen knife.

"This is your fault. You did this!" she snarled to me through clenched teeth. I just remember thinking... you've got to be kidding me.

"What the hell?" yelled Nick, picking up his shotgun and aiming it at the nurse.

She dropped the knife and I went to the floor. She looked furious at Nick for a moment, then she realized what she had done. You could see her strength just give out and she dropped to her knees and sobbed.

As I said before, people snap and lash out in very bizarre ways. I just wish she would have stabbed herself instead of me. Because, let me tell you, it hurt.

"What is wrong with everyone?! You're all crazy!" Nick was screaming and waving his gun around. I thought he was going to start shooting, infected by the madness that seemed to be filling up the place. But luckily, the police arrived.

I heard the sirens pull up to the front and the back of the building. Nick moved to the service window, looking out into the dining area. I took a towel off the table near me to tie around my wound. It was fairly superficial. I stood up, keeping my eyes on the pile of sobbing nurse, and hobbled next to Nick to see what was going on.

The police were already out of their squad cars with guns drawn. Bluthe's corpse most likely tipped them off to the danger in the area. "Hell, yeah!" said Nick as he moved to climb through the service window to go out to greet them. I snagged his arm.

"Nick. Stay here. The hound is still about," I said coolly.

"I know. We have to warn them!" He pulled his arm away from me.

Nick climbed through the service window, put the gun down on the counter and walked to the front doors. His hands were up in the air. The police shouted at him to get on the ground. He tried to warn them of the danger, of the dog, but it was too late. One of the cops screamed. I couldn't see what was going on. The scream led to one shot, then others. Nick ran back and climbed through the service window into the kitchen.

"Oh, God..." Nick mumbled under his breath.

"There is only one way to stop it. I know what we can do," I said in the most comforting way I could manage.

"There are more of them. I saw at least three of those things," said Nick, all hope drained away from his voice.

More of them? I thought. How could that be? As far as I knew, only one had been summoned, but perhaps more followed it. I didn't know what to do. My spell would only hold one of the creatures. There was no way that I could manage more. I had to be sure Nick wasn't mistaken.

"Nick. Help me move these boxes."

I slipped out of the kitchen door on my belly amidst the screams and the shooting. As I scooted on the floor to the window, the shooting stopped. I was afraid to look out, but I had to. I slowly looked up to see a blood bath. Three of the creatures were eating the fallen police. I noticed that they all had the same scar on the side of their bodies—the scar from Nick's shotgun blast. And then it dawned on me. There weren't three different creatures. *It was the same hound from different points in time!* These Hounds of Tindalos exist outside of time and space. If it decides to go after someone or something, it can come from its own future. I really needed to do that spell.

My shotgun wasn't far from where I was and I scooted over to grab it. As I did, one of the hounds seemed to notice me. It stepped sideways and vanished. The others moved in different directions and vanished as well. That sick feeling swept over me again.

"Nick! They're coming!"

I sprung up and ran to the back, though I was sure it wasn't going to do me any good. I waved my shotgun around as I ran, anticipating the creatures to catch me unaware. Unfortunately, it was there in front of me and it pounced!

I knew I had to try to redirect the attack as best I could. It had to weigh over 200lbs and it didn't seem too intimidated by my gun, so I just rolled with it. As I did, I fell over on to a table and lost my shotgun. The hound rolled off the table and vanished. I heard a blast from the kitchen. Nick!

I flung myself toward the kitchen, slamming through the door. Nick was standing there with brownish-pink ooze all over him and what seemed to be a dead hound. It looked skinny and frail and it had a massive hole in the side of its chest. The nurse was lying still on the floor next to the dead hound, quietly sobbing. The homeless man now had a fresh cup of coffee and a donut.

"I got it," Nick said with very little emotion.

I knew this was the creature from the end of its life. It had the same scar, but it just seemed older than the others—skinny with loose skin. It came here to die. But that didn't mean it wouldn't take us as well. I had to act quickly.

I ran and grabbed the marker and started making my symbols onto the kitchen floor. It was mostly a large circle, with markings along the outside.

"I don't think this is the time, man. We just have to get out of here." Nick breathed out as he spoke. He was desperate. I wished I could just tell him everything was going to be alright. But I knew it wouldn't.

There was a banging at the back door.

"Open up! This is the police!" screamed a disembodied voice from outside. Nick just stood there and looked at me. I ran over and opened the door.

The cop stumbled in with his pistol drawn. In the fluorescent lights, I could see he had blood on his arms. I closed the door.

He looked around the kitchen at Nick and I. He looked to be in his late twenties with short cropped black hair and a mustache. "Gomez" on his name tag. He looked around and saw the nurse crying, the quickly dissolving corpse of the hound, and the homeless guy. He looked at me and Nick.

"Is everyone okay?" Gomez asked, though he could tell we weren't.

"Those things are killing everybody. What are we going to do?" Nick pleaded.

"I've called for back-up. We just need to hang tight. Do you know what's going on?"

"My name is David Daniels. I'm a professor over at UCLA and I think these things are part of some bio weapon the government is trying to create. They escaped. I think..." I trailed off and tried to seem frightened and confused. Officer Gomez looked puzzled and horrified.

"Are you serious?"

"Forget back-up, call the National Guard!" I shouted. I knew we would all be dead or I would escape before anything like that happened, I just needed to buy some time with Gomez. He wasn't going to go for my spell-casting plan.

Gomez talked into his shoulder CB and repeated what I said in some kind of cop lingo. As he was talking, I looked through the kitchen window, past the dining area and out into the parking lot. There were some darkly dressed figures slowly moving towards the building.

Oh no, not them, I thought. They were the cause of all this. Fanatics ruled by their insane worldview. Nut jobs who will steal, threaten or kill to get what they want. They're the reason we were in that mess. They were the reason those things were on the loose.

I ducked down hoping they didn't see me.

"Kid. Nick, is it?" asked Gomez. He was trying to keep Nick calm.

"Yeah," mumbled Nick. I crouched there and kept quiet.

"Nick, it's going to be okay. We've got a lot of help on the way. We've got SWAT and if that doesn't work, the National Guard will be here to take these things down."

Nick seemed to perk up. "National Guard? You can do that?"

"Yeah. We just have to..." Gomez noticed the darkly dressed people walking up to the front of the shop. As he moved to the kitchen door, a wave of distorted space/time swept over me. The kitchen door flew off its hinges with a deafening bang. I think it was a grenade. Then there was a series of gun shots. I dove behind the boxes, lay flat on the floor and covered my ears. I didn't know what was going on, I just knew it was bedlam.

A few moments later it was quiet again, though my ears were ringing so loudly I couldn't really hear. I looked over to see Nick balled up in the corner. The nurse seemed to be hurt, but still alive, and the homeless man was just gone.

I scooted on my belly to peer through the opening where the door had once been. The place was a mess. No one was left standing. Officer Gomez was pinned under the door and apparently dead. The three darkly dressed men were all in pieces. From behind the counter a hound walked out with an arm in its mouth.

I froze. I didn't breathe. I kept thinking, don't look this way. Of course it did. The hound dropped the arm and looked right at me. Again, it didn't tense up or growl or move, it just looked at me with those dark, hollow eyes. I felt like I was looking into a void that was going to suck me into it. For a moment I thought I was going to fall. From the floor. Why wouldn't it attack me? I was just laying there. Then it moved in a blur, but not at me. Back into space-time, as the side of the counter exploded from a blast that came from behind me. It was Nick with that gun.

My ears were ringing so loudly by then, I was practically deaf. Nick said something to me, but all I saw were his lips moving. I stood up and walked over to him.

"Can you hear me?" I screamed. He looked confused.

"Yes!" he seemed to say.

"We don't have much time! I need you to stand over here by me and I need... I need to do... something. It will stop those things. I promise. Will you help me?"

"What?!"

"I said, 'Will you help me!'" Nick looked confused. I gently grabbed him by the arm and took him to the circle I had drawn moments before.

"Sit down!" I yelled in that monotone kinda way. Like when you're trying to have a conversation in a loud bar. I began the incantation. I needed Nick, you understand. It took two people to make the spell work and fortunately he didn't really need to do anything but be there. I yelled the chant out, knowing it wouldn't take too long. Just as long as we weren't interrupted.

I was a minute into the chanting when It walked in through the kitchen doorway. The hound. Nick raised his gun and pulled the trigger, but it only clicked. Empty. Nick started to scramble across the floor and the hound leaped on his back and bit into his neck. Nick screamed for only a moment as his head came apart from his body. I just stood there. The thing looked at me again. Its eyes had no expression, almost like a bug's. I swear it was almost smiling at me, like it was playing. It could have easily killed me a few times, but it didn't. Perhaps the Hounds of Tindalos are smarter than I thought. So intelligent as to have a cruel sense of humor.

I still had the pistol in my belt, but I'm not very quick on the draw. Then again, what choice did I have? I figured, "What the hell?" and I went for the gun. I would like to tell you I performed some slick, cowboy-esque maneuver. But no. I drew the pistol with such vigor and intensity, that I just threw it across the room. Very embarrassing.

The hound tensed for a moment as I flailed about, trying to catch the gun. Then it relaxed and looked at me with its head slightly cocked. I laughed. It actually looked kind of cute! As I laughed, something else caught the creature's attention. I couldn't see what it saw or heard, but the hound ran back out towards the dining area and disappeared. I looked outside to see even more police had arrived.

So what? The hound would still come after me, through time and space. I had to do the ritual. I moved, crouching, towards the dining area to get a better look at the police. The nurse stirred on the floor. I kept low and moved over to her.

"Are you alright?" I asked.

"My arm! My back... my leg..." she sobbed. She had some shrapnel in her arm.

"I know how to stop this thing but I need your help."

"Oh, God..."

"I just need you to sit in circle and I'm going to say some words and it should fix this whole problem. Will you help me?"

She wasn't reacting to me. She just cried and rocked. I didn't really need her to do or say anything, and at this point, I didn't care if she was willing or not. I grabbed her under her arms and dragged her to the circle. Her cries became screams as I moved her.

I could see police outside moving around and then I heard shots. And screams. And flashes. I looked away and focused on getting the nurse and myself to the circle. When we reached it, I sat her up in the center. She screamed out in pain.

"You have to sit up. Just sit here. I'm going to stand right behind you and say the words."

We were in position. I started the chant again. I tried not to focus on the second blood bath that was happening outside. I focused on my words and my energy. I channeled my thoughts and feelings into the circle. Time seemed to slow down. Perhaps it did. I had only a few more words to speak when the beast appeared. This time, it did not look amused. It looked furious.

I knew it was going to attack, so I reached behind me and pulled out my dagger. As I said the last word, the beast charged at me and I plunged the dagger into the nurse's chest.

The hound stopped. It was done. I had completed the spell and the sacrifice. The hound was mine to command and I commanded it take me away from that time and place. And it did.

I left the 21st Century and went back to Paris in 1922, to my grandfather. You see, Yog-Sothoth had a plan for me. That's why I didn't die that night. That's why the hound didn't kill me. It was part of the plan. If those investigators in black hadn't interrupted my followers as we performed the first ritual, things wouldn't have gotten so messy. They think they're protecting humanity? They have no idea what humanity's purpose is. Not that I do either. But Yog-Sothoth knows and that's all that matters.

The Host from the Hill

Dan Harms

December 19, 1828
Alsace Township, near Reading, Berks County, Pennsylvania

As he began his journey to the mountain of witches, Johann Georg Hohman heard hoof beats ahead on the hard-packed snow. Was it the fever, or a trick of the wind? No, it was real enough. He had scarcely left Rose Valley, but he could not be certain of his safety. He reined in his sway-backed horse and pulled out powder, ramrod, and shot. As he loaded with shaking hands, he peered into the pre-dawn glow.

Behind him, Hohman knew Anna, his wife, was waiting for him in the small log cabin that, if only for a few days, still belonged to them. Scant minutes ago, she had quietly checked his forehead, giving him a stern, loving, and yet accepting look. She would be fine; she knew enough brauch to keep herself and their homestead safe. He knew that she would hold together the strands of his life, as she had done a hundred times before, even if he did not return.

The snow whispered past Hohman's ears. Behind him, he could catch voices raised in a carol, likely from the hotel by the spring, but the wind and snow soon silenced it. Tiny crystals of ice struck his face, but his mind drifted.

Something jingled up ahead. Hohman stared at nothing for moment. Shaking himself, he pressed the flintlock's stock against his chest. His hands shook; the end of the barrel weaved.

Emerging from the curtain of snow was a man astride a fine bay horse and wearing an expensive frock coat and hat.

"Good evening, Mr. Hohman. I was on my way to meet a buyer for my shop for breakfast. I hope you are not trying to shoot me."

Jacob Boyer was one of Reading's most prominent merchants. In a happier time, Hohman had cured a sore on the leg of Jacob's son. He later borrowed money from Boyer to pay for his farm. Hard times came, and the sheriff would sell his property on Christmas Eve to meet the debt.

Hohman lowered the musket. "Good evening to you, Mr. Boyer." Holding open his satchel, he displayed brightly-colored pages covered with paintings of birds and hearts, with lettering in ornate Fraktur script. "Taufscheins. I paint them myself. I hope to make a little money for my family before the auction."

Boyer regarded the beautiful hand-colored birth certificates with suspicion. "Not many births in the winter, but I'll still want to see my fifty-two dollars and fifty cents. You may keep the proceeds from your sales— consider it Christmas charity." He smiled too broadly.

"Not charity enough to reschedule the auction, sir. A man's life should not be for sale on Christmas Eve. In our country—"

Boyer raised a hand. "I don't set the schedule, Johann. The sheriff does. And money is money, and a debt is a debt. If perhaps, you spent less time gallivanting about selling whispered prayers and worthless ballads, and more on your crops and—"

Hohman nodded curtly and rode past him. "Good day, sir." It was better to let Boyer speak and not regret his own words later. Time was short. Behind him, Boyer cursed quietly and rode toward the inn.

The merchant would have been surprised at Hohman's accoutrements that morning. The flintlock was strapped on his back once more—he had little powder or shot, but he would have no opportunity to reload. The metal of another weapon, specially prepared, was cold against his stomach, below the pouch with his rosary of well-worn wooden beads. In his satchel, beneath the Taufscheins, were a few days' provisions, a flask of holy water, his tattered family Bible, the letter from his professor, and a copy of his own book, *Der Lange Verborgene Freund*—the *Long-Hidden Friend*. Hohman could quote the statement at the end of the book verbatim:

Whoever carries this book with him, is safe from all his enemies, visible or invisible; and whoever has this book with him, cannot die without the holy corpse of Jesus Christ, nor drowned in any water, nor burn up in any fire, nor can any unjust sentence be passed upon him.

Hohman had found the charm in a book attributed to Gypsies. He had placed it in his own work, in hope that it would pass on some luck to his buyers. He now wished the same for himself.

Hohman was a braucher, one who used herbs, prayer, talismans, and the spoken word to ward off disease, misfortune, and the wiles of the Devil. Even among his countrymen such practices were regarded with suspicion, and his English-speaking neighbors scorned healer and client alike. They claimed that brauchers exploited the needy and helpless. Hohman had used his talents to make ends meet at times, but he saw it not as exploitation, but as a holy calling. People still called him from miles around, and they went away thanking him, often with no money at all changing hands. He had driven off fever or rash, cared for a sick horse or cow, and battled the malign devices of witches.

Witches? Oh, yes, they were real. Growing up in Germany, Hohman had heard many stories about them from his grandmother. They lurked in secret in every village and hamlet, making their secret pacts with the Adversary on dark nights in deserted graveyards. They blighted crops, tangled the manes of horses, and stole milk from cows. On the holy nights of the nearly-forgotten pagan calendar, they met on high peaks, most notably the Brocken in the Harz Mountains, for wild revels at which the Prince of Darkness presided.

Some said that belief in witches died in a small Massachusetts town called Salem nearly a century ago, but Hohman knew better. Did not the Bible proclaim their existence? Had he not seen the results of their handiwork in the suffering of his neighbors? Had he not seen a witch turn up at his clients' doorsteps to borrow a cup of milk or piece of bread, hoping to break the charm Hohman had turned against her? He had heard protest after protest from those who had been accused, stalwart members of the community and good church-goers, but he could see the fear in their eyes. Witches were real enough.

John Schild was proof.

One summer day, sixteen years before, Hohman was walking with a kerchief full of pears and apples to the Schild household. Schild had spent the past year following him on his curing appointments, hoping to learn some of the cures for himself. Schild went to the Reformed church up the road, but even the Protestants turned to Hohman's prayers when needed. He was a patient and careful learner, and the two had soon passed from an apprenticeship to a friendship. Perhaps, Hohman thought, he might leave a legacy in this world.

As he walked down the path toward the farm, something rustled among the trees on the hill nearby. Peering past the branches, he saw John's wife, lying in a pile of leaves behind a tree, each arm around two of her children. Their expressions silenced any questions Hohman could have asked. He dropped the kerchief and moved slowly toward the farm. The woman bit her lip but said nothing.

At the edge of the property, he saw a pillar of smoke. Breaking into a run, he found the barn aflame. The roof caved in, sending up a flurry of sparks followed by a pillar of flame. He called out for Schild. Accompanying the scent of burning wood was a crisp smell drifting from the cabin, across the vegetable garden. Hohman recalled a patient of his, a blacksmith who had dropped a hot iron on his arm. This smell was the same. He moved closer.

Outside the door was a small round object—a smashed pumpkin? They were not in season. Then he realized he was viewing the left half of the head of Andreas Schild, John's father. The remnants of his jaw hung slightly open, and a few flies had landed on it. A trail of gore led into the house.

Hohman squinted into the darkness. Littered about the cabin were the hacked-up portions of man and beast. Smoke emerged from the hearth, blackened bones protruding. He ran a short distance away and retched.

Still on his hands and knees, Johann heard footsteps in the grass. He flipped aside, just as an axe cleaved into the turf where he had rested an instant before. Over him loomed John Schild, his eyes dull. He pulled the axe out of the ground and swung again.

Hohman rolled, jumped to his feet, and ran. Schild was in better shape than he, so he had no chance of flight . Running to the woodpile, he grabbed a stout log and turned toward Schild, who ran at him. Hohman ducked to one side, catching him in the gut with the wood. Schild grunted. Hohman took the opportunity to dodge aside, looking for something else he could use.

Recovering from the blow, Schild brought the axe down again. Hohman, holding the wood in both hands, caught the axe at the cleft below the blade. Schild tried to wrench it aside, but Hohman pushed forward and up, stepping forward so that his face was inches from Schild's. He could see the flecks of blood in the man's beard, as Schild hissed in frustration. Before Schild could pull the axe away, Hohman whispered a charm against witchcraft.

Schild crumpled to the ground, sobbing. "The witches… the witches… I was strong… the cattle were sick… I thought I could…"

The axe had fallen to one side. Hohman slowly moved toward it, picking it up and tossing it away. He then put his hand on Schild's shoulder, quietly reciting the first holy words that came to mind. "The Lord is my shepherd, I shall not want. He leadeth me…"

Schild joined haltingly in the Psalm. Hohman quietly chanted, moving to the Creed, then to "A Mighty Fortress is Our God." Halfway through the second verse, he heard voices on the path.

Hohman thought of staying, but he had little patience for the courts' justice. The courthouse in Reading was not always kind to those who spoke in German. After muttering a farewell to Schild, he walked into the woods and made his way through them back to Rose Valley.

After what had happened to Schild, Hohman knew that he must go alone. Any one of his neighbors or fellow church-goers could be among the witches, and others would be vulnerable to their charms. One of the white-robed mystics of Ephrata would have been above suspicion—he had learned to trust them, despite their unorthodox beliefs—but the last of them had died fifteen years before. And the professor from Wurttemberg who had sent him was long gone.

The snowfall tapered as he continued on his journey, crossing the Saucony at Kutztown. He kept his hat pulled down on his chin. He passed the road houses along the route; they were too public. Outside Breinigsville, as the light faded, he noticed a barn, well off the road and away from the house. He hesitated for a moment, then pragmatism won out over scruple and he led his horse inside. It was easy enough to quiet the animals and push together a bed of straw. He ate two biscuits in silence, and then risked a candle. He smoothed the folds in the letter from his satchel and re-read it.

My dear Mr. Hohman,

I fear I have grim news to bring you, and a great responsibility to pass on.

I know you have expressed skepticism toward my findings when we met this summer. You will recall our discussion of the Old Ones, those hideous demons that dwell, not in hell, but in the deep seas and caverns of the world, or in the stars beyond, and who will one day return to take the world again in their possession. I have seen but the merest tendrils of their influence—but we have argued over this before. Despite your doubts, I would remind you that, even if these beliefs are the delusions of the Adversary, those who believe and worship them are real enough.

An associate at the Bibliothèque Nationale sent me a letter regarding a disturbing event. One day in early October, when the head librarian was out, one Frank Barnett from Britain came to that institution seeking the Necronomicon. I am certain you have never heard of that work, but rest assured it is one of the most blasphemous books in the world, penned by a mad Saracen poet over a thousand years ago. I know you will know whereof I speak when I say it is infinitely worse than Faust's Threefold Coercion of Hell or the Great and Powerful Sea-Ghost. The man viewed it for but an hour, under the careful eye of the assistant. When the head librarian returned, he questioned his assistant as to the exact pages consulted, found the visitor's name in the register and made enquiries at the docks. He uncovered that "Frank Barnett" was actually Francis Barrett, once an occultist and balloonist from

London who vanished some years ago, but whom rumor has since associated with Jacobins, Martinists, Satanists, and other disreputable sorts. He had set sail for Philadelphia with a formula in the forgotten Aklo language intended to raise the Sabaoth—a Hebrew word meaning "host"—from "the Hill." Though less powerful than those called "from the Air," they are nonetheless terrible in their coming and the effects on those who cannot escape.

Having read the Necronomicon, I understood the dire import of this phrase. I wrote a friend in Philadelphia, who confirmed my suspicions. Barrett had left the Mansion House Hotel on Third Street only a few days before, heading toward the Blue Mountains with a great wagon with unknown contents. I doubt he could go far in the present weather, but sorcerers hold the winter solstice—the longest and darkest night of the year—especially sacred. I made arrangements to follow, but pressing business has called Ladeau and me away.

I write you for two reasons. First, that you might know that such a dangerous individual is on his way to your country. Second, that you might find a way to stop him from his desperate act—he will need confederates, and you likely know better than I who they might be. After the incantation starts, Alhazred warns us, nothing but his death might bring it to its end.

Yours sincerely,

Friedrich von Junzt
Professor, Wurttemberg

Hohman blew out the candle and tried to be comfortable under his woolen blanket.

At three in the morning, he awoke, shivering uncontrollably as his mind turned relentlessly back, time and time again, to the phrase, "Host from the Hill," in a delirium that merely echoed, keeping him in the edge of false revelation. He burrowed deeper into the straw and pulled his blanket more tightly about him, thinking of the warmth of the hearth across the yard. He muttered a charm: "Abaxa Catabax, Abaxa Cataba, Abaxa Catab…" As the phrase diminished, so would the fever. It should work for a short time, he knew, but he had found himself remarkably resistant to the working of his own remedies. Nonetheless, his head ceased its whirling, and he fell into a dreamless sleep.

Schild's trial was a fair one, if one discounted the reality of witches who could drive men mad. His lawyers had kept him off the stand for fear of what he might say, and Hohman learned that his confession—the one that clever printers had not invented, at any rate—was carefully expurgated of all mentions of Satan's minions. What remained—wild protestations that he had killed various people, a belief that his wife had poisoned his tea—was more than enough for local sensibilities.

At the end of January, Hohman joined the milling crowd on Gallows Hill, listening to coughing and sneezing of the crowd and the cries of peddlers hawking broadsides. Schild walked up to the platform as the crowd sang a hymn. As the executioner was pulling the hood over Schild's head, Hohman could see his friend's eyes sweep the crowd. He knew that Schild was looking for him. Before their eyes could meet, the hood was on.

A short jolt later, Schild had gone to what reward God deemed him fit, and Hohman was alone once more.

Hohman awoke before dawn. He ate another two biscuits from his pack. He took out a dime to leave on the lip of the stall, and then thought better of it. He pressed on down the road, barely cognizant of his surroundings. The world had become a haze, with even the overcast light of the darkness. He could not continue in the same, cautious manner under these conditions. He mumbled questions to someone in Bethlehem; he could not recall the man, but the man knew him nonetheless. After he asked two or three times, they reached an understanding. An Englishman had come through town not so long ago, on a wagon filled with wicker and canvas. He had passed on; they did not know where. Hohman asked for the road to the Hexenkopf. After hesitating, the man pointed him toward a road leading through town, shaking his head.

Even in the gloom, Hohman could feel the Hexenkopf, the mountain of the witches, rising above him. The hill was spoken of in whispers, even as far away as Philadelphia and Harrisburg. It was not unknown for other brauchers, seeking a locale to which an illness might be transferred from a sick person, to send it into the looming crags of the hill. Others whispered that the place served as a meeting place for the witches, who would fly there on their unholy festivals to meet with the Devil as they had on the Brocken back in his homeland. Now, toward the top, he could see the glow of a bonfire and hear the shrieks and cries of abandon of the celebrants. If Barrett was to perform this ritual anywhere, it would be here.

He tied his horse to the tree, dismounted, and loaded the flintlock. He moved through the trees, as if stalking a pheasant or deer, watching the ground for roots or traps. Even this was a chore, and he hoped he would be up for the task.

"Jesus, God and man, do thou protect me against all manner of guns…"

He had assembled a repertoire of anti-weapon charms, but he had never any reason to use them before now. He recited every one he could remember, and then did so again for good measure. He hoped that at least one would be effective.

The top of the hill was near, the pounding of drums resonating in time with his waves of dizziness. The wind picked up, but the biting cold brought with it clarity. Hohman crept forward on his elbows and knees, holding his musket barrel up to keep it clear of debris. He lowered himself into a slight hollow and peeked out.

93

In the midst of the summit was a bonfire, built of logs stacked like a log cabin. Snowflakes hissed as they struck hot coals. The firelight touched dozens of naked bodies, whirling about each other. He glimpsed faces he had seen in Reading, while many were unfamiliar—this must indeed be an important gathering. About the circle stood large, burly men, cradling muskets in their arms. A table covered with wooden plates and goblets, bearing the remnants of a feast, sat farther back from the firelight.

At the edge of the glow stood a man, scarcely five feet high, in a black coat with a high collar and plush sleeves. He had been a handsome man once, with expressive eyes and a fine aquiline nose. Now his face was creased and sagging. A purple silk cravat protruded from the neck of his coat, and he held a cane clearly intended as fashion, and not for support. He looked with disinterest at the raucous crowd before him, crinkling a few sheets of parchment in one hand. Behind him, next to a smaller fire, loomed a canvas globe, rising in shadow above the scene, slowly shifting with the wind. A large basket was tied to its base, with small canvas bags attached to the sides. Hohman had never seen a balloon, but *Niles' Weekly Register* had described their ascents well enough.

Schild had once said that, if you really wanted to end an enterprise in disaster, you should find an Englishman. Hohman sighted the musket on Barrett. He could see at least forty men and women, five armed, with the dancers weaving across his target. Making his way about the perimeter would be risky, and it might take too long.

He aimed at one of the guards, but he could not fire. Sending a bewitchment back on its source was one matter; setting out to kill such a witch was another. He held still for a moment, wondering what to do.

He remembered sitting on a bench in a cabin near Lebanon. A young girl poured coffee into his tin cup. The father of the household looked at his hands, speaking of sick cows, failed crops, a business deal gone badly. The girl turned the spout over her father's mug, and the pot's handle broke. Rivulets of boiling coffee ran down her arm, and she screamed. Hohman grabbed her arm, ran his fingers over it, and chanted. He knew then what he would have to do for this family, that it would be long, that they would likely go away with resentment even if he succeeded. He also knew he would see it through.

Hohman thought of the girl's screaming face. He pulled the trigger. He felt the impact of the stock against his shoulder. The man toppled over.

Hohman stood up. Temporarily deafened by the shot, he could not hear himself howl. The entire crowd stopped its dance. Many broke and ran. Harsh voices called out, and two of the guards leveled their muskets and fired.

Hohman staggered back, falling into the hollow. He dimly realized that he was uninjured. He jumped back to his feet, reaching inside his shirt for his weapon. The men ran at him, pointing at his uninjured chest and drawing swords and cudgels. Some still looked about, anticipating other attackers. Hohman pulled out the sickle—no ordinary agricultural implement, but forged with a hint of silver and honed to razor sharpness. Would it be effective?

He found out quickly, as a hulking figure struck at his head with a cudgel. It glanced off, with not even the slightest impact. Hohman swung the sickle and caught the man in the stomach, slicing through muscle and viscera. Intestine uncoiled through the gaping wound. The man gurgled and slid to the ground. Hohman turned to the next attacker, who had circled around and hurled himself at Hohman from the side. Hohman swung upward, striking just under the breastbone and cutting upward, the sickle sticking in his ribcage. Hohman pulled back on the handle, finally wrenching it free.

Those witches who had not fled circled him, their bare feet padding on the hard ground. Through them strode Barrett. He stepped forward, his arms spread open, a grin on his face. Hohman swung the sickle at his face, catching it on the cheek. He heard a metallic snapping, and glistening shards fell to the ground.

Barrett gave a small, mocking bow. "Welcome to our revels, Mr. Hohman. As you can see, I've greatly enjoyed your book."

Something struck the back of Hohman's head.

Strong hands gripped Hohman's arms as he awoke, his mind swirling from the fever. He stood near the fire, a guard on either side. The other witches, reassembled, thrust their hate-filled faces toward him. Barrett stood before him. He grasped the braucher's chin and pulled it from one side to another. His vision blurred.

"Delayed eye movements, unfocussed pupils. You're not well, Mr. Hohman. A man in your condition should be in bed. Why you have chosen to grace our gathering with your attendance?" He chuckled. "I do not see the good professor with you. Perhaps he had something more pressing to do this evening than to save you?"

Should he remain silent? No—his only remaining weapon was his voice. He cleared his throat and tried to hold his head high. "One man of faith is enough against the forces of darkness." In this unholy setting, he did not believe it, though he knew he should.

Barrett looked at him. "Not tonight, it seems. Tonight—of all nights—the Prince of Darkness shall come up from his infernal palace! Not some cheap substitute, such as the man who these faithful servants followed until his deception was revealed!" He gestured off to one side, toward a small clump of black cloth, hair, and congealing blood. "Tonight, Lucifer himself rises from within the earth!"

"You think so?" Hohman's voice wavered, but he thought he could see an opening. "They have been fooled once—will they be fooled so easily again!"

Barrett smiled and motioned to two of the guards, who carried forward a heavy, clanking sack. "I am quite genuine, sir. The Dark Lord blesses those who honor him. Behold his bounty!" He reached inside, drawing out pieces of gold and silver plate, necklaces of pearls, and other finery that Hohman had not even seen on Philadelphia's most prominent citizens. He tossed these to his followers, their fingers scrabbling on the stony ground to pick up what they could.

Hohman's teeth clenched on his lip. He saw a silver tray glisten near his feet. That item, casually tossed on the ground nearby, would more than pay off his debt to Boyer.

"Shall we begin?" Barrett walked to Hohman, his face inches from that of the braucher. He whispered, "But an instant's worth of secrets will repay decades of research. Today, the Host from the Hill—the next, that of the Air. And who knows what next year—the reward of the Old Ones themselves?"

Barrett opened his hands; he held two pieces of wax. He plugged his ears with them and held up a wickedly curved obsidian blade. He waved it before Hohman. Holding up his left hand, he sliced it open. The blood spattered on the cold, hard ground. He began a chant, discordant syllables causing the air to ripple and bend. *Aklo*, Hohman thought.

The ground began to throb, first gently, but soon rising in intensity until Hohman could feel his teeth vibrate. The ground shook, cracked and crumbled. The fire crashed over, smothering much of the flame. Outside the remnants of firelight loomed large shapes that glistened as crystals. Stone shards shot out from the darkness, transfixing many of the witches where they stood. With them came a whispering, like an unseen cloud, secrets of distant worlds and the terrors of stygian grottoes and lonesome plateaus, flowing over each other. It was this, more than the Sabaoth's physical presence, that caused that crowd atop the Hexenkopf to shriek and flee. Those who ran toward the glistening shapes screamed, followed with the sound of snapping bones. As blood flowed, the voices grew more insistent.

Barrett had been slowly walking toward the balloon. Now he leapt into the basket and cast off the ballast. The balloon began to lift off into the sky, snowflakes swirling around the bag. No doubt he expected to escape the Host from the Hill by going where they could not follow.

As the whispering crept into the ears of the guards, Hohman felt their hands loosen. He wrenched his right arm free. He threw his weight against the other, knocking him over onto a burning piece of wood. The man screamed. The other grasped at Hohman, but he jumped away, weaving through the panicked worshipers to the other side of the fire. He found his eyes casting about for a gold ring, or set of sapphire-studded earrings. If he could find just one, it would solve everything. His horse was still swift in a pinch, and he could be away in but a minute…

He remembered Schild, and his wife, and the cabin back in Rose Valley.

He remembered his faith.

Hohman ran for the rising balloon. Dodging aside from the dark bulk of one of the Host, he grasped a rope trailing from its side, hauling himself upward. The entire balloon shuddered as it ceased its ascent and descended slowly, the winds pulling it away from the hilltop. Hohman pulled himself up, hand over hand. The wind, without any cover to lessen its force, blew around him, chilling him. The sweat on his shirt and in his hair was turning to ice. He would not last long.

The basket tilted toward Hohman, with Barrett lying on the slanted side. Still holding his cane, he thrashed wildly at Hohman, his blows raining down on the sides of the basket. One blow caught Hohman on the knuckles, drawing blood. He had no chance of climbing higher under the assault. He let go with the injured hand, flailing about for anything he could use against his foe. The ballast was already gone — Barrett must have dropped it when the balloon changed course. His weapons were long gone. He needed —

He touched the rosary in his pouch. Pulling it out, he flipped it up through the air. The first time, it struck Barrett in the face. He blinked and redoubled his efforts with the cane. Hohman pulled back his arm and tried again. This time, it caught around Barrett's neck. With one hand still around the rope, Hohman held on to the rosary and twisted it, using it to support his weight. The string stretched but did not snap.

Barrett coughed and hacked. One hand grasped at the beads, while the other swung the cane back and forth. It caught Hohman on the scalp, and blood seeped into his hair. He hung on desperately, forgetting the frigid air and the height. Barrett's flailing soon died down, his cane dropping from numb fingers into the darkness. He heaved once. His arms jerked once or twice, as Schild's had on the rope, and was still, his face blue, his tongue protruding from his mouth.

Something brushed Hohman's legs. He jerked them away, but he soon felt it again. Branches. He let go of the rosary, both hands now wrapped around the rope. When he struck the trunk of another tree, it was not enough. He fell, branches cracking and scraping about him, until he struck the ground. He was dimly aware of the balloon rising into the gloom.

It was bright and warm, and a presence was nearby. He drifted in and out of consciousness, not willing to leave the comfort of heat and ignorance. He finally awoke. He was in his small cabin, on a bench near the hearth. Anna leaned toward the firelight, his shirt and thread in her hand.

He sat up, with only a touch of dizziness. She smiled. "Welcome back, Johann. You have put quite a tear in this shirt."

"Anna, I—" He fumbled for words. He had gone through a night of fire, blood and madness, and yet, the condition of his clothes was suddenly of prime importance.

"You're back. That's all I ask." She put down her sewing and gave a slight smile. "And you are far more difficult to mend. A farmer coming home late found you in the woods near Hellertown, and your horse nearby. No one knows what you were doing, but likely the fever sent you astray."

So all of it—the balloon, the witches, and the gold—had passed unnoticed. He smiled. "Likely. What is today?"

"Christmas Eve." She put a hand across his chest and spoke quickly. "The auction is over, but the people prevailed upon Mr.

Boyer to let us live here until he found tenants. We will have to move soon, but we have a respite for now."

Hohman lay back down and stared at the planks in the ceiling. "A respite."

Only now did he realize how everyone was there as well. Professor von Junzt had been right: the Host and their masters would, indeed, return and retake the world. He had no doubts about that, after what he had seen. All that anyone could ever have was a momentary respite.

Hohman closed his eyes. For the moment, that was enough.

Breaking Through

Steve Dempsey

I went into the kitchen to get some more beers. The top of the fridge was stacked with overflow from the pile of washing up in the sink. Dirty mugs, take-away cartons and empty cans stood in precarious stacks. Some had spilled onto the floor. I couldn't remember the last time Tag or I had done any cleaning, or if we ever had. As long as we paid the rent on time, the landlord never came round. What did we care? The whole house was littered with the debris of our student life. There was a knock at the front door.

"Tag. Get that will you, mate," I shouted back down the gloomy corridor. I carefully opened the fridge, trying not to topple any more of the mess onto the floor. Tag didn't answer but I heard some noise. It was probably the TV, or some first year students come round to buy some E. We tried to stop them coming to the house but they never listened. I grabbed a couple of beers and wandered back out. Beyond the Seventies style archway into the living room the front door was open.

"Tag, you lazy git. Shut the..." I turned into the sitting room and stopped. Tag was lying on the floor on his back, his face a mess of red and black. A man stood there with his foot on Tag's neck.

"You must be the other little shit," he said. I froze and then turned to run but someone else had come up behind me and belted me one across the nose. The world flashed bright and then dark and I fell.

Later I came round sitting on the floor, my back propped up against the sofa. Tag slumped beside me. His hair was wet and matted and bubbles of almost black blood were coming out of his mouth and a gash in his cheek. I don't suppose I looked any better. My face felt as if it had been repeatedly stamped on. A man loomed over us. He was wearing brown corduroy trousers, a black leather jacket and a white shirt, now splattered with Tag's blood. The top three buttons of the shirt were undone, showing off his chest hair. The glare from the bare light bulb behind him hid his face. He had a baseball bat in one hand and poked me hard in the chest with it.

"You see your friend?" he said, with what a strong Mediterranean accent. "You wanna end up like him?" When I didn't respond he swung his bat round, catching me square on the elbow. Electricity jolted up my arm; I burst into tears. The man pushed my face with the bat, turning me to look at Tag, "You wanna end up like 'im?" he said again.

"No, No." I shook my head and cradled my elbow.

"So this is what you gonna do. You gonna give me all your drugs." I didn't answer quickly enough and he casually rapped me across the knuckles. I cried out in pain. "So?"

"Yes. Anything." I made to get up but he pushed me back with the bat.

"I have no finish. First you give me all your drugs. Then you make drugs for me. OK?" He sounded almost chirpy.

"OK," I said, like I had any choice.

"OK," he said. "You right-handed?" he asked. Puzzled, I nodded and as I did he brought the bat down on my left hand. I screamed and doubled over in pain. "Now you no forget," he said.

They, the leader Joe and his two helpers, took all our stock. That was about 4,000 pills, a month's work. They'd admired our lab set-up in the spare room and demanded the same number of pills each month with weekly pick-ups. I'd agreed. By that stage I didn't know what else to do and I needed to get Tag to hospital as quickly as possible. They loaded everything into an anonymous white van parked outside. As they drove away, Joe shouted, "See you next week."

In the front room, Tag lay on his side against the sofa. I sat down next to him and leaned over. I couldn't tell if he was breathing but the bubbles were still coming. I wanted to call an ambulance but I didn't want it to come here. They might call the police and I was in enough trouble.

"Your friend doesn't look very well," said a voice from the doorway. I looked up. A woman stood there, about my age, mid-twenties. She had long black hair, kohled eyes and lipstick redder than blood. She had those boots with the thick soles and towered above us in her long black coat. She carried a large bright red handbag, slung in the crook of her arm. It was decorated with tiny black flowers.

"Oh Christ," I said, "A witness, that's all I need."

"Oh, don't worry about me. I've shut the door. Now what seems to be the problem?" She came over to where we were sitting, squatted down and gave Tag a professional once-over. She smelled of incense. "I think he needs some help," she said.

"What? Who the hell are you? Just bugger off will you. I'm busy."

"Oh, I can do better than that," she said and reached into her bag. She pulled out a small vial. "We'll give him some of this."

"What the hell is that?"

"Medicine. When I medicine someone ..."

"... he stays medicined. Yeah, we all know the classics. Now what is it?"

"It's an old family recipe. Totally Class A of course. But it will perk Tag here up no end and I don't ask questions. The kind of questions the police ask. Even if you did call an ambulance now, I don't imagine he'd make it anyway. She gestured over and I looked down at Tag, slumped across my lap. The bubbling had stopped and his eyes had flopped open. I didn't seem to have any choice.

"OK, OK, just do it."

Very carefully—and it wasn't easy with her long black nails—she opened the vial and tilted it to Tag's cracked lips. A blob of white fluid oozed out and slowly drained into his mouth. After a few moments he shook his head, blinked, uttered a single "God" and fell back, breathing properly again. I found some blankets and together we moved him onto the sofa. She must have cleaned up his face because he looked much better already. I looked around the room, there were piles of magazines and pizza boxes either side of the TV and blood splatters on the grimy wallpaper. There were probably bloodstains on the carpet too, but it was too dirty to tell. And then I looked at ... at my new friend standing there like something out of the Halloween edition of *Good Housekeeping*.

"Don't worry," she said, "I'm not here to give you marks out of ten for tidiness," she looked around, "or the lack of. I'm Sarah," and she held out her hand. I wiped my hands on my jeans and shook her hand, holding it by the very finger tips.

"I'm Rich," I said.

"How about putting the kettle on and you can tell me all about yourselves?" We left Tag asleep on the sofa and went into the kitchen.

"So come on," I said plunking a mug of tea down in front of her, "who appointed you Fairy Gothmother?"

"I suppose I did rather turn up in the nick of time." She looked at the mug. "Quatermass and the Pit, nice. Actually I was coming to see Tag." She reached for her bag and pulled out a couple of books. "I brought these for him." She put the books on the table in front of me. There was a battered paperback *Chariots of the Gods*. It had a very Seventies gaudy turquoise cover. I laughed.

"How very undergraduate." Sarah frowned and punched me on the elbow which Joe had softened up with the baseball bat. I winced. The other book was a thick black hardback, *The Great Mother* by Erich Neumann.

"Been in the rolling stacks?" I opened a page at random, "*Mother, womb, the pit, and hell are all identical.* Nice. Hang on, listen to this, *The death of the phallus in the female is symbolically equated with castration by the Great Mother …*" Sarah took it out of my hands. "Not worthy?" I asked.

"Not if you're going to take the piss."

"So have you been seeing Tag?"

"Not exactly. I run a small group, a group of like-minded individuals. Tag has recently joined us. I wanted to find out more about him and I brought these for him to read." I frowned. "It's a spiritual group."

"With Tag! Tag's about as spiritual as …" Sarah put the books back in her bag and stood up. "I'm sorry. Come on, sit down. Fancy a smoke?'

I rolled a joint and we talked. Sarah was a bit older than us and doing post doc work in Theology, about new religions. It was one of the few jobs where she could dress like she did. She had heard about our little sideline. I told her how Tag and I, we were both postgrad students. He was doing Chemistry and I was an Engineer. We'd made a little ecstasy processing plant which ran on solar panels and supplies filched from the Uni. We'd started with just friends but now we were turning out enough to supply most of the local clubs in South East London. We hadn't really thought about it before but I guessed we must have trodden on someone's toes. We hadn't been careful and now were paying the price. I tried to get Sarah to talk about what she'd given Tag but she wouldn't.

"You are not yet ready," is all she would say in a funny voice. She left promising to return to check on her "acolyte" as she called him.

After she'd gone, I went to see to check on Tag. His injuries didn't seem quite so bad as I'd feared earlier and I cursed myself for having given in to Joe so easily. There had only been a couple of them, surely we could have made a better showing of ourselves?

The rest of the week was hectic. I had a meeting with my supervisor on Tuesday. He was happy with my work but worried that I was getting behind schedule. This meant that I had to spend the next three days in the lab, milling tiny components for my thesis on particulate handling. I felt exhausted and only returned home late at night to sleep. I didn't see much of Tag but he seemed to be over the worst of his beating. From the amount of blood, I'd expected a longer recovery. I suppose a little goes a long way. I left Tag in charge of the production, not that it required much work. You just had to make sure that the hoppers didn't run short or that any of the machinery broke. I'd built in an app that sent telemetry data to my phone, to ensure things were going well and to detect any tell-tale signs of wear and tear. On Wednesday I got a text saying the mixture was running a bit thick so I had Tag clean out the water feed but apart from that it was fine. Over the next week I saw more of Sarah but less of Tag. She would come round at odd times of the day or night and they would huddle in the kitchen or disappear off for "a walk".

By Friday I felt I deserved a bit of a rest so I didn't get up until almost noon. I was woken by noise from downstairs. Sarah was sitting at the kitchen table. She had toned down her look from the other night although she was still wearing the big make-up. She was talking to Tag in a low voice. They stopped as they heard me approach.

"Hello stranger," she said.

"If it isn't the Good Witch of the South. I was wondering when you'd come back.""Oh, I've been here a few times, haven't I Tag?"

"Yes," said Tag and seemed unwilling to say anything else. There was a silence so I put the kettle on. They watched me walk round the room.

"I'm having a day off today," I said as I waited for the water to boil, "Want to get drunk and test the merchandise?"

"Er, no," said Tag.

"What? You pop more pills than me, Tag."

"Er ..." said Tag and looked at Sarah.

"I think what Tag means," she said, "is that we need everything we have for Joe and his friends."

"Yeah," added Tag and looked relieved.

"Come on, it's not as if they are going to miss a couple. Do you really think they can count to a thousand?"

"You also need to check the machine," said Sarah calmly. "Tag told me that there was a problem and that he wasn't sure that he'd dealt with it properly. Isn't that right Tag?"

"Yeah, yeah," said Tag, getting more into his groove. "You know I'm not so good at the machinery, 'specially when I've been beaten round the head a few times." He pointed to his forehead. I couldn't even see a bruise but he did look a bit desperate.

"OK, OK," I said. "I'll go and check it over. We didn't lose much production did we?"

"I dunno," said Tag. He was supposed to take the finished product into Uni to put it through the pill counting machine. We couldn't afford one ourselves yet.

"Oh for fuck's sake! We are a team aren't we?" I tilted my head and then raised my hand. He hi-fived me.

"Yeah," we said together.

"Oh, boys," said Sarah, "I shall leave you to your domestics. I'll be back soon." She smiled at us and got up. Tag followed her to the front door and showed her out. When he came back I tried to talk to him about Sarah but he wouldn't be drawn. For someone who marked his conquests with a row of empty condom wrappers stapled to the ceiling in his room, he was being very coy.

On Saturday, I went to a party but I couldn't really get into it. I tried to figure Sarah out. She had Tag following her around like a puppy but she kept coming on strong to me. And then there was Joe. He was due round on Monday. I'm sure we'd have enough gear for him, but what about the money? Had our cash cow just dried up? I wasn't getting anywhere and being round so many happy people wasn't helping so I just sold a few pills and drank myself into a haze. It didn't work but I least I didn't really care anymore. I came back on the night bus, sitting on the top deck with the other drunks, reeking of cigarettes and pewk. About a mile away from home, the bus went past the abbey ruins, its walls tinged orange from the nearby street lights, like old broken teeth. I saw a small group of people, standing in the old shell of the chapel. They had built a fire. I couldn't hear what they were saying but there was some dancing and, it seemed, through the steamy windows of the bus, that I could make out flesh. I rubbed my sleeve across the window and before we disappeared up the road, I was sure I saw Tag.

The next day, about midday, I was in the kitchen making some tea and Tag came down. I asked him about his night at the abbey. He was non-committal at first.

"It was just a bunch of friends, having a drink," he said.

"But it was freezing last night. You could have come to the party. It was alright."

"We didn't fancy it." I handed him a mug of tea and leaned against the sink. He sat down and started loading sugars into his cuppa.

"Who's we then? Your, Sarah's little group."

"We're just friends," he said.

"God, it's like drawing teeth. C'mon. We are mates aren't we? I haven't done anything to piss you off, have I?"

He looked a bit taken aback at my outburst and thought about it for a bit, cradling his mug in both hands, elbows on the table.

"I guess not."

"So … hang on, what's happened here?" I looked round the kitchen. The sink was empty. All the rubbish that had been lying across the fridge, spilling on to the floor—it was gone.

"Have you had a tidy up? Is your Mum coming to visit again?"

"No. I just, I just wanted a change."

"Did Sarah put you up to this?"

Tag just took a long sip of his tea, and tried not to blush.

"Bloody Hell. She has got her claws into you, hasn't she?"

Tag slammed his mug down, tea splashed across the newly visible floor. He jumped across the room and I shrank back against the sink.

"Take that back!" he shouted. 'Take that back."

"Take that back? What is this, baby school?" Joe stood in the doorway to the hall, laughing. "Are you boys no longer friends? This is not right. Specially if it affect our supply. You shake and make up. You be good boys." Behind him in the corridor, his two helpers sniggered.

"You're early," I said.

"No, you late," said Joe and stood aside to let his men in. "Show us the stuff."

"It's alright," said Tag, "I bagged it up this morning, when you were asleep." He motioned to the front room and the duo followed him out. Joe crossed his arms.

"I like your friend," said Joe. "He good for business. So one tousand no problem for you? Next week, we want two tousand." And when I started, he added, "Or you make friends with my bat again." And he turned and walked out. Fuck. There was no way we were going to be able to turn that around, not if we wanted to make any money ourselves. But what else could we do? I was lost in thought when Tag came back into the room.

"That's that sorted then," he said. He seemed all together rather too happy with the arrangement.

"We're fucked."

"What? No, I had a word. Look." From his back pocket he pulled out a fat wodge of purplish notes. "They gave me this." I looked. Tag had a roll of about twenty twenty pound notes. No, they weren't twenties, they were euros. Five-hundrend euro notes. Ten grand. Ten fucking grand.

"Ten grand," I said, somehow making two syllables out of the last word. "What? Come on. You're kidding me, right?"

"Straight up," he beamed.

"You bloody marvel. Hang on. They gave you ten thousand euros? What, because they liked your smile"

"Sort of. You just have to know how to talk to people. I've been learning things."

"What sort of things?"

"Like I said, how to talk to people. How to get them to do things for you. We won't have any more trouble from them." Tag was smiling now. It was scary. He looked like one of those people on the bus who try to tell you how Jesus loves you.

"Tag. You're just not making sense. That's not how things happen for Christ's sake. The last time we saw them they took a baseball bat to your face, by way of introduction. Those kind of people, they don't … they just don't."

"Look," said Tag, "is this some kind of problem? Would you rather they just beat the shit out of us each week and took our stuff? Would you? Well, would you?" I shook my head. "Well then, this is better isn't it?"

"I guess so."

"Correct answer! Give the man a great big hand. And now if you don't mind, She is coming and I've got some friends to see." He counted out half the notes onto the table and then just dumped them all. "Buy yourself something nice," he said and left.

Tag wasn't making sense. I ran after him up the hall but he'd already gone, as had Joe. It was all getting out of control. I could make sense of Joe, but not Tag. I went upstairs. There was a short landing halfway up the stairs which lead to Tag's room over the kitchen. My room was further up, at the front of the house, over the sitting room with the bathroom between us.

The carpet was a dirty pale blue, covered in the scorch marks of dropped cigarettes and spilt chemicals. The ecstasy plant was in the bathroom, packed into the space behind the panelling around the bath. It was a nuisance getting it out each time we wanted to use it but we couldn't take chances with the landlord, if he ever turned up. I checked over the machinery. It seemed fine. Except, there was something strange in a hopper. The one which contained the bulking agent, usually chalk powder, was packed with ground up bits of dried herb. It had fronds, like the dill you get in pickles but it smelled extremely bitter. This must have been Tag's doing. It was all getting too much. I just had to find out what going on but each time I talked to Tag, or Sarah, I ended up none the wiser. Perhaps there was something to what Tag had said about knowing how to talk to people.

I walked back down the stairs and stopped outside his door. I wanted to look in but he was my friend, we trusted each other. But he was acting strangely and he needed a friend to keep an eye on him. I pushed the door. It wasn't locked, or even shut. His bed was along the left hand side of the narrow room with the window at the end and then his cupboard, desk and beloved swivel chair down the right. It was all very clean. He must have even hoovered, and the condoms were gone from the ceiling. Instead there was a poster of one of those swirly fractal things, like a big straggly star. It looked new. It was a funny place to put it. I lay back on the bed. It was one of those pictures where you had to squint to see a dolphin. I squinted. There was no dolphin although there was a strange smell. I rolled over and lifted up the pillow. There was nothing there but the pillow case had a greasy mark on the underside. I looked inside. Instead of the regular issue pillow, there was a tote bag. It was rolled up and filled with more of the same kind of herb I'd found in the bathroom. I pulled the bundle free. Its pungent, acrid smell enveloped me: cut grass, dirt, and, I swear, raw beef. At one end it was tied with red string and glistened with a white liquid, like the stuff Sarah had given Tag that time. I quickly wiped my fingers on the sheets. The odour was getting stronger and my head started to throb. I had to get out. I stuffed the bundle back into the pillow case. As I did, I caught a glimpse of the poster on the ceiling. Where there once was a random mess of colours and lines, now there was a dark hole, stretching up and through, swirling leaves and branches enfolded me, drawing me up, down even, I could no longer tell, into an all-encompassing, pulsating void. I felt my mind, my body reach out to the enormity that existed inside the fractal. Out there, beyond the edge of reality, it pooled massively around me, probing, forcing itself through the opening I had given it. But I was too small to contain it and I had not been made ready for it. I could not, did not know how to give in to it and revolted, fought it, flailing about, grabbing at the sheets, knocking over the chair. The noise was enough to bring me back for a second and I stumbled for the door and collapsed on the landing.

I lay there panting before rushing to the bathroom and, pressing knees against the base of the bowl, threw up in the toilet. Dear God. I felt tainted as if something dirty had been dragged round the inside of my head. I could still feel its tendrils, taste its wrongness in my mouth. Why would anyone want to even know about that thing? I had to find Tag and stop him, whatever he was up to. I went to my room and made some calls, mutual acquaintances from Uni, bar staff who looked the other way, regular users. No one had seen Tag, and then I got lucky. Craig, one of the electronics lab technicians who'd previously supplied me with components, had sold Tag some kit only just that week, an old Olympus MP3 recorder they no longer used. It was a start, but it wasn't much. I was going to have to look at Tag's emails. He'd never been security conscious before and I hoped his new found purpose in life hadn't quite reached that far. It would mean going back into his room but this time I was prepared. I found the scuba mask I'd used last Christmas in Egypt and got the pole we used for opening the attic trapdoor. I wasn't happy with the idea of touching the poster, but I didn't want it lurking behind me when I was using Tag's computer. Bracing myself, I put on the kit and burst into his room. I levered open the window, chucked out the pillow and dragged the poster down from the ceiling. I'd half expected something to jump out from behind it but there was just the old scratchy and yellowing Artex. The poster followed the pillow. And then to business.

As I expected, there was no boot password so once I started up the machine, I was in and straight into Gmail. Tag never used to be this busy. He had been a slacker with a loose sense of legality and a penchant for recreational chemicals but over the past week—no, past *month*—he'd been corresponding with a load of people I didn't know. I knew that his acquaintance with Sarah had started before Tag had his head bashed. He'd actually known her for quite a while before that and was in deep with her group, her coterie, her circle as she called it. It sounded like a made up religion, but they weren't Jedis. There was a lot I didn't understand written in a kind of code, "Shub-Niggurath fhtagn" seemed to reoccur but it didn't make much sense. Then I found a mass emailing of an MP3. Tag had sent the same email about twenty times, each to about fifty people, a thousand in all. Apart from the attachment, all it said was "Liverpool St" with a date and time. It was today and in less than an hour. I had to get down there. I sent the email to my phone and ran to the tube station as fast as I could, too fast as it turned out as I didn't quite have time to download the MP3 before I was underground. It would have to wait.

I wondered about the date and time. Today was October tenth and it seemed like a propitious date to do something. I remembered there had been some joking on the internet about 10/10/10 being Hitchhiker's day as 101010 was 42 in binary. Ten times ten times ten was a thousand, so what about the time? It had said 4:40pm. It took me until Angel station to get it. 4:40 was 1,000 minutes into the day from midnight. With the number of emails that was three times one thousand. I still didn't know what it meant but it sounded meaningful. It was the kind of time that might interest those kooks who think the world will end in 2012, the same people who thought their number was up in 2000. Whatever Tag and Sarah were up to, even if they didn't hurt anyone else, I didn't want them to do anything stupid. We had a good business going. I didn't fancy taking a McJob to finish paying off my studies.

The escalators weren't very busy at Liverpool Street. I ran up two at a time and out on the concourse. It was the usual Sunday scene of passengers reluctantly starting their journeys home, or standing staring at the massive indicator panel which stretched over a cross-walk above the concourse from my side of the station to the platforms. Suddenly there was a surge of people from all directions, up from the Tube or the overground trains or off the buses. The station was packed. There was a strange announcement over the PA, "Would Inspector Sands please report to the operations room immediately." One of those coded messages for staff, designed not to alarm the public. It was repeated again and then followed by a nervous "Passengers are reminded not to block gates and entrances." I fought my way to the stairs leading up to street level. I couldn't see Sarah or Tag anywhere and then I spotted him. Opposite me and above the gates to the platforms there was a row of concessions. Along the front of these was a walkway which connected out to the street at either end of the station. My view was partially blocked by the indicator panel but I could see Tag leaning over and looking down into the concourse. And then the clocks all clicked to 16:40. Instantly many of the passengers, singly or in groups of three or four, stood bolt upright and looked up towards the ceiling, through it and beyond. I looked up too but I couldn't see what fascinated them. And then I noticed they all were wearing earbuds, or headphones and they were mouthing something, a chant, but not like a hymn. It was more disorganised and quieter, like a hum but rising in volume, slowly gathering intensity as their mouths gradually opened wider and wider.

Across the other side of the station, Tag walked out onto the crosswalk. I ran down my side of the station and wheeled round to face him, fifty yards away. The station announcer asked passengers to evacuate the station but nobody moved. Those involved in the flash-ritual carried on regardless and others waited to see was happening. Tag had reached the middle and was looking down at his congregation. He was screaming with them, urging them on. Station staff were pointing and shouting but I couldn't hear them. The air was thickening, lights became dimmer. The chanting was starting to gather, to resemble words. I made out a "fhtagn", somehow now pronounceable, now redolent with meaning as if from a dream once forgotten and now remembered. I ran forward and leaped at Tag. He started and grabbed the handrail.

"She comes!" he screamed at me, his eyes bulging with intensity, his fists clenched. "We are her children and She comes to suckle us. At last She comes!" He wasn't making any sense. I punched him, right in the side of the head. He fell to his knees. His cheek caught a stanchion and ripped. Everything stopped.

"Tag! For God's sake, stop this. Now."

He looked up at me, blood seeping through the tear in his face. He smiled, pushed his tongue out through this second mouth and head-butted my knee. I pitched forwards and he grabbed my head, pulling it towards his face. I thought he wanted to kiss me. His eyes were gone, Tag was gone. There was something else inside him. I resisted, pulling back, and then snapped forward, my forehead catching him on the bridge of the nose. There was an awful wet sound as the bone gave and the fluids splashed down both of us. He reeled back, but only from the force of the blow. He no longer felt pain. And now, terribly, the whole front of his face had lost its shape, as if it had been smudged in Photoshop. I went cold, then hot. On my staccato breaths I could taste metal and a cloying milky sweetness. There was a vertical gash where Tag's nose and mouth used to be and in that hole dark things moved, pulling at the flesh, widening the opening, breaking through. I screamed and fled. Down below the chanting continued, more frenzied, the worshippers tore at their clothes and faces, the onlookers now heeding the announcements piled up the stairs and escalators. I ran past Tag and there was Sarah, laughing. Her handbag was still slung in the crook of her arm and from it she pulled handfuls of herbs and rained them down on the crowd below, gesticulating like a conductor. I skidded to a halt in front of her. The chanting from the mob was reaching a crescendo, their words now forming a whole, "Iä! Shub-Niggurath! The Black Goat of the Woods with a Thousand Young! Iä!"

"Oh Rich," she said, looking down at me, "thank you for not seeing what was going on. Thank you. If only you were pretty, it would make up for you being so fucking stupid." She stretched out her arms and her bag fell to the ground, her long hair boiled up in a great mass behind her head sucking the light into it. The ends of the hair flickered with dark energy, pulsing out of our world, into another and back. Her eyes emptied to blackness as she intoned the ritual.

"Shub-Niggurath! The Black Goat of the Woods with a Thousand Young. By Your foulness do I know Ye, by Your name do I call …"

I lunged and caught her round the middle. She crashed backwards onto the handrail, gasping for breath. I kept up the pressure, my arm now under her chin, and pushed her half back over the barrier towards the track below. The hair was alive. It gripped and wrenched my shoulder and I span round, almost off my feet. I managed to hang on, getting one hand across Sarah and under her armpit. And there was what was left of Tag coming across the walkway at us. His face was split completely in half, the two sides falling away from his shoulders as black ropes of flesh clawed up from inside his body and flailed around out of the stump of his neck. One grabbed my leg, searing through my jeans and flesh. Hair and tentacle pulled me this way and that; I felt ligaments snap and bones grind but still I clung on to Sarah. With a sickening moist sound, the rest of Tag sloughed away revealing the dark hairy body and cloven hooves of an enraged monstrosity. Great holes in its side with many teeth screamed and chattered. The tentacles struck out wildly and ripped me up into the air. I dragged Sarah up with me, tearing her prehensile hair where it clung onto the balustrade. The creature whipped us round and flung us far out, over and down onto the track. The 16:45 from Clacton was late and only moving at ten miles an hour but it wasn't going to stop for us.

Last Things Last

A. Scott Glancy

(based on an idea by Brett Kramer)

In the darkness, a cell phone is ringing. It squawks out "Hooray for Captain Spalding," Groucho Marx's theme music from *You Bet Your Life*. Agent Winifred struggles under her comforter to find the ringing cell phone. She brushes her own silent cell aside and digs for the burner her Cell leader gave her. That phone has never rung before, and after tonight's opera she'll drops it down a sewer drain and it will never ring again. When she finally finds her Cell's cell phone, she checks the caller I.D. It reads "ALPHONSE." She immediately answers.

"This is Winifred."

The computer-generated voice on the other end sounds as warm and avuncular as Stephen Hawking.

"Agent Winifred, execute identity protocol Kappa. Forty-six, left, thirty-two, three."

Winfred jumps out of bed and goes to a bookcase across her bedroom, withdraws two old volumes. She opens the first titled *Selected Prose and Poetry of Rudyard Kipling*. She opens the book to page 46, checking the left column she counts down to line thirty-two. The passage reads—

When you're wounded and left on Afghanistan's plains,
and the women come out to cut up what remains,
jest roll to your rifle and blow out your brains,
an' go to your Gawd like a soldier.

She reads the third word of the thirty-second line. "Wounded."

"Confirmed," answers the phone.

Winifred opens the second book, Dashiell Hammet's *The Maltese Falcon*.

"Protocol Theta. One eighty-five, four, five."

The anonymous voice squawks "Sap." Winifred checks the text. It reads—

I won't play the sap for you.

"Confirmed. You are go for mission details."

"You are cordially invited to a night at the opera," came the expected opening line. "Confirm your availability for a twenty-four hour engagement beginning immediately."

"I'm available for that window, but if I'm held over I'll need an intervention with my supervisor."

"That has already been arranged with your Special Agent in Charge."

"So what's the rumpus?"

"Agent Grendel will contact you at Jumbo's Clown Room on Hollywood Blvd. at 11:45 tonight. His contact code is 'Mamacita.' Your response is '*Chupa mi culo, hijo de puta.*' He will bring the script and play the lead. You are the understudy. Bring no registered weapons or ID. Sanitization is paramount. Dress for the office. Any equipment will be allocated from the local green box. Understood?"

"Understood," she says, checking her alarm clock. It was 11:04. "But I've never worked with Agent Grendel before. How am I supposed to find him?"

"He'll find you."

The caller disconnects without ceremony. Winifred puts down the phone and goes to the closet. Hanging among the conservative suits is a bullet-proof vest and a windbreaker with the letters "FBI" stenciled on the arm and back in yellow. She's dressed and in the car in ten minutes. In thirty she pulls up to the curb across the street from Jumbo's Clown Room, an inexplicable strip joint in a strip mall. As she crosses the street a nondescript car screeches to a halt right in front of her, cutting her off from Jumbo's. An old man with horn-rimmed glasses and steel-grey hair sticks his head out the window. He's much older than Winifred, perhaps by two or three decades. Where she is dressed in a conservative suit, he wears a corduroy jacket and jeans with no tie.

"Hey Mamacita! Jump in and we'll go for a ride."

"*Chupa mi culo, hijo de puta*," she responds dutifully but without conviction.

"It won't get you an Oscar, but good enough. I'm Grendel. Let's go."

"Winifred. What about my car?"

"Leave it. We are not leaving tracks tonight."

Winifred goes around the rear of the vehicle. Grendel watches her in the side and rear view mirrors. As she crosses to the passenger side he moves his sidearm from the passenger seat to a holster at his side. She gets in he pulls off.

"Is this stolen?" she asks.

"Registered to a dead person. I've got all the ID and papers we need to pass getting stopped by the cops. A Cell picks up the fees and makes sure the ID and car papers stay current. Hasn't your Cell-leader walked you through the process of making an invisible car?"

"We had other priorities on our last opera," she says coolly.

"How many is this for you?" he asks. It was the standard shoptalk for newly acquainted agents. It was also not supposed to happen.

"Four." L.A. flies past the windows in a blur.

"See any real action?" Grendel presses. "I mean, besides the one that got you recruited."

"Is this the part where you give me the buddy cop movie speech about how you're not my baby-sitter, my wet nurse or my Yoda and I'm going to have to pull my own weight around here?" she snaps. "If it is, I'd prefer it if you kept that shit to yourself."

Grendel gives her a tired sideways glance, but keeps driving. He breaks the silence after about a ten count.

"This is a blind date. I just want to know what depth you're pressurized to."

"Want a war story?" she asks.

"Sure."

"Last year my Cell busted up a genuine, no-shit, snuff porn operation run by a bunch of fat fucks calling themselves the Cult of the Feeding Hand. We didn't make arrests and we didn't make the papers."

"Did the avatar of Y'golonac manifest?" Grendel asks without skipping a beat.

"Avatar of what?"

"I'll take that as a no. Okay, so you're as cold and hard as a coffin nail. What's the rest of your resume look like?"

"I graduated Quantico four years ago. Before that I got an MS in computer sciences. I've clocked no time in the military so don't expect me to field strip an M-16 in the dark. So what's the op?"

"We're going to sanitize a former agent's apartment," Grendel says as he turns the car on to Hyperion Avenue and heads towards Glendale. "He dropped dead a couple days ago of a coronary. Landlord found him this afternoon. We had a friendly in the coroner's office take a look and it doesn't appear like anything more than an old guy having a heart attack. The next of kin have been notified and they're flying in tomorrow morning."

"A black bag job?"

"Yep. Go in, search the place for anything connecting the guy back to Delta Green, leave no sign of our search and send anything we find off to A Cell."

"Rule number one is no trophies, no souvenirs, and no diaries. He'd have to be some kind of idiot to keep that kind of stuff around his place."

"I worked with him a couple of time, back when he was my age and I was yours," says Grendel. "He cut his teeth back in the OSS. Didn't go to the corner store except by Moscow Rules. But even a guy like that might fuck up. Especially after A Cell moves him to the inactive list. People get slack, lazy or even, god forbid, nostalgic for the good ol' days... back when they got to go toe to toe with the shit nobody believes in anymore. Anyway, this is standard procedure. If you and the rest of the incoming class do your jobs right then someday you'll get to go through my shit to make sure I was a good soldier."

"No gold watch."

"No gold watch," Grendel agrees.

Grendel pulls the car up to the front gate of a 24-hour self-storage facility. Grendel punches in the code on the security pad and the steel gate rolls aside.

"Okay," he says. "Let's get tooled up."

Inside Grendel opens the six padlocks on the unit with keys on his keyring. "Is this your green box?" he asks Winifred.

"No, I've never used it before."

"You really should talk to your Cell leader about that." Grendel rolls the door up and pulls the string on the bare light bulb dangling from the ceiling.

The green box is a tangle of paramilitary and occult bric-a-brac. Shotguns and automatic rifles lean against bookcases filled with old books, ring binders and loose-leaf manuscripts bound in string. Some of the binders have titles on their spines like "How to Kill Things" while others are marked "Things You Can't Kill." An Ouija board with what look to be bullet holes in it is propped next to the binders. An M72 LAW anti-tank rocket is perched precariously atop a stack of steel ammo cases of various calibers. The steel shelves are filled with rolls of duct table, a pick and shovel, bolt cutters, an oxyacetylene blowtorch, and power tools with rechargeable batteries. A sawn-off 12-gage shotgun with a bouquet of withered roses taped to the barrel sits near a blood-spattered jacket from a floral delivery company.

A Tuxedo in a plastic dry cleaning bag hangs next to several military-grade biohazard environment suits. A shelf marked "Clean Up" holds bottles of bleach and glass jugs of sulfuric acid. Empty vials of injectable painkiller and antibiotics litter the floor along with dirty dressing and bandages around a blood-stained military cot.

As Agent Winifred marvels at the cache, Agent Grendel reads a clip-board hanging from the wall. "Check around and see if you can find any .40 caliber shells. There's a Glock 18 with a shoulder holster and two extra magazines in box seventeen."

Winifred starts opening the ammo cases and checks through the mismatched boxes of ammo inside. She comes up with two boxes of fifty rounds.

"Got it."

Grendel digs the pistol and shoulder holster out of box seventeen and tosses them to her. She slides it on and puts her jacket on over it. "Can you pick a lock?" he asks.

"Aced the course at Quantico."

Grendel tosses her a lock pick set. She puts it into her jacket pocket.

"That MS mean you can hack a personal computer? Do data recovery?" He grabs a small tool kit, a crow bar, a short sledge hammer, a stethoscope, what looks like a laptop computer, a bunch of cables, and stuffs them all into a black gym bag.

"I specialized in digital forensics. What's all that for?"

Grendel continues to pack tools and technology into the gym bag. A couple of flashlights and a pair of bolt cutters go in. "I'd rather bring a tool we don't need, than find we need something we didn't bring."

"Fair enough."

Grendel zips the bag shut and slings it over his shoulder. "Okay. Let's Watergate."

Thirty-eight minutes later Winifred pops the lock of their deceased colleague's Culver City apartment. It is sparsely furnished. There is a small television, a frayed couch, and nothing on the walls but a couple of bookcases. No signs of pets or plants. Any signs of life rest with the dirty dishes in the sink.

Winifred and Grendel carefully remove the police tape and step inside without a word, locking the door behind them. They snap on rubber gloves, close the blinds and draw the shades throughout the apartment before turning on their red-lensed flashlights. They search each room one at a time. They close the doors to each room to keep the light from spilling out into the rest of the apartment as they search.

They move from room to room, opening drawers and cabinets. Grendel unscrews the vent covers and checks inside the ducts while Winifred checks the toilet tank and medicine cabinet. In the bathroom Winifred finds the outline of a body marked in tape. There is a small bloodstain on the tile floor and dried smear on the edge of the sink. The tiles are ugly and the grout between them badly stained with mildew. Winifred wrinkles her nose at the floor. It's a shitty place to die, but she's seen worse.

Grendel searches the kitchen. He checks the cabinets, the oven, and refrigerator. He checks the seals on the boxes to see if any have been opened to conceal anything within. They look inside books, sift through an old green filing cabinet, but nothing incriminating turns up. Mostly it just looks like the sad refuse of a lonely life. Only one framed photograph sits on the dingy metal office desk. The photo shows a much younger man with his children. Winifred opens the frame and discovers that the photo has been folded so that the frame obscures the smiling woman embracing the children.

"Did he go through a nasty divorce?"

"No," Grendel answers. "Cancer got her. The kids are grown."

Winifred puts it back and keeps searching. While going through the filing cabinet she pulls out a file that contains bank records. Finding what she needs she puts it aside. The next file contains a deed and property tax documents.

"I think I've got something here."

"Any sign of a safety deposit box?"

"Not according to his banking records," she says, "but this isn't his only bolt-hole. He's got a cabin up in Arrowhead. Have you found any keys?

Grendel holds a ring of keys up and shakes them.

"Okay then. My turn to drive."

It takes another four hours for Winifred to wind the car through the fire roads and up the dirt driveway to the cabin near Lake Arrowhead. It's single story affair, well maintained, but drab, with a well-cleared lawn. Winifred kills the lights and rolls up the drive to within thirty yards of the cabin. They get out and approach the cabin cautiously, standing far enough apart so that anyone shooting at them can't cut them down with the same burst of fire. Grendel tries the front door. It's locked. He tosses the keys to Winifred and signals for her to wait a minute. Grendel tries looking through the windows but he can't see anything through the curtains. He checks around back and the back door is locked too. He comes back around and draws his weapon. She does too. She opens the door with the keys while he covers her with his pistol.

They play their red-lensed flashlights over the interior of the cabin. If anything, it is more barren than the apartment. The two agents enter the darkened cabin after checking for trip-wires or other booby-traps. The simple furnishings include a metal spring cot, a large, padlocked steamer trunk, and a folding card table with a propane lantern on it. Several open bags of cement, three large jerry cans of gasoline, some road flares, and a double-bladed wood axe are stacked against the back wall.

"Don't touch anything," Grendel hisses. "Check the other rooms."

Winifred goes to check the kitchen pantry and finds it filled with some canned goods on the shelves and a rusty wood stove. The beam of her flashlight reveals that the sink has been filled with cement. She quickly moves to the bathroom and finds that the sink, tub and toilet have been sealed in exactly the same way. She taps the cement with the butt of her flashlight to confirm that it has set.

"All clear," she calls out. "But you need to see this. Someone filled all the drains with concrete."

Grendel's hand trembles as he lights the lantern on the card table. The stick match jumps from his fingers. He stamps it out and sets his expression back to steely determination before he turns to face Winifred. He goes into first the kitchen and then the bathroom and looks over the cemented fixtures. He tries to look brave, but his expression is strained. He knocks on the pipe under the bathroom sink with his flashlight.

"Concrete goes deep into the pipe. Maybe all the way down to the septic tank, depending on how thick he mixed it."

The two agents return to the main room. Grendel hangs the lantern from a hook in the ceiling and looks around. The large ratty carpet in the middle of the room is strangely off-center. He pulls it aside and reveals an old dark stain in the middle of the wood floor.

"Ah, shit."

Grendel and Winifred kneel down to examine the stain. There are deep gouges in the floor, as if the boards were struck with a heavy, sharp instrument. Running her fingers over the splintered wood, Winifred looks at the axe propped against the wall. Its blade is stained with something black.

"Looks like someone used that axe to chop something up on the floor."

"Something or someone." Grendel's voice sounds as if he is being strangled.

"Think whatever got the axe went down the toilet?"

"Or got dropped into the septic tank. It still doesn't explain the concrete."

"Would a rotting corpse stink up the house if the gasses came back up the pipes?" she asks. Her time with the FBI hadn't been spent on death investigations.

"No, I don't think so. Otherwise the stink from the septic tank would too. Let's go see if we can find the access hatch for the tank."

The two agents scan the yard and quickly find the access hatch to the septic tank. It is slightly domed, made of metal and secured with a padlock. Winifred moves to examine it more closely but Grendel holds her back.

"Let's finish with one Pandora's box before we open another."

Back in the cabin Grendel opens the curtains to let as much of the pale pre-dawn light in as possible. Winifred works on the padlock that secures the large steamer truck closed. She unlocks it.

"Got it."

She takes out a flashlight and begins to examine the lip of lid for any signs of a tripwire. Grendel joins her and leans in close, his pistol free from its holster, but held down and out of Winifred's field of view. She slowly opens the truck a hair's breadth and leans in to look around the edge for any signs of a trip wire or booby trap.

"I think it's safe," she says. She carefully lifts the lid. Inside is an alchemist's workshop. There are glass vials containing colored powders. Beakers with strange fluids, sealed with lead stoppers and molten wax. Chalk, candles and a curved, ritual dagger are set atop a black robe covered in occult symbols. Resting on top of the supplies are two pages from an old book, sealed in thin plastic sleeves for easier handling. The pages are cracked and yellowed with age and hand-written in what appears to be a Cyrillic language like Greek or Russian. The ghastly illustrations could be from a book on human anatomy, but clearly aren't. Taped to the underside of the trunk's lid is a manila envelope. The only mark on it is a large green Delta symbol.

"This just stopped being low stakes," Grendel says, trying to keep his voice steady. "I guess that envelope's for us. You read it. I'm not in the mood." Grendel sits down hard on the cot, his pistol dangling from his fingers. He looks at the floor. Specifically at the odd dark stain.

Winifred reads aloud. "My Brothers. If you are reading this note, I have died or become incapacitated before I had the courage to complete my final mission for our group. I have done a terrible thing. I'm sorry. I couldn't help myself. I just missed her so much. The formula must be incomplete. I only had a fragment of the book it came from. She came back, but she came back wrong. Bullets were useless. I had to dismember it. But the parts kept moving. I put the pieces in the septic tank out back. When I came to, I could hear it, calling to me. It begged me to let it out. It used her voice. It knew just what to say to stay my hand. I couldn't kill her again. Not again. It must be burned to nothing. You will find twenty gallons of gas in the cabin. Pour them into the septic tank and ignite it. You'd be happier if you didn't look inside. Please make sure the remains are kept from my children. I am so sorry. Please forgive me." It is signed Clyde Baughman.

"Bastard!" Grendel shouts, making Winifred jump with surprise. "Fucking selfish bastard! How the fuck could you leave this for someone else to clean up? Jesus!"

"So he's crazy?" Winifred asks, not sure if perhaps her new partner doesn't have a little crazy in his pocket too.

"That'd be nice, but not the way my luck is running."

"So, what then? He brought her back from the dead?"

"No, no, no! Not her," Grendel spit the words out, trying not to trip over them. "Something that looked like her, sounded like her, but wrong! Something tainted!"

"Fine! Tainted, whatever. But you're still talking zombie here, right? George Romero? Eating brains?"

"No, we're talking about beating death." Grendel hauls himself to his feet and begins pacing furiously. "Anyone messing around with hypergeometry does it for power, but what good is all that power if you can't take it with you. The way to fix that, of course, is you just don't ever leave. You never die. West. Curwen. Munoz. Mason. Waite. Prinn. They all wanted it. Some of them even got it, for a while. It's the alchemist's holy grail. Eternal life. But it always finds a way to fuck you."

"He brought her back, from the dead?" Winifred says getting to her feet. "With a silly robe, some candles, and a magic wand?"

Grendel shrugs. "Looks more like a magic knife. Don't look at me like I'm talking crazy. I thought you said you'd been out on four operas?"

"Yeah, sure, but what I saw was from another world, not from beyond the grave."

Grendel stops his pacing. "Then it's about time you learned there's no difference between the two. It all comes from the same place." He stomps across the room, sticks the road flares in his belt and grabs up a jerry can of gasoline in each hand.

"Bring the axe."

Out in the yard the two agents cross to the septic tank lid, hauling their heavy load of gasoline-filled jerry cans. Grendel stops about twenty feet short of the tank lid and puts the cans down. Winifred does likewise. Grendel takes the axe from her and then hands her his handgun.

"Take the guns and put them in the car."

"Are you shitting me?"

"No," he says, his mouth as dry as sand. "Put them in the car. The note said bullets didn't do any good. With all the fumes we're going to kick up I don't want a muzzle flash to ignite the gas while I'm pouring it in there. I wouldn't like burning to death very much."

"I can keep my head," Winifred shoots back.

"Maybe I can't. If it gets out of the tank we run back to the car and get the fuck out of here. In fact, turn the car around so it's pointing towards the road. Leave the engine running and the doors open too. First one there gets to drive."

As Winifred runs back to the car to prep their escape route, Grendel eyes the tank lid and the padlock. He lays his hand on the surface of the lid, then hefts the weight of the axe, taking the measure of both. Winifred turns the car around and comes running back.

"I can't believe I left the guns in the car."

"How's this sound?" Grendel says, ignoring her. "I use the axe to punch a few holes in the top of the tank lid. Then I pour the gas in while you stand by with the axe. If it starts to force the lid, go for the hands. We've got to keep it in the tank. We don't want it stumbling around after us on fire."

"Sound like a plan," Winifred grumbles. "The kind of plan a crazy person would come up with."

"What so crazy about it?"

"The part with the undead wife in the septic tank."

"No plan is perfect. Ready?"

"Fuck no," she says. The look in Grendel's eyes tells her he isn't ready either, but there is no point in putting it off. Grendel raises the axe and brings it down on the lid with a resounding clang. He raises it again and again. The lid dents. A half-dozen blows later, the septic tank lid looks like a can opener has been at it. Grendel hands Winifred the axe and picks up the jerry can. Just as he's about to pour the gas in they hear a woman's voice, shot through with terror and desperation, from inside the tank.

"Hello? Hello? Who's out there? Who are you?"

"Wait! Wait!" Winifred says. "Do you hear it?"

"Please!" the woman shrieks through the perforated lid. "You've got to get me out of here! That crazy bastard locked me in here! He thinks I'm his dead wife's ghost or something! Please!"

"Don't listen!" Grendel bellows. "It's not human!" He starts pouring the gasoline through the holes he made in the lid.

"Oh my god, no! No please! What are you doing? Stop!" The shrieks rise to a crescendo of panic as the gas pours in.

"What the fuck are you doing?" Winifred shouts. "That's a woman down there!"

"No, it isn't," Grendel hisses between clenched teeth. "I've seen this sort of thing before. We've got to finish this."

"She sounds normal!" Winifred reaches out to stay Grendel's hand, but he turns his body to keep her from the can of petrol.

"It might not know what it is."

"I need to know what it is. I need to be sure."

"I know. I'm sure," he grunts, refusing to meet her eyes.

"What if you're wrong? What if Baughman went off his rocker and just kidnapped some woman and locked her in there?"

"He didn't. What he did was worse. And now we're going to fix it." Throwing the empty jerry can aside, Grendel turns to grab the next one and comes eye to eye with the Glock .40 cal he'd handed Winifred back in the green box. Winifred points it right at his face, using the professional shooters' stance they taught her at Quantico.

"That's supposed to be in the car, Fred."

"You are out of your mind if you think I'm letting you burn her alive. Not without being sure."

"We don't want to see what's in there, Fred. I don't want to see what in there."

"What's going on up there?" howls the voice from inside the septic tank. "Please! I'll do anything you want. Please don't burn me! Please!"

"Just a minute! There's been some confusion. We'll have you out in a minute," Winifred calls back, using her most authoritative cop voice.

"Oh thank you! Thank you! I was so scared. I thought I was going to die!" weeps the woman. Or the monster.

Winifred fishes the key-ring out of her pocket and holds them out to Grendel. "Find the key to the padlock and get it open."

Grendel carefully puts the gasoline can down and starts to take a step towards her to take the keys.

"That's close enough! Here!" Winifred throws the keys to him. Grendel catches the keys and immediately turns and throws them deep into the brush.

"I'm not going to help you kill us," he says grimly.

It takes a moment for Winifred to tamp down her anger. "That's not going to stop me. Get back. Move over to that side of the lid."

"Fred, it's not a woman! You have to believe me!" Grendel tries to sound brave. He doesn't.

"We'll know for sure in a minute. Now back off. Way off." Grendel steps back a few feet.

"More. More. Keep going. Okay, stop. Now, turn away from me, put your hands behind your head and interlace your fingers." Grendel does what she orders him to do. "If you turn around, or put your hands down, I will kill you. You got that?"

"Fred, if you let that thing out it's going to kill you."

"You just stay put." Winifred fishes her lock pick set out of her jacket pocket. She puts the pistol down while keeping an eye on Grendel. She takes out a pick and begins working it into the padlock. Grendel is not looking at her. He's looking at the car just twenty feet away, the doors open and the engine running. It won't be the first time he's left someone behind to die.

"What's going on up there?" the trapped woman wails. "Why did you pour gasoline in here? Oh god, the fumes! Please, it's burning my eyes!"

"Just hold on, I've almost got it." Winifred pops the padlock open and pulls it free. Just as she does, the septic tank lid explodes open and the dead thing inside snaps out like a trapdoor spider. Swollen, blackened, slimy hands with long cracked nails caked in dried shit grab both of Winifred's hands. The thing in the tank laughs, joyous and sadistic and louder than she could have believed. Winifred pulls but its grip is as firm as the grave. Her eyes dart to her pistol lying only inches away. The lid lifts more. Winifred screams as she looks directly into the eyes of the dead thing wearing Mrs. Baughman's corpse. Its visage is bone and meat smashed by an axe and re-knit by something that only vaguely understood human anatomy. Even so, it knew where to put the teeth. It starts to pull Winifred in.

The lid slams shut, Grendel's weight atop it forcing the horror back down into the tank. The steel lip of the lid bites into the soft, rotten flesh of the corpse-thing. The shock causes it to loosen its grip enough for Winifred to break free. The thing's arms, caught at mid-forearm, don't immediately have the leverage to force the tank open again.

"The axe!" Grendel screams. "Get the axe! Use it!"

Winifred scrambles to get the axe from where it lays just a few feet away. Even as Grendel uses all his weight and strength to hold the lid closed, the thing in the tank presses itself up, lifting him. "The arms!" he screams. "Chop 'em! Chop the fucking arms!"

Running on little more than adrenaline and panic, Winifred swings the axe down onto the thing's right arm and severs it at the edge of the lid. It flops onto the ground, trailing something black, thick and ropey, but not blood. Its wrist and fingers continue to move without coordination, but with a lively awfulness. Winifred swings again and lops the left hand off at the wrist. Grendel rolls off the lid and lets the screaming thing jerk its twitching stumps back under the lid. As soon as the lid closes, Grendel throws himself back on top to hold it closed.

"Get the gas!" he screams. "Come on! Pour it in!"

Winifred turns and snatches up the can of gas. When she turns back and sees Grendel is blocking the holes in the lid, she hesitates. The thing in the tank howls. It bangs against the lid as Grendel struggles to hold it closed. His eyes are wide with panic. If there is a smarter plan he can't think of it.

"Just do it! Come on! Do it!"

Winifred, her face a mask of white terror, pours the gasoline through the perforated hatch, getting plenty on Grendel, but most gets in the tank. The thing pounds against the lid, screaming incoherently about how it is going to kill them both. When the can is empty, Grendel rolls, gets to his feet and starts running. Winifred needs no encouragement. She runs too. Behind them the lid flies open again. Grendel stops, pulls a flare from his belt. He then realizes that he's wet with gasoline.

"Stop! Stop! Stop!"

Winifred stops running and turns. Grendel throws the flare into her hands. She catches it reflexively

"I can't light it! I'm covered in gas! Fucking light it and throw it! Now! Now! Now!"

Winifred pulls the cap, strikes it and the flare ignites instantly. Grendel runs away from her and the sputtering magnesium flare.

Winifred tosses it and it arcs right down into the open septic tank lid. There is a dull thud as the gas ignites. A fireball rises from the open lid followed by boiling flames and thick black smoke. The screaming goes on and on. It screams until its vocal cords blacken and snap. As the thing dies, it calls for its husband.

Winifred turns and walks back to the car, a little unsteady from the adrenaline. She turns off the motor. On the other side of the yard, Grendel bends at the waist and pukes. She comes back to see if he's okay. She puts her hand on his shoulder as he's spitting the last of it out.

"You all right?" she asks.

"It's just the fucking gas fumes… and the adrenaline. When the fire dies down I'll go get his resurrection kit and toss it in there. The bits you chopped off will have to go too."

"No. I'll get them."

"They're still moving."

"If they're still moving I need to see," she says. "I need to see what I'm going to be facing the rest of my life."

Grendel spits again and straightens up. "Welcome to the club, Fred. Now, if you'll excuse me I'm going see if I can wash some of the gasoline out of my clothes before the trip back to L.A." Grendel leaves Winifred alone to police up the bits and pieces and drop everything down the open septic tank lid. Eventually Grendel emerges from the cabin with the steamer trunk and together they drop it, the letter, the axe and even the bags of cement are dropped into the septic tank. Winifred picks up her gun and lock pick tools, even though the fire has damaged both beyond repair. It is well after sun up when two agents drop the last cans of gas into the septic tank and ignite them with another flare. By now they are dirty and sweaty and covered with soot from the fire. They get in the car and drive away as the fire continues to burn underground. Even with the windows down, the stink of gas fumes rising from Grendel's clothes is only bearable at highway speeds.

They drive back to L.A. in silence. Grendel pulls up in front of Winifred's car, still parked on the street across from Jumbo's

Clown Room. It's mid-morning and nothing much is moving in Hollywood.

"This is your stop."

Winifred doesn't move. Grendel looks away, straight ahead. He knows he's supposed to say something, but it doesn't come. He presses ahead anyways.

"Once you get out of this car, we won't see each other again unless A Cell puts us together on an op. That could be next week or next year or never. If you've got something you want to ask me, do it now. You won't get a chance until much — "

Winifred cuts him off. Her face streaked by soot and sweat but not by tears.

"Why? Why the fuck would he try to bring her back? You worked with him. You know he saw stuff. Real stuff. He should have known what would happen if he tried to bring her back. So why did he do it?"

"Fucked if I know. People do stupid things. The stupidest things usually happen because of love and hope. He loved her. Maybe he loved her so much he allowed himself to hope that this time he would be the one to get it right? That's all it takes, you know? Just a little bit of hope. With a little bit of hope you can end the world."

"You make hope sound like a weakness," she says.

"It is."

Winifred looks at Grendel with an expression of revulsion. Disgusted, she reaches for the door handle.

"Be seeing you," he calls after her.

Winifred slams the car door. Grendel pulls off before she takes five steps. She never looks back to see him go.

"Be seeing you," she says, hoping she won't.

A few hours later, Grendel enters his apartment. It looks uncomfortably like the one he searched the previous night. He crosses straight to his desk and turns on the lamp. He reaches for a half-empty bottle of bourbon atop the desk and pours two fingers into a dirty glass. He flops into the creaky office chair and leans back. Raising the glass, his eyes are drawn to the framed photograph of an older, attractive woman on his desk. The frame is gilded by a black ribbon. Locking eyes with her, he hesitates bringing the drink to his mouth. Putting his glass down Grendel pulls open a desk drawer and removes a heavy, badly tattered medieval grimoire. The script on the battered cover is barely legible Cyrillic. Opening the book, he turns to a series of pages that have been torn out. Reaching into his jacket he pulls out the plastic-sleeved pages that he and Winifred found at the cabin. Pages he told Winifred he'd burned. He places them into the book. The torn edges match like pieces of a puzzle.

Grendel looks at the complete resurrection spell before him. He knows he could do it. He knows he could make it work. Clyde was a fool to try it with only a fragment. But here it is complete. Grendel looks at his dead wife's picture and smiles sadly. He raises the glass and throws the bourbon back. He addresses the picture.

"Be seeing you."

He slams the book shut. For now, at least.

One Small, Valuable Thing

Chad Fifer

I.

The first time the old man looked at me, he was taking a piss in the snow.

I'd stepped out of the house for a smoke. It must've been ten or eleven degrees out there. The world was frozen over. Nobody was out. I was drunk. It was probably seven in the morning.

The old man appeared on the corner down the street, walking his dog, I don't know, maybe six or seven houses away? Bald guy, tall, black suit. The dog looked just like him: skinny, bony, all in black. Some kind of Doberman, I guess.

I watched him cross from one corner to the next, slow but deliberate. The dog didn't seem to mind the pace. They stopped and the dog sniffed around the bottom of a street sign while the man stared down at him. It looked peaceful. These two thin figures against the dead silent snow, like some kind of charcoal drawing.

Then the dog lifted his leg and did his business. There you go, I thought. Sweet relief in the morning. Better than anything.

As if he'd read my mind, the old man turned away from the dog, unzipped his pants and started pissing in the snow himself, right out in the open, still holding the leash in one hand. I couldn't believe it. He and the dog were facing away from each other like they were trying to be polite, this leash dangling in a smile between them. The scene had gone from serene to ridiculous and I kind of chuckled as I put out my smoke.

That was when the old man snapped his head to the side and looked at me. Impossible for him to have heard me laugh or anything, but that's when he looked, his hands tucking and zipping at his pants, independent of his gaze. I couldn't tell you what his expression was because of the distance, but I didn't like the feel of it.

The dog pawed at the snow around the sign. The old man continued to look my way, his body now just as frozen as the street.

I was back in the house before I could decide whether to wave or flick him off, slamming the door against the cold. Something had disturbed me about the situation, but I didn't know why. I felt light-headed.

There was a last gulp of Jack waiting in a measuring cup on the kitchen counter. I stepped over, knocked it back and pulled the sheet away from the window. It was too frosty to see much outside, but I felt like the old man had moved on. I looked a while longer for some kind of glimpse, but the frost just stayed where it was.

I wandered into the bedroom to tell Grace about the old man. She was asleep on our mattress, surrounded on three sides by electric space heaters. The bedroom was the only place with any warmth at all, and she was in the center. One of her legs was poking out from under the blankets, just a little brown calf tapering into a fluffy polka-dotted sock. I leaned over and pinched her big toe, swaying a bit.

"Hey," I said.

She kicked at me and rolled up from under the layers. I could see her face now, squinting.

"Shut up," she said. "What are you doing? What time is it?"

She burrowed back into the bed.

I took off the coat and the flannel, threw them against the chair and made my way into a sitting position on the floor, scooting over to the mattress.

"Hey," I whispered, leaning over her. "You won't believe what just happened."

She didn't respond but I told her about it all anyway. After I was done she waited a moment, then pulled the covers around herself and sat up a bit to look at me.

"He was bald? Like, he wasn't wearing a hat?"

"No."

"Who goes out in this shit with no hat? Who walks their dog in this?"

"Who pees outside in this?"

"You could pee all day in the middle of the street. Nobody's out there to see. I'm saying who goes out without a hat?"

"I don't know. Maybe he lives right there."

"Please," she said. "You're the only white guy living in this neighborhood. And the only bald guy."

She dove back down under the covers, making one last muffled comment:

"And the only *old* guy."

Grace is 19, I'm 23. That's all the difference there is but I guess it makes me the old one. She's black and Vietnamese, so she can get away with calling me white. But she's wrong about the bald thing. I *have* hair; I just choose to shave my head. Back in high school, I wore it long and dyed it black. All I cared about was drawing, talking shit, taking roadtrips. Drinking by the river with the guys. No consequences.

That was before the Army.

I was in my second tour when things got cut short. We'd only been in Kunar Province for five weeks. I was driving a truck with my buddy Gustavo riding shot. Our patrol had taken some small arms fire in the morning, but it was over for the time being and we were feeling relaxed, just bullshitting each other. I was actually goofing on the Pope when it happened. Gustavo grew up Catholic, so he was loving it. Then I hit the IED and we just fucking went boom. I honestly don't remember it. When I woke up, the doctor told me I was in Italy. I said no shit—I was just talking about the Pope. He got a big kick out of that. I'd been unconscious for a week. Gustavo didn't make it.

Coming back to Iowa after that, nothing was the same. I'd managed to keep all of my limbs, but I was spooky in the head and everybody knew it. Couldn't concentrate. My ears would ring. Sometimes I didn't know where I was at night, and I couldn't remember a goddamn thing. The pupil in my right eye had been blown when my head got knocked in, and it had never come back to looking right. I could see out of the eye okay, but the whole thing was practically black and it bothered my little sister, who didn't want much to do with me anymore. That was harder than anything, I suppose. The way she looked at me.

So I drank. I drank all the time. My parents had been keeping me in my old room but just couldn't handle it after a while, so they found me a bachelor apartment near Davenport West, my old school, and ponied up rent for a few months. It was on the condition that I worked this shitty security job in a parking garage next to a shopping center. I tried to do it their way but after a few shifts I said fuck it and never went back. I'm not lazy, I wasn't mad at my folks and I wasn't trying to get back at anybody. Maybe I was just humiliated. I don't know.

I met Grace right around that time, in the late summer, both of us trying to catch a ride home from a bar at two in the morning. Nobody would take us anywhere, so we ended up walking together and then sitting on some swings in the park, just like we were kids. It was one of those golden moments I didn't think could ever happen again. Four in the morning with the smell of grass in the air, staring at a girl's smile. Laughing. Bumping shoulders as we swung sideways and talked and swung sideways and talked. I mean, the girl was a drunk like me—it was obvious—but there was a light inside of her that warmed me right up. Something that made me feel like I should take a shot at life again. Like I could climb back into the driver's seat.

Grace moved into the bachelor with me a few weeks later. She'd been living in her ex-stepmother's condo but had to get out; the woman kept taking on cats and the whole place smelled like ammonia. On top of that, she had overheard the ex-step on the phone, telling a man that if he brought over fifty dollars and a bottle of something, she might have a girl for him. That was all it took. Grace punched the bitch in the stomach and hit the road.

Once my parents finally gave up on me and the rent stopped coming, we moved from the apartment into a nearby squat—this little house that had been foreclosed on in a neighborhood that's been rotting from the inside since I was a kid. It was supposed to be temporary while we cleaned up and found jobs, but we were still drinking with every last cent I had in savings. We just couldn't get to bed at night, walking around the house, talking it all out, everything either of us had ever thought or experienced. When we could wake up in time we'd get down to the library to use the computers and look for jobs, but we both knew we were dragging our asses.

Then the winter came. We were lucky that the power still worked in the house—for some reason it had never been shut down. I'd taken the space heaters from my folks and we were getting by with them but it was desperate, man. The cold was brutal. We knew we could lose the electric at any minute and freeze. Or we could get thrown out by the cops and freeze. Either way, we had to do something, and soon.

All of this was on my mind the morning I saw the old man, and when I saw him again the next day, a real bad idea started forming in my head.

I'm no thief. Even when I've been the most down and out, I've never stolen to pay my way. It's just not fair, I don't think, taking other people's shit. Like, when I was a kid, I used to wear my

Uncle Kip's dog tags. He'd given them to me after noticing all the tanks I was drawing on my grade school notebooks, all the guns I used to design in sloppy detail. I loved those dog tags—the way the small metal orbs on the chain felt, almost like a rosary—the way the metal was cold against my bare chest. One day in high school, I took them off and hung them in my locker during gym class. When I came back, the locker was kicked in and they were gone. I don't know who took them or why they would even want them, but I tried to beat the shit out of a Mexican kid in the next period, just because he'd shrugged when I told him about it. He put me in a headlock and nearly choked me to death. That's what thieving does, man. It's bad business for everybody.

But after I saw the old man a second time, I started thinking, what if we stole something *just once*, and not to support the drinking, but to get us out of the cold? Something that somebody didn't really need. Something that was probably insured. I knew that with a little dough I could get us back into my bachelor, and my old friend Jim Tingle told me he was always on the lookout for stolen shit if it was small and had what he called "demonstrable value," meaning you didn't need an outside expert to say it was worth a lot of money. He sold weed out of his van like a delivery service, but doing the fence thing was a good second income. Once a month, he would drive boxes of whatever shit he'd acquired up to Chicago and turn a profit through his connections with the Black Disciples. It was like the path out of misery had paved itself in front of me: grab some scratch, get my place back, find a job, and marry my girl. Easy.

So I started keeping watch at the window for my mark. And sure enough, every day, the old man walked his dog past the bottom of our street, always at different times, but along the same route. He never did the pissing thing again but he repeated that same slow, deliberate pace, always dressed in some spiffy black suit, no hat on his shiny bald head. Grace joined me by the window on the fifth day, both of us taking pulls from a nasty bottle of crème de menthe we'd found in the back of a cupboard.

"Tomorrow I'm gonna follow him," I said.

"Your new boyfriend," she said, and laughed.

The next day, I pulled on my coat and skullcap the minute I saw the man hit the corner. But before I could get through the door, Grace grabbed me, throwing her thick blue scarf around my neck and wrapping it across my nose and mouth. It smelled just like her, my beautiful girl. Her cocoa butter skin.

"To keep you warm," she said. But I think she already knew what I was up to.

I gave her a squeeze and hit the street, my face masked by the scarf. The man had a predictable stride and he never looked back—I mean *never* looked back—so the slo-mo pursuit was a cinch. I'd walk about a street's length behind him, careful not to make much noise even at a distance, pause to light a smoke when he'd turn a corner, then hustle a bit to catch up. The dog loped along right at his side, keeping just as steady a pace and ignoring the cars, fire hydrants, and snowballing kids along the way. It was hypnotic how they moved together, all smooth, like they were on one of those conveyer belts that people ride at the airport, those flat escalator things.

But the weirdness wasn't just in the style of the walk; it was in the goddamn *length* of the walk. That was the real surprise. I swear, we were trudging through the freezing cold for almost two hours. Two hours, this crazy old man walked! We weaved through the ghetto neighborhoods around my squat, down through Fejervary Park, and then sliced back and forth through neighborhood after neighborhood until we were miles away on the hills of McClellan Heights, where mansions look down on the icy Mississippi. I was beat by the time we got there, but the old man pivoted into his driveway without a single sign of fatigue, even though he must've walked at least *twice* as far as me if he was all the damn way out in my neck of the woods. All I could think was: how much exercise does this fucking Doberman need?

The house was a wide, two-story joint with about nine or ten trees on the sprawling front lawn, all reaching up to the sky with arthritic, clutching branches. It was well-kept but gray and a little bland for such a ritzy place. No lights were on inside, no smoke was coming out of the chimney, and nobody seemed to be waiting for the codger in a window. As I continued to stroll by, head down, nonchalant, I imagined a family could make a great home there. But with the man slowly creeping up to the door, unlocking it and leading the dog inside without saying hello to anybody, it only seemed like some kind of sad museum.

And museums are *full* of things with demonstrable value.

During our many drunken conversations in the squat, Grace had owned up to a whole load of shit she'd done before we met, from stealing earrings at the mall to siphoning gas in a church parking lot. I tried to play it cool when I came back from my long walk with the man, but she could tell I had crime on my mind.

When I borrowed my buddy Randall's car a few days later, she was the one who zipped up my coat, put a ball cap on my head and shoved a cardboard box under my arm. After seeing the old man float past our street with his dog in the morning, she handed me the keys and I drove right up to his house, parking on the street. I grabbed the box, walked up the drive to the front door, and rang the bell just like a delivery man. Grace had told me to be obvious when scoping a joint out. People don't notice obvious.

After a few minutes had passed and nobody came to the door, I wandered around the side of the house as if I were looking for a place to safely leave the package, scanning the surroundings for signs of nosey eyes. I probably looked guilty as hell, but the neighbors weren't watching as far as I could see.

Around the back, where the yard plunged down into a ravine and the river revealed itself in the distance, I found a point of entry after a quick search along the icy path that ran the house's perimeter. A small doggie door was built into the wall, almost hidden behind a large, chunky air conditioning unit. Its aluminum hatch only lifted outward, but after a few minutes of fiddling with my pocket knife, I was able to pull it up and peer through the opening at a darkened kitchen. I got to my feet and searched the yard quickly for a branch, being careful not to leave boot prints in the snow. Returning to the doggie door, I lifted the hatch again and pushed the branch through the opening into the kitchen, waved it around, then removed it and threw it back into the yard.

After ten minutes of waiting in the car, no alarms had sounded and nobody had come to arrest me. Okay. It seemed like the house could be entered through the doggie door without tripping alarms. But I could *never* fit through the door myself.

I passed the old man and his dog as I drove home to tell Grace.

Our plan was pretty basic. Grace would squeeze through the doggie door, find one valuable thing for us to sell and then slip out with it and drive home. On foot, I would follow the old man as he walked the dog so that we knew how much time she had. I spent some of our last money getting two disposable cell phones from Jim Tingle and told him I'd be back soon with something to sell him, if I was lucky. Randall lent me his car again, this time for a fictional doctor's appointment (the last time had been for "groceries").

Early the next morning, Grace drove off to park near the old man's neighborhood, and about two hours later, I gave her the call.

"I see 'em. He just crossed the bottom of our street. You're good to go."

"About time," Grace's voice whispered over the phone. "We'd better celebrate after this is all done."

"I promise," I said. She didn't sound nervous at all as she hung up. My girl.

The man and dog walked the route for the next twenty minutes. I followed them at a distance, doing my usual stealth routine. The phone vibrated.

"You think anybody saw you?" I asked.

"How do you get this fucking thing open?" I could hear my knife clacking against the doggie door.

"I told you. You have to be real gentle."

Clack. Clackety clack clack.

"Shit!"

"Grace, come on," I whispered. "Just take it easy. Poke the point into the right side and lift. You can't use a lot of force."

"Shut up. You're making it harder."

She hung up. An SUV blasting music rolled past the old man and the dog but neither reacted, gliding along at their slow, steady pace. Another fifteen minutes and the phone vibrated again.

"Okay, I'm in," Grace whispered, finally. "This place is huge. I'm tracking mud everywhere."

"We'll throw the shoes out later. Just keep your gloves on and find something valuable. Start from upstairs. Bedrooms and shit."

"It smells in here. It smells like something really spoiled."

I could hear her coughing.

"Grace."

"It's okay. Hold on."

Click. She hung up again.

I wished I'd gone to the bathroom before leaving. In all the excitement, I'd forgotten. It made the moments before the next call stretch on forever. I wondered if this was how the old man had felt that first day I noticed him, so uncomfortable that he was willing to risk his elderly dignity in exchange for relief.

At last, another vibration from the phone.

"It's really dark."

"Use the light if you have to. But hurry."

"I wish you could see these paintings of people everywhere. They look really old, like from George Washington days. Probably worth a fortune."

"I don't think you can get those through the hatch, baby. Don't waste time."

The dog was sniffing at a street sign and the old man stopped walking. I turned and wandered around the corner of an apartment building, keeping watch on the man out of the corner of my eye. The dog began to relieve itself and I envied the little bastard.

"The bedrooms don't have shit," she whispered. "I'm going to the room at the end of the hall. Hold on."

A long pause. Quiet, white noise from the phone, then:

"Whoa, man. This place is weird."

"What do you mean?"

"It's not a typical old guy's place. It's all black and... There are weird symbols all over the walls. Like all over the place. Even on the floor. This guy's a total metal head. Or super Jewish or something…""Just see if there are any jewelry boxes."

"There's a box in the middle of the room, like on a little pedestal," she whispered. "Hold on, I gotta use the light. It's dark."

The dog finished his business and turned, pawing at the snow to cover his mess. The old man stared down at his pet, still as a statue.

Grace again, in a whisper:

"It's not even locked. Big wooden box."

I heard a heavy creak from the phone. Then a sudden blast of air, like she'd crossed through a wind tunnel. Clattering sounds. I could tell the phone had fallen to the floor, and Grace's voice became distant.

"Holy shit," she said.

"What is it? Hey!"

She fumbled with the phone.

"Some kind of—I can't believe this. It's like a giant ruby or something. Or an emerald? I don't understand the color. It's like… it's like... ohmygod..."

Down the street, the old man suddenly snapped his head to the side. He seemed to be listening to the air, his entire body rigid and at attention.

"Just grab it and get out of there," I said.

"It's like it's glowing or something," Grace whispered. "It's like there's something moving inside of it."

"Grace, seriously. Just pinch it and let's go."

"What the fuck, man…?" Now she was frightened. "It's like it's looking at me. I don't like this. I don't like this."

"What's looking at you? Grace?"

A meaty *crackling* sound suddenly pierced the winter air—a bundle of bones snapping in two—and down the street, the old man dropped to all fours, tense like a great cat. Before I could even process what I was seeing, he launched himself across the snow and sped away between houses, legs over arms, lightning-fast. I reeled and blinked my eyes, trying to stop what could only be a hallucination, but the old man was history, leaving a settling cloud of glistening snow in his wake.

The Doberman unleashed a painful howl, ran around in a quick circle and then galloped away in the trail of its master.

Grace screamed through the phone.

"It's in my fucking head! *It's in my fucking head!*"

"Grace! Get out of there! He's coming home!" I broke into a run, shouting into the phone. "Get out of there now! Grace! GRACE!"

But the phone was already dead.

II.

In the hospital, I had what the chart called "frequent breaks with reality." I imagined I was a toddler in the deep end of a pool, paddling for the edge while an invisible hand tried to force my head under water. My legs pistoned desperately, but I was too weak and felt the life draining from my chest. I felt absolute panic. While under these spells, I'd lifted and swung my IV pole at the other patients so many times that the nurses started weighing the base of it down with sandbags. The reality of the long hospital room and the reality of the pool were indistinguishable; I wanted out of both at the same time and my body did the work it needed to do. I experienced it and watched it, but I had no part in the decision-making.

Up the hills, down the hills—cold sweat clung to my body as I sprinted under the glaring winter sun to the old man's house. When I finally arrived in McClellan Heights, I saw that our car was gone, or at least no longer parked in the spot we'd agreed on. I slowed my pace as I turned onto the old man's street, calling Grace's phone once again but getting nothing. The muffled sound of a loud, deep voice seemed to be coming from the man's house—some sort of shouting, or chanting. Was he shouting at my girl? How had he moved so fast? *Was I still in the hospital, even now?*

I stopped in front of the house and dialed the phone again, panting. A small *bzzzzhh* shot back from the man's yard. I crossed to the sound and saw it there in the snow. Grace's phone.

She'd made it out.

The shouting sounds from inside had stopped. Getting to my feet, I saw the old man wrench a curtain aside in the house's top window and stare down at me. His expression was obscured by the sun's reflection, but the sight of him filled me with rage. I thought about pissing on his lawn right in front of him, just to say *fuck you*—to let him know who I was. But I realized in that moment that my jeans were already soaked. I'd lost it completely on the run there, like an out-of-control child. I had to get home.

I vomited twice on the way back, nervous about Grace, sick with exertion and sure that a squad car would be driving up at any moment to stop me. What seemed like twenty years later, I made it to our house. The car was parked on the street. Tears welled in my eyes and I jogged inside.

"Grace?" No response. I hurried toward the bedroom.

"Grace?"

She was there, hanging by her scarf from the ceiling fan, the tips of her boots touching the floor and her knees bent, long black hair dangling from her head. A notebook was open on the ground, her limp arms extending toward it.

Touching her, hoisting her up and brushing the hair back from her face, I knew she was dead. No amount of kissing, no amount of crying, no amount of denial would make it not true. Clutching her by the waist with one arm, I tried to untie the scarf but it was too knotted up, and when I had to release her again to go at it with both hands, the way she swung lifelessly back into place made my heart plummet into my stomach.

Once on the ground, I untied the other end from her tiny neck and pulled her to me. Guys in the service had killed themselves this way, tying their throats to bed frames and leaning forward to choke out. It took enormous force of will, to make your body accept death. Grace's feet had been touching the floor. She could've stopped herself from dying. But she hadn't.

I lifted the notebook. The writing was jagged and hasty, but it belonged to Grace:

i'm sorry. you wont understand why but i cant be alive. ive seen what it will do. i love you but i cant look at you again or you might know it two. the burning eye is in my head even now like im sick with it. i hid the thing. i covered it blinded it stole it and hid it - i wont think or write where. its all i couldo to stop it. its seen me once and may come in the dark but it will never know the hiding place. its not ur fault. go away if u can. i love you forever. get away.

That was all. It made no sense. The invisible hand was pushing me under water once again and I was drowning. I was drowning.

The sound of the front door woke me. It was dark outside. I was crumbled on the floor with Grace, a string of drool leading from my mouth to her sleeve. I lowered her head to the floor and sat up, wiping at my face. Listening.

There were people in the living room, but nobody was calling out to me. Just footsteps on the floorboards, cautious, heavy. Couldn't be police. My joints cracked as I pushed myself to a crouching position and the footsteps stopped, a creak and then another creak. There were two men. I pictured their positions in the room. I'd been trained for this. Whoever they were, I was going to kill them.

When the footsteps started again, I scrambled to the wall, unplugging all of the cords and powering down the blazing hot space heaters. The men sensed me as well and hustled toward the bedroom. I pulled the comforter from the mattress and used it to lift the heaviest heater, a blocky industrial relic with a glowing metal grill. I flattened myself against the wall, and as the first man stepped into the doorframe, I swung around and slammed the heater into his face, throwing the comforter over him at the same time and using my weight to force his bulky body to the ground.

I heard his flesh sizzle as we fell, accompanied by hog-like shrieks from beneath the blanket. I looked up to clock the other intruder, a skinny guy in a black polo and ski mask. He was pulling a gun from his belt but had no coordination. Before he could level the thing at me I pushed off from his friend and barreled toward him. My shoulder caught him in the midsection and forced him into the wall with a satisfying *oof*, the gun dropping out of his hand and clattering across the floor.

His insect arms flailed as I grappled him, spinning him away from the wall and throwing him down. He fell flat on his back and I pounded the side of my hand into his ear, seeing the other man continue to struggle under the blanket in my periphery. With both men down, I took the chance to roll across the floor and grab the handgun, a 1911 with a well-worn grip.

But the thin man wasn't staying put. He leaped onto my back and wrapped his hands around my face, trying to get his bony fingers into my eyes. He was strong for a skinny guy but had no close quarters smarts, and in seconds I had him on his back again, pushing my forearm into his throat to hold him down. With my gun-hand, I pulled his ski mask away and screamed into his face, but my voice stopped short when his features became clear.

The man had no nose. A cheek was missing, revealing only bony teeth and a tongue rolling around like a burrowing worm. The skin around his eyes was jagged and worn away, and the eyeballs flashed back and forth in a revolting panic. Fear overcame me like electric shocks against the skin, involuntary panic in the face of disfigurement. It wasn't human.

The sound of a breaking window stunned me back to life, and I saw that the big man was gone.

"*Glaaaaaghh...*" The thing beneath me wailed, choking. The sound of it was infuriating. I looked down into its glistening sick eyes and felt no pity. I crammed the ski mask into its mouth to shut it up, pressed the muzzle against the fabric, and blew its fucking head off.

Chalky bits of skull flew around the room and I went deaf for a minute. Didn't matter.

I ran to the bedroom. The window was broken out. Grace's body was gone. The big man was gone. A wig was lying on the floor like road kill.

Flying back through the living room, I reached the front door in time to see a hearse pulling away from the curb, hasty and sloppy, the big man behind the wheel. I was halfway through the door before I remembered car keys and spun back into the living room.

As I ripped through Grace's purse to find what I needed, I saw the body of the skinny man still rolling and crawling around on the floor, headless but alive. Reality had broken forever, and I was living here now, wherever *here* was. It didn't matter anymore. I only wished I had time to kill the man again.

The hearse driver tried to weave his way through the neighborhoods, but he should've chosen busy streets if he'd wanted to lose me. Traffic kills a chase, but in neighborhoods there's space to move. I can find you.

I caught him speeding down an alleyway behind a Sizzler, headed for the old man's place just like I thought he'd be. He knew he was fucked as soon as he saw me squeal to a stop at the end of the alley, cutting off his exit. He hit the brakes, and in that moment we got a good look at each other. The marks of the heating grill were stamped across his face, another half-completed mug right out of Fangoria. This one had a nose and cheeks, but portions of his head were missing and his exposed brain rested within a crown of jagged skull fragments, pink and naked. The wig had been his.

The death-wagon flew into reverse and I maneuvered to bear down on it. I sped over the pockmarked pavement toward the car's nose, but Grillface backed out onto the street and threw it into drive before I could mash him. Punching the gas, I managed to clip his rear bumper. The hearse fishtailed on the slushy road, now pointing at the Sizzler parking lot. Grillface hopped the curb and flew through the lot, almost hitting an old lady and sending two teenage girls diving into the bushes. I skidded out, punched the gas again and popped over the curb, racing off after the long black car as it blasted onto the restaurant-lined avenue. It was the fastest goddamn funeral procession in history.

Once on the open road, I hauled ass to his tail lights, then swung into the left lane and sped up before Grillface could block me. I wanted to point my gun at the motherfucker's head, but as soon as I pulled alongside of him I saw that he had the same idea, the muzzle of a sawed-off shotgun resting in the crook of his arm, pointing through the driver's open window. The gun discharged before I could even think about shooting back, and glass blasted into the car from the windows on both sides of me, slicing into my face, cutting into my ear-drums and making me blind.

I tried to hold the wheel steady, but when I opened my eyes I saw that I'd drifted into the opposite lane. A teenager flying down the road on his bicycle threw up his hands, his mouth making a perfect O shape that would've been comical in any other situation. Yanking the lever for the emergency break and spinning the wheel, I tried to avoid the kid but felt the car lifting off of the ground. Then chaos erupted. This time I felt everything. I felt my nose hit the wheel twice in two quick bounces, smashing one side and then the other. The ceiling crashed down on my head like a steel anvil, pushing it to the side and stretching the muscles in my neck to the breaking point. Finally, something in my back gave way with a loud *pop* and numbness flooded my body like novocaine.

In a moment, all was still. The world was upside-down and rivulets of a thick warm liquid were crawling up my face. Through the window, a bicycle wheel was spinning and I saw the teenager crawling across the pavement, dazed. As I started to lose focus, I imagined I was back in Kunar. The boy was Gustavo, and he was alive. I wanted to laugh. It had all been a nightmare. My friend was alive.

And then everything faded away.

When the old man looked at me this time, he was inches away from my face.

"Tell me where it is." His voice was deep and slimy. "I know that you've hidden it. You and that mulatto whore."

I wasn't sure when I'd woken up or how long I'd been that way. I felt a total disconnection from my body, and could only stare at the old man in a daze. His skin was hairless and smooth, as if his jowls and wrinkles were sculpted rather than earned through long life. The spittle in one corner of his mouth foamed up more and more as he interrogated me until his tongue finally slid out to snatch it. But it wasn't a tongue. It was a more like a bundle of pink tubes, all squirming together to imitate a tongue.

"I will give you one chance to tell me. If you do not, you will live in one of my boxes underground, forever starving. But if you tell me now, I will give you relief."

Pain shot through my leg to my groin and exploded into a million stabbing clusters. I screamed so high and so loud that the echoes bouncing off of the walls sounded like a squad of witches buzzing a battlefield. The old man turned away, holding his ears, and I saw Grillface remove a long, long needle from the base of my foot. His exposed brain was covered by a black stocking cap.

Suddenly, everything was sharp again. I was naked, strapped to a table in a small, antiseptic room, the walls a thick white marble, some kind of furnace in the corner. The old man spoke to me, the spoiled air in his mouth spilling out like oil.

"All I have to do is say the words and you'll be free. Tell me. Where is it?"

"I don't know." My voice was hoarse, strange.

He closed his mouth and stepped back, his expression blank.

"Put him in the box and I'll call up the girl."

They worked together to undo the straps and Grillface lifted me in his arms. I ordered my body to attack him but it only trembled, seized by the paralysis of a nightmare. He shook his head at me and stepped toward the room's large, industrial door, throwing me over his shoulder so he could work the handle. None of my insides felt right. I was a ghost in a human suit.

He opened the door and I managed to lift my head a bit, just enough to glimpse the old man pick up a rusty Folgers can and pour what looked like ashes onto the table.

The door slammed shut.

Now we were in a cellar, probably below the old man's house. It reeked of death, a smell of rot that was almost physical. The old man's voice erupted into chants behind the closed door, stifled but audible. I felt myself being carried across the room, and then the world rolled over as I was dumped into a box.

It was a tight space, made of aluminum, probably a modified deep freeze. My body was folded in half, ass down, legs up, my knees facing my eyes and my busted up arms folded in between. Grillface turned away for a moment and then turned back with a padlock in his hand, looking down at me. He paused as he reached up to close the lid, staring down with an almost-human expression. Was it pity?

That was when I heard the scream, muffled from behind the door of the old man's torture room, but unmistakable.

It was Grace.

A sudden burst of strength filled my body and I clenched all of my broken muscles, lunging up and reaching for Grillface's stocking cap. I clawed my hand over it and got a tight hold on the jagged skull beneath. He slapped at my arm with his hands and squealed, taken completely by surprise. I wouldn't let go, and the grip gave me enough leverage to shake the freezer back and forth. Between my exertions and his struggles to get free, the box finally capsized, falling to the side and bringing the man down with it.

I let go of his skull and forced myself out of the box, stumbling like I was drunk as I climbed to my feet. Grillface stumbled as well but was quick to come after me. I fell back against a wall as he approached and did my best to put up my guard. He stopped in his tracks and looked at me, tilting his head to the side. Then he sidled over to an open cabinet, keeping his eyes on me as he removed his sawed-off shotgun.

He'd finally decided I was a threat. He pointed the gun at me and I pushed myself off of the wall, gathering strength as I moved toward him. The air ripped into pieces with the sound of the gun's discharge, and a heavy force punched me in the side, shocking me with intense pain and flipping me to the ground.

I looked down to see a frayed hole in the side of my stomach. Grillface stepped over to me and looked down again, this time empty of any pity. He pointed the gun at my head.

The door to the torture room swung open.

"What is all of this?"

Grillface turned his head and I heard Grace whimpering in the background. Drawing on everything I had, I raised my legs and wrapped them around the motherfucker's calves, rolling to the side and breaking his balance. He tipped like a tree and hit the stone floor hard, his grip loosening on the gun.

The old man stepped back, pointing his arm at me and spewing gibberish:

"Ogthrod ah eeeef! Gebble eeeehh!"

But it was too late for him. I'd wrestled the shotgun away.

Another earpiercing blast and the old man's head was gone. His body stumbled back, spasming, and fell against the wall. I flipped the gun around in my hands, the muzzle burning my skin, and started working on Grillface with the butt. His body continued to fight but I pounded his head to jelly, and after a minute or two I was able to stand and get away from him.

In the room, Grace was strapped to the table, naked. I did away with the straps as fast as I could and took her into my arms. She was weak and unable to move, only staring up into my face with an expression of crazy disbelief. My girl.

I moved as fast as I could through the cellar. Grillface's body twitched on the floor like a half-crushed scorpion, and against the wall, something was emerging from the neck of the spasming old man: a thick, fleshy tube that tapered into a pinkish-red point. I turned my face away and focused on escape.

Up the stairs, through a hallway, more stairs, then into the old man's house. I eased Grace onto her weak legs and wrapped us in dusty red blankets draped over a sofa.

"We're gonna make it, Grace. We're gonna get out of here."

"It doesn't matter," she said to me. Her voice was spacey and distant. "We're all going to die."

I pulled her close to me and placed a hand over the gaping wound in my stomach, the wound that hadn't killed me or kept me from moving. Just like the broken back hadn't stopped me. The broken back that had disappeared.

"We're already dead," I whispered to her. "Let's get a drink."

As we stumbled out into the frozen night, I noticed the Doberman watching us from the house's top window. We would be hunted, but I didn't care. At that moment, we had each other once again, and that was enough.

157

Wuji

Nick Mamatas

Roger Wu fumed silently. Friday nights were supposed to be fun—the usual crowd would pile into Chuck's dorm room because it was a single and in it he had a television with a pair of hot-rodded rabbit ears—and watch *The Green Hornet*. An excellent show, or parts of it were anyway: about a minute and a half of each episode, when Bruce Lee, as Kato, would let it rip. But *The Green Hornet* had done it again. Britt Reid was given a pistol as a birthday present, and it went off in his hand, killing poor old Eddie Rech. Kato didn't see anything unusual—he was too busy serving drinks.

Kato was even wearing a white suit jacket, just like a waiter or bartender might. Even if the next twenty minutes were wall-to-wall fight scenes, Roger's evening was ruined. Time for the old stand-by. "Did you know," Roger began, addressing Chuck and Stan and Lawrence and the two other white guys who were new to Berkeley this semester and whose names he had not yet committed to heart, "that in Hong Kong—"

"*The Green Hornet* is called *The Kato Show*," they chorused, even the new guys. Chuck hoisted a shot glass. "Drink once whenever Roger complains about Bruce Lee and the oppression of Asian-Americans on white supremacist television!" And they all drank, even Roger. And they drank again. Drink when Kato throws a dart! Drink when Casey sits down on a stool and crosses her legs! The best part of Friday nights was making up new rules to drink by. The worst part was Roger taking the bus back to Oakland Chinatown and bedding down in the same twin bed he'd had since he was three years old, while his friends made time with co-eds into the early hours of the morning. That's what he thought anyway.

At four in the morning, Roger was up again and mostly sober, in the small gym behind the United Methodist Church right on Shattuck. Sifu Wong noticed, of course, but he didn't mind. "You'll sweat it out," he told Roger every week, and Roger did. Holding stances till his legs quaked, then stomping across the room and back. Sifu Wong was in his seventies, but performed the drills easily, with the feet of a cat. Then there was form practice, and Sifu would bark at Roger to stop and hold an awkward position—thighs nearly parallel to the floor, most of his weight on one heel, hands "gentle, like a woman's" in Sifu's words, but always just a little wrong. Holding a posture was painful enough, but Sifu always found that extra inch of shifted weight, the tensed shoulder, the untucked tailbone, then adjusted Roger's pose to reveal a new level of agony in the core of his muscles. A grunt, and a wobble, and Roger was on the floor.

"All right," Sifu said. "*Tui shou.*" Roger took to his feet and lifted his arms to make the subtlest contact with his teacher, and hit the floor. Then again, and a second time. Sifu narrated. "Push, push," he said, and when Roger did, Sifu said, "*Lu…* lead you into void," and Roger found himself stumbling past his teacher, then skidding along the hardwood floor on his belly.

"Bruce Lee has it easy," Roger muttered to himself.

"An actor!" Sifu shouted. He heard everything, despite being in his seventies, and a veteran waiter of the noisy dim sum place where Roger also worked. "You think he has any real *gongfu*?"

Sifu waited for an answer, but Roger knew better than to offer one. "He does look pretty good," Sifu admitted, before tapping Roger on the chest with a knuckle and putting him on the floor. "*Dim mak*," Sifu said. "Makes the heart skip a beat."

"The death touch?" Roger said. His hands went to his chest, instinctively.

"Don't worry," Sifu said. Then he produced a small knife from somewhere in the baggy sleeve of his shirt. "It just stuns the body for a moment. Then you stab him with secret knife—everyone thinks you have real *dim mak*!" Sifu laughed for a long time. Roger couldn't but feel that the laughter was directed at him.

Roger was Sifu's only indoor student, the only disciple. But Oakland in 1967 wasn't China a century prior, so Roger didn't have to clean Sifu's home or keep the old man fed. At the Golden Dragon, they were both waiters in white jackets, taking orders in Cantonese and, increasingly, English; pushing dim sum carts; pouring tea; and after lunch was done and the carpet swept and tables pushed together for all-night card games, both kept an eye out for the Jackson Street Boys from San Francisco's Chinatown. They didn't come by often, but they did come by. More often, Roger kept his eye on the girls who'd come in after hours, though they wanted nothing to do with him. Why would they—he had no money, no good family name, no prospects, and even his illustrious teacher was a waiter here in America.

"Tonight," Sifu said, "think about this. The yin-yang are everything, but they are children of taiji. Taiji is the one, but where does one come from?"

"Uhm, the none?" Roger said.

"The wuji, yes. The void. The void from which everything springs. Where does movement come from? No movement. Where does no movement come from? Movement. In *tui shou*, you move, I send you into the void." He nodded, once. "Understand?"

"Sifu, I don't."

"Good. From no understanding—"

"Comes understanding?" Roger said.

Sifu shrugged. "Sounds good to me! Anyway, you watch the door. It's a lucky night for me, I think. I'm going inside to play cards." Roger stayed at the door, peering into the mostly empty street, trying to think of nothing, to no-think of nothing. It kept him awake, for a change, and when Sifu came out of the Golden Dragon an hour before dawn without a nickel to his name, he explained that keeping Roger awake had been his plan all along.

"So, the wuji, that's all..."

"It's all true, yes. But for now, it just keeps you awake," Sifu said. "Awake so you can breathe, breathe so you can collect chi, collect chi in your *dantien* to perform internal alchemy. Then you'll feel life inside you, where now there is nothing." Roger smiled at Sifu, confused, but Sifu didn't explain further, didn't shrug.

Roger took the bus home and slept for most of Sunday—anything to keep his mother from going on about his "dirty" white friends or lack of a "decent" Chinese girlfriend or his "lowlife" teacher—and he dreamed. But not of nothing. Roger dreamt of a great dark something, shiny and black with the outline of a roaring wave, and neither his own taiji nor Bruce Lee's snap kicks and chain punches could save him.

The hippies had found taiji and brought it over to the Cal campus. Roger was appalled at what he saw. Not only was the form simply *bad*—there was hardly anything to it other than an occasional dip, and a subtle shift of weight—there were girls doing it. White girls, who a week before might have been folk dancing, or performing yoga, or just worshipping their own yonis while squatting over a hand mirror. And Chuck. And those two new guys from Chuck's dorm. They wobbled on their heels like drunken ducks and snorted and giggled and breathed improperly. Their form was over soon enough; it only had a handful of moves. The class broke up immediately, and Chuck spotted Roger and smiled. One of the other guys waved.

"Whaa-taaah!" Chuck said, his hands up.

"Don't tense your mouth or neck when doing taiji. It ends up tensing your shoulders, which means you can't channel force from your legs."

Chuck kept smiling. "You're into this stuff, eh? You should meet the master."

"No, I don't think so. I do...something different."

One of the other guys from Chuck's dorm stepped up, to Roger, a bit too close. He had a pointed beard of the sort that Cal students who liked to think themselves intelligent often adopted. "Hello Roger," he said, as if he didn't believe the word *Roger*. "How are you doing today?"

"Fine, fine."

"Listen, I wanted to talk to you. About China. About the great things going on there."

"The mainland...? But my parents are from Hong Kong."

"Exactly!" he said. "Exactly!"

"Bernard," Chuck said. "Take it easy." Then, to Roger. "Bernard's on a Maoist trip these days. Even the form we were just practicing is Communist Party-approved." Roger smirked. That would explain it.

"It's not a trip—"

"It was Trotsky before. He still has the Trotskyite beard," Chuck said. Roger noticed that Bernard did put a self-conscious hand to his beard at that. "This is," Chuck said, hiking a thumb toward the dispersing class, "Communist Party-*approved* tai chi." Chuck said it like it was two words, like an American.

"Oh, is that why you're doing it too?" Roger said, an edge in his voice.

"Nah, I'm just trying to make a little time with Leslie."

"I have an interest too..." the third guy said. "Hello." He offered Roger a hand, it was clammy, like old sweat. "I'm sorry, I don't know if we ever really got to talk. Croshaw."

"It's his last name," Bernard said. "An affectation. *Bev* Croshaw."

"Well, uh, nice to meet you officially, Bev," Roger said. The scene was strange here, heavy. Did any of these guys have anything in common other than that stupid TV show, and failed love lives? Roger made his excuses, and left. For a moment he thought to tail the teacher, ask to do a little push-hands, but decided against it. Then Roger realized that he was being tailed himself. He was ready to turn on his heel and palm-strike Bernard right in the nose, but it was actually Bev.

"Roger, please..." Bev said. He was such an ordinary-looking guy, this Bev. His picture could have been in a brochure for the college. "I'm sorry," he said.

"You apologize a lot," Roger said.

"Oh, I'm sorry...uh, I mean, I am from the Midwest, you know."

"Okay," Roger said.

"I took that tai chi class today because it seemed like something I once saw in a book!" Bev blurted out suddenly. "An old book, not something one can buy in a store—an ancient text. Well, it's not a text, really, but more of a collection. Like the Bible, it's an anthology of myths and correspondence, and pseudo-histories, and even poems and—" Roger started stepping backward, so Bev stopped and apologized again. "I'm sorry, it's just...you know more about this than anyone else, probably." Bev took a breath. "Not because you're Chinese or anything; I mean, you seem very interested in martial arts."

"Let's start over," Roger said. Nothing was worse than hearing some "tuned in" white guy talk about how Roger being Chinese was utterly unimportant. "What's your major?"

"Classical languages," Bev said. "Western languages."

"Econ." Bev had nothing to say to that. He didn't even nod. "Well, I guess I can take a look Maybe show it to shi—my teacher."

"Well, come on then!" Bev said. He nearly grabbed Roger's hand.

"Now?"

"Yes!"

Roger blew off a class to go through microfiche with Bev, who whispered excitedly the whole time about the "mad Arab" Abdul Alhazred, who supposedly wrote, or found, or compiled the book — the Book of the Names of the Dead, which sounded spooky enough to be interesting.

"Abdul Alhazred *doesn't even make sense as a name*," Bev said, without explaining what he meant. The original language of the text was lost, but there were a number of diagrams that Roger admitted did look familiar. A man in a bow-legged stance, tentacles spiraling along his limbs and across his waist. There was something like that in Chen Xin's manual — a depiction of *chan si jin*, coiling power. Dragon power, after a fashion. Another image of a spiral, black and white interlaced — like the *taijitu* symbol Roger had been so annoyed at finding tacked up on storefront windows, on crazy hippie pamphlets next to crosses and stars of David — but exploded and swirling ever outward.

"Roger, do you know of the theory of Alexander? He conquered the world, and his troops brought with them their martial tactics — boxing, and wrestling, and pankration. That's an all-in no-holds-barred martial art. The ancient Greeks believed in *pneuma*, or breath —"

Roger snorted. "Who doesn't believe in breathing?"

"Do you really want to know?" Bev asked. He sounded serious.

"What!" Roger slapped his own hand over his mouth. It hardly mattered though; the library was basically a hang-out for students sleeping off the previous night's adventures until finals. "What, just go on."

"Breath. Like chi, which is Chinese, yes. I'm sorry, I don't mean to tell you about your cultural beliefs —" Roger just stared. "Anyway, it's the same concept. An energy, gathered from the entire universe and stored within ourselves, to fuel acts of both creation and destruction." Bev continued. "Alexander made it as far as India, the birthplace of Buddhism. And from India came Bodhidharma, who then traveled to China and transmitted Chan to the people who would later become Shaolin monks. And he brought with him from India the art of kung-fu."

"Where did you get all this?" Roger said. "A secret tome out of the back of a comic? 'Forbidden Oriental Fighting Arts' for three ninety-eight and a thirty-day money-back guarantee?"

"You mean it's not true?"

Roger shrugged. "Maybe? There are lots of stories about lots of things. Maybe it's all true, or none of it is, or some little grain of it is." Roger wasn't going to give this kid anything. Let *him* show up before dawn to practice six days a week for three years before hearing any of the secrets of *gongfu*.

"Well, it explains these pictures, doesn't it? In the *Necronomicon*. From Greece, through India, perhaps then to China, then back to Northern Africa—Arabia, essentially—and then the West."

"But this," Roger said, tapping the microfiche screen with a fingernail, "isn't Shaolin. Or anyway, it's a lot closer to taiji than Shaolin, and taiji is Taoist, not Buddhist. But sure, Wudang Mountain isn't far from Shaolin, and in China everyone's a Buddhist and a Taoist and a Confucianist and a Legalist and a Communist and runs a small business on the side...well, until Bernard's new best friend Chairman Mao gets wind of it."

"I'm sorry, but what do you mean?" Bev asked. His enthusiasm soured in a moment—enflamed yang receding into yin with a single turn of the head.

"Something my teacher told me: people have four limbs, one trunk, and one head. Fighting always looks the same at a high level because we all bring the same tools, and the same weaknesses to a fight. There's no trickery, no secrets, just practice. 'No hit, no teach' he says. And then he hits me." Roger patted the top of the machine. "But this is cool though. Looks kind of Chinese to me, but I'm no expert." Roger felt just a bit malicious, so added: "I'm just the only Chinese guy you know, except for Bruce Lee."

Bev muttered more apologies and offered to buy Roger a drink sometime. "I'll see you Friday," Roger said, and he left the microfiche room but not the library. After seeing Bev walk down the steps, Roger slid back into the microfiche room and located the sheets labeled *Necronomicon*, then dug some change from his pocket and made Photostat copies of the pages he wanted.

Roger had his Friday nights free. After two more episodes—a dumb two-parter about scientists pretending to be aliens in order to steal an A-bomb—*The Green Hornet* was canceled. So much for Bruce Lee. Chuck decided to get high and stay high full-time, Bernard vanished into politics, and Stan and Lawrence retreated into friendly nods on campus and the occasional discussion of *Star Trek*. "Didja see it?" Roger did. He liked it, especially when Spock would do the Vulcan Nerve Pinch. A fake *dim mak*, but Roger was sure he had the real one. Every Friday night he practiced the postures on those pages from the *Necronomicon*. One Friday afternoon Roger saw Bev in Oakland and thought to wave for a moment, but held his arm down. Bev walked right past him without acknowledging Roger at all. Better that way, Roger decided.

Roger didn't tell Sifu, didn't mention the pages to anyone. He even kept a bottle of booze under his bed in order to replicate his once-typical morning breath for the early Saturday sessions. Roger didn't notice that others noticed the changes in him. Sifu got rougher with him; the old man needed to just to keep up. Roger's father hid behind his copy of *The Pacific Weekly*, his mother made excuses to visit friends, and ordered in from restaurants rather than cooking. That was fine with Roger; he could take the little paper containers up to his room more easily. Everyone noticed the *imbalance*, for lack of a better word. Spring was turning to summer, but Roger was always a bit chilly; his room, damp and cold. He was nervous, always chewing his lip; Roger could barely have a conversation or walk around the neighborhood on an errand without stopping to rest. Only when he pushed hands with Sifu was Roger invigorated.

On Saturday nights, he found it easy to contemplate the nothingness from which everything springs. Just standing on a curb, hands in his pockets, Roger discovered the *wuji*. And he dreamt, for long hours about the wuji. About swimming a black ocean for endless years, his limbs dead but still moving thanks to some force not his own.

Roger was sure he had the dim mak. He just needed a reason to use it. And that reason was coming. The Black Panthers were on the streets, and they hardly liked the Chinese any more than they liked whites, Roger thought. The Jackson Street Boys had made more incursions across the Bay. It was supposed to be the Summer of Love, but the only people getting any action were the radicals and their smelly white women. That was fine. All the martial artists believed in preserving their *jing*, their precious life energy. Had Sifu ever seen *Dr. Strangelove*? Probably not. Power roiled in Roger's belly, in the depths of his *dantien*. It was like a baby, a baby made of *yang* that left Roger nothing but *yin* for himself. When Roger contemplated the wuji on Saturday nights, he felt himself vanish and a pulsing red fetus, all knobs and pseudopods, remained to levitate several feet over the hot pavement.

It's still not completely clear to most people what happened outside the Golden Dragon. The English-language newspapers were silent on the subject; the Chinese-language articles hard to translate thanks to the use of several obscure—some might say esoteric—characters in the vital explanatory sentences. It was August when the Jackson Street Boys made their move, but it wasn't a direct one. The East Bay tongs were weak, and the Panthers were strong, but not as strong as the Oakland PD or establishment politicians. The Jackson Street Boys made contact with the right people in town—we'll defend you against the blacks, they said. Just let us in. The Golden Dragon gang found themselves without a clientele, and blamed for the violence that the Boys brought with them. And then there was Bernard, who Roger saw sniffing around town, though the man had never been south of Woolsey Street before.

The situation came to a head one broiling August night. Roger wasn't perspiring at all. It was almost like a musical number in a Technicolor spectacular. The Jackson Street Boys ten abreast on one side of the street, the Golden Dragon bunch in a loose semicircle around the entrance to the restaurant. The car traffic was light, but Roger knew that there was something going on down at the end of the street, down at the end of Franklin Street. If he looked, the Jackson Street Boys would charge, he was sure of it. So he looked and saw Bernard, hoisting a Pepsi bottle with a flaming rag in it overhead and rushing up the block. "For the people!" he shouted. Three dark figures, Panthers in black sweaters despite the heat, sidled up the sidewalks. They had rifles. Probably just looking to pick off who was left standing, take the neighborhood for themselves. The Boys roared and charged, knives out. Roger heard Sifu inhale sharply, deeply, like his last breath needed to be his best. A deep shiver flooded Roger's limbs, but then with his next breath his veins were aflame. The Molotov hit the street, several feet short of the Dragon gang's rear. A Panther leveled his gun and cut Bernard in half. Roger was sure he heard someone shout *Thanks!* in Cantonese-accented English. The Dragons opened fire with pistols, brandished hatchets and butcher knives.

Roger could see a bullet blooming out of the back of one of the Golden Dragon waiters, wide as a saucer. He put a hand out and it shattered against his palm. He ran down the street, bursting through his own line, and rushed a machine gun, his chi high, his chest an iron vest. With one punch he stove in a Panther's head. A turn on his heel, a low kick, and a second went sprawling into the puddle of flame, then yelped and rolled away. A Jackson Street Boy came roaring over a parked car and got nailed by the last Panther. Roger turned to see Sifu tied up with men on three of his limbs—the old man shook off one of them, tripped another and sent him headfirst onto the pavement, then tussled with the larger, better third. The son of the Golden Dragon's owner fell at Roger's feet, his neck open and smiling. The last Panther was taken out by a lucky knife to the eye, but he had five men on the street around him, their limbs splayed against the asphalt like the rays of red stars.

Roger looked around again. Sifu did something complicated to his opponent's neck, and the guy fell like his bones had left him. Four Jackson Street Boys flanked Sifu—one of them had a revolver. Police issue? Anything was possible now. Roger rushed to help. Sifu fell to one knee. Roger had his hands up, looking to touch. One guy ducked out of the way, another didn't. The tip of Roger's fingers on the man's jaw. Then a great black whip of night split the man in half.

Sifu's eyes widened. "No," he said. He reached to touch Roger, to shoot a spear-hand up to Roger's groin. The lower *dantien*. Roger clamped his palm on Sifu's face and didn't bother to squeeze. The old man fell backwards; his head sounded like a melon against the pavement. Roger grabbed a wrist holding a knife and twisted, feeding a spiral from deep within himself into the man's elbow, shoulder, spine, ankles. Roger smiled. He thought he was going to live through this.

In the end, it took all of them to bring Roger down. The Jackson Street Boys fell like extras in a Hong Kong movie, but that gave Chuck the time to get into his car and slam it right into Roger's back. Poor Chuck, he flew through the windshield like he'd hit a tree. Roger was stunned, both by the impact and at the vision of his stupid old friend flying overhead. Seatbelts weren't commonsense then. Stan was there too, suddenly, and Roger hesitated for a moment. Stan had one of the Panther's guns and pumped a few bullets into Roger's temple. That put Roger back onto a knee. Lawrence just ran off into the restaurant, which was a mistake since Bev had sliced the gas line open while waiting for the brawl. He must have lit a cigarette or something—smoking during a stressful situation still was commonsense then—and then the ground under me shuddered; the sides of the Golden Dragon puffed out, but held. The street was painted a flickering red. Roger grabbed Stan's ankle and yanked it hard, slipping the rug right out from under him. Roger saw a new opponent, and the bizarre dagger in his hand, and went for Stan's gun.

"Bev."

"I'm sorry," Bev told him. "I need what's inside you. The something that springs from nothing." I heard Bev's voice clearly. These were the first words I was able to make out. He wasn't really sorry. "The book told me what to do with it, how to grow that spiritual baby within you, to make it strong through conflict and strife, so it could defend us from..." Bev seemed to forget the language for a moment. "Things."

Roger held up the gun. "Put down your weapon."

"This?" Bev said. "It took me a year to make this." He turned the blade in the light and it glittered as if faceted, but at the same time it wasn't. "I'm a double-major, actually, Classical languages and physics. It's a seven-dimensional blade." Bev looked at Roger, expectant. "Oh, I'm sorry," he said, finally, "that means it works from over here." And then Bev sliced through the air and cut me out. "Sort of like a phaser, or Hornet's Sting," Bev told Roger's corpse. Then he dropped the knife, which sliced into the air and *left*, and picked me up and took me in his arms.

Forty-five years, Bev cared for me. Feeding me, reading to me, nurturing me into a being worthy of defeating the Outer Gods who even now reach out across the inky blackness of space toward your planet. But like most precocious children, Bev had misunderstood the details of childbirth and rearing, and conceived a fantasy to fill the black hole of his ignorance. What he midwived was an Outer God, or the teensiest phalange of one anyway. And I am here, sprung forth from the *wuji* and into the world, to return the world to *wuji*. It's a cosmic cycle billions of years in the making, and no human agent could ever possibly intervene. The universe grinds away at itself. Why tell you all now? Well, I've been among you for years — in my time I've learned the animal joys of strife and anguish. Do not hate me for long. It will all be over soon.

The One in the Swamp

Natania Barron

Georgia was nothing like the Arizona Territory, and my sister Cassandra was nothing like herself by the time we got there.

We jumped off the train just south of Waycross, and I was full of regret. The entire trip from Arizona was on account of an argument between Cassandra and our oldest sister, Elizabeth. Cassandra figured Elizabeth had to be following us, and no matter how many times I explained how unlikely it was—considering Cassandra had shot her in the leg—she'd hear nothing of it.

In truth, I wished that Elizabeth would have followed us. I wished that we could skip back a few weeks, and go back to the way things were, back when we just killed things and never asked questions. I wished that Cassandra's heart hadn't gone hard, and she was back to the delicate, laughing, flirting sister I knew. Even if I resented her for all her beauty, I'd have paid anything to see her smile again.

"Keep up, Lydia," Cassandra called back. She was making for the trees and she cut a dark shape before me, ill-shaped with her gun under her duster.

"I'm going as fast as I can," I said.

"Well go faster," Cassandra said.

She vanished into the tree line and I followed behind her, almost losing my footing on the steep incline. I had to keep moving or else I'd lose Cassandra to the trees.

The air was so thick in the wood that I about near choked on it. Going from the desert air to this was a terrible adjustment, and no matter what we did we were always sweaty and hot.

A few minutes of walking and the ground went mushy, water filled my boots, and I let out a groan.

"Cassandra?" I called.

"Hsssh!" she hissed, followed by the sound of her safety disengaging. Then I heard the charge of the secondary barrel on her shotgun, the one that I installed. I'd modified it so she could provide a considerable electrical charge along with a barrage of bullets.

I never could leave a weapon well enough alone. That's what Elizabeth used to say.

As for me, I didn't have any of my more impressive weapons in easy reach, so the Starr revolver was going to have to do the trick.

Ducking down, I closed my eyes and turned my ears, tilting my head just so. My hat helped amplify what was out there and sure enough I heard it.

I've heard ungodly things before. Profane things. I've heard the chittering of creatures so heinous I can't even put it into words. It's part of the territory, being in my family. We're good at finding trouble. But the sound I heard in the swamp was a growing noise, a moving noise. A knowing noise, unlike anything I'd ever heard before.

I glanced over my shoulder, certain I'd see someone standing there, but there was nothing save more trees and vines, closing in behind.

We'd traveled from Arizona to Georgia on our own, and we thought we left all the worst of it back home. Turns out we were picking up where we'd left off.

The leaves and vines around us slithered and whispered, shifting unnaturally.

Cassandra barreled forward, revving up the gun, toward something I could not see.

In my hesitation, worrying after my sister, the vines found their way to me. My left leg was completely entwined before I had the presence of mind to do anything about it.

Cassandra let out a short cry which was followed by a resounding sound like a thousand dragonfly wings beating at once. Or a flight of locusts. Or demon's breath. It burrowed into my ears, making my head vibrate and my eyes water. The vines had wrapped mostly around my pack, and I'd have to let it go or else perish.

Cursing my luck, I cut myself from the vines and my pack, making use of one of the smaller knives I kept in my boot. Something hot and wet spilled out around my shin when I severed the vines, but I didn't think twice about it then. I had to get to Cassandra, wherever she was.

The forest floor moved under my feet, and just as I was about to reach Cassandra—I'd seen the flare of her gun go off some paces before me—a vine wrapped around my leg and I tripped, skidding face first into the wet ground. A horrible taste filled my mouth, like sucking the bottom out of a cesspool. I was sick, instantly; there was no way to stop it.

I retched until I saw stars. But when it was over, for a moment I was blissfully clear-headed. I could see Cassandra, standing some feet away from me, the blue-green glow of the shotgun, setting her lovely features alight.

She'd come to save me.

I thought I heard a goat bleat. And then, I was gone.

The waking was painful, and at first I was only aware of heat. My skin was raw to the touch, my throat dry as desert sand, and I was trembling all over.

Someone touched me. Not Cassandra. Then I fell asleep again.

This happened a few times, until at last I awoke more lucid. It was welcome. I am not used to being conscious and without my faculties; I might not be the most talkative of my sisters, but I've always been an observer, someone who appreciates thought and consideration above idle chatter. But in my moments of this strange illness, not even that was a possibility.

"There she is," said a voice, cracked with age and unfamiliar. "Take a sip now, won't hurt 'cha."

His accent was thick, every word drawn out near to the point of obscenity.

I drank. The water was cool, but it made me shiver.

"Reeves, you go get the other girl and bring her here. Let her know her sister's well up," the old man said.

I wanted to see Cassandra, but when my vision cleared all I saw was a wizened old Negro man, squinting at me like I was some sort of specimen in a sideshow. The room was dim, poor, and unremarkable.

"You're strong for being so slight," the man said. "And so young."

I wanted to tell him that I was nearly twenty, and not so young as I looked, when my vision swam. The pressure in the room changed, and Cassandra stood over me.

"Lydia?" she asked.

That was her. That was my sister. I smiled to hear her voice. She was concerned. She loved me. She needed me. Her heart hadn't hardened completely.

"Cass…" was all I managed.

Her hands were in mine, her dark hair falling in ringlets over our clasped hands. Young men always went head over heels for that hair of hers, so thick and curly. But to me her hair smelled like home, and memories, of evenings curled up in bed together to keep out the cold, whispering in the dark.

"Don't cry," she said. "You're going to be fine."

"Took a nasty spill down over yonder," said another woman behind Cassandra. She was of mixed race, her hair tied up in a rag, her face lined but not old. Not like the old man. "Ain't many who come back from something like that. We thought for sure you'd be dead come morning."

"I fell," I said, remembering. "I got sick… the vines…"

"The vines got you," the old man said. He hissed through his teeth, what few he had. "But all's well for now."

For now.

On the third day, in the middle of the night, I awoke to the sounds of water somewhere outside my window. Not constant water, but water coming in spurts. Like someone priming a pump that wasn't working. I could hear the mechanism groaning in response to someone struggling to make it work.

I knew that sound. The piston was jamming against something, and the seal wasn't good enough.

By the time I made it to the pump, whoever had been struggling with it was gone. There were a few old buckets and a dipper cast about the bottom, almost hastily. I looked around, but no one was there to notice me.

Under the moonlight it was hard to work, but it was satisfying to be using my wits and my hands again. After about an hour of fiddling with the various bits and bobs, water was coming out again in a steady stream. It was just a matter of calcium buildup and a badly done piston. Whoever was in charge of parts was not exactly an expert.

I was just adjusting the handle when I heard someone behind me.

"You're supposed to be in bed."

Cassandra.

I used the pump as leverage to stand. "You know I won't sleep right if I think something isn't working as well as it should."

"Did you even ask if you could fix it?" she asked, taking a closer look at my handiwork. She patted the top of the pump in approval.

"Well, no," I admitted. "But chances are I'm the best shot they're gonna get for a long time at fixing this. It's sure remote out here."

"You need to get back to bed."

I held my arms out by my sides. "I'm right as rain." But I was trembling so fiercely I warrant I wasn't terribly convincing.

Cassandra tossed her braid over her shoulder and looked away from me, out across the cluster of ramshackle buildings that made up the village and into the swamp and trees surrounding it. "We can't."

"What d'you mean?" I asked. "You said we had to get to Savannah, to Aunt Sibyl. That's why we left Arizona in the first place."

"I mean, we *can't* get out. Unless you want to go through the swamp."

"Surely there's a road."

"No road. They're surrounded here during the flood season. They're people who want quiet and removal from everything out there."

"And now the swamp is strangling them out," I said.

"Yes."

"And you want us to help them."

"They saved your life, Lydia. If they hadn't…" Cassandra's voice got tight, but she cleared her throat and spoke stronger. "They say we're the only ones ever to have come out of there alive. And this has been happening for months, now. People go in, never come back. The whole village of Marlow is starving to death."

I sighed. "I'm not in any condition to be fighting right now."

"I don't need your gun, Lydia. I need your brain. I've got something to show you, and after you've seen it I don't think you'll be able to say no."

"What is it?" I asked.

"Right now you need to get back to bed. Even in the dark I can tell you're white as a ghost."

I had to agree with her.

When I woke again, it was evening, and the old man was fussing over something at the hearth. It smelled like meat, but it had that almost floral hint to it that spoke of game rather than anything particularly domesticated.

"Here. Eat." He handed me a clay bowl full with frothy brown soup. Or stew. It was hard to tell.

While I took an experimental bite—it was bitter but not intolerable—he left through the front door and I was left to wonder again after these strange people and their even stranger problems.

For a moment I thought someone was peeking in the window, but when I went to look it was most certainly vacant.

Not two minutes later, Cassandra came back in.

"How're you feeling?" she asked.

"Still sore," I said. I smoothed my hand down my bare leg. The skin was mottled and dark, scabbed and scarred where the vine had broken against me.

"You up for a walk?" she asked. "It's not far."

She brought me to a half-collapsing barn some distance from the nearest pen. There was no livestock to be seen or heard, and what I could see of the ground showed signs of abandonment. No prints, and the grass was growing back.

The barn doors swung open on rusty hinges and I noticed light at the far end. I was reminded immediately of my shop back home, where I spent the majority of my time fixing things, and felt heart-sick over it.

Across the way a young man and a woman—the one I had seen upon waking—stood, hovering over a lumpy mass on the ground. It was covered in white muslin, but there were dark stains on it.

I staggered as I got closer, my leg buckling under unexpected pain.

"You sure you're well enough?" Cassandra asked.

"I think so," I said, stopping to rub my leg. The scar tissue was swelling, hot to the touch. My eyes welled with tears against the pain, but with a few deep breaths it seemed to lessen.

"Good to see you up," said the woman. She was dressed in ochre and red, her hair tied up and bundled in a heap behind her head. "You probably don't remember me, but I'm Mrs. Jess. I helped you a bit when you were sick. Made you some broth."

I remembered the broth, spiced with a concoction of herbs I could barely recognize.

The young man turned to look toward me. No, that wasn't right. He turned to look at Cassandra. And he smiled, then pretended not to.

"That's Clell," Cassandra said, gesturing to him. She was bored with him, I could tell. "His father was one of the first to be lost."

"Y'all are the first to have escaped alive," Clell said. He had a shock of brown hair, and front teeth that were too large for his small mouth. But he had kind eyes, if a little dull.

I felt my skin crawl, and my wound throb. The skin on my neck prickled, and I glanced to the door to see if someone was standing there.

"Lydia?" Cassandra asked.

I cleared my throat. "Before we get to this gruesome business, shouldn't you inform me on just exactly what's happening here?"

Mrs. Jess clicked her tongue and folded her hands in front of her chest. "Started with a thunderstorm, worst we've ever had. Winds loud enough to be a damned hurricane. When it blew over, our goats were gone. Every last one."

"We could hear bleating in the swamp, weeks later," Clell said, "but even when we called, they wouldn't come."

"I'll be," I said. I was far less impressed than they thought I should be, I could tell that much. They exchanged glances. "And this thing here?" I pointed to the heap.

"I was hoping, Lydia, that you could take a look at it and see if you could make more sense of it than the rest of us," Cassandra said.

I would have laughed, but Cassandra had clearly given them the impression that they should put their hope in me. That was a burden I did not want to bear.

The thing under the muslin smelled like singed hair and sewage, and I was not looking forward to seeing what lay under the cover, that was certain.

Clell and Mrs. Jess moved away, and I reached over and pulled.

There was some resistance, since much of the cloth was stuck with something black and tacky. But slowly the creature was revealed. A goat, but nearly the size of a small horse. Its entire body was anomalous, its head having swelled far past normal proportions, and its eyes receding entirely into its skull.

And strangest of all, its feet didn't end in hooves. They ended in vines. Which I wouldn't have noticed so quickly except for the fact that they began entwining around my ankles.

I startled back, kicking off the vines, cussing colorfully but glad the vines were nowhere near as strong as those I'd encountered earlier.

"I thought you said this thing was dead!" I said.

Clell looked like he was going to faint, and Mrs. Jess just shook her head.

"It's dead. Felt for the heart myself. I'm the resident livery owner. I should know," Mrs. Jess said.

"Well, only way I can figure this out is to cut into it. Anyone have a scalpel?" I asked.

Thus began the dissection.

As I cut into it, the blood ran dark greenish black, and I was thankful for the pair of thick gloves I wore. The volume of blood was far more than expected and, in addition to the proliferation of veins, which I will touch upon again in a few moments, I found a network of thin, delicate webs wound throughout the body. I could only surmise that these were the nerves.

In general, the veins on the beast were hardened, the walls twice as thick as they ought to be. And they had rearranged, somehow. Instead of all flowing from the heart, the arteries traveled down into the legs and then, after some transition, became more like tubers and flowed into the vines still reaching out for me.

The thin nerves collected into thicker clusters in the legs and tail, and then branched out toward the central cavity of the beast. It was there, after some rather unpleasant rooting around, that I discovered the heart.

Except it was not a heart. It was a brain.

It was larger than a goat brain ought to be, about the size of half a loaf of bread. But it was not a complete brain, not at all. It was greatly mutated.

"What's the matter?" asked Clell.

"You mean other than the fact that this exists at all?" Cassandra said.

I held up the beast's brain. "All that's here is a rudimentary brain stem, and the part of the brain that is in control of vision."

"Where's its heart?" Cassandra asked.

"I'm going to try and find out," I said. "Seems to me there's a chance they might have swapped places."

Cassandra's shot pierced just north of the thing's heart-brain, but she'd also shot it in the head. Chances were the bone fragments had ruined most of what was in there.

I was getting more and more exhausted by the moment, but there was nothing to be done of it. My leg throbbed, and I had the sense that we were being watched. Maybe it was just curious villagers; maybe I was just too tired. But I kept looking behind me at the wide-open barn doors expectantly.

"Here we are," I said, peeling away the tacky shards of bone. "Bring the lantern down. I need a better look."

The gloves were thick, impeding my sense of touch, but I didn't need to root around for long to know I wasn't coming up with anything. I pulled back, only to find my glove stuck with more of the weblike nerves. The head was entirely empty.

"I always said goats were the dumbest creatures on earth," I said, "but this one takes the cake."

"Nothing?" asked Mrs. Jess.

"Just more of this stuff," I said, finally standing up and walking away from the creature. I had no idea what time it was, but by the time I reached the barn doors I noticed a pale blue glow on the horizon.

They were talking behind me, and I was trying to think. To consider everything I'd seen. I thought of all the weird and heinous creatures I'd come into contact before, but none of them had been this puzzling. They were biological, for the most part, or at least once were. They adhered to certain rules. While their interiors might not have mapped out precisely to the sorts of animals found in our day-to-day lives, they still had hearts, and blood, and brains, more or less in the correct placement. And they never grew vines instead of hooves.

"I need to rest," I said, turning around. They were all staring at me. Hopeful. "I'm tuckered out."

"Did it tell you anything?" asked Clell.

"It told me nothing more than what you saw. That it's an abomination of a proportion even I can't make sense of," I said. He cast his eyes down when I could not give him the answers he was searching for.

I slept. I dreamt. In my dreams, I was being watched. But I could never see the face of who watched me so close. I could hear her whisper, feel her breath on the back of my neck, but every time I turned to see her, she was gone.

I awoke to the sound of the water pump.

"Lydia?"

Cassandra's voice interrupted the sweet rhythm of machinery. She was at the hearth, stirring some soup. It smelled spicy, smoky.

"We're going to have to go back there," Cassandra said. "And I'd hate to think we don't have an advantage now."

"I've never seen something like that before," I pointed out.

"But isn't that how it always works? I figure we've seen so much strange, something eventually was bound to top it."

The pump worked outside, sighing and sucking, and it struck me as clear as a bolt of lightning.

"The pump…" I said, standing and going to the window.

"It's not broken again, if that's what you mean," Cassandra said. She was definitely cross with me; but then again, she always got cross when I didn't think fast enough to suit her.

"No, no. The goats. What if the goats work like a pump?"

"… like a pump…" Cassandra's eyes almost went cross, and she was clearly concerned for the state of my sanity.

But the idea had hatched.

"The goats. Their veins, they're like pipes. I think they're animated with pressure, water pressure, that vile venom stuff that got all over my leg. And they're controlled with the webs. They don't have enough of a brain to do it themselves but..."

"But?"

"My guess is that there's one of them, smarter that the rest. A center of thought and intelligence. Judging by the brain I examined, it'd be something with a far more complex mind, something able to control two dozen goats at a go."

Cassandra was silent, pacing. "Bigger, maybe?"

"Maybe... why, did you see something out there?"

"I thought I did. But it was hard to say, Lydia. I was concentrating on getting you out alive."

"If we're to get rid of this thing, we've got to get the center. Kill the brain."

"And how the hell do you propose that we do that?" she asked.

"With fire. And blades," I said. "Not so different than how we usually do things. Except more tactful this time."

She smiled. "You've got a plan?"

"I do." I closed my eyes, considering. "There's a stream heading into the swamp, isn't there?"

Cassandra nodded.

"Good," I said. "Should do perfect. But first I need to build a boat."

It didn't take a technical genius to recognize that so long as the vines had traction, they'd do us in. So I was going to have to fashion something that would clear the way for us through the swamp. It would have to be a boat to ensure proper mobility.

First, I knew I wanted to lure them. From everything I heard, the beasts preferred a good bit of fresh blood. So I made simple clockwork blood grenades we could throw into the water to tempt the murderous goats. We'd bring the fight to us, if we could.

My initial design for the boat was to have two rudders, equipped with repurposed scythe blades, rising just under the surface of the water to cut away any of the errant vines in our way. But cutting a path deep into the swamp was only part of the equation; I doubted that simply clearing vines would be enough to give us leverage against our foes, so I devised two separate mechanisms for the side of the boat, sticking out to the starboard and port sides.

My thinking was this: if we were able to pinpoint a moving vine, we'd catch it—somewhat like catching an eel in the water—and hook it to the mechanism, which was a rudimentary winding gear. They could accommodate at least thirty feet of rope in my tests, and I figured that would be long enough to try and get one of those goats in range of Cassandra and some of my altered weapons.

The boat took the most time to get right. It had to be wide and low, and since we were relying on mechanized rudders, there wasn't any room for paddles. It took some work, and some scrounging, but at last I was able to combine a steam-powered motor with a basic pump system, allowing for both water and steam propulsion. It would be steady enough and, with the right hands, variable.

As for weaponry, I had chemistry. It's amazing what one can do with lime and fire, eggshells and vinegar. Before long I had quicklime and acetone, which I would put to good use.

The villagers watched me go about my work with wonder. And while I was tired, it was easy to forget. I ate more and gathered what strength I could.

In the space of six days I had everything in order, though I was tuckered beyond belief. Still, once the boat was finished, the majority of the town—about twenty individuals all told—came out to the barn to have a look.

It was agreed that Clell and Mrs. Jess would come with us, considering they had the experience with firearms and both were willing to go.

The crowd dispersed once the decisions were made, and I went about checking the vessel for the last time. Time was wasting; Cassandra and I had other places to be, at last other places I'd hoped we'd get to.

It was Reeves who came to me last.

"M'dear," she said. "You holding up?"

"Much as I can," I replied.

"The leg?"

"It hurts," I said, reaching down and massaging the muscle beneath the scar. Sometimes it felt as raw as the day I'd been wounded.

"It's a gift," Reeves said. "That wound. They'll respect you, out there."

"Somehow I don't think they respect," I said, as kindly as I could manage. Her rheumy eyes searched mine and she looked pained.

"They are only part of it," Reeves said. "You know that. You feel it, too."

I didn't answer. Didn't want to answer. I'm too practical a person to heed the warnings of an old woman far past lucidity. So I gave her a nod, and thought about that feeling I hadn't been able to shake since I got hurt. The watching. The knowing. The sense that these beasts were but part of a far greater view, of which even my mind could never comprehend.

"Well, thank you. You didn't have to do none of this," she continued, starting to walk away.

"You saved my life," I said.

And she shrugged in a way that said I had no idea what I was talking about.

We pushed off on a narrow tributary that soon opened up to a southward-flowing rise. It was mid-morning by the time we left, and Cassandra was back to her quiet self. It took some work to get Clell accustomed to the steering mechanism on the boat, but once the boiler was good and hot we had no problem at all. He was a natural on a boat, his balance far better than my own.

All was quiet but for the lapping of water and the hissing of the engine as we made our way deeper. The year had record rains, and the going was relatively easy at first.

I didn't think the goats would be out until it got dark.

"Look," Mrs. Jess said. "Up over there."

I followed the angle of her finger to a pair of horse skulls nailed up to a tree. They were old, by the look of them, bleached in the sun and crumbling with age.

"That's foreboding," I said.

"Indians," Clell said. "This is Skull Lake. Sacred ground. Mrs. Jess, you said we weren't gonna go through here."

The livery owner fussed with the gun at her side. "I must have navigated wrong."

"Best keep forging ahead," Cassandra said. "Nothing to do about it now."

Dusk came, and my leg started throbbing again.

"Lydia?" whispered Cassandra, batting away a fleet of mosquitoes.

"Get ready," I said. "All of you."

We'd seen snakes and gators as we'd progressed, but when the water started bubbling fierce, we knew the time had come.

My heart pounded in my chest, and I scurried to lower the scythe rudders and reels into the water. My leg started aching, and the hair on my arms went up as that creeping sense of being watched came over me again. It wasn't dread so much, but curiosity that came over me.

Biting the inside of my cheek hard enough to draw blood—and help me focus—I put down the anchor and took position behind Cassandra. The boat was sturdy, made to glide softly across the water, but with all the bubbling around us it was far more precarious a position than I'd have liked. I'd fought on rail cars before, even on horseback. But never on a boat. Falling into the water didn't just mean vines, it meant meeting scythes, too.

Cold sweat trickled down my back and Clell yelled, "Got one!"

The pole I'd put together consisted of a simple hook at the end of a long wooden dowel, and if twisted just right the hook would close on the prey; in this case, it would grab the vine.

"Bring it here," I said. Clell complied and I fed the vine down through a loop on the side of the boat, and let it go; the spring had built up plenty of tension, and started pulling the vines toward us.

Wet leaves slapped against the side of the boat, and in the distance bleating started. Bleating and growling, followed by the wetness of vines coming at us from every angle.

Thankfully, the mechanism worked. Mrs. Jess screamed as the figure of one of the goats came into view, half dragging through the water, and the scythes engaged. The water around us frothed and the boat rocked as the blades cut through the vines encroaching on the port side.

Starboard, where the reel was doing its job, was another story altogether.

"There's another," Cassandra shouted, "being dragged behind this one—they're roped together. Shoot when you can, Mrs. Jess."

Cassandra let out two shots in quick succession, and the first beast's head exploded some distance from us in a spray of black and white fluff.

"Not the head—the heart!" I shouted.

Cassandra shot again, Mrs. Jess following suit this time but her aim going wide. The trees rustled behind me, and I turned to see nothing but the darkening sky.

The water continued to bubble and gyrate, the detritus of the shredded vines rising up around us filling the air with the familiar stink of it. I should have been more afraid, but I was not trembling for fear. I was trembling for excitement.

The second beast propelled into view, and a third was behind it. I used the pole to secure another vine as the first sunk into the water, one of Cassandra's incendiaries blasting it to bits below. I wasn't sure how much more vine length the mechanism could take in on this side.

"Grenades!" I shouted, and Clell obeyed through a haze of fear.

The water sprayed up and around the boat, and I prayed that the venom from the severed vines in the water was too diluted to do any harm.

Overhead the grenades arced, raining down drops of blood all about us. Blood sprayed in all directions, sprinkling our faces. Not two heartbeats into the explosion of blood and the water began churning, a renewed frenzy. The vines sought us out, driven by the promise of fresh blood, and only Cassandra's steady shooting kept us from being overwhelmed completely.

We summoned six beasts with those blood grenades, and we killed each and every one. Then, the water just stopped churning. The last goat snapped its vine as we brought it close, and it dragged no others with it. For a moment, we all stood, taking it in, taking in greedy breaths of air and waiting.

It was full night. Clell was half sobbing, half gasping. Mrs. Jess's eyes reflected off the moonlight.

"Holy hells." Cassandra was looking back behind me.

The boat shuddered, and I turned to try and dislodge the reels, but I froze.

Something rose up from the treed area before us. There was a passage in the lake, narrow enough to get us through, but the rising horror before us was blocking the way. We were all too tired for another onslaught of those goats, but this thing moved slowly. Smartly.

Then I threw a handful of quicklime forward. I had to have a better look, and wanted to surprise the creature, this Goat King, before we lost our chance.

In the quicklime's brief glow at least ten legs flinched. A half dozen heads startled. Horns protruded near everywhere. But that wasn't the worst of it by miles. It seemed that over time, this central beast had accumulated odds and ends from various warm and cold-blooded creatures, including gators, birds, and human beings.

Heads and eyes, hands and feet, claws and teeth, all turned toward us, vines keeping everything together in a hulking mass that continued to rise skyward.

"Clell! Fire!" I shouted.

I heard him pull the valve on the rudimentary tank I'd put together back in town. The acetone—which I'd distilled back in Marlow—was fed through a long pipe, and with Cassandra's help, Clell ignited a ball of fire in the direction of the creature.

But seeing the Goat King again, this time brought to life for more than just a flash, was too much. Clell took one look and fell forward into the water and the scythes, and Mrs. Jess screamed after him. The fire died.

"You mush-head," I called as he went down.

Mrs. Jess went to pick up her shotgun. I grabbed her shoulder as she dipped forward, just in time to see Clell's face rise up to the top of the water, eyes wide open, mouth bleeding black and horrible.

Then went Mrs. Jess. She fell out of my grasp, losing her footing and crashed into the water, vines encircling her and then bringing her into the mass of the beast.

Another one. Gone, just like that.

Two of Cassandra's deadly rounds had taken off chunks of the Goat King, but it was keeping its distance for now, rearranging its bulk to take another host into account.

The mouths on the Goat King began speaking and braying and bleating, a chorus of words I could not understand. Yet they spoke to me. Somehow, they spoke to me of terrible thing, of hidden, dark things. Of forgotten, monstrous things. I did not want to listen, yet could not prevent myself.

"Lydia!" Cassandra shouted, her voice bringing me out of my stupor.

It was just the two of us.

"I'm going to throw the tank," I said, gathering what wits I had left. "Wait for my signal to shoot!"

I trailed off because the back of the boat was being wound round with more vines. Cassandra aimed her sights at the Goat King, who was slowly approaching the boat, waves of water coming from his hulking body. Something kept thumping against the bottom of the boat, and I didn't dare to think what the scythes had done to Clell...

All the Goat King's mouths screamed in concert; some were human voices, others animal. Beneath it all there the same buzzing, dying, hellish noise I'd heard the first time I'd encountered the vines.

"Lydia… I…" Cassandra was shaking. I had never seen her so afraid.

The presence was behind me again, waiting. Watching. Amused.

I threw the tank with all my might. It flew across the water, and for a moment I was certain I hadn't put enough heft behind it. But it landed in the middle of the vined monstrosity, clocking one of the human faces right on the forehead and sinking further down.

I had some quicklime left over, and I threw it up into the air and disengaged the flame gun. The quicklime went vibrant bright, flaring out and around, spilling light into every corner of the swamp. Bugs kindled in the air, and every face and tooth on that hideous Goat King came to view.

I screamed. I laughed. I was strong and sure, clever and brave. But I was being watched, I was being challenged.

Reeves was right: I was respected.

"Now! All out!" I shouted.

Cassandra didn't hesitate. She shot at my order, but the tank would not explode.

The monstrosity lumbered toward us, waves of water crashing against the boat until we were shoved up against the tree line. Flames rose and smoked, the smell of meat and vegetable and burning all around.

It would fall on us, smother us to bits. I tried in vain to get the scythes moving again under the boat, but everything was waterlogged and jammed. We were almost out of ammunition, and the monstrous creature was gaining on us.

And still the chorus continued, that monotonous refrain of terror.

"No!" I screamed.

Then the acetone kindled. I fell back; Cassandra tumbled on top of me, her gun engaging somewhere up into the trees. Then my face burned with heat from the flames, as the creature burned. Behind it, nodes of fire flared up all around the swamp; I counted over a dozen through the trees and vines.

They burned. All of them burned.

Cassandra held me, weeping. I watched the fires turn to smoke, watched the hulking mass of the Goat King sink into the swamp.

If she had heard the words, she did not understand what they meant. But the fear was enough. God knows, the fear was enough.

But She was still there, still watching. Still waiting.

We drifted in the boat until morning, making ground by a long pier. In the distance I saw the lights of a passing train, heard the whistle, and welcomed it.

"We can't go back to Marlow," I said to Cassandra, who woke and was looking around bewildered.

"I know," she said. She narrowed her eyes as we got off the boat, checking our guns and supplies. "Poor Clell."

I sighed. Cassandra had found her heart again, it seemed. But I'd left a part of me in that swamp that would never come back. Could I tell her that I sensed something greater even than the Goat King? Some hovering presence that now and again whispered to me, that I could sense at the edge of my consciousness?

No. I had survived. And She, whoever She was, was larger and more unfathomable than any technological mystery.

We walked toward the train tracks, toward civilization.

Elizabeth, our eldest sister, would be waiting for us at our Aunt's house in Savannah. She and Cassandra would make up. And we'd go back to Arizona where we'd resume our duties until we all got old enough and the world changed.

But I would never forget the one in the swamp. Not the one we killed, but the one that watched.

Infernal Devices

Kenneth Hite

A shotgun hangs on the wall of Veterans of Foreign Wars Post 393, in Lebanon, Montana. It measures a little over five feet in length, with a wooden stock and grip of carved beech (with stag-horn inlays) running almost to the end of the barrel. Or rather, barrels, as it has two of them, mounted in an "over-under" configuration. In modern terms, its bore would be considered a little larger than 12-gauge, but its wheel-lock mechanism— or again, mechanisms, as each barrel has its own lock—is far from modern. A typed card mounted below it identifies it as the "Donation of Staff Sergeant Lewis Parchwell, of the 13th Infantry Regiment, taken in battle on November 28, 1944." Elias Hornby, the Recording Secretary of V.F.W. Post 393 for nearly thirty years, and a self-taught hoplologist who had presented papers not just at Montana State University but at the regional Gun Collector's Show in Denver, dated the gun to 1531 based not only on certain specifics of the mechanism common to early 16th-century arquebuses, and on the absence of the characteristic flared "blunderbuss" barrel end (which appeared only tentatively in the 1530s but became much more common later), but on the letters "AN.DOM.MDXXXI" carved into the left side of the stock near the butt.

For several months his dating, though duly published in the minutes of the Colorado Firearms Collector's Society newsletter the following fall, rested in undeserved if unsurprising obscurity. Then, by chance, it drew the attention of Dr. Anthony Fetterman, the staff historian at the National Firearms Museum, at that time (1971) located in Washington, D.C., and then (as now) operated by the National Rifle Association as a means of, among other things, inculcating a proper respect for firearms history among the American public. After a hasty correspondence with Recording Secretary Hornby, Dr. Fetterman flew to Butte at his own expense, catching the bus to Lebanon the next day. Upon his arrival, the anxious historian set immediately to work making his own examination of what, if Hornby's dating was correct, would be the oldest shotgun known to exist in the world, predating the Saxon fowling-pieces on display in Birmingham and Augsburg by several decades.

His examination triggered (unfortunate pun aside, there really is no other word for it) a heretofore unprecedented rift between Post 393 and the National Rifle Association, a rift that tore throughout V.F.W. posts all over eastern Montana as tempers flared and enthusiasts took up sides. Based on the remarkable preservation of the high-carbon iron barrel and the bronze fittings, to say nothing of the nearly pristine steel lock mechanisms, Dr. Fetterman concluded that the shotgun was a museum replica not much older than 1930. He was wise enough to publish that conclusion only upon his return to Washington, but he did so in the pages of the National Firearms Museum's historical journal, *The Arsenal.* In response, the officers and members of V.F.W. Post 393 closed ranks around their Recording Secretary, rejecting the implicit argument that Hornby was a fool or a hoaxer. After some persuasion, Hornby wrote a lengthy rebuttal of Fetterman's findings to be published in the same journal: to wit, that Dr. Fetterman had made no actual chemical analysis of the gun, that no museum would commission such an unusual piece as a replica, that the backs of the barrels (and to a lesser extent, the priming pan) were scorched and scored to a degree indicating repeated heavy fire, and that the steel of the lock was of a variety unlikely to have been easily to hand in 1930.

The controversy eventually led to the return of *The Arsenal* to a biannual publication schedule, to fourteen lifetime N.R.A. memberships being ostentatiously cancelled in Montana, and (rumor had it) at least one protest vote for George McGovern in 1972, McGovern having (unlike Dr. Fetterman, as a Montanan unkindly pointed out upon hearing the rumor) actually served in combat during World War II. Dr. Fetterman's request for renewed access to the gun for chemical testing having been indignantly (and unanimously) rejected by the members of V.F.W. Post 393, his final letter to *The Arsenal* contained little but querulous restatement of his earlier findings, unconvincingly leavened with unctuous assurances of his own unvarying faith in Elias Hornby's good character.

There the controversy, for lack of further fuel, finally banked and, like George McGovern's presidential ambitions, eventually faded into nothing more than a rancorous memory.

At first, Hulda Richter thought nothing wrong when the man in black appeared in the clearing, accompanied by a shaggy, horned figure holding a long staff. Of her ninety-one winters, she had spent nearly eighty holding esbats and sabbats in this clearing, for the surrounding forest was one consecrated by massacre to She Where Three Roads Meet, and the ring of stones to the Lurker at the Threshold and to the Treader-Out of the Stars. In those winters, and in that forest, she could smell when something was wrong, smell it deep in the squirming marrow of her bones, in the places where her skull itched to elongate and deform like a basket at the bottom of a tarn.

And nothing was wrong, or rather, nothing was Wrong. There was no singing agony along her jaw and forearms and pelvis heralding the coming of the Black Ram of Haddath, no wave of corruption on the wind flowing from Her Thousand Mouths. Only the sound of Latin, on the night breeze off the pines, and a sudden alarum of bird-calls. And then a crack like a thunderclap, and the spatter of Horst's blood and pulverized bones on her skin.

It would be overstating the case to say that Albert Kohl barely felt the recoil. He was a big man, almost six feet tall even ignoring the fringed and antlered hunters' hide he wore. And much of him was muscle, but that just let him handle more gun. The gun kicked like a horse losing patience. But Albert had been kicked before, and his feet were well planted, and he postponed noticing the blow until another time. For now, he pulled the barrels back into line before Doktor Wiese got to "maleficium" in his peroration, and tried again to aim at the old crone glinting at him with a gaze that glittered and shone like moonlight on marsh water. He slowly tugged the little iron bead on the front of his gun toward the witch with the Evil Eye.

Albert had carried this fine fowling piece with Doktor Wiese for three years. Before that, he had carried a glaive, and before that a boar-spear. Whatever the weapon, in those many years he had not earned his share of the rewards nervous burghers gave to witch-hunters by leaving the task of discerning true witches solely in the hands of the good Doktor. Well he knew the difference between some rat-ridden beldame who the village simply wanted out of the way, or a thumb-fingered herbalist whose potions had worked too surely on the wrong patient, and the true witch-servant of Satan. To be sure, the towns paid the same weight in silver to dispose of any and all of them, so Albert seldom applied such fine distinctions to the matter at hand.

But the Evil Eye was serious business, because it had seen visions the Devil had shown it, and it could look on you and send you to Hell. And for the real witches, the initiates of the primal cult that both Catholics and Protestants desperately strove to burn out of the lands they warred over, the Evil Eye was just the beginning of their vileness. So whereas in most cases, Kohl let the Doktor get all the way to the third "anathema" before even pointing the gun at anyone who looked like trouble, when the Evil Eye winked at him, he fired without thinking about recoil or anything else.

And this time, the shot had spread wide to the right and torn out the chest and shoulder of the burly plowman standing next to the gnarled crone he had targeted. That happened sometimes; the loads were necessarily uneven, and the wind in the clearing had been freshening. But more often, there was another cause, as indeed there was in this case. From about a third of the way around the ring of witches came another hateful vulture gleam, this one in the eye of a woman who would be handsome but for her short-cropped hair; a prostitute from the river towns, most likely. That made this coven quite a haul, potentially: it had intercourse with foreigners, not merely wicked locals. Put to the question, they would give names of other cult members, and of cult members in a richer town than Monschau or even Aachen.

With such a diverting prospect at hand, Albert decided merely to cripple the whore, emptying the second barrel into her leg.

The second thunderclap crashed out, and Hulda saw a wave of gray smoke drift toward her. Now Margrethe was down, thrashing and clutching a leg turned to useless chopped meat. The coven wavered, on the edge of scattering into the forest. Suddenly, Hulda smelled a reeking stench she could barely place: burnt charcoal, perhaps, and sulfur? For a few nervous seconds, she wondered if the churchmen had managed to actually call up their own imaginary Devil to pursue her and hers, but then she recognized the smell from the musketeers' camp eight years back when the wars of the League had touched Monschau: this was an arquebus, or some device similar.

Shamed by her own momentary fears, Hulda fixed her sight on the glittering amber eye of Arcturus, hanging above the tree-line. She raised her voice in the ululating call of the cult, a call that was old when the One later called Pan had revealed it to the first mystai: *Iä! Iä! Shub-Niggurath!* And then, as the blackbirds cawed wildly, she croaked one of the True Names, the One that indwelt here and now: *Lloigor Cf'ayak!*

From eleven throats (even Margrethe gasped it out) came the return: *Lloigor 'vulgtmm! Aï! Aï!* New power cracked and bent Hulda's limbs, and one of her few remaining teeth popped out of her writhing jaw in a freshet of pus. Her vision, normally clouded with cataracts, suddenly cleared even as it seemed to rotate up and to the side of her head, and suddenly the tree line glowed with bluish fire. She happened to be looking at the man in black when she stopped moving her head, and the fire crackled from his own eyes and his open mouth and then turned deep red and bright violet at once as his shrieking howl of agony at the same time pierced the sky like glass and dropped like lead into the stones of the earth.

The witches yowled their demonic cry and began to rush across the clearing toward Albert.

This is what happens when you let mercy distract you from your duty, Doktor Wiese would have said, chuckling as they spent their silver on hot wine or nutmeg-and-ale in Aachen. But Doktor Wiese was gone, torn to powder by demons and dragged to Hell in an eyeblink. No more would Albert hear that chuckle, or the confident bray as the Doktor explained to a new client that he had trained under both Paracelsus and Agrippa. The Doktor was dead, Albert fervently hoped, because after too much hot wine one night, the Doktor had hinted at the things besides death that could happen to a man who the witches caught unwitting at a time and place favorable to their arts.

This is why the Doktor brought him along, why he had recruited him five years ago: Albert Kohl was the best poacher in the Palatinate, and he was never caught unwitting at someone else's favorable time and place. Albert always scouted their destination before the sabbat; by the time the moon was new and the witches showed up, he knew the ground around their monolith or their bald heath better than their own fathers did.

So now Albert turned and ran toward the slot in the woods around the clearing. He had noticed the dry spring two nights ago in the waning moonlight, breaking the sharp slopes of scree and twisted roots that heaved up against the clearing's sides. Now he ran down it, skidding on the dirt clods and gravel, but gaining time and space on his pursuers. He needed enough of both to reload.

As he hoped, they began to split up as they got deeper into the woods: amateurs thinking they were the beaters and he was the fox. They were wrong. He was the hunter, and they were the birds. The forest was suddenly full of birds, he thought, hearing the twittering of chaffinches and the sobbing of wrens from all directions. Well enough. The noise would hide his passage. He shrugged out of the heavy leather hide, needing speed more than concealment or protection. Then he slung his gun and fell back toward where he had left the axe at moonrise.

Two of them were still moving vaguely toward him. Not close enough to offer them any real advantage, but it did mean Albert would have to kill both of them before either one got off a shout of alarm. If they actually managed to converge on him, he might have more in common with that fox than he liked. He shifted his grip on the axe again and waited for the first to pass him. He had left his gun hidden under a trailing bush, and was glad of the freedom of movement, much though he missed its comforting bulk. The second witch passed him; he erupted from behind a thick fir bole, swinging the axe in a perfect arc into her spinal cord. Instantly paralyzed, she couldn't shout a warning. Albert ran down her partner (a squat man with a goiter) and smashed in his skull. Now, he had time to recover his gun and reload.

Albert poured black powder out of one end of his shot belt into the metal cup on the other end. One charge, into the first barrel. Then he fingered out a handful of lead from the belt's middle packet. Like most hunters with a fowling-piece, he bought his lead from printers, who had lots of lead sheets they had run to almost paper thin-ness, smashing and pressing against the type. Stamp or cut those sheets, sometimes with the impress of the Bible or the treatise or the proclamation still on them, into squares, or close enough. Tumble the squares a bit in a churn to blunt the corners, and you had shot. Dump a fistful of shot on top of the measured powder, tamp it down with a rod, cover with a little piece of wadding, tamp that down. Do it again on the other barrel. Check both locks. Check the rotation of the barrels. Check the cover of the priming pan. Pour out primer. Check the flint on the hammer. Albert had practiced that little liturgy every day but Sunday for many years, now. He was devout.

He shot one in the head as they walked down parallel deer paths, waiting until a particularly thick and rustly hemlock blocked almost all the starlight and much of the noise. The birds drowned the rest of it.

He shot the young boy right in the chest, coming upon him by surprise as they both rounded a moss-covered plinth of limestone, jutting like a tooth from the soft ground where the trail looped around and met the ravine again. That shot echoed up and down the riverbed, raising only one or two plaintive caws in response. Albert's advantage of surprise was as dead as the boy, for a while anyway.

He missed one, but it was a running shot at a running witch, back into the woods.

Albert briefly clutched the bag hanging from a thong around his neck and prayed to St. Eustace, patron of hunters, to guide his aim. Then he moved his hand from the bag to flip up the rear sight he'd had a tinker in Aachen put in. The bead-sight on the muzzle end was usually enough, but the rear sight helped with long shots like this one. The knucklebones in the bag must have been authentic relics, because the witch sprayed blood and toppled into the rocks she sheltered behind. It was almost a hundred yards down the ravine to where the witch had been crouching, certain that nobody could creep up on such an exposed, though strong, position. Now, Albert could move past that position as fast as he wished, to fall on the witches across the ravine, deeper into the woods.

He shot one in the back, an old man who wasn't carrying a weapon.

He shot another one in the stomach, and chopped him in the face to finish the job.

Fewer birds called with every shot, it seemed. He hadn't heard a wren in an hour.

He very much wished he hadn't lost his axe. He had hacked open one witch's shoulder, then spun around to chop the second only to find his hand empty. The blade had stuck in the witch's arm, the thick chest muscle clamping spastically down onto the steel. The witch fell, twisting and pulling the axe handle up out of Albert's hand, and the second witch had a very long knife. Albert had to back up once, twice, three times before he could trade a long cut in the side (stopped from gutting him only by his second shot belt) for a straight-arm smash and a kidney punch. The second witch was down but far from out, and shouting for a third friend. Albert turned and loped away, once more trusting his knowledge of the woods.

In a small clearing between two beech trees, Albert stopped moving. He knew where they were, but he couldn't do anything about them. They were keeping together, keeping each other alive and in sight so he couldn't ambush them. He reached for his shot belt, and it felt lighter than it should. The second belt must have fallen off, cut nearly through by the knife as it was. He only had one shot belt, the one he'd already charged his gun from six, eight times. He was getting tired, the strain beginning to tell. He wished Doktor Wiese were here to tell him to forget about it and go home.

After checking the belt twice, Albert still had barely enough powder for one more charge, and no more shot at all. In truth? No more? He was always finding single stray squares of shot when he didn't want them: in his bread bag, or in his pockets, or in his bedroll. Now he felt every stitch, every fold of his trews and tunic and coat. He opened up the shot belt completely, slitting its seams, unrolling the leather and picking through it for singletons.

He found eleven little lead squares, looking even more warped and uneven in their isolation. He dropped them in on top of his last charge of powder. He also had six silver pfennigs, small enough to fit inside the gun's bore. If he didn't get out of this forest, he couldn't spend them; down they went. He still couldn't chance three witches, even if he had crippled one already—not with one shot and only a paring knife for close quarters. But perhaps he could still kill the old witch who he had missed at the beginning of all this, the one with the Evil Eye. She couldn't have gone far, and unlike her fellow witches, Albert knew exactly how to get back to the clearing.

But he'd missed her, from a prepared position with a full load and minutes of aim. He needed an edge if he was going to hit her when he was tired, from an angle he hadn't sighted in, with this last chancy, underpowered charge. The knucklebones of St. Eustace—they were small enough to fit down the barrel. He opened his relic bag, saying a brief prayer for forgiveness. St. Eustace was a hunter, though; he would understand. The knucklebones were colored like honey, once incised with crosses but now worn almost smooth. Lying in their midst was a weird little talisman, inscribed with unreadable runes. Doktor Wiese must have slipped it in without telling him; some sort of extra philosophical protection. It was slim and rounded, and the gray-green stone slid easily down the steel bore. Albert tamped the uneven load home, and moved silently up the ravine, back toward the clearing.

Hulda knew when the hunter had circled around to her. Three of her fellows were still stumbling around in the woods, hopelessly lost and far from Hulda's aid. Hulda was alone now — she had opened Margrethe's torso at the end, aiming the ribs and long bones and other parts in the correct directions to prepare the Angles without the full coven. She started with a quickly murmured *Iä* sequence but soon lost herself in the Dhol chants, rhythms and formulae she had burned into her brain, but never until now uttered. As the blue flames began to flicker in her sight, she could see the trees and standing stones begin to refract and multiply, splintering like spilt sugar on a hot ladle. Her vision bounced and skittered from the smoothly shining trunks, mirrored from the lattice of branches and stones, and she could see the hunter standing where he thought he was hidden, holding his foolish weapon.

I'll show him hidden, she thought with a sharp, personal viciousness that was very unlike her. I'll show him hidden indeed. Hulda's mouth fell open and as she began to intone the proper notes and tones in her throat, pieces of Margrethe's liver spilled out over her numb, slack lips.

If Doktor Wiese — who, after all, could confidently state that he had trained under both Paracelsus and Agrippa — had survived to see what Hulda was doing, he would have similarly confidently stated that she was summoning a demon. If a physicist of the 21st century could be persuaded to opine on the matter, he would say, possibly less confidently, that she was rotating a superstring containing a separate universe into her local space. By the 50th century, the sages of Tsan-Chan can discuss the matter without superstitious referents.

Lloigor merely perceived, and it was so. This was/is/had been/will be true for longer than the Earth exists.

At first, he thought the trees themselves were moving to block his shot. The old witch couldn't have moved; she barely looked like she could stand up. But suddenly, there were trees between him and the witch, between his last charge of shot and her Evil Eye. But they weren't trees. They moved against the suddenly icy wind, and they melted in the suddenly blazing starlight, writhing like eels mating, and they towered above him and slid below him, and they had branches and limbs and planes and surfaces and oh yes eyes. So many eyes, and now the branches and other things were toppling and rippling toward him and the eyes burned into him and the wind pinched and pulled like talons and something reached for him from every angle, elongated and gaping and he was stumbling back and he couldn't move back any more.

He had one shot left, and everything he could see was a smashed nightmare joined at angles that stabbed at his flesh. His ears roared with the piercing wind-call and his legs were numb or dislocated or not there any more. Everything smelled like burning tin, but Albert gripped the barrel of his gun with hands gone wet and salty.

Doktor Wiese had always been very clear that suicide was a mortal sin.

Albert raised his shotgun, hand over hand, moving his fists down to the stock and the lock. He let the barrel fall forward, leveled it at the many-angled Thing rising before him, and squeezed the trigger. He never felt the recoil.

Lloigor felt His first volcanic bolide approximately one and a half billion years after the Earth formed. He felt His first lightning strike 18 million years before that, and His first axe blade around 165 million years before humanity evolved. In all those cases, the term "first" is one of those superstitious referents that the sages of Tsan-Chan deplore, because He felt/feels/will feel all of those things simultaneously, for as long as they occurred, and for as often. And because He is the Many-Angled One, He simply transected/projected/assumed/extruded a surface that quenched bolides, grounded lightning, and splintered axe-blades as though turned by a shield of oiled diamond. And again/always/before for every other single thing in three dimensions intended to wound, burn, freeze, disintegrate, or sublime: He already solves/solved/will solve the precise configuration of Angle and Surface needed to dampen or deflect or counterbalance the attack, and so such a blow was/is/can only be a nullity to Him. Indeed, He even will/has/is obliquely refracted from the death of planets in a red star's senile embrace, Arcturus and Sol and suns not named in this universe. Almost nothing is/will be/has been unknown to Him.

Except.

He felt His first round lead shot in 1294, fired by a Mongol warrior in northern Burma; He felt His first grouping of round lead pellets in the Snowdon Hills in Wales in 1597, aimed by a hunter freezing to death and mad with hunger. Hollow lead balls, pointed lead bullets, pointed silver bullets, steel shrapnel, depleted-uranium shells, titanium needles: He has/will/is resisting them all forever/now, because He already did/will/is.

But only once—only at 2:54 a.m. on April 19, 1534, in the cursed stand of woods just southwest of Monschau in the Duchy of Jülich—has He been hit with eleven irregular geometric lead rhomboids and six worn silver-and-pewter alloy discs tumbling on entirely chaotic approaches, combined with two human knuckles and two pieces of carefully dyed ivory, and a small ovoid of gray-green moldavite, most importantly all of them inscribed with polysemic and alphanumeric payloads, and all of them moving at just under 1,200 feet per second.

Lloigor shrieked. Colorless blue fire enveloped the entire forest. Hulda died instantly as her bones and lungs suddenly lost all their directionality and expanded randomly for nine seconds; the three remaining witches lost, on average, forty percent of their skin and senses.

In front of that scream, Albert Kohl was like a leaf in a torrent, battered but intact, spreading himself over the pressure wave and tumbling along it bathed in the brilliant violet edges of the ice-blue rage of the god, stretched and pulped along His perceptions until He had to/had to/had to close them off, to stop them, to end the moment of pain and singularity and *not knowing*.

Lloigor blinked.

In an ultraviolet screech, Albert Kohl blinked out.

The forest was empty of sane life for miles. It no longer touched the Many-Angled One.

After three straight days of combat in the Hürtgen Forest, with about three hours of sleep all told, PFC Pete Larsen ignored the weird purple light suddenly flickering in his eyes. It was either a hallucination or the krauts throwing out something else to keep this godforsaken stand of woods Yank-free. Either way, the solution was the same: squint away the exhaustion and try and drive the balky Sherman tank forward another few yards.

It must have been a side-effect of sleep deprivation; Larsen must actually have nodded off for several seconds to have missed seeing the big blond guy with the gun come out of nowhere. Probably simple-minded, drafted into the Volkssturm at the Reich's last gasp—he didn't even have a uniform. He was dressed like a hayseed in a homespun shirt, and gaping like a man who'd just seen all the elephant he could handle.

Wherever he came from, he was going to Hell. Larsen reached down and squeezed the trigger on the M2 machine gun mounted on the turret. The .50 caliber stuttered out a few rounds, Larsen corrected the aim with a tug, and the big guy went down with four or five holes in him.

After that burst, a kind of thick stillness lowered itself over the woods. Even the artillery strikes sounded muffled; heavy weather coming in, maybe. Nobody followed the hayseed, so Larsen climbed down out of the tank to stretch his back and unkink his hams. The shotgun lying by the big guy's cooling body looked kind of interesting close up—nice carvings, a real antique.

Two months later, Larsen lost the shotgun in a poker game to a REMF sergeant from Montana named Lewis Parchwell, leaving him nothing to show for two pair (queens and eights) and almost a week's straight fighting in the forest except a real distaste for cold weather and a persistent violet light that he saw in the corner of his vision whenever he was very tired.

Walker

Dave Gross

It's not a nightmare that wakes me but another seizure. I count the sound of passing cars until the spasms stop. When I can stand again, I slouch away from the others who lie twitching in their fractured slumber.

Half an hour later, I stand in front of the mirror for an hour, trying to remember the name of the woman I see there. I roll out when I smell crack smoke from one of the stalls. I can't be here. I can't be anywhere the cops might see me, recognize me.

They won't recognize me unless I give them an excuse to get close. I already look like one of the lost. Two weeks since my last shower, I definitely smell like one.

I shuffle down The Ave, cycling nonsense rhymes through my mind to protect my thoughts from eavesdroppers. The citizens cross the street when they see me coming. One barefoot kid puts a handful of coins and a crumpled bus transfer in my hand. I look at the time stamp and wonder whether there's anywhere I want to go.

There isn't.

Beck is slipping away. When she's gone, all that anyone will remember are the official lies. I need to write down what happened while I can still get it straight.

Soon I will *be* one of them.

No, I'm kidding myself. The truth is I've been one since the day I ran over the homeless guy.

Traffic was insane. Barely past the intersection, Rebecca Eames stopped again. The morning fog was dense for early March. She could barely see the next red light past the line of cars.

At the signal she turned off Pine. Forget the highway, she decided. It was a parking lot by now.

She needed to reach the North Precinct in the next fourteen minutes to look busy before the lieutenant rolled in. Every morning since the transfer, she'd been at her desk when he walked past, saluting over his right eyebrow with two fingers. He did the same thing when he went off shift, only he said, "Be seeing you."

Rebecca knew the catch-phrase from the old *Prisoner* TV show, which her father enjoyed while he still lived with her in the condo. She decided it was better not to let on. The lieutenant might think she was kissing his ass, or he might decide she was a geek. If nothing else, he seemed to enjoy his private joke, and Beck decided not to disturb it. Little things like that counted at review time.

It was her own fault she caught rush hour. She shouldn't have stopped for coffee, or else she should have bought a cup of drip instead of the skinny half-sweet double mocha. Fancy coffee needed to go on the list, along with dinner out and gas for trips out to the Peninsula. If it wouldn't add another three years to the plan, what she really needed was a car that got better mileage.

She'd circle back to 23rd and cut north across Montlake. Traffic wouldn't be great there, but it couldn't be any worse.

She floored the gas, and the big cruiser leaped forward, knocking her latte out of the shallow cup holder. She reached down for the cup and leaned harder on the accelerator.

A man ran in front of the car. Before she could move her foot to the brake, he came up over the hood. She heard his head strike the windshield, and he vanished, leaving only a blood smear on the glass.

Rebecca squealed the car to a halt. She called her location to dispatch, asked for medical assistance, and was out the door.

The man lay across the curb, his faded duster pulled up to reveal rumpled flannel and denim beneath. His hair was a golden brown mop head.

Her first thought was that she'd run over Eddie Vedder. Bobbie Felton had taken her to the Pearl Jam concert at Key Arena a few months earlier. Rebecca had been mesmerized by the singer's growling baritone, at least when she wasn't avoiding Bobbie's persistent attempts to slip his hand into her back pocket.

But only the man's hair was the same as Eddie Vedder's. Rebecca's immediate impression was that he was too good-looking for a homeless man. He had fashion-model cheekbones and an action star's jaw. His pulse was strong and fast. Rebecca detected no trace of alcohol, but she didn't like his pallor.

She didn't like the blood on his ear, either.

Rebecca knelt for a better look at the wound. It wasn't large, but like all head wounds it bled a lot. He was breathing, thank God. She lifted an eyelid when she heard a sound from the alley he'd run from.

She felt it before she saw anything. Her eyes stung. The pain reminded her of tear gas, which she'd last experienced a couple of years earlier during the WTO protests. But the smell was different, like the sharp pong of mold in an abandoned house.

The thing emerged from the narrow lane, bobbing tentatively like a sagging helium balloon. Rebecca blinked, but the creature appeared blurry even as the image of the nearby buildings remained sharp. What her eye perceived made little sense by the time her brain tried to parse the code.

She had the impression of an enormous lobster with the wings of a damselfly, but with a spongy surface the color of wet pavement and bruises. Its crustacean limbs ended in digits—not claws and definitely not fingers—in which it grasped weird metal objects so tight that they appeared to transfix its flesh. Rebecca winced, thinking the thing resembled a cluster of genital piercings gone septic.

She drew her service revolver and aimed at the center of the mass.

"Halt, Seattle Police!"

She felt ridiculous as soon as she spoke to this object, but it stopped moving forward. With a nauseating start, Rebecca understood it was a living creature, not some papier-mâché Halloween ornament left to molder in the rain.

"Drop your weapon."

Again she felt vaguely foolish, but her training took over. What was this, some radio-controlled toy? It had to be, but it looked—it smelled—like nothing she had ever seen. Rebecca watched for any sign of aggression and realized she had no idea what that would look like.

Rebecca heard police sirens four or five blocks away.

Beside her, the injured man stirred and mumbled. She could barely understand his words. "…On the twenty-sixth … got to stop it … the kingdom …"

She glanced down at the man and back at the thing. A neon green reflection glimmered on the metal object(s) it held. She knew intuitively that it was not a reflection. It was some sort of emission.

A painful jolt shot through Rebecca's body. She convulsed, her arms and shoulders twitching. She turned the pistol away from her target, toward the man on the ground.

It was not her will that guided her hands, and the horror of what she was about to do sent a spike of adrenaline through her brain.

She corrected her aim and squeezed off three shots at the thing.

The gas or mold or whatever it was that stung her eyes intensified until she wiped away the tears with her sleeve. When her vision cleared, she could no longer see the thing she'd shot. She knew she'd hit it. She was positive, and she was sure it was the right thing to do. Whatever it was, it was not something that should be here. It was not something that should exist. If it returned, she'd shoot it again.

She held her revolver steady at the place where the thing had been until red and blue police lights lit up the morning fog.

Fourteen hours later, Rebecca's certainty that she'd done the right thing had all but dissolved. It began to crumble when she tried to explain what she'd seen to the first responders. Howe and Jarvis took one look at her face and sent her to the ambulance for an eye wash and a shock blanket. Afterward, she'd hesitated too long in answering Howe's questions, so they sent her to the hospital along with the homeless man.

The longer she had to think about it, the more Rebecca knew she couldn't make an honest report without ruining the plan. The moment she described what she'd seen, they'd be drawing blood to test her sobriety. They'd have done it already if she weren't police.

If only she hadn't fired, she could have managed the story. The guy had been chased by kids, or another homeless person, or he ran from nothing at all. She didn't have to lie. She could keep it vague, but three rounds fired demanded a story better than "novelty balloon."

Administrative duty she could live with, and there was no avoiding that, but she wanted nothing to do with the department shrink, much less IA. Either one of those would also ruin the plan.

No matter how she thought it through, she couldn't figure out a way to explain those three shots that wouldn't get her locked up or shut down. Fortunately, no one had been hit. There'd been no blood at the scene and no complaints from the public. So she relied on the escape clause.

"I don't know," she told the investigating officer. "Everything is still so confused."

It was bullshit. The other cop knew it was bullshit. But it was legally acceptable bullshit, a delaying tactic more likely to get you a consolatory drink from the old guard than any serious trouble with IA. All she had to do was get things straight within a day or two.

She surrendered her gun to ballistics, a formality, and bummed a ride home from her partner Patrick. She wanted to talk with the man she'd hit, but despite the leeway she enjoyed as a cop, she knew that wouldn't be permitted. Fortunately, she and Patrick got along well enough that she could ask for a small favor and expect to receive it. He swung by her apartment after his shift. She heated water for the French press while he filled her in.

"Guy's a regular on The Ave and Capitol Hill. ID reads Henry Robert Walker, but it's bogus. The birth date is 14 July 1938. Looks just like him, but there's no way he's sixty-two."

"So it's his father." She took the kettle off and let it calm before filling the carafe.

Patrick nodded. "Must be a Social Security scam, although he works construction now and then. Yandel's looking into it. If Mr. Walker is picking up daddy's check, it's not to buy booze. Connie recognizes him from her beat, says he doesn't seem to drink, and he's not one of the aggressive panhandlers. No record, just a few warnings for loitering. He stays in various shelters but never spends more than a couple of days at the same one."

"Is he talking? What's he say?"

Patrick looked her in the eye for the first time since sitting down. She looked back, letting him try to read her face while she stirred the coffee.

"They're keeping him awake to monitor his concussion, but he hasn't said anything about the accident."

"He said some weird stuff this morning. I just wanted to know what he was running from."

"Listen, he's listed as stable. You're not looking at vehicular homicide."

"That's ..." Rebecca had been focusing on making sense of what she'd seen and how to explain it. Until now, the enormity of hitting a man with her car had not sunk in. Of course there'd be charges, a citation at least. A civil suit could wipe her out, erasing any memory that she'd even had a plan, yet all she could think about was that impossible thing she'd seen. All she wanted was to know what it was and why it had come to ruin her life. "That's good news. That he's stable, I mean. I should send... I don't know. A card or something."

"Now, Beck," he said. "You stay away from him. Just get your statement squared away and let your union rep handle the rest."

"You're right," she said. She pushed down the plunger and poured a cup of coffee, but Patrick waved it away.

"Too late for me. I need to get home to supper." He hesitated a moment. "Want anything from the store? You know, until you get your car back?"

"No," said Rebecca. "I'm good."

Now that the plan was a wash, she decided, there was no reason she couldn't afford a taxi to the hospital.

Rebecca introduced herself as Sara Walker, Henry's sister. She held her breath, hoping the duty nurse wouldn't ask for an ID, but she didn't. There was no need. Walker was gone. He hadn't checked himself out, the nurse said, he'd just left.

"He needs to come back here," she told Rebecca. "The doctors want to monitor him for at least forty-eight hours. If you know where he is ..."

"I don't," said Rebecca. "But I'll ask around."

She started on The Ave, since it was closer. It hadn't changed as much as she'd expected from the complaints that competition from University Village and Northgate had drawn away shoppers. This summer she knew the city would start repaving, adding street lights and benches. She doubted the makeover would do much good.

Outside the bars, gauntlets of smokers attracted the occasional homeless person hoping to bum a cigarette or some change. Rebecca recognized a few of the older ones from her brief stint on the beat. One with a nicotine stained beard nodded as she walked past. She'd responded to the report of his third heart attack a few years ago. She remembered his name as Abbie and wondered how his liver had held out another year.

A handful of the seeming homeless were middle-class kids panhandling for beer money. They were the ones most likely to become belligerent when refused or ignored. The only time she'd ever had to draw her sidearm was during a dispute between one of these Ave Rats and a motorist whose car he'd tried and failed to jump on his skateboard.

The weight of the Glock 21 under her arm was reassuring. A gift from her brother, she used it for target practice before their monthly beer sessions. Except for its olive color, it was identical to her service pistol. She wanted to avoid flashing her badge. While most of the subjects she was likely to question would recognize her as a cop the moment she spoke, she expected the rest would recognize the lump under her jacket.

She wished she'd brought a photo of Henry Robert Walker, but she couldn't risk returning to work to open his file. At best, she'd give the impression she was trying to lean on him to absolve her of the accident. At worst, she'd create more suspicion.

Instead, after she'd strolled up to 52nd and back down to 41st, she changed fifty bucks into fives and bought a couple of packs of cigarettes to use as an entrée.

She started with the older indigents, those who'd spent more than a few months on the street. She described Walker and inquired about the names Henry, Hank, Hal, Harry, Robert, Rob, or Bob. Almost everyone claimed to know a man matching the description, hoping Rebecca would offer more incentive to remember more. If she had her detective's shield, she could request CI payments, but as it was she doled out her cash like a miser.

After forty bucks and three hours, Rebecca learned little more than what Patrick told her earlier. Walker had been around for years, although he didn't socialize with the other old-timers. He haunted The Ave only once or twice a week, spending the rest of his time near the Market, Belltown, Capitol Hill, and Pioneer Square.

He didn't claim a spot for his own and avoided trespassing on the claims of other homeless people, sometimes holding a cup as he stood on the sidewalk but never initiating conversation. One Native American woman considered him creepy, but she couldn't explain why beyond saying that he said too little and watched too much.

"Most days he just stands on the corner. It's like he's waiting for someone," she said. "Or waiting for something to happen."

She wasn't the only one reluctant to talk about Walker. Rebecca noticed a reticence in several of the people she questioned. She was used to that, but she had a feeling it was not the result of an aversion to the police, or to questions. It happened only when she saw in their eyes that they knew the man she was asking about.

The day's events began to weigh on Rebecca. She'd intended to try Belltown and the Market next, but fatigue was clouding her mind. She decided to go home. She could walk Capitol Hill for an hour or so before bed. She reached for her cell to call a taxi, but her habitual frugality kicked in again. Maybe the plan was dead, but it wouldn't kill her to take the bus back home.

As she approached the stop, Rebecca spotted Abbie putting the touch on a man stepping off the bus. The rider's goatee and elbow patches gave him a professorial look. Rebecca read that academics were statistically more likely to give, but he waved Abbie away and hustled off to a nearby brewpub. He must not teach statistics, she thought.

She offered Abbie the remaining cigarettes.

"God bless," he said, bobbing his head in thanks as he stepped away. He caught a glimpse of her face and hesitated. He stood there a moment, cupping the flame of a cheap lighter in his palms. He drew in a lungful, held it a second, and let it out with a pensive expression.

"You're looking for the walker."

"Henry Robert Walker," said Rebecca. "Do you know him?"

Abbie shrugged and took another drag. "Can't say as I do. But I seen him around. He did me a good turn when I got bit by a mean dog. Let me sleep under a tarp he'd fixed for himself."

Rebecca took the last two fives out of her purse. "Where did he keep this tarp?"

The Queen and East precincts took turns flushing the squatters out from under the interstate overpasses. No one enjoyed the detail. It wasn't difficult—the indigents were used to being roused from their nests now and then—but it was pointless. The same people came back after a few days, sometimes only a few hours.

There hadn't been a sweep since before winter, so the concrete slope was home to nine or ten homeless men and women. None of these were thrill seekers like the Ave Rats. They were the damaged and discarded, mentally or physically ill, junkies and alcoholics, unwilling or unable to accept help from a shelter or one of the city's charities.

Walker huddled in a green tarp on the far southern edge of the concrete. He was sitting up and seemed alert. In fact, as she came closer Rebecca saw he was watching her, as if he'd been expecting her arrival.

He had only a small square of gauze taped to his forehead. Rebecca could have sworn the wound was worse than that. The EMTs had mentioned broken ribs, and Patrick said something about a CT scan. It was crazy to think he'd walked out of the hospital under his own steam, but here he was.

"Did you bring a gun?" he asked.

The question alarmed her, but Rebecca controlled the impulse to reach for the Glock. "Why, do I need one?"

He shrugged. Rebecca opened his mouth to speak, but he interrupted. "Here's what you need to know."

He unspooled a tale of profound and schizophrenic paranoia. Walker wasn't his real name, he said. It was his avocation. He and others like him patrolled the cities infiltrated by alien beings — creatures like the one Rebecca had seen. He and his colleagues traveled on foot because so many of the clues the enemy left behind were too subtle to notice by those speeding by in cars.

Rebecca liked this detail. She'd burned enough shoe-leather walking a beat to see the truth in it. But she had also dealt with enough mentally ill people to recognize the power of a compelling detail to make the most absurd fantasy irresistible to a tractable mind.

With their advanced technology, Walker explained, the aliens had transplanted their brains into the bodies of key government officials to ensure their goals would be executed. He admitted he did not know the exact nature of their designs, but he believed passionately that the aliens saw humans as little more than beasts or tools.

Walker had been one of a cell watching for alien activity in Seattle, and he'd found it. For the past two years he'd been stalking city government functionaries, consulting fellow "walkers" who kept an eye on contractors and other key business leaders. Putting the clues together, they discovered that the creatures intended to activate a massive machine on March 26 in the Kingdome.

Not "the kingdom," as Rebecca had misheard. This second nice detail gulled her momentarily into thinking she was talking with a sane person.

She knew now that she should go home and leave a tip for social services to pick him up in the morning. That's exactly what she would have done, except for one thing.

She'd seen the alien.

"What exactly is this machine supposed to do?"

"I don't know," said Walker. "But you've felt what the small version of the machine does. What do you think it's for?"

Rebecca thought of the stinging in her eyes, the confusion in her thoughts as the green luminescence pulsed on the metal device. Did it affect her mind? What would have happened if she hadn't fired those shots? Would the aliens have controlled her mind?

She shook her head, frightened to realize she was thinking of Walker's aliens as real beings, not the products of a psychotic break. But if they were delusions, she could not explain why she too had seen them.

Maybe she was the one who needed a visit from social services. One thought of the stigma of a visit to the department shrink for anything other than her annual checkpoint squelched that notion.

Walker could not be delusional, because what he described was the same as what she had seen, and Rebecca knew that she was not delusional.

She decided that was enough existential crisis for one night. While she still felt some equilibrium about her own mental state, she would get a good night's sleep and decide what to do tomorrow.

"Where can I find you tomorrow afternoon?" she asked.

"Give me your cell number."

"Give me yours," she countered.

"Can't," he said. "Haven't got one yet."

In the end, Rebecca chose the hooded man with a firearm story. It was weak, even the union rep said so, but it was unlikely to get her charged. It was, however, certain to cost her the bump to detective and the pay increase that was the lynchpin of her five-year plan.

What she needed was a new plan. After a night's sleep, she realized how perilously close she'd come to losing her mind to Walker's crackpot story. She'd put the world's shittiest day behind her. Maybe it would be seven years until she could move out of her father's condo and buy a house in Ravenna. She hoped it wouldn't be ten.

Regardless, she felt a great weight come off her shoulders as she left the interview room. Through his office window, the lieutenant nodded as she returned to her desk to put her files in order for Patrick. She'd spend another nine days on leave before returning to work, with or without a reprimand. Probably without, if the description of her assailant was sufficiently vague. At least she didn't have to worry about Walker's turning up to contradict her story. He'd exhibited no desire to press charges for the accident. Still, it was good to be sure.

She stuck her head in the lieutenant's door on the way out.

"Any word on the poor guy I ran into?"

He looked up from his monitor and smiled. "Looks like you scared him back to California. Our Mr. Walker bought a bus ticket under his own name a couple of hours after he left the hospital. He's SFPD's problem now. I doubt we'll see him again."

Rebecca failed to conceal her surprise.

"Don't worry, we all have a few smudges on our sheets. This one won't amount to much by the time the next review rolls around." He winked at her, a cold gesture devoid of sexual innuendo and thus all the more chilling.

Rebecca smiled a straight line and bobbed her head. "Thanks, Lieutenant."

He touched two fingers to his brow. "Be seeing you."

Rebecca's hands and feet felt cold as she stepped out of the station. Minutes after her interview, she'd received an email notification that her car was ready for pickup—another favorable sign—but instead of catching a ride to impound, she took the next bus back home.

She sat by the window and watched the buildings and alleys go by, surprised at how often she spotted an unexpected walkway sheltered by the boughs of a tree, or a door where she'd never noticed one before. Sometimes she caught a brief glimpse of a building hidden from the street and craned her neck for a better look, but it was gone before she could see just what it was.

She got off near Harvard, half a mile from her condo, and walked the rest of the way. She noticed the circuit of cables that joined the houses to telephone and power lines. Their patterns were more intricate than she had ever realized. Following them, she began to perceive the subtle relationships between buildings, their dependencies and secrets. With every block she saw some feature she had never before discovered, and she felt as she had the first day she stumbled upon Freeway Park, that startling maze of trees and flowerbeds perched directly over the I-5.

She spent the rest of the afternoon tidying the condo, alphabetizing her bookshelves, culling the boxes of magazines that had accumulated in her home office—anything to stop thinking of the queer lie the lieutenant had told her. Anything to stop wondering what she would say to Walker if he called.

But no one called for the rest day, and at last she finished a bottle of Chardonnay and fell asleep under the gentle radiation of the muted television. She dreamed of the drone of insects.

She woke in the dark to the buzzing of her cell phone.

"Meet me at the Pergola."

"Listen …" said Rebecca. She wanted to say she shouldn't have given him this number, that he could call her at the station if he had anything to say, but that was stupid. She had already thought about two or three reasons why the lieutenant would have lied about Walker's leaving town, and none of them was any good.

"Today is the twenty-sixth," said Walker.

Rebecca stepped off the bus right beside the Pergola, the Victorian canopy that had been the neighborhood's principal landmark for over ninety years. Hours from now, tourists would take each other's photo beside the wrought-iron structure as they waited for underemployed stand-up comics to guide them through Seattle's Underground. Until then, most of the residents were homeless people shuffling awake after sleeping in the nearby park.

She'd seen Ghost Mountain clear as a postcard picture on the ride over. That's what her father called Mount Rainier, which was invisible in the distant gloom so many days of the year. When it materialized in the southern distance, he called it an omen. He would never say whether it was a good omen or a bad one.

Rebecca saw Walker round the corner with a coffee cup in either hand. He'd showered and shaved since she last saw him. Years of living rough left a specter on his face, but he looked less like someone she'd meet on a call and more like someone she might see on a date.

He offered both cups, allowing her to choose one. The gesture took her off guard, and she realized it hadn't occurred to her that he might have drugged or otherwise tainted one of them. When she picked one, he produced packets of cream and sugar from his pocket, but she shook her head. Then she tasted the coffee and changed her mind. After two creams and a sugar, the stuff was drinkable.

"Whatever they're doing, it's today," Walker said without preamble. "Most of the security has left the site. Last night I cut through one of the fences, but I decided to call you before going in."

"Slow down. You're still talking about the Kingdome, right? What's going on in there, and what do you expect me to do about it?"

The place had been closed for renovations since early January. Over thirty years old, the place was starting to fall apart. Calls for repairs or replacement of the entire facility had grown louder since another ceiling tile fell on the fans five or six years back.

"I know how nuts it sounds," he said. "The truth is I don't know exactly what's happening in there. They aren't renovating the place, that's for sure. What I need is a credible witness. You've seen one of the mi-go, and I can tell you haven't written it off as a hallucination. Maybe you've heard and seen some other strange things. You're a cop. Of course you have."

He asked for so little, Rebecca felt suspicious.

"Put your coffee down," she said, assuming her work voice.

"What?"

"Hands on the wall. Spread 'em."

He did as she directed. She patted him down and found nothing dangerous.

"All right, we'll take a peek." When they found nothing unusual, she'd give him a card for social services and wash her hands of him.

They walked the six blocks to the Kingdome, but Rebecca instantly saw that something was wrong. Despite the signs declaring the renovation and the names of the three contracting firms involved, there was no equipment on the lot. Even the foreman's trailer was missing, and not a single vehicle was parked within the chain-link security fence.

Rebecca felt Walker's eyes on her. She had the feeling he was appraising her reaction, maybe even reading her mind a little. That idea did not disturb her the way she thought it might. There was a vast difference between human empathy and whatever that—it was difficult even to think the nonsense word—that *mi-go's* green energy device had done to her.

Walker led her to the place where he'd cut the fence. He'd left the bolt-cutters on the ground. Rebecca wondered briefly where he'd gotten them and decided it was not an urgent question. He picked them up and held the fence open for her as she slipped through.

They walked across the empty parking lot. There was no point trying to sneak across the barren space in the clear morning light. They reached the northwestern entrance unchallenged. Walker cut the chain on a service entrance. They went inside.

Rebecca had expected silence, but an electric hum filled the interior. They followed it past the ticket gates, where Walker touched her arm. The gesture startled her, but he pointed toward the food court ahead. There stood a bald man in the uniform of a private security company. He wore an automatic weapon slung over one shoulder.

Rebecca recognized the weapon as an Uzi.

No security firm in the city was licensed to carry such weapons.

She drew her Glock and gestured for Walker to follow as she retreated to the next arena entrance. They remained close to the wall as they descended the stairs and looked around.

There'd been no renovation work, although thousands of uniform holes had been drilled and plugged all over the walls and ceiling, where patches of water damage and missing tiles were obvious even in the upper gloom. All the light came from the floor level.

Throughout the arena sprawled a vast tangle of electrical and hydraulic cables. Pools of yellow fluid leaked beneath a few junctures, glimmering under blue-white lights that reminded Rebecca of the fluorescent tubes of old office buildings. Countless metal canisters lay on the seats of the lower spectator level and on bare catering tables forming five or six rings around the arena floor.

All of that mad business was little more than a matte painting in a science-fiction movie compared to the monstrous spectacle in the center.

Hundreds of half-naked bodies, maybe over a thousand corpses, lay in neat rows on the arena floor. Each of their heads had been shaved just enough to clear the way for a large incision on the back of the head. Fascination gained the upper hand on revulsion, drawing Rebecca closer to the ghastly pile. There she saw the purpose of the incisions: the brains had been removed.

Walker tugged at her sleeve again. He pointed upward at the holes Rebecca had noticed before. She looked to him for an explanation.

"The place is rigged for implosion," he said.

"How do you know that?" She remembered he'd done construction work and said, "Never mind. What the hell are they doing with these ... remains?"

She couldn't bring herself to say "brains."

"Their devices affect our thoughts. You felt it, but you stopped the thing before it could control you. Maybe this is some way of affecting many people at once."

"The whole city," Rebecca whispered. She tried not to imagine the effect, but thoughts of plague and Hiroshima roiled in her imagination.

Walker dropped to the floor. She did the same before following his gaze to another arena entrance.

A pair of hovering mi-go glided down the stairway. From the semi-crustacean limbs of one dangled a coil of cable and a pair of plastic grocery bags. The other dragged the limp body of a man dressed like the security guard they had spotted earlier.

"They're eating their own," whispered Walker.

Rebecca sensed that he was correct and that it must mean they were near to ... what? Broadcast? Detonation?

She had no idea which would be worse.

More importantly, she had no idea what to do about either prospect.

"Can you —?"

A spray of automatic fire covered them in fragments of concrete. Walker jerked to the side. Rebecca crouched and raised her weapon, seeking a target. The bald security guard stood at the top of the ramp. She squeezed off two shots. He withdrew behind the corner.

Walker took a step and fell. Rebecca pulled him by the shoulder of his jacket and retreated to the stands. When Baldy poked his head around the corner, she fired another round. His head snapped back and he hit the floor.

The gunfire alerted the mi-go, who dropped their burdens and floated away from the commotion.

Rebecca lifted the hand Walker pressed just above his left hip. It was a clean wound, through and through. Not good, but not as bad as it could be.

"We've got to get out of here and report what we've seen."

He barked his astonishment. "To whom?"

Rebecca blinked at his exacting grammar, but she got the point. Even if she was wrong about the lieutenant, it took a lot of clout to allow a thing like this to happen in the Kingdome of all places. If the issue was as urgent as she felt, she'd have to deal with it herself.

"Can you blow this place?" she said.

"Probably, if we can find the detonator."

She scanned the arena and saw no sign of the mi-go. "Start looking."

Rebecca ran over to the fallen guard. Her shot had struck him in the cheek, and the exit wound had sprayed a ragged cone on the floor behind him. She collected his machine gun and tried not to think about the fact that this was her first kill.

Walker was already hustling around the ring of canisters. He paused to open one, his fingers twisting and pressing at catches she couldn't see. At last the cylinder split vertically, releasing a pink-gray mass of exactly what she had feared was inside. A high pitch whine rose from the table he had disturbed. An alarm.

"Forget that," she said. "Follow the explosives."

She followed about ten feet behind Walker, keeping her eyes on the entrances. When she caught a flicker of green light from above, she realized her mistake. By the time she raised her weapon, the nauseating sting was in her eyes.

Rebecca aimed at the center of the green blur and fired a round. She blinked, fixed on the target, and fired two more.

It felt as though a cold hand slipped inside the back of her neck and gripped her spine just below her brain. For an instant she saw it all in perfect clarity.

She and a thousand like her would be the conduit of the message. Their thoughts, harnessed and aligned, would inform the thoughts of every human mind watching listening reading the television radio Internet. She could not know the content of the message, but every atom of her body yearned to deliver it.

And yet not every atom of her body was necessary to the conduit. A facilitator would arrive to divide her useful essence from the dross. Before the facilitator could approach, however, she had to remove the interference.

She aimed the Glock at Walker and fired. The shot missed him by yards. His eyes widened, and he dove behind the cover of the arena seats. She fired again, again, each time closer to his last position.

Rebecca realized what she was doing and tried to throw the gun away. She managed to point it at the ceiling before she paused, reconsidering her action.

What was it she was supposed to do here?

The heckling laughter of automatic fire interrupted her reverie. Another security guard had appeared. He stood over the limp body of the man the mi-go had dropped and shouted, "Steve, what the fuck? What the fuck, Steve!" He fired into the upper stands, spraying bullets across the area where Rebecca had last seen the green light.

The feeling of a hand on her spine relaxed.

"Walker, are you all right?"

He did not raise his head, but she heard his muffled voice reply, "I'm okay."

"I'm going to get away from you and find some more of those things. You try to blow this place."

She ran for the nearest entrance, but Steve's buddy spotted her movement. He swung his Uzi in her direction, but she was faster. She threw him three quick rounds from the Glock, and he hit the floor grasping his belly.

Rebecca put her back against the wall of the entrance and holstered the pistol. She raised the Glock and scanned the upper rings for movement. When she saw a dark crustacean shape floating thirty yards away, she fired a burst. She held the trigger longer than she'd intended and lost count of the rounds. Six or eight, at least. Enough to make the thing withdraw.

She ran out of the arena into the outer hall. There she surprised another security guard, leveling the Uzi at his face before he could raise his weapon.

"Drop it," she said. When he complied, she said, "Get the hell out of here."

The man fled. She took his weapon.

The panic of surrendering to the alien impulse subsided. She didn't think she was a danger to Walker any longer, but she was reluctant to return to the open space of the arena. She could at least clear more of the guards or their masters from the perimeter.

She continued the circuit with the extra Uzi slung around her shoulder. When she saw a green reflection on the walls ahead, she fired several bursts and kept running forward. With every second, she doubted her choice. She should be with Walker to protect him, or else she should run. Even if she couldn't find help, she could at least get away from those canisters. She would rather die than become a bodiless prisoner.

Walker's voice called out, barely audible above the buzzing inside the arena. Rebecca followed it to the next entrance, paused at the corner to check for enemies, and ran inside.

His voice came from an unexpected direction, a trick of the acoustics of the stripped-down arena. "Found it."

"Good. What do you think, ten minutes? Five? How far away do we need to be?"

"Go now," he said. "I'll be right behind you."

At the time, it seemed only reasonable. When Rebecca felt the inaudible buzzing of the mi-go approach, she ran for the outer doors. The fifth one she tried wasn't locked, and she burst out into the sunlight. Across the parking lot, she saw the guard she'd released running to the east. She went west, toward the fence Walker had cut.

She almost made it when the shock wave threw her against the chain links and pushed her through the ragged gap. For an instant she saw the blue sky, and then she saw only smoke. She heard a dull thrumming in her head.

Then she heard the buzzing that was not a sound but a transmission.

There's an election coming, if you can call it that. It's all the other walkers talk about, until they notice I'm nearby. Some of them blame me for what happened to Henry. Or Harry, or Hal, or Hank, or whatever he called himself. I'm sorry I never found out his real name. He was nice.

Most won't even listen to me anymore. They must think something happened to me when the Kingdome went down. Some of them know what really happened, but they don't let on. They pretend it was all a planned demolition, like the broadcasts showed them. They don't remember that no one mentioned a new arena before March 26, only afterward.

Oh, sure, you can look it up online. I suppose you can even find a copy of the newspapers they manufactured after the explosion. But you couldn't do that before. It's all after the fact.

Just like me. I'm after the fact.

Sometimes I take the bus or walk back to my old condo. There's a new couple living there now. I could have gone back, but I knew it was a trap. It's enough to have a look once in a while to remember how dangerous it is.

That first night they were waiting for me inside, so I didn't linger. I found Walker's tarp where he'd left it. It isn't warm, but it keeps the damp off, and I feel safe there when the seizures are bad. I don't remember having them before the kingdom fell, but I have them all the time now.

For the rest I make do with what change people can spare.

I watch the faces of the people who go by. I listen for the buzz that isn't a sound, but I still don't know what message it transmits. I'll figure it out one day, when the seizures let up. It's easier when I keep moving. I like to take the bus around the city, but most of the time I walk.

And I Feel Fine

Robin D Laws

I'm climbing up up up up up UP up up UP through sudden
twilight. Grabbing girders. Wriggling through jabbing lengths
of exposed, twisted rebar.

Pulverized grit showers down. Hits me in the face. Gets in my
eyes.

It feels like forever, but has really probably been minutes, since
I was strolling through level three of the underground parking
lot, having slammed shut the door of my champagne-colored late
model mid-size fuel efficient family sedan, laptop bag slung over
left shoulder, travel mug of rapidly cooling Timmy's in my right
hand, thinking about the paper trail for the Lennox and Euclid
property line dispute, thinking about the kids' soccer schedule,
thinking about possibly ditching the lunch she packed for me in
favor of the new Korean place down in the food court

When WHAM

The world upends.

Breaking it down, because likely it will prove important, when
I get up top, if I get up top, to understand the nature of the calamity
and navigate accordingly:

Felt it first in my feet. A shifting. Not like the gentle wuss-ass earthquakes we oh so rarely get around here. A wrenching back and forth of the concrete beneath my sneakered feet. (Thank goodness, by the way, for the habit of putting on the dress shoes only upon arrival in the office. The pebbly worn undersurface of my Chuck Taylors coping surprisingly well on bent steel and crumbling concrete.)

After the tremor, the sound. Distant and all around me all at once. Omnidirectional. It comes from below, from the sides, from above. Registering in my bones and in the pit of my gut before I can hear it as a sound. Running up the tonal scale from subliminal bass, crescendoing, crescendoing, from roar to screech. When it hits the high notes my knees give out. I fold. Lie on cold parking surface, hands covering the sides of my head. I realize I am wailing along with it. My screams echoing the world's. Dampness on my palms: I check them and, yes, it's blood. Pouring from my ears, drenching my neck, soaking into the collar of my shirt, the collar of my jacket.

Then the instant of silence, the oh shit silence, the calm before the cataclysm. Then everything coming apart. The girders and beams of the structure's metal skeleton, shaking itself like a wet dog. Shedding concrete blocks, wiring, light fixtures, signage, junction boxes.

Explosions of sparks.

Fire.

Ceiling chunks whump down onto vehicles. Car alarms chorus. I *can* hear and *can't* hear. The sound underwater, muffled, overwritten by a cycling cicada buzz.

I crawl under an SUV. Hope it doesn't collapse. Hope it doesn't catch fire. The structure pancakes down.

Lying flat, I see the dead. Heavy woman in security guard uniform by the elevator door. Blond ponytail woman, paralegal-looking, by the wheel of a minivan, legs broken and splayed. Part of a business-suited torso.

Gilbert from document management still alive by the handicap spaces. Debris pins his legs. Eyes bolted open. Screaming like

I am screaming. I consider crawling out and rescuing him. My body won't let me. *You're going to fucking survive this.* From deep within the voice emanates. Like from my center of gravity. *Think of her. Think of the kids. Fuck Gilbert. Gilbert shares none of your DNA. Fuck everyone else. Them only. Survive for them. Survive for their survival.*

Plummeting rubble renders moot the one-sided internal debate. It pulps Gilbert's shrieking head.

SUV shock absorbers shudder as more debris lands on the vehicle roof. I flatten. The car holds.

Then the dust cloud. Powdered building floating all around. The falls let up. A great groaning overhead. Won't hold for long. The survival voice tells me it's time. Time to get out.

It is not a level of underground parking anymore. It is a column of collapsed materials. Small pockets of space between disarranged building elements.

I can hardly see. Faint beams of light moting through the gathering dust. Piercing from above.

Climb up into those spaces, the survival voice tells me.

You've got to be fucking kidding, I tell it back.

So it disables my faculties of higher reasoning. My inability to process, my unwillingness to suspend disbelief—these are not positive traits in this situation. The voice rewires me.

I find myself hopping onto the caved-in SUV roof. From there onto a minivan. From there onto a Prius, which is flipped onto its passenger side, which has been thrown onto the driver's side of a crumpled sporty mid-life crisis urban pick-up truck. Cherry red, it looks like.

The Prius topples beneath me but by then I am holding onto a dangling electrical bundle. On one level I am thinking that what I am doing is crazy. The insistent voiceover that has commandeered my head instructs my incredulous prefrontal cortex to STFU.

From there I don't so much listen to the voice as obey it unquestioningly. And that's how I am climbing up up up up up UP up up UP. Girders, rebar, grit. Wriggling, pulling, resting, anticipating its shifts, waiting them out, moving on. There are still aftershocks, or writhings, or whatever they are. Below my feet the spaces I crawled up through have pressed themselves shut.

Something is strange with my feet. My first thought is, I've injured them but I'm not feeling them because I've gone into shock. The sneaker has entirely come off my left foot. The right sneaker is ripped and bursting. Are they swelling? Slashed open? It's hard to tell, because they're covered with dust. They're cremains-gray. The nails look extra long and yellow, like the toes are extruding them. It's weird, because I clipped them just the other day. Maybe it's the other way around. The flesh of the toes is retreating from the nails, making them look bigger. They feel off but then all of my body feels that way.

More shifting above. New spaces open up. The survival voice scuttles me up through them. I see the same illusion affects the nails of my hands. They too seem longer, yellower. And jagged and bloody, of course. This climbing is tearing them up. I scrape and stretch through snapped spears of stress-graded lumber, through cement chunks, through painted tarmac. I clamber through a layer of cars. To get to one space I open the rear door of a tuna-canned Chevy Malibu and lever myself through its popped trunk. Stereo cords constrict around my legs. I rip them loose.

A childhood dream dredges itself from the memory vault. I am buried and digging to the surface. Through earthen tunnels my kid frame motors. With oak roots for handholds, I heave myself toward a faint and distant light. I displace stones and sticks and bones. All roll beneath my shoeless feet. Giving me traction. Lending me purchase.

Epiphany klaxons. I used to have this dream all the time.

Though you think it would be, it was never a scary dream. It was fun, it was playing. I would wake up from the dream with excitement raging through my veins. Like in my sleep I'd eaten a dozen candy bars. Yet instinctively I knew it was a secret, not to be shared with Mom or Dad. Mom because she was frightened of me being frightened, always hiding from me horror images and monster stuff, no matter how mild. Dad because he was frightened of Mom, or at least of her displeasure.

It doesn't go with my job description as an expert in real estate and property litigation, but on occasion I wonder about psychic stuff. What if premonitions are the terrible events that happen to you, rocketing backwards through time, to reach you as a warning?

In other words, the dreams of happy tunnel-crawling, the fearless movement toward the light: was my trauma in this moment sending them back to my past self, to my childhood bunkbed, into my dreams?

Or did I know then what would happen now. Were they a rehearsal?

Option two is the more optimistic one, so I decide that. I let my body fall back into the state of those dreams. Embrace whatever instinct they encoded in me.

The way becomes harder, but the progress swifter.

I hear street sounds. A new round of alarms. Sirens. Moans. Intermittent impacts. The shafts of light transition from very dim to a little less so.

Physically, I am definitely messed up. When the shock wears off the check's gonna come, and it will be a motherfucker. It's exhilaration now, but beneath it the signals are beyond haywire. I've been rearranged like this former parking garage has been rearranged. My bones twisted like its girders. The muscles stretched and bruised around them. I am an adrenaline throb. Even my face feels wrong. Like it is elongating, pulling my nose and teeth forward, my ears back. I could swear to you my brow is sliding down, my eyes pushing back to shelter themselves beneath its expanding shelf. My ears wrapping back. The skull flattening.

This isn't possible, is it?

I'm delirious, hallucinating.

Maybe I'm still back under that car. Crushed and dying. The climbing, my personalized white-light tunnel. The debris column, my Owl Creek Bridge.

Don't think about that now, the survival voice tells me.

It blankets me with determination, concentration. It shuts off the eternal processing of the internal monologue. Upward it pushes me, through another floor of rapid-junked cars. Scrabbling and squeezing.

I grab onto what I think is a cord and it's a woman's dead slim arm. Hunger wracks me. The human body is a crazy thing. It must have twigged to the energy deficit I'm putting it through.

Panicking, I try to get her blood off my face and hands. I only end up smearing it on me. Some gets in my mouth. It's coppery. The image of the steak from last night's partners' meeting pops to mind. Ultra-rare. Sprig of rosemary on top. The secret's in the garlic rub.

Another rush I didn't think I had. Up up up up up. Clawing, pulling, flattening. Stuff falls upon me as I tear at the wreckage it rests on: a fire extinguisher, half a GPS tracker, a miraculously untouched full box of Krispy Kremes, scalp bits. Up UP up up up.

And I'm out. Nosing from the ruins like a gopher from a hole. Chunks of mortar rolling off my suit-jacketed back. Like the departed burrowing from their graves on resurrection day.

I expect rescuers, cops, ambulances, hard hats, urgent shouts, flashing lights, bullhorns, sparking saws slicing through rubble. Nothing but eerie quiet. Where are the first responders, and why are they not first responding?

Then I see: it's not the building. It's the whole city.

It has to be a war. This can only be a bomb. The nuke plant out in the exurbs couldn't do this degree of damage, not here, not even worst-case. So scratch that. It has to be The Bomb.

The mental disconnection goes loopier. Here I am, swaying, wounded, mere shambled steps from my exit point, and the processor kicks in, and all it has to contribute is: *the geopolitical situation had its kinks, but I sure had no inkling this was coming.*

The survival voice puts the intellect back in its box for the duration. It says:

You've got to keep moving.
This is not safety.

Getting yourself out was step one only.
You've got to find them.
It's about them.
They are your DNA.
Family, if you want to call it that.

Survival voice interrogates intellectual processing while leaving it constrained in its box: *Where are they?*

Luckily, replies intellectual processing, it is a PD Day at school, so they're home with her. All of them are home together.

Then we're going home, says survival voice, and I hurl myself, staggering, limping, onto the pitched-in street.

Only then do I look around, and at that strictly to assess routes and degrees of hazard.

Hearing is still shot, a dulled electronic flatline overlay obscuring everything. Beneath that: keening metal, shattering glass, heaving pavement. Beneath that: weeping, groaning, and a distant half-song. This last noise bores into me. It scares the part of me I identify as myself. It also scares the detached overseeing impulse I have hived off and am referring to as survival voice. There is so much weirdness to grapple with. The fact that somebody has chosen, in response to this unfolding disaster, to make music. The droning notes themselves, both vocalized and not, like Enya crossed with death metal. If it's words they're singing it's not in any language I understand.

And yet, I do.

I shrug off the sound. I ignore the smells, which are the blood and dust coating my nostrils from the ascent.

Visuals. The towers of the financial district sway like plastered drinking buddies. They shuck off their windows, their metal framing. A crevasse widens in the street, as if it's been sliced open on the lane dividers. Pavement pulls away from the streetcar tracks as it drops into the hole. A streetcar teeters on the edge. The handful of people still in its seats are either unconscious or dead. The driver's body—headless for some reason—pitches forward. The streetcar pitches forward. Its dedicated overhead power lines snap. They wildly whip-snake across the street. I duck back. The end lashes past me, zapping around a marble stanchion.

Smoke envelops the disappearing streetcar as it slips into the hole. Empty trucks and cars, doors flung open, follow it down.

This street is toast. I get the eff out of Dodge. My gait is completely screwed. I'm still not hurting yet, which is simultaneously a godsend and alarming as crap. Weirdly, I'm fast, but in a hunched-over, loping way. I check the soles of my feet. The other shoe is gone, too. If I were remotely aware of my own condition I'd double over and hurl. The layer of ground-in debris jammed into the skin is almost sole-thick. It's glass mostly, with concrete pebbles and fragments of melted plastic thrown in for variety. The toes still look too long, the nails longer still. The thought that this is an elaborate hallucination crowds in again until survival voice bats it away.

The moment I'm no longer in any building's shadow, I stop to orient myself. My heart should be a raging industrial press but I can't even feel it pump.

It takes effort to straighten my spine. I three-sixty the city. Gray-black billows veil the skyline. It's hard to tell but it seems like a bunch of the landmark buildings are gone. Like teeth punched out of a guy's mouth.

A shockwave sends me airborne. I land on chin, chest and elbows. Rolling, I see that the Commerce Court has fallen.

Home is north. I need the shortest route with the lowest density. Smaller buildings equals less to fall over onto me. I'm on foot so I don't have to worry about traffic. A bunch of sideways jogs will get me out of the downtown and into a circuit of residential neighborhoods.

I speed my lope.

In the square up ahead I see my first living people since Gilbert cashed out. A pair of cops and a couple dozen civilians huddle on the pavement. They cluster on the part of the square closest to the street, out of topple range of the city hall building. All of them ghosted by a thick layer of dust. The cops wave shotguns like aimless pointers.

Maybe they have water. Or a medic and an aid kit. I stumble their way. The civilians stand. They're shrieking, as if something awful looms up behind me. I whirl but see nothing, so I continue on toward them.

The cops aim their shotguns. Stupidly, I turn again. What can I be missing? Then off blasts a round.

Survival voice: *Move your ass, nitwit! It's you they're shooting at!*

I try to shout at them but produce only strangled, high-pitched garble. Has my voicebox been crushed? The shot goes way wide. I think I might be out of range. The cop is definitely shaking and so are the concrete slabs beneath his feet.

I bound a retreat. I can't go south; there is no south anymore, just fallen skyscrapers. Crazy shotgun cop's crazy shotgun cuts off my desired route west and alternate route north. He's leaving me no choice but to go east, deeper into the commercial district. There's a park a few blocks away. Maybe I can deke north through it, then into a different residential zone, then make my way east further up.

A wind descends. It blows dust and shards at my back. Overhead billows part. The sky is red and orange. It swirls like one of those sixties rock band light shows. Red blobs eat orange blobs. Orange blobs explode as seeds within them, popping the red blobs. Then all over again.

Bodies strew the street. A few wounded people shelter in front of shattered shop windows. Some shrink back when they see me. Most stare inwards, completely shut down. I'm not here. They're not there. I want to yell at them to get out of debris range of any building. Their stunned faces tell me I won't get through. Even if I can force decipherable sounds from my larynx.

Up ahead a streetcar lies on its side. A hunchbacked figure scuttles at it. His clothes have been blasted off and he's a mess of open sores. He punches in a window. Reaching in, he starts scavenging. I react initially with outrage—he thinks this is a looting opportunity? Then I figure he must be replacing his missing clothing and see his side of it. Then I see blood spurting onto his arms and face and go far, far past outrage.

Finally it starts to seep in that whatever is happening belongs to some other frame of reference entirely. This isn't a person raiding the fallen streetcar. He tears at dead flesh—what I hope is dead flesh—with elongated arms. Clawing nails slice and dice. The hairless face mixes features of dog and caveman. It's hard to tell with the gobbets of meat on its face, but the mouth looks like a freaking snout. Legs fold beneath him, lever-legged like a toad, reverse-kneed like an ostrich.

I've tottered closer to it. Only a few dozen yards separate us. The mechanics of those legs could send it leaping onto me in a few easy hops.

Intellectual processing re-emerges to toss a question at survival voice: *Why the hell didn't you pull me out of this?*

The scavenger takes notice of me. Locks eye-contact. A gnawed ear falls from the grip of sharkish teeth. It plops onto his clawed foot.

The ghoul produces a sound: *Meep.*

Then the shitstorm. Non-metaphorical. Loose stool precipitates from the brown and roiling sky. Fecal clumps thud like hail. They smack against fallen, leaning shards of plate glass. Explode on ruptured pavement. They slick surfaces. Shuffling survivors slip and slide. It's not a pissing rain, it's raining piss. Steaming, acidic urine sheets down.

I run for cover. I lose my balance. I carom off the pavement. I bump into a wall and hit my head. I stagger up. I learn to use my new leg configuration. I leap. The shitstorm is localized. I outpace it.

I reach the park.

A block further down lies the blazing hospital. An enormous object juts from a blown-out window bank. It's a long tube, glistening like fish-skin. Spot fires dot its scales. The end of the tube puckers. Hooks and suckers line the rim. Battered survivors, heads bobbing as if hypnotized, form a queue before it. At the head of the line stands a lithe, short girl with a ballet dancer's body. She throws back her arms and raises her swanning neck. Feelers enfold her. They push her into the hooks. They pierce her flesh, forcing her onto the suckers. Together the appendages shove her through a bony mesh. It's like those baleen things that whales use to scoop up plankton. Just before she liquefies, the dancer recovers her senses and fights back, wailing. Then she's blood spray. The person in line behind her doesn't flinch. A salesman type in suit and tie. He relaxes his frame and leans into the tube's embrace. Feelers enfold him.

The survival voice says: *That's a god.*

Or part of one.

They're worshiping.

I run.

I zig through the park, around crisped trees, over blackened grass. A landmark stands at the heart of the park: a towering church. Yellow-brown bricks pelt down from it. Creatures stick to its roofs and steeples. They're escapees from a deep-sea nature documentary, blown up as big as buses. With crayfish claws they cling to its green copper spires. With translucent appendages they tear at its window frames and wrench loose its guttering.

Why is all this happening?

For no reason at all, the survival voice answers.

For no reason at all?

It's just what happens.

But I have to understand.

You can't and you won't and it doesn't matter.

I hit the street adjacent. Past burning pawn shops, crumpled nail salons, collapsed variety stores. Buildings here are three stories, tops. Half are already rubbled. Blocked by smoking, overturned cars, I skitter up a slope of stone facing and pavement chunks.

There is one thing you do have to understand, the voice tells me.

A crazed melee breaks from a half-extant newspaper office. The crowd divides into beater and beaten. They drop a television set on an elderly woman's head. They're smashing a baby stroller. If I knew who to pray to, I'd pray for it to be empty.

Turning west will take me back toward the high buildings. East will divert me even further from my destination. I decide to chance the mob. They're busy whaling on each other. Maybe they won't come at me.

I skulk the perimeter of a caved-in parking lot. Crouching behind the remains of the attendant's booth, I wait for a moment of maximum chaos. Then I'll make my sprint for it.

Closer up, I can see that not all of the people in the flailing scrum are people. Not any more. They used to be, judging from the scraps of clothing still clinging to them: distended T-shirts, scraps of sports sock, bits of jewelry, tattoos stretched out of shape on impossible flesh. Some are man-apes now: sprouting coarse hair, baring dagger teeth. Others fuse features of human, frog and fish. They're devolving on the spot. It's these beings who lead the rampage. They howl in pain and visit that pain on the ones who aren't changing. Two of the fish-men pick up a goateed bike courier and pull him apart. The entire crowd, including them, pauses for a gasp of collective revulsion. Courier viscera spatters broken tarmac. The ape-men notice the fish-men. The fish-men notice the ape-men. The ape-men hiss. The fish-men gurgle. They launch themselves at one another. They rend and bite and slash. The undevolved crawl away sobbing.

This is my moment. I sprint around the skirmish. A wounded man on hands and knees changes course to avoid a falling fish-man. I clip him with my foot. He tumbles. I tumble. I'm up on my feet seconds later but the devolved have spotted me. I belt it out of there. Objects hurl at my back. They hit my neck and shoulders. A car mirror bounces off my head, drawing blood. I find more speed. A clarity descends on me as I give in to the exertion. Soon this is going to cost me. One body can produce only so much adrenaline. There is so much running left to do.

I scan the avenue ahead. Smoke clouds restrict visibility to a few blocks. No signs of mob scenes. People gather in twos and threes. Nobody's on the move. Finally I can close some distance.

Survival voice repeats a statement from before the mob attack: *There's something you have to understand.*

I have to get back to them, I think. The workings of my dissociation do not concern me. I am not asking myself why it knows stuff I don't.

You're going in here, it decides.

Seizing control of my gross motor functions, survival voice steers me over the demolished threshold of a décor shop. I wade through ankle-deep glass shards. At the back of the store there's a wall of mirrors and miraculously a couple of them are still mostly intact. I see myself.

I'm an exact double for one of the creatures back there. The solitary one feeding off the streetcar victims. It's a point-for-point match. The elongated snout. The recessed eyes. The pulled-back ears. Clawed fingers, clawed feet, the reversed lever legs. I tug at my rubbery hide. I expose a mouth of blackened gums and gator teeth. Thick tears occlude my vision. A grotesque self swims back at me.

I've devolved.

Why?

It's always been in you.

Memories flash. Mental locks untumble.

My mother, at the kitchen table, the plastic tablecloth with the apple and pear design. Late grade school. As a project, I'm supposed to research our family tree. She's discouraging me from covering her side of the family. "Do your father's instead," she tells me. She says it's more interesting—there's the founder of a town and a cabinet minister. I do not think this is more interesting, because I've heard hints at gatherings, about a crazy uncle who got in trouble selling coffins dug up from cemeteries. That's not as good as a horse thief or pirate, but it will do. Then another flash: I'm working on the project and drawing in the entry for the founder and the cabinet minister.

Ahead six years: my mother dead. I'm lying on my bedroom floor, over the heat register, listening to an argument between my dad and my maternal grandmother. My dad wants an open casket, like his family has always had. Grandmother says under no conditions and in fact Mom will be cremated, in accordance with her wishes, as her family has always done. And there will be no headstone, no burial of the ashes. Grandmother warns him of consequences. He scoffs. But flash ahead to the memorial service: she's on a plaster pedestal, in a marble urn.

I'm in your blood, says survival voice. *Many thought themselves wholly human, but had a trace of other pumping in their arteries. Until today, when the other broke loose.*

No, I think. At long last the crash of exhaustion comes. I fold. I throw myself into the only unbroken chair: a faux antique of wood and leather. I can't imagine moving. I have to rest.

No, says survival voice. *You have to keep moving.*

I can't.

You must.

I physically can't. Hard to believe I got this far.

You must. The voice swivels my head.

Poking out from behind the counter, I see a slender, gore-specked arm.

No.

You must.

I can't.

You can.

I won't.

You will.

Then I am over at the woman's side. She's not moving. With my new clawed hand I try to find a pulse. I was never any good at this before.

She's dead. You know this. The smell tells you. It's instinct.

No.

Yes.

There's a cleaning rag behind the counter. I lumber to the bathroom, in the back. Pour water on the rag. Go back and clean the fine white particulate from her arm. I undress her. I bite down, starting with the forearm.

I am moving again. The feed has replenished me. Days may have passed now. It is hard to judge. Since the disaster there has been no sun. The sky irregularly shifts from the swirl of red and orange to blackness. Bloated new stars hang low over the toppled city. I haven't seen a functioning clock since I left the downtown core.

Visions from the journey crowd my head.

In the sky, black-winged phantoms glide and caterwaul.

The horizon shifts. I turn on my heels to face the waterfront. A vast shape rises from the lake. Fat stars dance around it. The ground rumbles as more buildings drop.

Fluids rain down. Blood. Sputum. Bile. A clear and ropy substance I don't want to think about. Where it lands, the plants transfigure. There's a color in them I've never seen before. That's not supposed to be possible.

On a grade school track field, writhing figures furiously copulate. Their heads split open and blossom like meat flowers. They keep at it.

Tracked vehicles mobilize down a residential street. I duck behind a low stand of Chinese sumacs. Soldiers and irregulars perch on top. Assault rifles in hand, they strike vigilant poses.

I wait till they're out of sight before moving again. Not long after, I hear screams and autofire from their general direction. The screams outlast the autofire.

A fish-man hangs crucified on an electrical pole. They used a nail gun. It croaks at me. I trot on past it.

The residential areas are not quite so hard hit as the downtown. Maybe one in five homes is burned out or flattened. The destruction is randomly distributed. Cars choke some streets; others are clear. The dead have been piled on the curbs, like banks of snow.

Suddenly ravenous, I stop to haul a fat dude in flip-flops and a jam band T-shirt into an open tool shed. This time I do not bother with the washcloth before cracking his ribcage.

I reach my neighborhood. I haven't been letting myself compute the odds of their being okay. On that one, the survival voice and I are in agreement.

Finally, I turn onto my street. There's a commotion at the end of the cul de sac. Hollering. Rocks thrown against brick. Breaking bottles. A rhythmic pounding on recycling containers.

They're in front of our house. A crowd of a couple dozen, give or take. The words are tough to discern.

I hear, "Get out!"

I hear, "You can't be here!"

I hear, "Monsters!"

I hear, "Ghouls!"

I put it together. If the disorder is in my blood, it's in the kids' blood, too. They've devolved, just like Pop. The nabes have seen them. The nabes are restless.

They must still be alive.

Is she?

The mob is so intent on the house that none of them are looking behind them. I stalk up the middle of the roadway. Nearing my destination, I can see that the roof drips with water. It's been hosed down, as protection against Molotov cocktails and other flaming projectiles. The kids could never have thought of it or pulled it off. That has to have been her. She's alive too. Unless they got her in the interim.

In their hands: metal pipes, kitchen knives, two-by-fours. There's only one gun I can make out. Thank goodness this isn't Detroit.

Is this happening in Detroit?

Is it happening everywhere?

I'm nearly on them when one guy turns around and yells. It's Mr. Friedrichsen, who wears a farm equipment baseball cap even though he's a retired actuary. "Holy shit it's another of them! They're coming! They're coming!"

He swipes at me with a cleaver. I snarl and stomp a foot toward him. Mr. F blanches and leaps back.

He's cleared the way for the guy with the gun. I don't recognize him. He might be one of the recent move-ins who bought the Melkus place.

I try to duck but you can't duck a gunshot. The moment of impact is like a wallop with a board. I stagger back but stay upright. The bullet hole sizzles between my second and third ribs, on the left hand side. So much for the survival voice.

I wait for the gusher of blood.

All that leaks out is a clear, mucus stream. The hole spits out the bullet. Its rubber edges seal up.

I leap onto the gunman, knocking him down. I tear the pistol from his hand. I beat him in the face with it. His jaw cracks in two. He slumps. I smack him a few more times.

Everyone else stands there, stupid with incredulity.

My altered hand is no longer designed for a pistol grip and trigger. Awkwardly I thread my claws around and through. I wave the gun around. The muzzle aims at whoever's closest.

I try to reason with them but the sounds come out burbled. One genius locates the nerve to edge up behind me. I smell him coming. I turn and gut-shoot him. He drops. It's Sam Peterson, who organizes the annual street festival.

The crowd surges in. I empty the pistol at them. About half of the rounds land true.

Bodies all around me. Instinct begs me, wheedling, cajoling, to hunker down and start chowing. It's freaky and deep but I suppress it.

A woman throws a frying pan at me. I duck. It hits Todd Lobke, who has been trying to get a headlock on me. In the moment of distraction I dig claws into his throat. The woman barrels at me, weaponless. I grip her forearm and snap it.

Blows land on my shoulders and kidneys. They're smashing me with fists and goalie sticks. I whirl around, slashing blindly. There's pulped tissue in my hand. An eyeball stuck on the nail of my right index finger. I flick it off, appalled. Now it's my turn to pay the price of distraction. I take a shot to the face. I blur down. I'm on my knees. I'm about to pass out.

Imagine what will happen to them if these people get inside the house.

There's a booted foot kicking at me. I bite into the ankle. My snouted jaws go clean through. I bat the foot away. Its owner falls. It's Stanton, from across the way. I grab his body to use as a shield against further blows. Some neighbors stop hitting, others keep on. Stanton bleeds out, twitching. Behind him I see Ronna Adkins, the student who rents our basement apartment, slip on his gouting blood. Clamping hands grab me and pull me out from under Stanton's body. Already it smells dead and fortifying. It's Ted Nolan hauling on me. He gets his face in mine. I bite it off and spit it out. I clamber up, grabbing Mr. Falcioni, who shares his pears in the fall. It's his arm I have in my grip, and I pop it from its socket. He collapses; with a swift kick I rake his balls off.

"You were going to kill my family!" I try to yell. It's all meeps and murmurs.

Most are running away now but a few have yet to get the message. They've lost their fucking minds, I guess. I stuff both my hands into Molly Hohman's mouth, smashing through teeth on the way in. Then I pull them apart. Dan DeVille I slash open from hip to collar. It's like turning him inside out. The Ward kid is trying to light a Molotov. I bound at him and one-eighty his neck. The lighter catches the rag as he dies. I hurl it at my retreating neighbors. Mr. Hay, Mrs. Rose, and Tad Hentges run around burning.

They're all fleeing, except for some slackjaw teenager I don't recognize. He's reaching for the gun, not getting that it's empty. I only break his wrist, crushing it with my springy heel.

I burst through the door, my white-green hide painted blood-red. The kids recoil, even though the resemblance between us has never been tighter.

She's there, too. She has a flare gun from the cottage ready to go. It fits poorly in her clawed fingers.

More flashes: no one ever got us as a couple. We never really got us. Why we were drawn together so completely, so immediately. Despite our lack of apparent compatibility on every outward metric: money, heritage, education, looks, age, biography, resumé, temperament.

The connection was in our arteries.

I pull her close. We cry, as best we can.

She licks the blood off my snout.

Months later, only the survival voice is left. The sky is always red. We've found a safer den. It hooks up to tunnels. They in turn lead to a land of dreams. That isn't what it used to be, we're told, with most dreamers dead.

On the bright side, there's lots of food. The youngest comes in with a charred hand. He's taken a few chews out of it. We're teaching him about sharing.

The bounty of corpses won't last forever. The remaining humans aren't reproducing much. So there are long term worries. A civil war might be coming, between the original ghouls and all of us new ones. No point worrying about that until it comes, though.

We're together, and that's the important part.

Welcome to Cthulhuville

Larry DiTillio

The tropical sun felt good on Santiago's face. Heat nourished his soul. He cracked one eye open to glance at his wife, Marisol. She was at the edge of the shoreline playing with their six-year-old daughter Esmeralda. She was a beauty when he married her and the last ten years had only added to her splendor. Watching them laughing together in the surf, he felt like the luckiest man alive. Not bad for a poor *nino* from East L.A. he thought, as the cabana boy approached.

"Can I get you anything sir?" Santiago smiled. Not bad at all.

He ordered three Chi-chis, one virgin. The cabana boy nodded and turned away. As he did, Santiago noticed what looked like a brand in the shape of an octopus on the boy's shoulder. As he looked at it, it looked back at him and the sky darkened. Santiago heard screams. He turned and saw a vision from hell.

Pouring down from the firmament were black, faceless things with large bat-like wings, and curved tails. They swooped over the beachfront, carrying people away. One took Marisol; another seized Esmeralda. Santiago jumped from his chair, grabbed a chunk of driftwood and raced toward them. One of the things came for him.

He crushed what passed for its head with the driftwood, but it was too late. The creatures holding his wife and daughter soared away, their screams echoing in his mind. He sank to the sand, praying to God to save his family.

Santiago jerked awake from the recurring dream, with an anguished cry, a cry gagged by a sudden mouthful of hot blood. He retched up the meager contents of his stomach and fell face forward into them. Ugly laughter cackled in his ears as he struggled to his knees. Then he saw the blood was not his own. It spouted like a human fountain from a jagged neck wound on the decapitated torso of a heavyset man. His head lay at his own feet, dead eyes gazing comically at his mutilated flesh. Santiago rolled away from the corpse and found himself at the feet of a hulking brute with a gore-stained machete in his hand. The brute sneered down at him; displaying teeth filed to points, and spoke.

"You trying to suck up my red, dog shit!?"

Santiago didn't quite get it but he knew it meant trouble. He looked up at the brute with hard eyes, gathering what strength he had left. The brute hesitated for a moment, as Santiago's gaze bored into his; then with a smirk, raised the machete.

From his knees, Santiago smashed his balled left fist into the brute's *cojones*, doubling him over. He caught the man's descending jaw with a right uppercut, knocking him to the ground. The machete flew from his hand. Santiago dived for it as the brute began to rise. The feel of the blade in his hand gave him new hope. He whirled as his foe charged with a howl! He side-stepped the move and buried the machete in the brute's shaven skull. The man swayed for a moment, eyes wide with surprise, then toppled. Santiago roared skyward, pumping his fists in victory until something hard hit him just behind the left ear.

He stumbled forward and as fog began to fill his brain he thought he heard cheering.

Mac McMahon studied the man asleep on the makeshift cot. He seemed to be in his early thirties, his brown skin and facial features suggesting a mix of African and Hispanic. He was some six feet tall and in better shape than most of those who found their way to Canyon Haven. His muscle tone indicated an athlete, body builder or perhaps a convict. He had killed Farrow's Chief Guardian easily, as if he were used to killing. Mac hoped that was not the case. There were already far too many such men in the Canyon.

He rummaged through the man's blood-soaked clothes, which had been removed to dry. He found a hooded jacket, some worn blue jeans and a Lakers T-shirt from the 2014 NBA finals. Mac smiled as he remembered watching Game 7, a great game. It seemed so long ago now. Mac let it go. He couldn't think that way. For better or worse, this place was his world now. He turned back to his examination of the new arrival, distracting himself from the bleak reality that was 2015.

There were several old scars on his body, three from what looked like knife wounds, one from a bullet. There were also tattoos: a professional heart on his left shoulder with the name "Marisol," and three tear-drops on his right forearm that were definitely prison work. Mac shook his head; just another lost soul. He left the stranger to his rest and exited the small cavern to get some food for him.

Moments later, Santiago awoke, head pounding like a conga drum. His eyes fluttered open to see a small cavern, dimly lit by glowing fungi. He was on the floor, lying on some kind of strange ass smelling bed and naked save for his socks and sneaks!

He tried to sit up but made it only part way when his head began to swim. He lay back and shut his eyes but the swimming continued. The glowing mushrooms made the cave look like some insane Flintstones *discoteca*. He wasn't sure if he was dreaming again when he smelled something, something like... hot food! His stomach's rumble echoed like an ogre's laughter in the small cavern.

"Sounds like you're hungry son," said a kind voice.

Santiago dared to open his eyes. Looking down at him was a tall, lanky white man in his mid-seventies with Irish eyes, white hair and a moustache that crept across his face like a scrawny albino caterpillar. He was dressed in a tattered white shirt, stained black slacks and Dr. Comfort shoes. In his hands he held a stone bowl of some steaming liquid. This he set upon a low stone table a few steps away from the cot.

"This should quiet your belly for awhile," he said. "Can you stand?"

Santiago wasn't certain he could but he was not going to show weakness in front of a crazy old man. He took a deep breath and rose carefully from the floor. He swayed a bit but didn't fall. He looked down at himself and back toward Mac.

"I could use my clothes, man." Mac lifted a sopping garment from the pile he had searched. Multiple cascades of water fell on the stones of the cavern floor from it.

"Still wet. Wear this until they dry."

Mac threw a small bundle to him. Santiago caught it and untied the length of rope holding it together. It was a worn blanket with a hole in the center, a makeshift poncho. He slipped it on, tied the rope around it, went to the low stone table and sat. Mac stood watching him, as he looked warily into the stone bowl. It contained a lumpy reddish brown stew, with an enticing aroma.

Santiago poked at it. It seemed to be mainly mushrooms, the same ones that lit the cavern by their shape. He licked some off his fingertip. It was a bit salty, but not bad. He lifted the bowl, took a bigger swallow. The mushrooms were meaty in texture and felt good in his long-empty stomach. He consumed the rest in one greedy gulp and burped with great satisfaction.

"I don't know what the hell it is but it hit the spot, *vato*." Mac extended his hand.

"The name's McMahon. You can call me Mac." Santiago shook his hand and replied in kind.

"Santiago." Mac commented on the name.

"It means St. James you know." Santiago laughed.

"Everybody in East L.A. is named for a saint or the Virgin."

"You're from California then?" asked Mac. Santiago sighed and spoke, the ordeal of the past weeks spilling out of him.

"I was, before the big one. It was days before I dragged myself out of the fucking hole that used to be L.A. Weird thing is, everything was gone, like it had just been erased. No roads, no cars, no buildings, no people, *nada*! I was hoping to find a coastline but I never did. I just kept moving until I couldn't go on. I guess I must have passed out. When I woke up I was here, wherever here is.."

"We call it Canyon Haven. It's a survivor's camp," Mac replied. "It has a primitive ecosystem capable of sustaining human life. Just food and shelter at the moment but it will do until we can find out what's happened in the rest of the world. Would you like to see more of it?"

Santiago hesitated. He'd seen his family taken but the fact that others survived gave him a modicum of hope. He nodded affirmatively to Mac. Mac smiled and moved to a small niche in one of the cavern walls. He drew a folded black jacket from it and put it on. From the pocket of the jacket he drew a clerical collar which he fastened about his neck. Santiago's eyes widened at this.

"You a priest, man?" he exclaimed!

"For what it's worth, yes," sighed Mac as he started out of the cavern. Santiago followed, chuckling to himself at the irony of a priest in hell.

The cavern mouth was on a slight downhill slope at one side of the Canyon. Santiago emerged and saw what looked like a gruesome parody of a Stone Age movie.

Canyon Haven consisted of an asymmetrical box canyon of black basalt. Its walls rose from thirty to two hundred feet high and showed no obvious break. At the base of the walls sat cave mouths, some big, some small. The bottom of the canyon, the size of four *futbol* fields, was dotted with patches of thick black moss. A few odd trees stood here and there. Small black fruits hung from their gray branches.

Hundreds of people milled about in the canyon. They represented a cross section of society but no young children, fewer women than men and almost no old people. Most of them moved in a listless fashion, performing some task or other with languid movements. Others pranced about like broken puppets, chanting in a strange tongue. They were all watched by armed men with shaven heads. These were obviously compatriots of the brute Santiago had slain, confirmed when one of them noticed him and slashed a finger across his throat. Santiago clenched his fists but Mac gripped his arm tightly and spoke firmly.

"No more trouble. There's too many dead already." He knew Mac was right. If he were to survive in this place, he didn't need enemies. The shred of hope he'd carried into the canyon was gone. He felt empty now.

A teenage Japanese-American boy in an anime T-shirt and cargo pants approached them. "Farrow's ready for you guys, Father Mac."

"Thank you Shige," said Mac. The boy looked at Santiago, excited and a bit fearful, but spoke up in a gushing tribute.

"You killed Andreas good man. That was peench!" He held up a high-five and Santiago slapped it. Mac dismissed the boy with a frown of disapproval. Santiago responded with a sheepish grin as he followed Mac toward one end of the Canyon.

"I'm guessing Andreas is the *cabron* I killed. So who's Farrow?"

"He leads the Brotherhood. They run the camp."

"I hope you don't mean the Aryan Brotherhood," laughed Santiago. Mac rolled his eyes, as they continued across the floor of the canyon.

Farrow sat regally in a throne-like chair of carved stone. He was a tall, lean man, attired in a full length black and red djellaba. His skin was the color of copper, his features angular; his eyes black as a raven's feather. They were accentuated by thick black eyebrows, the only hair on his bald head. His long fingers ended in two inches of talon-like nails. These he waved toward the Guardians attending him as Mac and Santiago entered the cavern. They bowed briefly and left. This encouraged Santiago. Whoever this obvious nut job was, he didn't seem to be afraid of him. Big mistake! Mac stepped forward.

"Farrow, this is Santiago. He came from Los Angeles. He..." Farrow's voice interrupted the priest. It was an unpleasant voice, a rustle of dead leaves.

"That will suffice, Father. First we must discuss the matter of Andreas."

Farrow rose from the chair. Santiago weighed his options at light speed. He could run or take Farrow as a hostage. Farrow was as tall as he was but obviously many years older. There were only some ten paces between him and the throne—and then there weren't....

Farrow's face was somehow an inch from his own, his black eyes staring into Santiago's. It felt like ants crawling into his eye sockets. More dead leaves rustled.

"So tell me Santiago how is it a starving man who has traveled so far kills my Chief Guardian in a few seconds?"

Santiago chose his words carefully and delivered them calmly.

"The muthafuka was trying to take my head off. I took his first. Sorry."

Mac sucked in a breath. There was an eternal moment of silence, then, amazingly, Farrow stepped back, and laughed!

"Excellent answer, honest and to the point," he said.

Santiago was still wary.

"So we're good, right homie?" Farrow smiled; took a step closer to Santiago and whispered into his ear.

"Andreas was blood sick and stupid. But he was my best. So I must have something—homie."

Farrow flicked his finger across Santiago's left cheek, drawing blood. This he delicately licked off his fingernail. In his mind Farrow saw Santiago's whole life in a matter of seconds. Every misdeed, every lie, every beating, every killing. And with his family gone, hate was the dominant emotion in his heart. He was perfect for what Farrow had planned.

"What the fuck was that for?" spit Santiago.

"To remind you that actions carry consequences even in this insane world," replied Farrow. 'Now go. We'll decide how we can best use your skills here later. You can bunk with our good priest for the moment, if it's alright with him."

Mac nodded and Farrow grinned—the latter a sight Santiago hoped to never see again.

That night Santiago had a dream. It started as usual, with the memory of his wife and daughter being taken but then came a new twist. He heard a female voice, mysterious and sultry.

"Santiago, I weep for you," it purred. He turned and saw a woman in her late twenties coming toward him on the now abandoned beach. She seemed to glide over the sand, her black maxi dress fluttering around her like angel wings. Her hair was dark with a streak of white and fell to her waist. Her left eye was deep blue, her right jade green. Her mouth was a sensuous slash of red. She hovered before him and spoke again.

"Come to me Santiago. I hunger for you. Let me be your Marisol now."

Santiago could feel the heat radiating from her lovely body and it aroused him. He moved to embrace her but she was already floating away, holding out her arms to him, her voice fading to a siren whisper as she moved toward a huge dome atop a cliff overlooking a dark sea.

"Come, Santiago; let us lay together in New R'lyeh."

As she vanished thunder rolled and lightning crackled. In the brief flash he saw something unimaginably massive blotting out both the huge dome and the cliff. A voice spoke, an unearthly voice like the singing of a million whales.

"Santiago, you are my sword."

He woke, trembling and confused. Then he heard another horrid sound nearby. He turned fearfully but it was only Father Mac, snoring like a bull moose in heat. Santiago let the priest sleep and lay back down on his cot, struggling to make sense of the dream.

In his dream, Father Mac witnessed a scene of unfathomable carnage. He was on a hill looking down on an endless array of slaughtered bodies. Many were Roman soldiers. Most were men, women and children dressed in the fashion of the ancient Middle East. Then he heard a gentle voice behind him.

"Father, why hast thou forsaken me?" Trembling, Mac turned and gasped as he saw Jesus, nails in his hands and feet, thorns in his head, looking down at him from the cross. He was on Golgotha, the place of the skull. He knelt reverently before the Christ and cried aloud.

"Lord I haven't forsaken you. I just don't understand why this has happened? So many killed. So much human accomplishment and potential wiped out. Is this really an act of God?" Jesus laughed and looked upon the priest. His voice became harsh, mocking.

"How long did you think God could ignore your incessant wars and numerous crimes against your fellows and your planet? Time to pay for your *own* sins, old school style!"

Jesus pulled his right hand free of the crossbar and pointed to the horizon. Mac looked and saw the silhouette of something massive approaching, something so big he was seeing only a small fraction of it. Jesus laughed again.

"God wants a word with you," he said. Mac's eyes were fixed on the strange shape moving slowly over the immense field of corpses. Then God spoke in a voice like a million chapel bells tolling.

"McMahon, you are my Priest. The book shall show you the way."

Mac awoke weeping softly, torn by horror and hope. He did so until morning.

What passed for morning in Canyon Haven was a dull swirling gray mist offering a few rays of weak sepia-toned light. Santiago and Father Mac stepped out of the cavern into it.

Neither had spoken more than a few words, after being awakened by the boy Shige and told to report to Farrow. They walked to Farrow's cavern in silence.

There they found Farrow talking to a hearty-looking man in his thirties. He was dressed like a farmer: overalls over a wool shirt and sturdy work shoes. Farrow welcomed them as they entered.

"I trust you both slept well?" The question seemed to imply he knew about the dreams, a thought that discomfited them both. Mac and Santiago simply nodded. Farrow turned to the other man and made introductions.

"Elijah, this is Father McMahon and Santiago." The man extended his hand and spoke with a definite New England accent.

"Elijah Whateley. Everyone in New R'lyeh is anxious to meet you both." The words exploded in Santiago's mind, the words from his dream.

"What's New R'lyeh?" asked a confused Mac. Farrow answered.

"It's another survivors' camp," said Farrow. "They need someone to help them translate a book in Latin; a task Father Mac is well suited for.."Mac suddenly remembered the words in his dream. Was this a sign, he thought?

"Fine for Mac but what do I do there?" said Santiago. Farrow replied bluntly.

"Provide company for the good Father and get out of Canyon Haven. My

Guardians are still angry about Andreas. I think you'll find New R'lyeh better for your health." Santiago smelled the scent of a dozen rats but he was more than happy to leave Farrow's domain.

"What do you think Mac?"

Mac was torn, weighing the obvious dangers outside the Canyon against his desire to see the book told of in his nightmare. But like Santiago he was growing tired of this place and its odd master.

"So when do we leave?" he said.

"No time like the present," laughed Whateley. He nodded to Farrow and beckoned them to follow him. They went down a tunnel that led to a large ledge. Whateley reached in the pocket of his overalls, extracting what looked like a curved piece of bone. He put it to his lips and blew a high-pitched whistle from it. In response there came a frightening screech from above. They looked up to see a formation of three creatures with leathery wings, wasp-like bodies and raptor-like heads descending toward them. All three landed before them. Whateley went to the one in the middle and mounted it, then pointed to the other two.

"If you'll just hop on Merry and Pippin here we'll be off," he said. Mac and Santiago exchanged a dubious glance.

"No way," said Mac, "I don't even like to fly in a plane."

"Uhhh, they smell like rotting flesh," added Santiago as he drew close to one of the things.

Whateley replied in a matter of fact tone, "New R'lyeh is over three hundred miles from here. The Byakhee can get us there in less than an hour."

With no real alternative, Santiago followed Whateley's lead and mounted one of the beasts. He could feel it vibrating beneath him. Mac crossed himself and followed suit.

"How does this work exactly?" ventured Mac, already in terror.

"Just hold on," replied Whateley demonstrating how to grip the creature's slim waist with both hands. When they followed his lead, he blew another blast from the whistle and all three creatures soared upward with ear-splitting screeches. They flew so quickly they were out of sight of the Canyon in a matter of minutes, during which Father Mac's screams and Santiago's whoops of joy were heard in equal measure.

Some thirty minutes later they spotted a series of cyclopean cliffs at the edge of a dark sea. On the largest of them Santiago could see the dome from his dream. The Byakhee slowed then, gradually leveling off to land near the dome. When their riders dismounted, the odd flyers immediately took off into the air and abruptly vanished from sight as Mac and Santiago marveled at their first glimpse of New R'lyeh.

Unlike the primitive conditions in Canyon Haven, New R'lyeh's residents lived in rows of small picturesque cottages, facing a larger building. The edges of the town teemed with numerous gardens in which vegetables and fruit trees grew, while a wooden corral near the large building boasted a small herd of peculiar goat-like beasts. An old fashioned stone well with a bucket hanging from a wooden crank adorned the center of the town. Some twenty five people could be seen moving about the area. They represented many races and ranged in age from about twenty to eighty. They were attired in motley fashion that went from casual wear to business suits and went about their various tasks with enthusiasm. Mac addressed Whateley with unbridled amazement.

"How did all this survive the disasters?" Whateley smiled broadly.

"Hard work and a little help from God," he replied as he started down a path leading down to the town. Santiago breathed in the cool sea air as he and Mac followed. He was tired of mysteries and dreams. The seeming normality of this place put him on edge. Mac was grateful for it.

When they reached the town the residents quickly swarmed around the visitors with cries of welcome. These ceased as a distinguished silver-haired man in a blue suit stepped forward and extended his hand.

"I'm Tobias Mason, Head of the Order of the Radiant Circle. We welcome you both to New R'lyeh." Mac shook his hand. Santiago did likewise. His grip was as firm as his tone.

"Is that like a religious order?" asked Santiago. Tobias smiled.

"In a way, yes. But you must be hungry. Let's talk over a hot meal."

"I think I'm gonna like it here," said Santiago.

Mason led them to the large building which functioned as the town hall. Inside was a long wooden table set with pewter plates and utensils. At one end of it sat a short black man, his hands resting on a large cloth-wrapped package. Tobias introduced him as N'doko. They took seats around him as two townsfolk emerged through a door, toting platters of steaming victuals. It was simple fare: vegetables from the gardens and thin slices of meat. Santiago dug into it with his usual gusto. Mac was more interested in the package N'doko held. Noting this, Tobias spoke.

"N'doko, the book please." N'doko set the package on the table and carefully opened it. It was a thick tome bound in a copper colored material. Etched into the cover were the words "Liber Ivonis." The book reeked of antiquity, filling Mac with joy and anticipation. He'd always loved old books and this was a prime specimen.

"The Book of Ivonis. May I…?"

"Of course," replied Mason. N'doko gently slid the book across to Mac. The priest opened it and glanced through a few passages.

"It's very old, I'd say perhaps 9th century…"

"Exactly," said Tobias, pleased with the priest's knowledge. "So you would have no problem translating it?"

"I could but it would take months, considering its size."

"We don't require an entire translation. Just a single chapter will serve our purpose." Tobias moved to Mac and carefully flipped pages until he got to the final chapter. "This one," he said. Mac read the chapter's title aloud.

"The Last Prophecy?"

"I believe you'll find it most interesting."

In truth, Mac's heart was pounding at the thought of what might be revealed in the book. He was eager to begin.

As for Santiago, he had paid little attention to the conversation thus far and now, belly full, he grew weary of listening to old men talking about old books. He rose from the table, with a satisfied belch.

"Seems like you dudes got work to do and my Latin sucks. I think I'll take a look around, if that's okay with you?" This last bit was directed at Mason.

"Please do. You'll find our little town to be quite friendly." With that he returned to the discussion and Santiago exited the building, determined to find the woman in his dream.

When Santiago stepped out of the town hall, the sky above him was twilight purple, but then he saw something shining through the dark clouds. He realized it was the moon, a muted blue in color. It was first he had seen of it since the end. Then he heard strange words chanted in a familiar voice. He moved toward the sound and saw her. She finished the chant and without turning toward him whispered his name.

"Santiago."

He came to her then and she embraced him, pressing her lips against his in a long, succulent kiss. Santiago felt a wave of sensual energy course through his body. When the kiss ended she looked deep into his eyes.

"Who are you?" he said.

"I am Selene, High Priestess of Great Cthulhu. He has chosen you for me. Come."

She extended a hand to him and he took it. They walked together through New R'lyeh, the townsfolk greeting them with sly smiles. She led him to one of the cottages and entered. The room was lit by several pillar candles and burning sticks of incense gave it a warm, exotic smell. She went to a bed and with one easy motion let her dress fall to the floor. Her body was magnificent; his desire a hot flame. Hungrily she stripped the clothes from his body, pushed him down on the bed and mounted him, crying out as he entered her. Their lovemaking continued throughout the night, driving all other thoughts away in sheer ecstasy.

Mac labored on his translation of The Last Prophecy. It went slowly at first but as he read more, the book seemed to come alive, the words imparting their meanings as if speaking directly to him. He began to write furiously, ignoring fatigue and doubt as his obsession with the text spurred him on. At times he felt on the edge of madness as the ancient words told of hideous deities bringing humanity to the brink of extinction. Each mystery he struggled with led to more secrets and more revelations, each draining mind and soul, until he finally came to the end and the grandest disclosure of all. He slept then, his head resting on the book.

When Santiago awoke he found himself alone in Selene's cottage. He looked about the room and saw his clothes folded neatly on a chair. He left the bed and slowly dressed, savoring delicious memories of the night's activity. Then the door opened and Selene entered. She crossed to Santiago and kissed him. He loved the feel of her body against his and tried to draw her closer but she backed away, scolding him in a gentle tone.

"Not now. There's much to do. Find the priest and bring him to the dome. I'll meet you there."

"What's in the dome?" he asked.

"Your destinies," she replied.

Father Mac was still asleep when Santiago found him. Santiago shook him gently. The priest shifted his head and mumbled something but did not open his eyes. Santiago shook a little harder.

"Mac, wake up!' There was more shifting and mumbling and finally the priest opened his eyes. They were bloodshot from a long night of reading but something twinkled in the dark pupils, something odd. Mac smiled as he recognized Santiago and began to speak with a messianic fervor.

"Santiago! This book, it explains everything. God hasn't forsaken us. He's yet to come. It's not the end, it's a new beginning!"

Santiago had never seen McMahon like this. It was as if the book had driven him insane.

"Whoa chill out Padre, you talking *loco* here," he said. Mac considered it and for a moment the odd spark in his eyes was gone. He spoke haltingly.

"I know it sounds crazy but somehow I feel it's true." Santiago put a reassuring hand on his shoulder.

"It's just words in a book, Mac."

"Words in a book have changed the world before," said the priest.

Santiago shook his head. Mac was obviously convinced by what he had read.

"Come with me. You need some air and there's someone I want you to meet."

Mac nodded as he looked down at the book. He felt a hunger for it he couldn't explain.

"I think that's a good idea," he said softly.

The sky above New R'lyeh was a brighter gray this day. Looking seaward Mac and Santiago spied reddish clouds moving lazily in their direction. The enormous dome, its surface encrusted with an eon's worth of shells and seaweed, loomed above them. There was no apparent entrance but, as they drew nearer, a section of the dome wall vanished. Selene was revealed there; breathtaking in a ceremonial robe of sea green embroidered with mystic symbols. Mac's eyes grew wide as he saw her.

"Father Mac I'm so pleased to meet you. I am Selene Curwen. Welcome to the Temple of the God Who Sleeps. Come, meet him."

The wall section re-appeared behind them as they followed Selene up a sloping hallway which led to the interior of the dome. There stood an enormous cylinder of thick glass filled with sea water. Floating in it was a colossal mass of gelatinous green flesh. It grew and shrunk, pulsating, twisting and ripping itself into gruesome parodies of faces, mouths, eyes, wings, tentacles and things too insane to define. It was at once fascinating and utterly repulsive.

Mac and Santiago struggled to look away but even then they could feel the presence of the god. Santiago once thought he feared nothing but this made him cower like a frightened child. Father Mac had fallen to his knees, blinded by tears of utter madness.

It was then Selene's voice called out, "Great Cthulhu, hear my words, your priest anoint, your sword forge!"

She followed this with a strange incantation and suddenly what little sanity Mac and Santiago had left exploded. In their minds they saw dimensions collide and the Earth swallow all trace of human civilization. They saw loved ones die in chaos, terror and madness. They saw and felt the end but more importantly they saw the faces of those whose actions triggered it. The faces were familiar.

The members of the Order of the Radiant Circle, now attired in ceremonial robes, gazed upwards in eager anticipation. The sky was thick with crimson clouds. Several stars could be seen as the moon began to rise, shining like a ball of blood. Tobias spoke to them in a triumphant voice.

"The Blood Moon rises, as the prophecy says."

There was a murmuring of wonder and excitement from the crowd as grotesque shapes began to form in the red sky. The first was a massive, ever-shifting collection of glowing globes of light. The next was a vile amorphous monstrosity attended by nine smaller horrors that played ghastly music on whining flutes and muffled drums to which their master writhed in a gruesome mockery of a dance. More hideous things followed every moment, the sky teeming with them like some unholy audience to what was to come.

"The Gods come to bless the awakening of Cthulhu," shouted Tobias joyfully, "we must go to the dome."

Inside the Dome, Selene, Mac and Santiago conferred as they awaited the arrival of the Order. Both men were calmer now, their madness bringing them clarity of purpose.

Selene alone harbored doubts. She'd been told the opening of the gateway which had brought the world of humanity to ruin was the work of the Brotherhood and other cults loyal to the god Nyarlathotep. The Curwen family had been loyal servitors to the Order for centuries and she saw the lie as a betrayal.

Santiago, tired of playing a pawn in a game of gods, suggested a plan. It would take courage and all of their skills to implement but if it worked they might save what was left of humanity. They looked to each other; grim determination evident on all their faces. Selene declared it.

"Time is short. We must make our preparations quickly."

When the Order reached the dome they found the entryway open. They filed in, ascended up a sloping hallway to a large octagonal area covered with mystic symbols. There were numerous small grooves on the floor of the octagon all leading directly to the cylinder in which Cthulhu slept. Selene, Santiago and Mac stood casually beside it. The two men were now garbed in the ceremonial robes of the Order. Tobias stepped up to them and addressed Selene.

"Are you ready to begin Priestess?" Selene nodded and Tobias commanded his flock to take their places. They formed a circle around Selene, Santiago and Mac. Selene spoke.

"Tonight we fulfill the last prophecy. Focus your power to the utmost so Great Cthulhu may walk among us again."

The members of the Order clasped hands and shut their eyes. gathering their sorcerous energies. Unknown to them, Mac was whispering words in Latin, as Selene began whispering a spell of her own. Then an all too familiar voice thundered loudly.

"Mere power is not enough Priestess." All turned to see Farrow, moving slowly towards them.

"You are not welcome in this place," cried Tobias.

Farrow stopped, smiling a thin smile as he spoke.

"Welcome or not, I am here. And I say again power is not enough. The Last Prophecy demands blood as well." Selene spoke in a contemptuous tone.

"Perhaps you would care to provide it?" she retorted. Farrow laughed out loud and answered.

"With the greatest of pleasure!"

The loud report of a sawed-off pump shotgun followed. Tobias Mason's head erupted, splattering flesh and brains in all directions, as five of Farrow's Guardians rushed from hiding. Two held shotguns, the other three knives and machetes. The surprise attack disrupted Mac's intended spell and panicked the members of the Order. Ten of them died before one of the gunmen erupted into blackened ash. Blood began flowing through the grooves in the floor into the cylinder, reddening and roiling the green water.

Selene began to cast another spell as the remaining gunman leveled his shotgun at her from behind. Suddenly he dropped it to the floor, howling in wracking pain as a spell blasted him. Selene looked toward Mac, his hands still glowing with power and nodded thanks. Santiago grabbed the shotgun as a Guardian came at Mac with a knife. Santiago blew him across the blood-slick floor. He looked to the Guardian still howling from Mac's wrack spell, smashed his face in with the butt of the shotgun and swiftly turned it on the rest of Farrow's brutes, killing them all.

Farrow had yet to take a hand in the fray but he did so now. With arcane gestures he sent a cloud of demon locusts toward the remaining members of the Order. The insects ravaged over them, stripping the flesh from their bodies in a matter of seconds. Farrow basked in their dying screams for a moment and then turned to face Selene, Mac and Santiago.

"Thus ends the last prophecy and the Order of the Radiant Circle," he said.

"I still live," replied Selene.

"And I would have you remain so," said Farrow, "so long as Great Cthulhu continues to sleep."

"Leaving your Brotherhood to rule the world in his absence," said the Priestess.

"Just so," Farrow replied, "but I offer you the chance to rule at my side."

"I am consecrated to Cthulhu. I can serve no other, least of all you," said Selene.

Farrow sighed and spoke. "A pity to waste such skill and beauty on a sleeping God, but if you will not serve me in life, you will do so in death." Suddenly Santiago spoke but his voice was now deep and dark resonating throughout the dome.

"I don't think so," he said as his eyes began to glow with green light. For the first time he saw doubt creep into Farrow's eyes.

"What trickery is this?" Mac answered him with delight.

"Cthulhu sleeps but his sword awakes."

Santiago thrust his left arm out to the side. It transformed into a long curved sword, glistening with power. He stalked toward Farrow, a savage smile on his face. Farrow backed away, his hands making quick gestures as he spoke the words of a spell but Santiago leapt up and over him, the spell missing by a wide margin. One swift blow separated Farrow's head from his body. It landed on the floor, eyes wide with surprise. And then it spoke.

"Foolish mortal, it is time to see who you really face!" His head and body shimmered and with a cackling laugh began to transform into something monstrous. Selene cried out, recognizing the form as the God of the Brotherhood.

"Nyarlathotep!!!" Yet even as the form began to take shape, the walls of the dome shook and cracks began to appear in the cylinder. A voice like the wailing of a thousand banshees spoke.

"The sacrifice is acceptable!" A horrid shrieking sound came from the still coalescing shape as a huge tentacle emerged from the cylinder, grasped Nyarlathotep and pulled him into it. Gouts of blood filled the green waters as the massive form within smashed through the top of the dome. The entire structure began to sway, sending large chunks of stone and metal to the floor. Selene, Mac and Santiago ran for their lives.

As they reached the exit, they heard a gigantic cracking sound as the entire pillar on which the dome rested began to topple. Selene quickly extracted a small statuette from her robe, spoke the necessary words and hurled it down onto the shaking ground. In a flash of yellow light, a dragon-like creature appeared before them. They clambered onto its broad back and flew upwards watching as New R'lyeh sank beneath the dark waters. Then their eyes moved to the sky where an incredible event was in progress.

Cthulhu, savoring the taste of his traitorous messenger Nyarlathotep, was now feasting on the attending gods after his long sleep. He first devoured Azathoth and all his pipers and drummers and then moved on to entire pantheons of Other Gods. Some fought, most fled and so the ravening continued for many days after, the only survivors being The Great Old Ones and Yog-Sothoth whose existence was necessary to the future designs of Great Cthulhu and his minions.

Every human being on Earth had witnessed the slaughter in the heavens and many had been driven mad by the sight. Thus it was no surprise that the citizens of Canyon Haven fled into their caves when the dragon-like creature landed. But when Selene, Mac and Santiago dismounted and the creature flew away, a few brave souls emerged. One of them, the boy Shige, rushed up to Mac and Santiago.

"Wow that was so cool," he cried. "Where'd you get a dragon?"

"It's called a Shantak," said Selene. The boy's eyes grew wide at the sight of the Priestess.

"Man, you are smoking hot!" Selene blushed a bit and Mac gave the boy a not so gentle rap to the head. By this time most of Canyon Haven's people had gathered around the trio, welcoming them and asking questions. Then suddenly, a quintet of Guardians pushed their way in.

"Where's Farrow?" said their leader.

"He's dead and as of now the Brotherhood is too."

"Says who?" the brute replied reaching for the butcher knife in his belt. Santiago clasped his wrist in an iron grip and looked into the man's face, his eyes glowing green.

"Great Cthulhu," he replied in a deep voice, as he snapped the Guardian's wrist like a twig. The man fell to the ground screaming as the other Guardians ran in terror.

From that day forward, Selene, Father Mac and Santiago ruled Canyon Haven with a gentle firmness and a commitment to saving all survivors of the end. Selene's magic proved valuable in tracking down other camps. Within ten years humanity thrived and grew strong. It was not the world they once knew but in many ways it was a better one.

Great Cthulhu, now worshipped by all, was not seen again, except in dark dreams. Some say he returned to R'lyeh and continued his sleep, others claimed he went back to the stars which spawned him and still others believed he would one day come to Earth again and start the cycle of prophecy anew.

End of White

Ekaterina Sedia

Coronet Kovalevsky had never expected to find that land was finite. It seemed so abundant to him when he was younger, something you could never possibly run out of—or run off of—that the very suggestion seemed ludicrous. Yet there he was in the summer of 1920, teetering on the precipice of the Crimean peninsula, with very little idea of what to do after Wrangel's inevitable defeat and his own presumed tumble into the Black Sea. He had decided that he would not join the Bolsheviks—not so much out of any deeply held belief but rather because of his inherent disposition to avoid any large amounts of soul-overhauling work. He appeared committed and idealistic from the outside, even though inside he knew it was mere laziness and ennui.

So he lingered with the rest of his regiment in the small Crimean town (more of a village, if one was to be honest) named N., close to the shore, away from the invading Red armies and the dry, fragrant steppes that smelled like thyme and sun. At first, the officers kept to themselves, spending their days playing cards in the town's single tavern, and waiting for the news from the front. The evacuations of Murmansk and Arkhangelsk had already started, and the British hospital near N. promised the same opportunities for salvation, if the things didn't go the way Wrangel wanted them to. They waited for the fighting, for some way to end this interminable standoff. Kovalevsky hoped that his demise would be quick and, if not glorious, then at least non-embarrassing.

But the days were warm, the house he stayed in had white curtains on its tiny windows, cut like embrasures in thick clay walls—walls that retained pleasant coolness long into the afternoon heat. A split-rail fence half-heartedly guarded long rows of young sunflowers and poppies, with more mundane potatoes and beets hidden behind them, and a couple of chickens scratched in the dust of the yard. It was not unpleasant, if overly rustic.

The owner of the clay-walled, thickly-whitewashed house was one Marya Nikolavna, a small and disappearing kind of woman who seemed neither overjoyed nor appalled to have an officer quartering in her house; but nonetheless she frequently brought him homemade kvas and ripe watermelons, their dark green skins warm from the sun and their centers cold as well water, red and crumbling with sugar. She did not complain when Olesya started to come by.

Oh, Kovalevsky could tell that there was gypsy blood in Olesya—there was wildness about her, in the way the whites of her eyes flashed in the dusk of his room, the way her pitch-black braid snaked down her back, its tip swinging hypnotic as she walked. It took him a while, however, to recognize that it wasn't just the wild gypsy fire that smoldered hot and low in her blood, it was something else entirely that made her what she was.

It was a cloudy, suffocating kind of day in July, when everything—man, beast, and plant—hunkered close to the ground and waited for the relief of a thunderstorm. Unease charged the air with its sour taste, and Kovalevsky, feeling especially ill-disposed to getting out of bed that day, watched Olesya pad on her cat-soft feet across the wide floorboards, her half-slip like a giant gardenia flower, her breasts, dark against the paler skin stretched over her breastbone, lolling heavily. She opened the curtains to peer outside, the curtain of her messy black hair falling over half her back. Her profile turned, silver against the cloudy darkened glass. "It's going to rain," she said, just as the first leaden drops thrummed against the glass and the roof, formed dark little craters in the dust, pummeled the cabbage leaves like bullets.

And just as if the spell of heavy, lazy air was lifted, Olesya straightened and bounded out the door, shrieking in jubilation.

Kovalevsky, roused from his languid repose by the sound as well as the breaking heat, sat up on the bed, just in time to see Olesya running across the yard. He cringed, imagining her running through the village like that, half naked—not something he would put beyond her—as she disappeared from view. She soon reappeared, fists full of greenery, and came running inside, her wet feet slapping the floor and the black strands of her hair plastered to her skin, snaking around her shoulders like tattoos.

"What's this?" Kovalevsky asked, nodding at the tangled stems in her fist beaded with raindrops.

"This is for you," she said as she tossed a few poppies, their capsules still green and rubbery, at his bed. "And this"—she held up dark, broad leaves and hairy stems of some weed he didn't know—"this is for me."

She found his pen knife on the bed table and drew crisscrossing lines on the green poppy capsules, until they beaded with white latex. Kovalevsky watched, fascinated—the drops of rain, the drops of white poppy blood... it made sense then when Olesya drew the blade along the pad of her left thumb, mirroring the beaded trail in red. And in this cut, she mashed a dark green leaf, closing her eyes. She then wadded up the rest of the leaves and stuck them behind her cheek, like a squirrel. She tossed the pearled poppy capsules at Kovalevsky. "Here."

He wasn't naïve, of course—he just didn't feel any particular need for additional intoxicants. But under Olesya's suddenly wide gaze, her pupils like twin wells, he drew the first capsule into his mouth and swallowed, undeterred by its grassy yet bitter taste.

His sleep was heavy, undoubtedly aided by the monotone of the rain outside and by the drug in his blood. He dreamed of waves and of Olesya, of her bottomless eyes. He dreamed of her wrapping his head in her white underskirts so that he became blind, mute, and deaf, and his mouth filled with suffocating muslin. He woke up, coughing, just as the moon looked into his room through the opened curtains and opened window. Olesya was gone—of course she was, why wouldn't she be? Yet, he was uneasy, as he stared at the black sky and the silver moon. He imagined it reflecting in the sea, just out of sight, in parallel white slats of a moon road. It was so bright, the large fuzzy stars in its proximity faded into afterimages of themselves.

The opium still clouded his senses and his mind, and he lolled on the border between sleep and wakefulness, his mouth dry and his eyelids heavy, when fluttering of curtains attracted his attention. He peered into the darkness and managed to convince himself that it was just the wind, a trick of light, but just as he started to drift off, a spot in the darkness resolved into an outline of a very large and very black cat, who sat on the floor by the foot of his bed, its green eyes staring.

Now, cats as such were not an unusual occurrence—like any place that grew crops, the village was beleaguered by mice, and cats were both common and communal, traveling from one barn to the next yard, from a hay loft of one neighbor to the kitchen of another. They were welcomed everywhere, and their diet of mice was often supplemented by milk and meat scraps (but never eggs: no one wanted the cats to learn to like eggs and start stealing them from under hens). Yet, this cat seemed particularly audacious, as it sat and stared at Kovalevsky. He stared back until his eyelids fluttered and gave out, and he felt himself sinking into his drugged sleep again; through the oppressive fog, he felt the cat jump up on the bed and he was surprised by its heft—the bed gave and moaned as the beast, soft-pawed, kneaded and fussed and finally curled next to his thigh.

The next morning came with no traces of the strange cat's presence—or Olesya's, for that matter. Kovalevsky felt rested, and decided to visit the only drinking establishment the village possessed—indicated only by a faded and yet unusually detailed sign depicting a black goat with what seemed to be too many limbs, a fancy often found in rustic artists. The tavern was located in the same building as N.'s only hotel; it was a wide, low room housing a series of rough tables and serving simple but filling fare—borscht and dumplings swimming in butter and sour cream, then black bread and pickled beets and herring. This is where most of the officers spent their days—at least, those who had not been lucky enough to take up with one of the local sirens.

To his surprise, the tavern was quiet; the owner, a well-fed and heavily mustachioed Ukrainian named Patsjuk, lounged at the table nearest to the kitchen.

Kovalevsky asked for tea and bread and butter, and settled at the wide table by the window. The grain of the rough wooden slats was warm under his fingertips, a tiny topographic map, and he closed his eyes, feeling the ridges, willing them to resemble the terrain they had covered. There was just so much of it— on foot and horseback, on the train, sleeping in the thin straw, next to the peasants and lost children crawling with typhoid lice. The railroads and the regular roads (highways, dirt paths, streets) went up and down and up again, wound along and across rivers, through the mountains, through forests—and his fingers twitched as he tried to remember every turn and every elevation, until Patsjuk brought him his tea and warm bread, peasant butter (melted and solidified again into yellow grainy slabs) piled on the saucer like stationary waves.

"Where's everyone?" Kovalevsky asked. His tea smelled of the same heavy greenery that tainted Olesya's breath last night, and he wondered about where she went — to what Sabbath.

Patsjuk shrugged and leered. "Wouldn't know. Your Colonel was by the other day, but he's just about the only one who even comes anymore. I suspect the rest discovered the moonshiners, or some other nonsense abomination." He spat.

Kovalevsky nodded — Colonel Menshov was just the type to keep to the straight and narrow, away from any shady liquor, very much the same way as the rest of the regiment were likely to do the exact opposite. Kovalevsky could only assume that he hadn't heard anything of the matter due to his recent discovery of novelty intoxicants, of which Olesya was not the least.

One needed intoxicants at the times like these — at the times when one's army was all but squeezed between the pounding waves and the impossible, unturnable tide of the Reds, and the matters of being compressed like that (and where would one go under such circumstances) seemed impossible to ponder, and Kovalevsky tried his best to let his gaze slide along the ridges and the valleys of the yellow butter, to distract his uneasy mind from things that would make it more uneasy. To his good luck, an outside distraction soon presented itself.

Colonel Menshov walked into the dining room, in a less leisurely step than the circumstances warranted — in fact, he downright trotted in, in an anxious small gait of a man too disturbed to care about outward appearances. "Kovalevsky!" he cried, his face turning red with anguish. "There's no one left!" "So I heard," Kovalevsky said. He slid down the long, grainy wooden bench to offer Menshov a seat. "Patsjuk here says they fell in with the moonshiners." "Or Petliura got them," Patsjuk offered from his place behind the counter unhelpfully.

"What Petliura?" Menshov, who just sat down, bolted again, wild-eyed, his head swiveling about as if he expected to see the offender here, in the tavern.

"He's joking, I think," said Kovalevsky. "Symon Petliura is nowhere near these parts.""In any case, it's just you and me." Menshov waved at Patsjuk. "If you have any of that moonshine you've mentioned, bring me a shot of your strongest."

Kovalevsky decided not to comment, and waited until Menshov tossed back his drink, shuddered, swore, and heaved a sigh so tremulous that the ends of his gray mustache blew about. "What happened?" he said then.

"Darkness," Menshov said. "Not to mention, everyone except you is missing.""They'll come back.""I'm not so sure." Menshov gestured for Patsjuk to hurry with another drink. "Demons and dark forces are in this place, you hear? It's crawling with the unclean ones."

Kovalevsky looked at Patsjuk, who busied himself pouring a murky drink from a large glass bottle, and appeared to be doing everything in his power to avoid eye contact. Kovalevsky guessed that he probably played not a small part in straying Menshov off the straight and narrow.

"What led you to that conclusion?" Kovalesky asked.

"Cats," Menshov said, and waved his arms excitedly. "Haven't you seen them? Giant black cats that walk on hind legs? These are no cats but witches."

Kovalevsky felt a chill creeping up his spine, squeezing past the collar of his shirt and exploding in a constellation of shivers and raised hairs across the back of his head. He remembered the nightmare weight of the cat, and Olesya's smolder stare, her hands as she cut the poppies, how they bled their white juice... He shook his head. "There was a cat in your house?"

"Last night." Menshov slumped in his seat. "The awful creature attacked me as I slept—I woke and was quick enough to grab my inscribed saber. I always have it by my bed."

"Naturally," Kovalevsky said.

"The cat—and it was large, as large as a youth of ten or so—swiped at my face, and I swung my saber at its paw. It howled and ran out through the window, and its paw... it stayed on the floor. God help me, it's still there, I didn't have the bravery to toss it or to even touch it. Come with me, I'll show you, and you'll see that this is a thing not of this world—that it has no right to be at all."

Kovalevsky followed, reluctant and fearful of the possibility that Menshov was neither drunk nor addled. The fact that he even entertained the thought showed to him how unhinged he had become—then again, months of retreat and the trains crawling with lice would do it to a man. He wondered as he walked down the dusty street, large sunflowers nodding behind each split rail fence, if the shock of the revolution and the war had made them (everything) vulnerable—cracked them like pottery, so even if they appeared whole at the casual glance, in reality they were cobwebbed with hairline fissures, waiting only for a slightest shove, a lightest tap, to become undone and to tumble down in an avalanche of useless shards.

Menshov stopped in front of a fence like every other, the wood knotted and bleached by the sun, desiccated and rough, and pushed the gate open. It swung inward with a long plaintive squeal, and Kovalevsky cringed. Only then did he become aware of how silent the village had become—even in the noon heat, one was used to hearing squawking of chickens and an occasional bark of a languid dog.

"You hear it too?" Menshov said. "I mean, don't hear it."

"Where's everyone? Everything?"

There was no answer, and one wasn't needed—or even possible. The house stood small and still, its whitewashed walls clear and bright against the cornflower-blue of the sky, the straw thatched roof golden in the sunlight. Kovalevsky knew it was cool and dry inside, dark and quiet like a secret forest pool, and yet it took Menshov's pleading stare to persuade him to step over the threshold into the quiet deep darkness, the dirt floor soft under his boots.

He followed Menshov to the small bedroom, vertiginously like Kovalevsky's own—square window, clean narrow bed covered with a multicolored quilt—his heart hammering at his throat. He felt his blood flow away from his face, leaving it cold and numb, even before he saw the grotesque paw, a few drops and smudges of blood around it like torn carnations. But the paw itself pulled his attention—it was black and already shriveling, its toes an inky splash around the rosette of curving, sharp talons, translucent like mother-of-pearl. If it was a cat's paw, it used to belong to one very large and misshapen cat.

"My God," Kovalevsky managed, even as he thought that with matters like these, faith, despite being the only protection, was no protection at all. His mind raced, as he imagined over and over—despite willing himself to stop with such foolish speculation—he imagined Olesya leaving his house that morning, the stump of her human arm dripping with red through cheesecloth wrapped around it, cradled against her lolling breast.

"Unclean forces are at work," Menshov said. "And we are lost, lost."

Kovalevsky couldn't bring himself to disagree. He fought the Red and the Black armies, and he wasn't particularly afraid of them—but with a single glance at the terrible paw, curling on the floor in all its unnatural plainness, resignation took hold, and he was ready to embrace whatever was coming, as long as it was quick and granted him oblivion.

He tried to look away, but the thing pulled at his glance as if it was a string caught in its monstrous talons, and the more he looked, the more he imagined the battle that took place here: in his mind's eye, he saw the old man, the hilt of the saber clutched in both hands as if he became momentarily a child instead of a seasoned warrior, his naked chest hairless and hollow, backing into the corner. And he saw the beast—the paw expanded in his mind, giving flesh and image to the creature to which it was attached. It was a catlike thing, but with a long muzzle, and tufted ears and chin. It stood on its stiff hind legs, unnaturally straight, without the awkward slumping and crouching usually exhibited by the four-legged beasts, its long paws hanging limply by its sides for just a second, before snatching up and swiping at Menshov.

Kovalevsky always had vivid imagination, but this seemed more than mere fancy—it was as if the detached paw had the power to reach inside his eyeballs somehow and turn them to hidden places, making him see—see as Menshov staggered back, the saber now swinging blindly. He propped his left hand against the bedpost, gaining a semblance of control, just as the monster reached its deformed paw and swept across Menshov's bare shoulder, drawing a string of blood beads across it.

The old man hissed in pain and parried, just as the creature stepped away, hissing back in its low throbbing manner. With every passing second, Kovalevsky's mind imagined the creature with greater and greater clarity, just as the still-sane part of him realized that the longer he stared at the accursed paw, the closer he moved to summoning the creature itself.

He clapped his hand over his eyes, twisting away blindly. Whatever strange power had hold of him deserved the name Menshov gave it—it was unclean and ancient, too old for remembering and cursed long before the days of Cain.

Menshov's mind was apparently on a similar track. "If we die here," he said, quietly, "there's no way for us but the hellfire."

"Would there be another way for us otherwise?"

Menshov stared, perturbed. "We've kept our oath to the Emperor. We fought for the crown, and we fought with honor."

"That's what I mean." Kovalevsky forced his gaze away from the paw and turned around, as little as he liked having it behind his back. "Come now, let's see who else can we find. And as soon as we do, we best leave—if they let us, if we can."

They searched for hours—but no matter how many doors they knocked on, only empty shaded coolness greeted them, as if every house in the village had been gutted, hollowed of all human presence, and left as an empty decoration to await a new set of actors. And the more they saw of it, the more convinced Kovalevsky grew that the buildings must've been like that—empty, flat—before they have moved in. Where were the villagers? And, most importantly, where was Olesya? Was she just a vision, a sweet nightmare created from his loneliness and fear, aided by the soothing latex of the poppies in the yard and Patsjuk's dark green tea?

"Was it always like this?" Menshov said when the two of them finally stopped, silent and sweating. "Do you remember what this place was like when we first got here?"

Kovalevsky shook his head, then nodded. "I think it was... normal. A normal village."

He remembered the bustling in the streets, the peasants and the noisy geese, bleating of goats, the clouds of dust under the hooves of the White Army's horses when they rode in. Did they ride in or did they walk? If they rode, where were the horses—gone, swept away with everything else?

And then he remembered—a memory opened in his mind like a fissure—he remembered the view of the village and how quiet it was, and how he said to a man walking next to him (they must've been on foot, not horseback) that it was strange that there was no smoke coming from the chimneys. And then they walked into the village, and there was bustle and voices and chimneys spewed fat white smoke, and he'd forgotten all about it. "Maybe not so normal," he said. "I remember not seeing any smoke when we first approached."

Menshov nodded, his gray mustache shaking. "I remember that too! See, it was like an illusion, a night terror."

"The whole town?" Kovalevsky stopped in his tracks, his mind struggling to embrace the enormity of the deception—this whole time, this whole village... It couldn't be. "What about Patsjuk and his tavern? We were just there. Is it still...?"

"Let's find out."

As they walked back, the dusty street under their feet growing more insubstantial with every passing moment, Kovalevsky thought that perhaps this all was the result of this running out of land—running out of the world. After all, if there was no place left for the White Army, wouldn't it be possible that some of them simply ran and tripped into some nightmare limbo? It seemed likely, even.

The tavern stood flat and still, and it seemed more like a painting than an actual building—it thinned about the edges, and wavered, like hot air over a heated steppe. Illusion, unclean forces.

Patsjuk sat on the steps, and seemed real enough—made fatter, more substantial by the fact that Olesya perched next to him, her round shoulder, warm and solid under her linen shirt, resting comfortably against the tavern's owner's. Both her hands were intact, and Kovalevsky breathed a sigh of relief, even if he wasn't sure why.

She grinned when she saw Kovalevsky. "There you are," she said. "See, you took my medicine, took my poison, and now you're lost. The loving goat-mother will absorb you, make you whole again."

Menshov grasped Kovalevsky's shoulder, leaned into him with all his weight. "Why?" he said.

A pointless question, of course, Kovalevsky thought. There were never any whys or explanations—there was only the shortage of land. By then, the ground around them heaved, and the dead rose, upright, the nails of their hands still rooting them to the opened graves, their eyes closed and lips tortured. The streets and the houses twisted, and the whole world became a vortex of jerking movement, everything in it writhing and groaning—and only the tavern remained still in the center of it.

Kovalevsky's hand, led by a memory of the time when he cared enough to keep himself alive, moved of its own volition, like a severed lizard's tail, and slid down his leg and into his boot, grasping for the horn handle of the knife he always had on him.

He hadn't remembered it, but his body had, and jerked the knife out, assuming a defensive, ridiculous posture. He swiped at the air in front of him, not even trying for Patsjuk's belly, then turned around and ran.

His boots sunk into the road as if it were molasses, but he struggled on, as the air buzzed around him and soon resolved into bleating of what seemed like a thousand goats. Transparent dead hands grasped at him, and the black thing, more goat than a cat now, tried to claw its way out of his skull. Kovalevsky screamed and struggled against the wave of ancient voices, but inhuman force turned him back, back, to face the horrors he tried to run from.

So this is how it is, Kovalevsky thought, just as Olesya's face stretched into a muzzle, and her lower jaw hinged open, unnaturally wide. Without standing up, she extended her neck at Menshov. The old man grasped at his belt, uselessly, looking for his saber, even as Olesya's mouth wrapped around his head.

On the edge of his hearing, Kovalevsky heard whinnying of the horses off in a distance, and the uncertain, false tinny voice of a bugle. The Red Armies were entering the town of N.; he wondered briefly if the same fate awaited them—but probably not, since they were not the ones rejected by the world itself.

Kovalevsky closed his eyes then, not to see, and resigned himself to the fact that his run was over, and at the very least there would be relief from the sickening crunch that resonated deep in his spine, from the corpses and their long fingernails that dragged on the ground with barely audible whisper, and from the tinny bugle that was closing on him from every direction.

Biographies

Natania Barron is a word tinkerer with a lifelong love of the fantastic. She has a penchant for the unusual, and has written tales of invisible soul-eating birds, giant cephalopod goddesses, gunslinger girls, and killer kudzu. Her work has appeared in *Weird Tales, EscapePod, Steampunk Tales, Crossed Genres, Bull Spec,* and various anthologies. Natania's first novel, *Pilgrim of the Sky,* released in December 2011. She is also the co-editor of Bull Spec. When not venturing in imagined worlds, she can be found in North Carolina, where she lives with her family. Her website is www.nataniabarron.com.

Steve Dempsey lives in England with his wife Paula and more books than a house should sensibly hold. In their spare time they attend esoteric lectures and poke around in second-hand bookshops, just in case someone has a tome they don't already own. Steve is a government analyst and when he's not correlating the contents of restricted databases, he plays games and writes short stories. The one in this anthology is his first to be published.

Dennis Detwiller is a writer, artist, tabletop game designer and video game producer. His tabletop games have won major industry awards; his video games have sold millions of copies worldwide. Along with John Scott Tynes and Adam Scott Glancy he co-created *DELTA GREEN*, the widely acclaimed setting of modern-day Cthulhu Mythos horror and conspiracy.

Larry DiTillio has been a professional media writer since 1973. His script work has appeared on *Babylon 5, Hypernauts, Captain Power and the Soldiers of the Future, The Hitchhiker* and *Murder She* Wrote. He also writes animation and has scripted over 130 teleplays in that genre including *He-Man, She-Ra, Princess of Power, Conan the Adventurer* and *Beast Wars: Transformers."* He's also (gasp!) a gamer and wrote the classic *Call of Cthulhu* scenario *Masks of Nyarlathotep.* Philosophy of Life — To live is to undo your belt and look for trouble. "This story is dedicated to my dear friend Maurice 'Mac' McMahon, High Priest of Games, lover of people and all things Cthulhu. Rest in Peace."

Chad Fifer is one of the minds behind The H.P. Lovecraft Literary Podcast (hppodcraft.com). Each week on the show, he and co-host Chris Lackey take a critical and irreverent look at one of Lovecraft's stories, using atmospheric music and talented guest readers to breathe unnatural life into the work. Chad is also the author of the coming-of-age novel *Children in Heat* and was the resident humor columnist at criticism magazine *The Simon* for eight years. He co-wrote animated feature film *The Chosen One* with Lackey and is currently developing a number of film projects. He lives in L.A.

A. Scott Glancy had played the *Call of Cthulhu* roleplaying game for decades before co-authoring *DELTA GREEN*, a gaming supplement that married the gritty spy thrillers of John LeCarre with the cosmic horrors of H.P. Lovecraft. He joined Pagan Publishing in 1998 to work full time developing new *Call of Cthulhu* products. Delta Green remains his first love. Little is known of Mr. Glancy's career plans prior to his joining Pagan Publishing, save for his cryptic references to the collapse of Soviet Communism as "the day those drunken Bolsheviks fucked my employment plans into a cocked hat."

Dave Gross was born in Michigan but grew up in Virginia. After earning a Master's degree in English, he worked as a technical writer and teacher before moving north to edit magazines for TSR in Wisconsin. Later he moved west to do the same for Wizards of the Coast and Paizo Publishing in Washington, writing fiction on the side. He is the author of the Pathfinder Tales novels *Prince of Wolves* and *Master of Devils*. With Elaine Cunningham he co-authored *Winter Witch*. Dave now lives in Alberta, Canada with the best things in life, his wife and their small menagerie. You can track Dave @frabjousdave on Twitter or at frabjousdave.blogspot.com.

Dan Harms is a librarian and author living in upstate New York. He is best known for his books *The Cthulhu Mythos Encyclopedia* (Elder Signs) and *The Necronomicon Files* (Weiser). He has written numerous pieces for the *Call of Cthulhu* game and served on the editorial boards of such august publications as *Worlds of Cthulhu* and *The Unspeakable Oath*. At this time, he is finishing work on an annotated edition of *The Long-Lost Friend*, the author of which is the protagonist of "The Host from the Hill." Dan's blog, Papers Falling from an Attic Window, can be read at http://danharms.wordpress.com.

Rob Heinsoo obtained a pseudo-classical education as a first-wave D&D gamer in the 70's and studied social anthropology in college to obtain his intellectual poaching license. His game design credits include *Epic Spell Wars of the Battle Wizards: Duel at Mt. Skullzfyre*, the upcoming *13th Age*, *Three-Dragon Ante*, *D&D Miniatures*, *Dreamblade*, *Inn-Fighting*, lead design of the 4th Edition of *Dungeons & Dragons*, and pieces of *Shadowfist* and *King of Dragon Pass*. He lives in Seattle with his wife Lisa and is lead game designer at Fire Opal Media. You can find him storytelling and discussing new fiction projects at robheinsoo. blogspot.com or follow @robheinsoo on Twitter.

Kenneth Hite has designed, written, or co-authored more than seventy roleplaying games and supplements, including the *Star Trek Roleplaying Game*, *GURPS Infinite Worlds*, *Day After Ragnarok*, *Trail Of Cthulhu*, and *Night's Black Agents*. Outside gaming, his works include *Tour de Lovecraft: the Tales*, *Cthulhu 101*, *Zombies 101*, *Where the Deep Ones Are*, and the graphic illustrated version of *The Complete Idiot's Guide to U.S. History*. He writes the "Lost in Lovecraft" column for *Weird Tales* magazine, and his essays and criticism have also appeared in *Dragon* Magazine, *Games Quarterly* Magazine, *National Review*, *Amazing Stories*, and in anthologies from Greenwood Press, Ben Bella Press, and MIT Press. He lives in Chicago with his wife Sheila, two cats, and many, many books. He blogs at princeofcairo.livejournal.com.

Chris Lackey is the co-host of the H.P. Lovecraft Literary Podcast, animation and film director and ukulele enthusiast. Look for *Deadbeats,*a graphic novel he co-wrote with Chad Fifer, from Self Made Hero Publishing. Chris has directed his own animated feature, *The Chosen One* (2007), and worked as a producer on the H.P. Lovecraft Historical Society's *The Call of Cthulhu* and *The Whisperer in Darkness*. Chris is an American who lives in Yorkshire, England. He likes the rain.

Editor and Stone Skin Press Creative Director **Robin D. Laws** is an author, game designer, and podcaster. His novels include *Pierced Heart*, *The Rough and the Smooth*, and *The Worldwound Gambit*. Robin created the *GUMSHOE* investigative roleplaying rules system and such games as *Feng Shui*, *The Dying Earth*, *HeroQuest* and *Ashen Stars*. He is one half of the podcasting team behind "Ken and Robin Talk About Stuff." Find his blog, a cavalcade of film, culture, games, narrative structure and gun-toting avians, at robindlaws.com.

Nick Mamatas is the author of several novels, including the Lovecraftian Beat road novel *Move Under Ground*, and with Brian Keene the Lovecraftian gonzo journalism tract *The Damned Highway*. He's also the author of over eighty short stories, some of which have appeared in Asimov's Science Fiction, Tor.com, and the anthology *Lovecraft Unbound*. Nick's work has been nominated for the Bram Stoker award five times in five different categories, including achievement in short story for "The Dude Who Collected Lovecraft" co-written with Tim Pratt; he won a Stoker in the anthology category for *Haunted Legends* co-edited with Ellen Datlow.

Ekaterina Sedia resides in the Pinelands of New Jersey. Her critically acclaimed novels, *The Secret History of Moscow, The Alchemy of Stone, The House of Discarded Dreams* and *Heart of Iron* were published by Prime Books. Her short stories have sold to *Analog, Baen's Universe, Subterranean* and *Clarkesworld*, as well as numerous anthologies, including *Haunted Legends* and *Magic in the Mirrorstone*. She is also the editor of *Paper Cities* (World Fantasy Award winner), *Running with the Pack* and *Bewere the Night*, as well as forthcoming *Bloody Fabulous*. Visit her at www.ekaterinasedia.com.

Kyla Ward is a Sydney-based creative who works in many modes. Her novel *Prismatic* (co-authored as Edwina Grey) won an Aurealis Award for horror. Her short fiction has appeared in *Ticonderoga Online, Shadowed Realms*, Gothic.net and in the *Macabre* anthology amongst others. Her short film, *Bad Reception*, screened at the 3rd international Vampire Film Festival and she is a member of the Theatre of Blood, which has also produced her work. Poetry, articles, rpgs, art; if you can scare people with it she probably has, to the extent of programming the horror stream at the 2010 Worldcon. To see some very strange things, try www.tabula-rasa.info.

The Lion and the Aardvark
Aesop's Modern Fables

These confusing times of Internet trolls, one-percenters, toxic fame, and impending singularity cry out for clarity—the clarity found in Aesop's 2,500 year old fables. Over 60 writers from across the creative spectrum bring their modern sensibilities to this classic format. Zombies, dog-men and robot wasps mingle with cats, coyotes and cockroaches. Parables ranging from the punchy to the evocative, the wry to the disturbing explore eternal human foibles, as displaced onto lemmings, trout, and racing cars. But beware—in these terse explorations of desire, envy, and power, certitude isn't always as clear as it looks.

ISBN: 9781908983022

Publication date: December 2012

Available to order from the Stone Skin Press website

www.stoneskinpress.com

The New Hero
Volume 2

Every generation fits the time-honored constants of the hero tale to its own needs. Today's serial adventurers, whether they burst from re-envisioned histories or ply the humming foredecks of an imagined future, ride a cresting cultural wave. Through thirteen thrilling stories of threatened identity and vanquished disorder, The New Hero 2's diverse cast of top writers slices, dices and recombines the limits of the form.

Grab camera, medkit or mystic tome and rush to your rendezvous with the heroes of tomorrow.

ISBN: 9781908983039

Publication date: December 2012

Available to order from the Stone Skin Press website

www.stoneskinpress.com